DECEPTION

SCATTERED STARS: CONVICTION BOOK 2

DECEPTION

SCATTERED STARS: CONVICTION BOOK 2

GLYNN STEWART

FAOLAN'S PEN
PUBLISHING

faolanspen.com

This edition published in 2020 by:

Faolan's Pen Publishing Inc.

22 King St. S, Suite 300

Waterloo, Ontario

N2J 1N8 Canada

ISBN-13: 978-1-989674-05-5 (print)

A record of this book is available from Library and Archives Canada.

Printed in the United States of America

1 2 3 4 5 6 7 8 9 10

First edition

First printing: July 2020

Illustration © 2020 Jeff Brown Graphics

Faolan's Pen Publishing logo is a trademark of Faolan's Pen Publishing Inc.

Read more books from Glynn Stewart at faolanspen.com

1

"ATTENTION ON DECK!"

As the sharp-voiced command echoed across the flight deck, it was easy for Commander Kira "Basketball" Demirci to see who was new aboard the mercenary carrier *Conviction*.

The old mercenary hands, the ones who predated her own arrival on the carrier, barely shifted in response to the command. Most of them had been military at one point, but they'd all served as pilots and copilots on the mercenary ship for at least four years.

Her own people, once the elite pilots of Apollo's Three-Oh-Three Nova Combat Group, still had *some* instincts, but they had been elite nova fighter pilots. The Apollo System Defense Force had allowed its nova fighter squadrons to get notoriously unmilitary.

The newcomers, though, were all locals from the Redward System. All of them were formerly of the Redward Royal Fleet, some more recently than others, and the Redward Royal Fleet wasn't letting its tiny handful of nova fighter pilots go yet.

They all snapped to attention at Kira's command, and the tiny officer, the carrier's Commander, Nova Group, grinned as she walked into the middle of the rough circle of pilots and copilots. From there, she could see all thirty-five of her people and all twenty-four of her nova fighters.

"Vacation is now officially over," Kira told them all. "We were *supposed* to be having a nice comfy briefing in the flight country briefing room with coffees and snacks and all that, but, well." She shrugged.

"*Conviction* is one hundred and sixty-seven years old, people; shit happens. Our briefing room currently has no lights and is roughly forty-five degrees Celsius. The snacks the stewarding crew put together are *ruined,* and I don't plan on melting us all to death. So…get over here, all of you."

Despite the lack of formal attention she'd gathered from the mercenaries, everyone gathered around her in the middle of the flight deck as she waited for them.

"So, boss, do we get to play with the new toys?" one of her oldest friends asked. Joseph "Longknife" Hoffman commanded the newly constituted Memorial-Bravo Squadron. He was a gaunt man of average height with pale skin and blue eyes. His second-in-command—and boyfriend, mercenary fighter wings being even more relaxed than elite military wings—Dinesha "Dawnlord" Patel shared his height but was dark to Hoffman's pale.

"We do," Kira confirmed, looking around the room. "We have to," she said more loudly. "Too many of you have too little experience behind the stick of a nova fighter."

She gestured widely at the starfighters around her.

"We're nowhere near what *Conviction* can carry, but we already have more nova fighters than we can really fly," she noted. The flight group now consisted of twelve Hoplite-IVs, the top-of-the-line interceptors she'd stolen from Apollo when she'd left home, and twelve PNC-115s, "Parasite Nova Combatants," fighter-bombers *Conviction* had acquired from a more technologically advanced power thirty years ago.

Of course, seven of the Hoplites and five of the PNC-115s were knockoffs, built with plans extracted from *Conviction*'s repair fabricators. The class two nova drives at their hearts were difficult to build and rare, especially out there. The Redward System was part of the

Syntactic Cluster on the edge of the Rim, the outer limit of human civilization.

No one out there could build class two nova drives…no one except Redward, thanks to a fabricator Kira and *Conviction* had helped them acquire two months earlier.

"Four of you are on my rolls as pilots but can count on your fingers the number of times you've flown a nova fighter in real space," Kira said grimly, nodding toward that group. The four Redward natives were still clustered together, looking awkward.

They'd flown gunships for the RRF and passed her tests in simulators or they wouldn't *be* there, but they still looked unsure of themselves.

"Seven of you were copilots aboard *Conviction* before we acquired the new birds," she continued. "You've *been* on nova fighters in real space, but you haven't flown in combat. And, of course"—she grinned and waved at the freshly fledged collection of copilots—"we don't have a single copilot aboard our PNC-One-Fifteens who has flown in combat."

It was a far cry from the wing she'd taken into the Battle of the Kiln two months earlier. She'd gone into that fight with fourteen nova fighters, but every one of her pilots had been a combat-hardened veteran.

"None of you would be getting into one of my fighters if I didn't trust that you could do the job," she told them all, her tone suddenly hard. "I will tolerate no hesitation, no lack of confidence. It's your job to tell me you're ready. It's my job to tell you when you're wrong. You are *fighter pilots*. You have a long tradition of being arrogant jackasses to live up to; am I understood?!"

It took a few seconds for everyone to catch up and start laughing, but she got the result she was after. It would take time to get them all on board, but hopefully they'd *have* that time. The Syntactic Cluster had been quiet for the last couple of months.

Kira didn't trust it. She knew too much about what had been behind the rise to power of the Warlord they'd crushed at the Kiln— the KLN-35XD System. She didn't trust the shadowy players her Captain had once worked for to stay quiescent for long.

"WALDROUP, this is Basketball. Are we clear for launch?" Kira asked.

Her callsign reminded her that she hadn't had a chance to get on the court as much as she'd like. She was capable of playing circles around most people on a basketball court, regardless of their height. It was good exercise and often handy for putting foolish subordinates in place.

"Basketball, this is *Conviction*," her deck boss, Angel Waldroup, replied. "Are you green?"

Kira's headware was interfacing with her Hoplite as she checked over the nova fighter's systems. Redundancy and safety meant three-quarters of the information was displayed on the screens around her anyway, and all of it *could* be accessed with physical controls, but the mental connection helped update the pilot faster.

"Memorial-Alpha-One is green," Kira confirmed. "I have green lights on the rest of the flight group as well. Can you confirm?"

"We show all markers green and you are linked in to the system," Waldroup told her. "All fighters are under deck control."

There were times for manual launches and manual landings; and Kira would insist her pilots train for both. Right now, when she was taking the entire fighter group out for a mass exercise on the edge of a star system, was not that time. Even a small error in lining up a nova fighter before bringing the Harrington coils online could see the fighter impacting the inside of *Conviction*'s hangar at several dozen kilometers per second.

With twenty-three other fighters behind Kira in the launch order, all fully fueled…it would turn into a cascade disaster that could easily kill *everyone* aboard the sixty-thousand-cubic-meter carrier.

Kira checked the link and watched a green indicator appear on the front of her starfighter cockpit. Everything around her was virtual projections and viewscreens. The fighter itself was a deadly wedge of metal that averaged three meters thick, tapering from a barely flat nose to a ten-meter-wide base fifteen meters back.

Her cockpit was in the exact center of the spacecraft, as protected as physically possible in a relatively tiny vehicle. There were no windows showing her the outside world, only the screens. They showed her a lot of information right now, but they also showed her the carrier deck around her.

And that green indicator on the window into space at the end of the deck.

"I have the ball," she told the control center. "Initiating launch cycle in five."

"We have you on the line," Waldroup confirmed. "You are green."

"Bounce the ball...*now.*"

Kira's order was for the computers involved, not the humans. The entire process of flinging her starfighter out of *Conviction*'s hangar bay with a controlled gravity well and bringing up the fighter's own Harrington coils took under a hundredth of a second. Even with headware and neural interfacing, there was no way any human could exert control of that process.

By the time she took direct control of the fighter, she was already over fifty kilometers clear of the carrier, spinning the Hoplite-IV in place to slow and watch the rest of the fighter group launch.

Today, *Conviction* was in the extremities of the Redward System. The gas giant Lastward, the main fuel and supply depot for the Redward Royal Fleet, was visible as a thumb-sized blotch in the distance. The rest of the system's planets were invisible.

Redward didn't want to advertise their newly acquired ability to manufacture nova fighters. While *Conviction* wasn't part of the RRF, they were under a retainer contract with King Larry's government. When they started showing off extra nova fighters, people were going to wonder.

That wasn't going to stop Kira or her boss using every one of those fighters to achieve their missions, but they would give their employers' request enough credence that they would *practice* with them in private.

More starfighters were streaming out of the carrier as she watched. This part was easy enough, run by computer control.

"All fighters, form on me as you reach clear space," she ordered. That should *also* be easy enough. She'd see how her new people did. She was honest enough to admit she'd poached the best of *Conviction*'s

PNC-115 copilots for her own squadrons, but she needed *everyone* to be good.

The twelve Hoplite-IVs of the two Memorial Squadrons directly belonged to Kira and her own mercenary company. They were contracted with *Conviction*, but Memorial Squadron Limited Liability Corporation was a separate legal entity owned by Kira and the five other ex-Apollo pilots.

She'd only been a mercenary for a few months, but she definitely had the impression that complicated ownership structures and legalese were normal. At least she and the other survivors of the Three-Oh-Three Nova Combat Group had been well set up, with a lawyer ready to guide them through the process.

Another debt Kira owed her old squadron commander. She'd love to pay it back with interest on the people who'd killed him, but she knew that Jay Moranis had wanted them safe. He'd sent them to the edge of civilization, to the old friend who ran *Conviction*.

Which made keeping her people alive the only way Kira could repay her debt. So far, they were working with her on that one.

Twenty-three fighters followed her out of *Conviction*'s launch bays, one by one. They could do a faster cycle on the launch or even launch multiple fighters at once. They didn't need to today, so a fighter left the ship every ten seconds or so.

They took up formation around her with fewer problems than she'd feared. Even the gunship pilots could fly in normal space, after all. They were used to ten-thousand-cubic-meter pocket warships, not nova fighters, but they were still pilots.

"All right, everybody," she greeted them. "If you check your systems, you'll see a beacon with your name on it about ten light-seconds away. Everybody pinging their beacon?"

One of the toys she hadn't even realized she'd been missing until she had them again was *shuttles* with class two nova drives. There were two of them aboard *Conviction* now, and they'd spent the morning laying out the targets for everyone.

"Your guns are in training mode and the beacons can pick up if you ping them," she continued. "No jammers for this. Straight nova, shoot and scoot. I want to see you all back here in ninety seconds with your target 'destroyed.' Any questions?"

Silence answered her and Kira grinned in anticipation.

"Lock in your targets. Timer on my mark...*mark*. Break and attack!"

KIRA KNEW the drill as well as anyone. The moment she was finished speaking, she threw her fighter into motion. She'd already calculated the three-million-kilometer nova and triggered it. A wave of intense discomfort flashed over her as she novaed, and then she was *there*, ten thousand kilometers from the beacon transmitting her ID.

Aboard a proper starship, usually ten thousand cubic meters or bigger, the nova didn't have any detrimental effects. Part of it, she understood, was the nature of the class two nova drive, a side effect of the process that allowed the drive to recharge from a short nova in sixty seconds instead of ten minutes. Part of it was just that a nova fighter had that much less shielding.

The stomach cramps were an old friend now, and she ignored them as she focused on the task at hand. Her mental triggers twitched and light flickered across space. Her plasma guns were shut down right now, but the ranging lasers were enough for the beacon to register the hit.

She flipped in space, twisting around the beacon and firing again. She tagged the target four times as her nova drive recharged, and she reversed her fighter's position.

Then the nova fighter informed her that the drive was charged and she triggered it again. Another three million kilometers vanished and she was back beside *Conviction*.

Kira gently rotated her Hoplite-IV in space, looking to see who was back with her.

This time, she hadn't been expecting everyone to pull it off perfectly. Her five Apollon pilots were with her instantly. Galavant and Swordheart, the two copilots she'd borrowed before the last of her Apollons had arrived, were trained up to her expectations and were only a moment or so later.

The mercenary veterans filtered in over the next three seconds, along with one of the former gunship pilots. The ex-copilots and the rest of the gunship pilots followed, and Kira checked the timer as the last nova fighter emerged from nova.

"Back in formation, everyone," she ordered. "I make it eighty-seven seconds for the sweep, which is within what I told you." Kira paused, then shrugged as she decided to be honest with her pilots.

"It takes sixty seconds to cycle your nova drives," she told them. "That firing pass should have lasted exactly sixty seconds. Every second we spend in the battlespace is a vulnerable moment. The less time we spend in combat, the better.

"Today, I said ninety and you hit ninety. Tomorrow, we'll aim for eighty. Next week, seventy. Eventually? The target is sixty-five seconds in and out. At *most*."

The targeting beacons' data was trickling into her headware now that they'd been back for over ten seconds, and she concealed a grimace.

"I now have our targeting data as well," Kira told them, and the silence on the channel told her at least some of them were guessing what came next. "Across twenty-four fighters, we fired just over ninety times. Each of those would represent a quarter-second or so of pulses from our actual guns. The extra speed of the lasers washes out with the spread of the pulses for accuracy in my experience, so we call it close enough to assess accuracy."

She paused, letting that all sink in.

"We hit sixty-three times," she told her people. "Not quite a seventy percent hit rate...which would be bad *enough*, except that not everyone managed to hit their own target. Had we actually just made a firing pass on an enemy formation of twenty-four targets, two of them wouldn't have been touched."

Everyone had at least hit *something*, which was better than some training exercises she'd run in Apollo.

"I am not, today, breaking down those accuracy rates and misses by pilot," Kira said quietly. "This is your freebie. We're going to repeat that run, without jammers, a few more times and see if we can at least manage to hit every target.

"Tomorrow, we cut to an eighty-second in-and-out and I *do* start tracking who is shooting other people's targets," she continued grimly. "I do not expect perfection today. I don't expect perfection tomorrow, even. I *do* expect continuous improvement.

"We don't know how long we have until we need to go into action. Best-case scenario, we're up against pirate gunships again—but someone brought real modern nova fighters to the Kiln. Which means, people, I'm going to *train* you to fight real modern nova fighters."

Because if she didn't, she was going to find herself training a new set of pilots.

And she'd attended enough funerals in the last year already.

2

"SO, HOW ARE THEY DOING?"

Kira shook her head as she took a cup of coffee from her boss. Captain John Estanza was a solidly built middle-aged man of around seventy—she still didn't know his exact age—with neatly kept shoulder-length silver hair.

When she'd first met him, he'd been drunk. He'd *stayed* drunk for several weeks, until the death of his previous Commander, Nova Group had forced him to return to sobriety. Kira had been well on her way to falling in love with Daniel Mbeki, but he'd been almost a son to John Estanza.

The thought of the man still hurt, but not as much as it had. Kira knew better than to mention him to Estanza, though.

She considered her answer to the Captain's question as she glanced around the office. It was even plainer than it had been the first time she'd visited Estanza, mostly because the one decoration then had been a wet bar.

That was now in a storage closet somewhere, and Estanza appeared to be living on the coffee his steward was delivering. One of Redward's exports, the coffee was *very* good, and she sipped it appreciatively.

"Twenty of my pilots saw the elephant at the Kiln," she finally said.

"Including me, that is. Seven of them might have only been copilots, but they were there and they went toe-to-toe with modern Brisingr fighters in the hands of Costar Clan pilots."

"And three of your new copilots were aboard *Conviction*," Estanza said. "None of that necessarily tells me how they're shaping up as a squadron and a flight group, Demirci."

"They're rough," she conceded. "*Really* rough. I had to split the old Memorials and Darkwings up, so it's not even like I have a solid squadron I can rely on. None of them are bad, but half my pilots need work. I need a week to work them up, boss."

"You have tomorrow, then you're back in simulators," her Captain told her. "It draws a lot of attention, having the most powerful warship in thirty light-years swanning around the outer system. Redward *really* wants to keep their new nova-drive plant secret."

"The biggest threats already know," she said. "We *stole* it from Equilibrium, after all."

Estanza nodded, sipping his own coffee as he leaned back in his chair and sighed.

Once, long before she'd met him, John Estanza and Jay Moranis—her old Apollon commanding officer—had served in a mercenary force called Cobra Squadron. Cobra Squadron had, in turn, been a false front for an organization called the Equilibrium Institute.

Kira *still* wasn't entirely sure she believed everything Estanza had told her about his former employers. It was hard to conceive of an organization moving money and ships to influence the politics of the entire Rim and Fringe, the outer half of the human sphere.

But when they'd moved against a Costar Clan pirate warlord, that enemy had been in possession of military shipyards and a class two nova-drive factory, plus modern Brisingr warships. The nova-drive factory had been staffed by a team of engineers who had turned out to explicitly be Equilibrium Institute agents.

Hard to deny the existence of an enemy who came right out in front of you. On the other hand…

"It's not like I told Redward about them," Estanza said. "I'm careful about who I loop into my crazy conspiracy theories, Demirci. Even now, I only have so much proof."

"I need more than two days to drill this bunch, boss," she said. "Even the ex-RRF set have solid basic skills, but right now I have thirteen elite pilots and eleven wild cards. Even then, seven of my veterans have wild cards for copilots."

"Are you saying that Galavant and Swordheart are wild cards?" the Captain asked.

Kira chuckled. Those were the two pilots who'd flown for her before, PNC-115 copilots who'd flown Hoplites for a single mission under her command. They'd chafed at her training regimen then but were taking to it like ducks to water now.

"Fair. Nine wild cards—but the copilots are still fresh," she countered. "Thanks to Swordheart and Galavant, my Memorials are probably deployable. Except, of course, we don't officially *have* twelve Hoplites."

"And that's the problem," Estanza agreed. "And I'm going to throw you another headache: Redward is going to have another shipment of nova drives for us in fifteen days. That's the last set, but you need to sit down with Angel and decide what fighters you want her to build."

Conviction's fabricators had been updated more recently than her hull, which meant they were significantly better than those available to Redward. Redward had all of the *designs* of the Hoplites and PNCs, but their fabricators weren't truly up to duplicating the more modern nova craft.

The carrier's systems could. Angel Waldroup and her team had built every one of Kira's new fighters—which had taken most of the last two months.

"I'm not sure how quickly we'll be able to turn them into real fighters, but I'll talk to her," Kira promised. "I have no idea where we're going to find pilots for them."

"We might need to head coreward for recruitment," Estanza admitted. "Ypres might have some actual nova-fighter pilots who've drifted outward like your people. Or maybe we should even consider sending recruiting agents toward the Inner Rim."

Kira grimaced. The agents would need to travel at least a hundred light-years to get to anywhere where nova fighters were common. At that point, they might as well go the extra few days to reach the Apollo-Brisingr sector and see if they could recruit pilots familiar with the Hoplite.

She couldn't go. Brisingr still had a dead-or-alive bounty on her head, illegal as that was in just about any civilized star system.

"I'll think on that too," she said. "You're more experienced on that front than I am, though."

"I might send you or maybe Gizmo to Ypres before we start trying to recruit from farther coreward," Estanza admitted. Gizmo was the man Kira had put in charge of her two Darkwing Squadrons, the PNC-115s.

"In that case, we need more time," Kira countered. "I don't want to leave the fighter group until I'm comfortable they can go into a battle without me—and I don't want to give up my one Group Commander before then, either."

Conviction had an oddly flat hierarchy for a warship. Technically, she and Gizmo were both "Commanders," the only actual *rank* the mercenary crew's officers seemed to have. Distinctions inside that rank were by role, which still felt awkward to her.

But *Conviction* was John Estanza's ship, not hers. If it worked, she'd work with it—and it seemed to work.

She'd instilled a few more specific divisions in her fighter group, but that was for *her* people.

"You have the simulator pods," Estanza told her. "I know it's not the best option, but part of the deal with Redward is that we don't flaunt the new fighters." He shrugged. "I'm honestly surprised they were as bad as you say. The sims should have prepped them more effectively."

Kira nodded grimly.

"I don't think we were doing enough nova-and-attack simula-tions," she admitted. "More standard dogfighting scenarios. I'll change up the simulator curriculum, but it's not the same and you know it."

Her boss was an ex-fighter pilot, after all.

"We're looking at a patrol contract in the near future," Estanza told her. "That will give us lots of opportunity for you to carry out real-space maneuvers and exercises. We'll need to be careful about who's around, but this is the Syntactic Cluster." He shrugged. "There aren't that many people at a given trade-route stop."

The safest novas were made to and from carefully mapped points in deep space with no nearby stars. Those "trade-route stops" often had refueling and recreational infrastructure in more civilized space, as it took hours for a standard class one nova drive to recycle.

Here in the Syntactic Cluster, all you could really say for them was that they were mapped and *usually* patrolled by Redward or one of the other handful of systems with warships. Most of *Conviction*'s work for their employers out there was sweeping the trade routes when there were signs of trouble.

"That'll help, I suppose," she allowed. "It's not like I didn't know this was only going to be two days, but I was hoping we'd make it a regular occurrence."

"If we're home-based for an extended period, we probably will," Estanza told her. "It's not like we've had the full fighter group for long, after all. You got the last knockoff PNC, what, five days ago?"

"Four," Kira corrected with a small smile. "Angel took her time; she wanted to make sure we had no problems."

"Which was the right call," her boss agreed. "And some good news I picked up just before we headed out here is that the locals finally have combat-ready models of their own nova fighters. They're calling them the Sinister and Dexter types, a fighter-bomber and an interceptor respectively."

"How do they stack up to the originals?" Kira asked.

"Now, now," Estanza grinned. "They are most definitely *not* ripped off from stolen designs from Apollo and Griffin; why would anyone suggest that?

"To answer the question, though, they're not quite up to the weight of our birds," he concluded. "The systems they acquired with the nova-drive plant have helped them upgrade portions of their military-fabrication plants, but they're still a Far Rim power. They're a bit slower and a bit less heavily armed than ours—but they're better than the handful of ancient fighters they used to have."

"So, we might have real nova-fighter backup next time we get in a serious scrum," Kira said. "That's good to know."

"And they might be hiring you and the other vets to train *their* nova fighter pilots," Estanza told her. "No one has mentioned that to me yet, but you demonstrated at the Kiln that you know this game better than anyone else in this sector."

"Except you," she pointed out. "I'm good. Cobra Squadron were *legends*."

Her captain shrugged diffidently.

"I prefer to let that particular legend stay buried," he admitted. "If we keep dragging it out, our involvement in some of the uglier parts of that war might come out."

Kira nodded her understanding as she finished her coffee. Cobra Squadron, after all, had truly fought for Equilibrium, not Griffon—and *everything* they'd done had been part of a carefully choreographed campaign to turn the Star Kingdom of Griffon from a wealthy, near-pacifistic, merchant state into a dominant hegemon that brooked no violence in its sphere of influence.

And when they'd achieved that, they'd undercut Griffon to make sure it didn't have the strength to expand its sphere, turning it into another of the Institute's carefully balanced regional powers.

3

"BOSS, WE HAVE A PROBLEM."

"Get in here and close the door," Kira ordered as she gestured one of her oldest friends in from the hallway. "What's up?"

Mel "Nightmare" Cartman was her wing pilot and her strong left hand. Hoffman commanded Memorial-Bravo, but Nightmare was in charge of Alpha when Kira was too focused on the bigger picture to take care of the squadron she technically also ran.

She was a tall and lithe blonde woman, towering a head above her petite commander and with a grace and curves that attracted gazes away from Kira. Cartman was far happier to attract those gazes than her boss was, though the death of the friend she'd traveled to Redward with had slowed her down for a while.

"We're dangerously low on beer," the woman said seriously. "There might only be four or five weeks' worth left in the flight country bar!"

Kira stared at her subordinate and friend for several long seconds, then snorted and dropped into her chair. The office she'd taken over aboard *Conviction* was ridiculously plain. There was a undecorated metal desk in the middle of the room and two chairs and that was it.

Conviction's CNG was more comfortable with working entirely in her headware than most. She could create screens, images, maps—

whatever she needed wherever she needed it. Now she opened the consumables status report for flight country's mess and bar and shared it with the other woman.

"You are trying to give me an entirely unneeded heart attack," she said. "Do we *actually* have a problem?"

"A few, but none are really major," Cartman replied, taking the spare chair. "Though that report is out of date. The heat-control issue fucked the mess's fridge. If it needed to be cold, it's trash."

"I'll talk to Labelle and Vaduva about that," Kira said. "Thankfully, the food comes out of *Conviction*'s budget, not the Memorials', so I don't need to fight over who is paying for it."

"Any idea when flight country is going to be habitable again?" Cartman asked.

"Soon," Kira promised. "Last I heard, Labelle was rebalancing the entire ship so we don't have hot spots. Everywhere is going to be a few degrees warmer than usual, but nowhere is going to be over thirty degrees anymore."

Flight country, which was directly beneath the heat-radiation system that had broken down, was still going to be the warmest part of the ship. Parts were being fabricated as they spoke, though, so Kira hoped things would be fixed by the time they made it back to Redward.

"Good. Otherwise, I'm going to start wandering around flight country naked and see if I can kick off an orgy."

Kira was silent for a moment as she judged her second-in-command, then sighed.

"Why do I put up with you, again?" she asked.

"So that we can rotate which of us is being the angsty one over dead friends and lost homes," Cartman said in a sudden moment of dead seriousness. "You get mopey every time you walk into this office, and the distraction is good for you."

"Fair," Kira acknowledged. "But no orgies."

"Drat."

The other woman grinned for a moment, but it faded back into her serious expression.

"The other problem I have is our new blood," she admitted. "I'm keeping an eye on the ex-RRF pilots as you asked, and I'm worried."

"They all came well-recommended and none of them have really screwed up yet," Kira said. She might have promised not to judge her pilots based on the first day of exercises, but that didn't mean she hadn't run the analyses. "No worse than some of the ex-copilots, anyway."

"Not really their skills I'm worried about," Cartman said. "Even the new copilots I'm not overly concerned about. It's specifically Harriman and Zulu."

Kira nodded slowly. Ansigar Harriman and Patrick Zulu were the two younger pilots she'd hired who'd served in the RRF. Both had graduated from the academy and served a six-year tour of duty in the gunship flotillas. They were fully qualified for the job, but they were also young blood.

And perhaps her biases as an ex-lifer were speaking, but she always questioned why anyone would leave a military service after only one tour of duty.

"They're the youngest pilots in the flight group. I think," Kira noted. "Other than that, what's the worry?"

"Part of it is wondering why someone would leave the military after one term to go civilian and then sign up with a mercenary company inside a year," Cartman said. "I think both of them are in this for money over anything else, which could make them brittle when the push comes."

"We're all at least partly in it for money," Kira replied. "I can't blame them for that."

"I know," her subordinate agreed. "That pair…I'm not sure they really expect to see fighting. They're in this for a paycheck and a chance to fly a fancy spacecraft. I'm not convinced they'll stick it out… and I'm a little worried that someone might be able to buy them."

"That's a hell of an accusation to throw based on some itchy hunches, Mel," Kira pointed out. "I'm not saying you're wrong to worry, but without something solid…"

"I know, I know." Mel raised her hands defensively. "I just got used to flying with people I knew inside and out, you know? The Dark-wings were bad enough, but at least they ticked the way I expected.

"Now? Now we've got a whole mess of people, and I don't know a bunch of them at all. Those two are just the ones that bother me the most."

"Watch them for me," Kira ordered. "And talk to Gizmo and Ratchet."

Marjut "Ratchet" Shelby ran Darkwing-Bravo, making her Kira's fourth and most junior squadron commander. She was a long-standing Darkwing ace, though, with ten kills under her belt in one fight or another.

"They're both under Ratchet, so make sure she knows to keep her eyes open," Kira concluded. "We're not going to throw anyone under the bus because we're feeling itchy, but I see no reason to leave any openings, either."

4

THE THING that still caught Kira by surprise every time she returned to Redward was how small everything was. Flying escort for *Conviction* as the carrier gently decelerated into orbit gave her an incredible view of the orbital infrastructure around the planet, and she kept expecting there to be more. Redward was, after all, one of the richest systems in the Syntactic Cluster.

But there wasn't. There was the single orbital, Blueward Station—barely two-thirds the size of any of Apollo's *four* orbitals. There was a loose ring of industrial platforms, barely worthy of the "ring" label. The entire fleet positioned in high orbit would have made for two carrier groups at most—and the "carriers" were retrofitted freighters, still full of sub-fighters, the nova fighters' sublight and drastically inferior cousins.

A single Apollo or Brisingr carrier group could have taken out the entire Redward Royal Fleet. Two carrier groups could have secured control of every trade route in the Cluster. Even some of the planets in the Cluster were backward enough that their orbitals would be vulnerable to those carriers.

Redward wasn't one of them. No one in the Syntactic Cluster could build a nova drive that could jump more than sixty thousand cubic meters. At seventy-five thousand cubics, *Conviction* was bigger than any vessel in the RRF—and she was *dwarfed* by the four asteroid fortresses anchoring Redward's orbital elevators.

Even a hundred-thousand-plus-cubic Brisingr assault carrier or battlecruiser would falter against the defenses of a civilized planet. Kira suspected that there were warships from the Meridian or closer to Sol that could take down Redward's defenses, but those ships weren't going to make the thousand-light-year voyage to the edge of civilization to pick a random fight.

It was the key rule of interstellar warfare: planets were functionally invulnerable not only to peer powers but to powers several tiers up. Apollo and Brisingr were, arguably, seventh-tier powers. Redward was something like *ninth*-tier, but her defenses could stand off the nation Kira came from.

The asteroid fortresses above Redward were the standard linchpin of those defenses. Each of them was easily a kilometer across and packed with the most powerful weapons Redward could build. The RRF was docked at those stations, their warships spending their time at home under the guns of those near-invulnerable defenses.

Conviction, on the other hand, docked at Blueward Station at a rough arrangement of docking tubes that had once served a squadron of nova gunships, the ten-kilocubic light warships that were even more ubiquitous than the asteroid fortresses.

"CAP, this is *Conviction*," Commander Zoric's voice said in Kira's headware. Kavitha Zoric was *Conviction*'s XO, Captain Estanza's right-hand woman and the one responsible for running the carrier while Estanza ran the mercenary company. "We are secure with Blueward Station and inside the RRF's security perimeter."

Zoric coughed.

"They haven't *quite* said they're insulted that you're still flying CAP, but they *did* suggest it was unnecessary."

Kira laughed. There was really no reason for her to keep a Carrier Air Patrol in space at all inside the Redward System beyond habit—but she had no intention of letting her fighter pilots *or Conviction* acquire bad habits.

"I'm just enjoying the view, *Conviction*," she told the other woman. "Nightmare, Indigo, RTB on the ball. I'm going to loop the station to check for problems and follow you in."

Mel had been flying on her wing and they'd brought along a PNC-115 just in case. If something *did* go down, neither of the Hoplite-IVs carried torpedoes. Indigo's fighter-bomber had been loaded with a full three torpedoes and she'd been one of Mbeki's veterans.

Between the three of them, even a serious warship would have had a bad day while the rest of the fighter group launched. Which was, of course, the entire point of a Carrier Air Patrol.

"Are you looping the station *just* to point out that you don't answer to the RRF?" Zoric asked as the two nova fighters broke off to follow Kira's return to base order.

"*Maybe*," Kira said with a grin. "But also to burn a bit of time. I have three whole hours before I have to meet with Dirix and Pree!"

PRIAPUS SIMONEIT HAD BEEN the first person Kira had met in the Redward System, the lawyer that her old commanding officer had sent her to with the money and information to set up what had become the Memorial Squadron Limited Liability Corporation. He was an old man with visible liver spots and a taste for white long-tailed suits that had gone out of fashion in Apollo twenty years earlier.

Simoneit didn't work full-time for Kira, but he handled most legal affairs for the Memorials as well as the significant personal estate she'd inherited from Jay Moranis on Redward. The planet had been the old pilot's emergency bolthole, and he'd left Kira his personal property and finances there.

Stipan Dirix *was* a full-time employee of the Memorials, a two-meter tall slab of muscle formerly of the Redward Royal Army who ran Kira's dockside office.

Between the pair of them, they handled everything Kira needed handled in the star system. Not least of that was making sure that she and her people could move around safely—there was still a death mark on her and the rest of her Apollo comrades.

Brisingr's reach had proven far longer than she'd ever feared, but illegal bounties were a thankfully minimal threat so long as she moved around with escorts and kept in touch with Station Security.

"We're going to need twelve more pilots," Kira told the pair of them as she took a cup of coffee from the coffee machine in the corner. It had started brewing the cup the moment she'd entered the outer office. If she took any sweetener or cream, it would have added that before she took it, too. Simoneit's office had all the features, even if they were often slower or more obvious than Kira was used to.

"That's not going to happen," Dirix said bluntly. The big man leaned back in his chair and spread his hands in a wide shrug. "Not pilots that are worth the plasma to blow them away, anyway. I figured you weren't done with the recruiting drive, so I was keeping my ear to the ground."

"And?" Kira asked, though she suspected she knew the answer.

"Anyone I would have figured had the skills to pick flying a nova fighter and sufficient integrity that I'd try to hire them is suddenly employed," her manager told her. "It's all very quiet and hush-hush, but my read is that the RRF showed up at their door with re-signing bonuses no one could say no to."

"Fair. We'll need to expand the net, then," she told him. "Estanza wants to send one of us to Ypres to recruit there."

"You're not even surprised, are you?" Dirix asked. He shook his head. "Which means that wherever your mysterious new nova fighters came from, the RRF has a line on the same source and is recruiting up their own nova-fighter wing."

Kira raised a sharp finger at the two men.

"That's speculation, Stipan," she told him. "And it *stays* speculation and in private, clear?"

She turned her gaze on the lawyer, who smiled thinly.

"Everything we discuss is privileged," Simoneit reminded her. "My lips are sealed."

"I get it, boss," Dirix said with an almost-exaggerated nod. "Do you need me to arrange private transport to Ypres for someone? Or, hell, I guess I could go."

"No offense, Dirix, but you don't know a nova strike from a

bombing run," Kira said. "We'd need to fly your recruits back here and test them before hiring them. If we're not sending me or Gizmo, we're just wasting everyone's time."

"So, ship and escorts to get a senior *Conviction* officer to Ypres?" he asked.

"This one's a *Conviction* problem, so Vaduva gets the work and the bill," she replied. "Are you getting bored, Stipan?"

"I'm watching an accountant and four part-time bodyguards," Dirix admitted with a snort. "I'm busy enough, but if my job gets exciting, something's gone very wrong."

"So, you're bored," Kira concluded. "It's just: you're okay with that?"

"Basically," he agreed. "But if you need me to do something a bit different, I'm down for that, too."

"We carry on for the moment," she told him. "Pree, anything going on I need to know about? *Conviction* is spinning her wheels for the moment, waiting for a contract. We could be stuck here for a week, we could be novaing out tonight."

"We shall see," the lawyer said calmly. "The annual management meeting for your condo is in three days. Do you have any interest in attending?"

"Are they likely to break anything if I don't?" Kira asked. Jay Moranis had come from wealth and spent his life turning money into more money, about as much via canny investment as via violence for hire. His concept of acceptable accommodations for his bolt-hole had been a top-end luxury penthouse that was far beyond Kira's needs— even if she spent more than one day in fifty on the planet.

"Hardly," Simoneit agreed. "We have a property manager under contract. They can attend the meeting on your behalf and forward minutes if anything unusual occurs."

"Works for me," she said. "Anything else?"

"I'm not sure," the lawyer admitted. "I received some interesting inquiries as to the best method to reach out to you on personal matters."

"Define *interesting*," Kira said carefully. "Everyone in this system

I'd call a friend is either on *Conviction* or in this room. Or, I suppose, on an RRF warship," she said after a moment.

"It was lawyers talking to lawyers, Kira, which tells me quite a bit even when they say nothing," Simoneit told her. "Unless I miss my guess, in which case you may dock my monthly retainer, Queen Sonia is looking to reach out to you."

Kira blinked in surprise. She'd *met* the Queen of Redward, in the memorable covert planning session that had led up to the Battle of the Kiln, but it had been a very busy meeting. She didn't think she'd made *that* much of an impression.

"What does the Queen need?" she asked. "Something blown up without involving her husband?"

Simoneit looked pained and Kira concealed a smile. She was *reasonably* sure the lawyer had picked up on Queen Sonia's secret role as her husband's head of intelligence, but she was also sure it fell under the category of things he couldn't admit to.

"While I suppose that is possible, my impression is that the Queen's people were mostly laying groundwork for where to send invitations," he told her. "Her Majesty is known to invite assorted leading figures in the Redward System to small parties where she introduces them to each other. Rarely men, mostly women and nongendered individuals.

"Bluntly, it is a way for her to build a network of support for both herself and her chosen allies," Simoneit said. "If she is considering including you in that circle, Kira, that will be of immense value to you."

Kira shook her head.

"*Politics*," she swore. "I can do parties, but that will require me to be in-system. Can you act as my contact point?"

"That is part of what you pay me a retainer for, Kira," he said with a smile.

Further conversation was interrupted by a buzzing alert in Kira's headware. She grimaced, shaking her head as she checked the message.

"Does either of you have anything urgent?" she asked the two men.

"I just got an update from Captain Estanza: we have an urgent contract and he's recalling everyone to *Conviction*."

Her people weren't ready...but while *Conviction* might be military for hire, she was still military. Sometimes, *ready* had to be what you had, not what you wanted.

5

THE SMALL MEETING room felt cramped with everyone Estanza had summoned. *Conviction*'s use of *Commander* as the only officer rank sometimes left the question of "who should be in meetings" with an odd answer.

Kira could mandate that she was the only person from the combat group attending the command meetings, but it was damn useful to have her squadron commanders fully in the loop. That meant the fighter wing alone brought four Commanders to the meeting: herself, Commander Ruben "Gizmo" Hersch from Darkwing Alpha, Commander Joseph "Longknife" Hoffman from Memorial-Bravo and Commander Marjut "Ratchet" Shelby from Darkwing Bravo.

The fifth flight group person probably technically had the title, but the broad-shouldered deck boss Angel Waldroup had never gone by anything except "Deck Boss" since Kira had first boarded the carrier.

If they counted Captain Estanza as separate from the ship/flight group divide, Kira's people outnumbered the ship officers present. Only three of *Conviction*'s officers present held the Commander title: the XO Kavitha Zoric, the ground commander Caiden McCaig and the chief engineer Lakshmi Labelle.

The last member of the senior staff was Yanis Vaduva, the swarthy and always-smiling purser who ran the mercenary company's finances. Like Waldroup, he probably had the title Commander on some table of organization somewhere and never used it.

The meeting room was attached to Estanza's office, a breakout space designed for small meetings just like this. With the expansion of the fighter wing, the Captain had opened the wall to his office to allow them slightly more breathing room.

If Kira was getting two more squadrons' worth of starfighters, she was either going to have to give up on bringing all of her squadron commanders or she and Estanza were going to have to negotiate the meeting location.

For now, she waited patiently as an artificially stupid robot rolled around the outside of the room, supplying mugs of preferred beverages. With McCaig sitting next to her, she could smell the rich tones of the chocolate mixed into the big man's coffee.

With her new need for bodyguards, Kira had become familiar with the type of man she mentally classed as "meat slab." McCaig dwarfed them all at just over two and a quarter meters tall and broad for his height. She suspected there *had* to be some genetic tinkering in the ground commander's background, but the caloric needs of that mass explained the chocolate.

And, well, asking if someone had genetic tinkering was only slightly more polite than asking if they still had their birth gender. A lot of information was readily available the moment your headware was in direct contact range of another person…and a lot of information was nobody's business.

"If everyone is sufficiently caffeinated and sugared, as the case may be, we need to get started," Estanza told them. The Captain stood from his chair in an unassuming movement that still managed to capture every eye in the room.

Kira had seen John Estanza drunk and hopeless in an office. The transition back to the effortlessly charismatic commander had been a shock for her—but *Conviction*'s long-standing crew had always known that man existed, and the new crew had never seen anyone else.

This was the man, the legend, the second-in-command of the mercenary squadron that had won five wars. The drunk she'd first met had been the aberration, lost to his fears and leaning on his protégés.

She just wished they'd found a better way to bring the true Estanza back than having one of those protégés killed.

"First off, McCaig, your people are going to need to start prepping for boarding actions," Estanza said. "I know that's what you train for, but we might actually need it this time. Search-and-rescue focus, most likely."

Kira laser-focused on her CO. That meant a ship was missing.

"The Redward Royal Fleet destroyer *Hope* is one hundred twenty hours overdue from a standard patrol," Estanza told them all. "She's a *Sensibility*-class ship, the RRF's most advanced destroyer."

The Captain gestured and an image of the ship appeared in the middle of the conference room.

"In fact, from what I can tell, the three *Sensibility*-class destroyers are the RRF's most advanced warships, period," he noted. "They're fast and well-armed, twenty-eight thousand cubics with a crew of one hundred and fifty-five."

Twenty-eight kilocubics was on the small side for a destroyer by the standard Kira was used to. A quick check of her headware files on the Syntactic Cluster suggested it was actually on the large side for the Cluster. Her instinctive reactions hadn't caught up yet.

Fast and *well-armed* also had different meanings as she skimmed through the specifications on the *Sensibilities*. An Apollo destroyer of the same vintage would have taken *Hope* apart. It wouldn't have done so without damage, but the end result wouldn't have been in question.

"Her patrol was out to the Otovo System," Estanza continued. "The entire trip should only have taken twelve days there and back, including a stop to discharge static in Otovo. For her to be five days overdue strongly suggests she ran into something along the way.

"Unfortunately, the RRF doesn't have a lot of resources to spare at the moment," he told them. "The transition from paper to reality of the SCFTZ is placing a lot of demands on King Larry's fleet, especially his mid-weight units."

The Syntactic Cluster Free Trade Zone was a fledgling trade union that had been the baby of the kings of Redward for a generation. If they could bring the seventeen inhabited systems of the Cluster together in a mutually agreed low-tariff zone with coordinated anti-piracy patrols, every world would reap dividends.

They'd initially go toward the richer systems who *had* the freighters to take advantage of the FTZ, but those systems were also the ones who'd be putting up the ships for those anti-piracy patrols. Ten-kilo-cubic gunships couldn't secure trade route stops against pirates who'd have similar ships.

"So, they're hiring us," Vaduva concluded for his Captain. "This is why they have us on retainer."

"Exactly. The terms are reasonable; the RRF and I have a pretty solid shared understanding of what's worth taking *Conviction* into space for now," Estanza told them. "There is a codicil in the contract that we attempt to keep fighter deployments to twelve or less."

He shrugged.

"*Attempt* is the key word there," he said. "They don't expect us to risk our people or *Conviction* herself to maintain that impression. Our retainer is sufficient that I don't intend to expose Redward's little secret just yet."

"So, what's the plan?" Kira asked.

"We follow *Hope*'s patrol route exactly," Estanza said instantly. "It's not a direct route; it's set up to pass through a few extra trade-route stops. Eight novas there and back. We will also discharge static in Otovo."

"I'll set up fighter sweeps for each stop," she confirmed. "We can do that without drawing attention to our numbers. Two PNCs for CAP, two Hoplites for search and rescue. We keep the rest of those two squadrons on standby in case we find somebody hostile who needs punching, but they stay aboard the carrier and don't draw attention."

"*Hope* is a new-enough ship that we might be looking at a pure systems failure, in which case we hope we get there before she runs out of oxygen," the Captain said grimly. "I'm *hoping* that's all it is."

"What else could it be, sir?" Hoffman asked. "The Costar Clans aren't going to pick a fight with a destroyer, not after the Kiln."

The Clans mostly had the standard ten-thousand-cubic-meter gunship. Every human colony had been set up with enough of a tech base to build the hull, Harrington coils, and nova drive for a ten-kilo-cubic freighter. So, of course, every human colony also built ten-kilo-cubic gunships as the most basic type of FTL-capable warship.

The Costar Clans were a loose alliance of abandoned mining stations, forgotten and marginal habitats, and similar groups that couldn't afford to buy their needs for whatever reasons. Redward—and now the SCFTZ—were working to salvage many of the habitats and stations and bring them to a level of stability that precluded raiding.

Right now, the Clans were the biggest threat in the region—and most of their heavier ships had been swept in a recent attempt at conquest under an Equilibrium-assisted warlord. Any Clan ship that could have seriously threatened *Hope* had died at the Battle of the Kiln.

"There is always the chance that *someone* picked a fight with an RRF destroyer," Estanza said grimly. "Our employers don't currently have any serious enemies on the board, but that doesn't mean there's no one who means them ill. We keep our eyes open and we watch for trouble."

"Redward is trying to change things," Kira reminded the others. "That always pisses some people off—and while Redward might be the biggest dog in the Cluster, there's plenty of people out there with the hulls and guns to take on a single destroyer in the wrong place at the wrong time."

"But why one destroyer?" McCaig asked. "Especially one of their more-advanced ones? That's a risk."

"Potentially, to get their hands on that very advanced tech," Labelle noted, their voice soft. "Even if they can't get into the ship's fabricator templates, someone could learn a lot about Redward's R&D by tearing down *Hope*."

"There's a lot of reasons why someone might have taken her down," Estanza agreed, meeting Kira's gaze. She knew the *other* reason, too: the Equilibrium Institute believed that projects like the SCFTZ created more problems in the end. They wanted *someone* to step in and be the dominant power enforcing the rules.

As far as the Institute was concerned, Redward would either become that power or be used as a foil to *create* that power.

"Regardless of what happened, our mission is to find *Hope* and rescue her crew," the Captain concluded. "We'll complete the same patrol along the way, which will help secure those trade stops, but our objective is to find Redward's ship.

"We have bonuses in the contract for every crew member retrieved alive as well as for retrieving *Hope* in various states of intactness." He paused, then smiled. The expression was slightly sad but honest.

"It says a lot about King Larry and his people that we'll get paid more for bringing home all of *Hope*'s crew than we would for bringing the ship back intact without them," he noted. "We get paid best, of course, for bringing home both.

"If someone came after *Hope*, they'll find out we're a lot bigger and a lot more dangerous than she was. If *Hope* is having problems, we'll get her and her crew home. Either way, the first step is to *find* her.

"We nova in ninety minutes."

6

NOTHING.

Three novas and two trade-route stops had shown the same result. The fourth nova had just finished as Kira's Hoplite kicked into space, but she already knew what they were going to find.

Nothing.

The trade route they were following was roughly thirty degrees off the direct course toward the Ypres System, generally regarded as the gateway into the Syntactic Cluster from more coreward stars. Of the systems reached along this set of five trade-route stops, only Otovo couldn't be reasonably reached from a different route.

That meant these trade-route stops were surveyed and safe to nova into, but almost no one was using them. There'd at least been *some* ships at the two previous stops.

This time, Kira's scanners showed a complete blank as she pulled the fighter into formation "above" *Conviction* and waited for her wing pilot to join her. That took a few seconds longer than it might have but not as long as she had feared.

Suman "Clanker" Chaudhari had been a copilot on one of the Darkwing PNCs, so they had a decent handle on how a nova fighter operated. They were still one of Kira's newbies in Memorial Squadron, normally flying under Hoffman.

So long as this mission kept being this quiet, Kira was going to take advantage of the relative calm to test her pilots. She was keeping a close eye on everyone she was sending out—and on the time.

Sixty hours so far. *Hope* had been one hundred and twenty hours overdue. They were moving at the same pace the destroyer had been using, which meant they were always seventeen days behind the RRF ship.

"I'm not seeing anything out here, Commander," Clanker's voice told her over the flight link. "No ships, no jamming, nothing. *Conviction*'s scanners don't pick up anything either."

"I see the same," she confirmed. "But we sweep anyway, Clanker. The last thing we want to do is miss a crippled ship because she's gone cold. I'm sending you coordinates; we nova on my mark."

It took the class two drive sixty seconds to cool down from anything less than a one-light-minute nova. The bigger class one drive took multiple minutes, limiting the in-system—or in-trade-route-stop —use of novas.

Of course, the six-light-year standard nova took twenty hours to cool down from, so the bigger ships were stuck at sublight speeds anyway.

"I have the coordinates," Clanker replied. They at least sounded calm and ready. "I make a standard sweep at twenty light-minutes. Confirm?"

"Confirmed," Kira said. They'd nova out in one-light-minute chunks, to make sure they found anything, and then bounce around the exterior of that sphere for several hours. By the time they returned to the carrier, they'd know if anything was anywhere inside the surveyed trade stop.

Like Clanker, Kira figured she knew the answer—but they had the time to spend anyway.

"Maintain formation and...nova."

TEN HOURS LATER, a second set of Hoplites passed Kira as she and Clanker returned to *Conviction*. They would stick with the PNCs, providing the CAP around the carrier. All ten hours of scanning had done was confirm what they'd already known: this was a half-forgotten trade route with nobody there.

Their scans would be sold to the various civilian databases and make the trade-route stop a tiny but measurable bit safer for the next ship that novaed there, though. It wasn't a complete waste of a stop.

Conviction's computers took over and gently guided the two nova fighters to rest. There was a time for manual landings, but these days, Kira scheduled those in advance. Occasionally surprising people was all well and good, but too many of her pilots were too green for her to risk surprise drills that could wreck the carrier!

Waldroup was waiting for Kira as she dismounted the fighter, the deck boss wordlessly falling into step beside her as the teams took over the Hoplite.

"Problem, Boss?" Kira asked.

"Licensing," the other woman said flatly.

"Licensing?" Kira echoed as she doffed her flight helmet and placed it in her locker. She was perfectly capable of removing her flight gear while talking, but she wasn't sure how licensing was a factor yet.

"Our fabricators run complex digital-rights software to make sure we don't make anything that isn't licensed," Waldroup reminded her.

"Yeah, we had to crack it to get the Redward R&D teams enough pieces to make new nova fighters," Kira remembered. "If we cracked it, why is it a problem?"

"Because there's a bit we never had the code for," the other woman told her. "The fabricators you brought with you were designed to repair Hoplites, not build new ones. We filled in the gaps with what we had, and the biggest one is the Harringtons."

Harrington coils needed gravity to be manufactured. They couldn't be built in a spaceship fabricator, so Kira supposed there was no point in the parts fabricators for her fighters having the designs.

"And?" She waited for Waldroup to get to the problem.

"We didn't notice until we had a lot more flight data, but that's one of the benefits of these sweeps," the Deck Boss told her. "The Harring-tons we're using are Redward-built. With the repairs, two of the existing Hoplites are running Redward Harringtons too, but it's most obvious on the new-builds."

"*Obvious* is a problem," Kira conceded. If it was *obvious* to an external observer that half of her Hoplites had never seen the Apollo System, that would start raising the questions Redward was concerned about.

"Exactly," Waldroup said grimly. "I just went over the data for your flight with Clanker. We can't do that where anyone can see it."

"Mix an original bird with a new one?" Kira asked. "That obvious, huh?"

"If we've got two original birds, even if one has refitted coils, they look close enough," the Boss told her. "If we've got new-build birds, no one can pick out the difference because they don't have a comparative.

"But we can't fly new-build next to original, not without drawing attention."

"Fuck." Kira considered that. "It could be worse," she conceded. "So long as we *can* still fly the new-builds?"

"Unless we're running into somebody who'd have detailed sensor data on Hoplites, we're fine," Waldroup confirmed. "It's only putting them next to each other that will flag an anomaly."

"What about the PNCs?" Kira asked.

"Griffin is four hundred light-years from here, not a hundred," the other woman said with a chuckle. "I don't *care* if we piss them off. More importantly, none of our PNCs are running original-installation Harrington coils."

"Where the Hoplites were brand-new," Kira agreed. "All right. Would it help if we refitted all of the originals to Redward coils?"

"Not enough for it to be worth it," Waldroup said. "The Redward Harringtons cost us a bit of efficiency, too. We're making up for it by running more power to the coils, but it's costing you a small but noticeable chunk of your flight duration."

"I know," Kira admitted. "It's small enough that I'm not worried. Yet."

"I'll watch it all and let you know if we have more problems," the engineer replied. "Just...keep in mind that the new-builds look different to people looking with the right scanners."

"It's annoying, but it's better to know it than not," the CNG said. "We'll make it work, Angel. Thanks for keeping me updated."

7

EIGHT NOVAS and six days brought *Conviction* to the Otovo System. None of the six stops along the way—four along the trade route from Redward to Otovo and two along a detour close enough to check—had held any sign of *Hope*.

Across six trade route stops, they'd only seen five other ships, too. Kira found that a grim reminder of both how poor the Syntactic Cluster was in general and how poor this particular corner was. The Otovo System was a signatory of the Syntactic Cluster Free Trade Zone, but she suspected desperation was what was driving their involvement.

Like most systems colonized by humanity, Otovo had a midsized gas giant in the outer system and a slightly-smaller-than-Earth planet in the liquid-water zone. People needed habitable real estate to live on, and nova ships required the gas giants to discharge the inevitable tachyon-static buildup in the nova drive cores.

"Is there...nothing at the gas giant?" Cartman asked.

Kira and her usual wing pilot were standing in flight control, watching as Longknife took command of a four-fighter mixed CAP. Following on from Waldroup's concern, Memorial-Bravo's

Commander had borrowed one of the new-build Hoplites as he and Galavant joined two of the PNCs to watch over *Conviction*.

"There's a fueling station above the larger moon," Zoric pointed out from the bridge. There was a live connection between the three "command spaces" of the carrier: the bridge, flight control, and the carrier's lightly used combat information center.

"I meant defenses," Cartman admitted. "I'm used to seeing a couple of asteroid fortresses and a few monitors at least."

Like the asteroid fortresses they supported, sublight monitors were often *much* bigger than nova warships. They were part of the equation that rendered most worlds nearly invulnerable to attack.

"We're picking up a few things around the fueling station that might be weapons satellites," the carrier XO replied. "But so far as we can see, Pilot Cartman, you're right."

Kira shivered. Otovo had a second gas giant, but this one was closest to the inhabited planet most of the time. Usually, that would mean both more extraction infrastructure to feed the planet's power needs and the accompanying defenses to keep that infrastructure safe.

"We're moving in to drop our discharge cables," Zoric continued. "The Captain is trying to make contact with the locals and see if they heard from *Hope*. He said to have you stand by, Commander Demirci. He figures he'll want you and I on the call if he manages to find someone in authority."

"I assume that fueling station is run by somebody, if nothing else," Kira muttered. "I'll watch for his word, Commander," she promised. "I keep forgetting how damn poor the Cluster is. Redward's bad enough some days..."

"And Redward is rich to most of these people," Zoric agreed. "They're trying to lift everybody else up to a point where they can at least buy Redward's coffee. But...this is the end of the civilization out here, Kira."

"And this is the *coreward* side of the cluster," Kira muttered. "You'd think they'd find somebody to work with."

"You forget, Commander, that the Cluster is doing *well* by the standards of this far out in the Rim," Waldroup said softly, the deck boss looking over her shoulder. "They're close enough together to enable the trade routes to be mapped and maintained locally. That's not true of everywhere fifteen hundred light-years out."

Kira grimaced. Even a hundred and fifty light-years closer in, Apollo and Brisinger were a step above this. She could barely conceive of what being *worse* than the Cluster looked like.

But then, she knew there were people—untold billions of them, in fact—to whom her home would look as backward and underdeveloped as Otovo did to her. That was almost as hard to wrap her brain around some days.

"EM DREESSEN, these are my senior officers: Commander Kavitha Zoric and Commander Kira Demirci," Estanza introduced Kira and Zoric a moment after they joined the virtual conference.

Kira's headware updated her on the androgynous individual across the computer-generated table. Harper Dreessen's loose hair hung down to cover their face as they bowed their head in acknowledgement of the introduction.

"Commanders," they greeted the new arrivals. "Captain Estanza. My people tell me you have urgent questions."

"Yes, Em Dreessen," Estanza confirmed. "The Redward Royal Fleet hired us to investigate the fate of their destroyer *Hope*. We understand they docked seventeen days ago?"

"*Hope*." Dreessen suddenly looked very tired. "Yes, Captain Kopp and her vessel were here on schedule. They discharged their static and purchased fuel from the station. They've gone missing?"

"When we left, she was five days overdue for her return to Redward," Estanza said. "Did anything out of the ordinary happen while they were here?"

The administrator shook their head.

"*Hope* arrived and fueled on schedule," they repeated. "Our parent corporation has a standing contract with the RRF to provide provisioning for their vessels in the Otovo System. They proceeded from here to Otovo itself, which the RRF ships do about half of the time."

"I see," Estanza said. "Anything else of note that we should be concerned with?"

"That depends on what you're looking for," Dreessen said grimly. "Otovo is not a rich system and we do not see many visitors, Captain Estanza. I am aware of several problems in the region, but I can't be certain if my government asked *Hope* to investigate any of them."

"I take it the Otovo System doesn't have sufficient forces to investigate much on their own?" Estanza asked.

Dreessen laughed bitterly.

"Captain, unless your ship's sensors are far worse than I expect, you realize that my refueling station has a grand total of six defensive satellites that might, between them, manage to convince a particularly aggressive chicken to leave us alone. The rest of the system is not significantly better defended."

They shrugged.

"I believe we have four gunships," they concluded. "We do have a small fleet of nova-capable ten-thousand-cubic freighters, which this station was built to support. They're mostly engaged in hauling raw materials from some out-system operations...and several of *them* are overdue."

Kira heard Estanza grunt in reaction. That wasn't promising.

"Who would Captain Kopp have spoken to on Otovo?" Estanza asked.

"I don't know," Dreessen admitted. "In theory, she's a junior captain from an allied power and would talk to some functionary at the Navy Department. In truth...quite possibly the President."

"All right. Thank you, Em Dreessen," Estanza told the administrator. "My purser will be in touch shortly to organize our own refueling, but we will be on our way shortly."

"I hope Captain Kopp is all right," Dreessen told them. "We truly appreciate the RRF sweeping our trade routes, Captain Estanza. Without their help, I'm not sure anyone would ever show up in our corner of the galaxy."

ESTANZA HELD Zoric and Kira in the call as Dreessen cut out, the virtual conference switching from a standardized meeting room to a more casual hunting-lodge-den setting with overstuffed chairs and a roaring fire.

From the surprised glance the Captain gave the fire, that wasn't *quite* what he'd been expecting.

"Captain?" Zoric asked.

"I think I need to talk to Labelle," Estanza said slowly. "I think my *casual office* setting got randomized again."

"We have a casual office setting?" Kira replied.

"You can set up whatever you want," the Captain told her. "But *Conviction*'s computers might decide you're wrong and reset the settings. *This*"—he gestured around them—"was one of six the *original* Captain kept in a random rotation for more casual virtual meetings."

That was…strange. *Conviction* had been built for the Starmichael Trade Security Forces over a hundred and sixty years earlier. She'd been a third-tier ship for that Meridian power then and was utterly obsolete by their standards now.

But there shouldn't have been personal files from the original Captain on board after a century and a half!

"She's getting quirkier, sir," Zoric said quietly. "The radiator failure was weird."

"She's getting old," Estanza admitted. "We're well past the point where entropy set in, Kavitha. There's only so much we can do to hold the old girl together without plugging her into a serious shipyard for a complete rebuild…and there isn't a yard within three hundred light-years of here that could actually do a good job at that."

He sighed.

"*Maybe* Crest or Apollo," he conceded before Kira could say anything, "but only their *military* yards, which aren't going to take on a mercenary ship. We keep her going. Labelle is good at it, but sometimes odd things happen."

The Captain's virtual avatar gingerly took a seat in one of the fur-covered chairs.

"To the business of the moment, my *suspicion* is that the Otovon government asked *Hope* to go out of her way to investigate something for them," he told the two women. "Captain Kopp would have done so; there's no question. One of Redward's biggest concerns is that the poorer nations being drawn into the SCFTZ might see themselves as being exploited.

"I can't see them running into anything here that could take out *Hope,* but we are on the coreward side of the Cluster. Someone might have gone rogue and ended up in our space. Whatever happened, we need to find out—which means we need to know where *Hope* went."

"We're still at least eighteen hours from being able to nova," Zoric pointed out. "A short nova to Otovo won't cost us much time, but it would have to wait. Or we'd have to talk to them by radio."

"I have a better plan," Estanza said. "Kira, I want you to take two of the Hoplites to Otovo. It's a thirty-light-minute nova, so you'll be able to return well before we nova out. You'll need to make contact with the Navy Department and the government, work out who talked to Captain Kopp and what they told her."

"I can do that," Kira promised. "Not quite my expertise, but I imagine they want to be cooperative."

"Almost certainly. Whatever *Hope* was supposed to deal with for them, I suspect it's still a problem," Estanza said. "Which means the next people they're going to ask to deal with it are *us.*"

8

KIRA MADE certain that her arrival in Otovo orbit came *after* a long-enough wait that the lightspeed message announcing her mission was there ahead of her. Any sane government would react to the appearance of unannounced nova fighters in orbit of their planet with immediate and severe prejudice.

Upon arrival, she realized that she probably hadn't needed to worry. It wasn't that the Otovo defenses were incompetent. It was that the single asteroid fortress and half-dozen undersized monitors were sufficiently out of date that she wasn't sure they would be able to *target* her ship...and that was with her battlespace multiphasic jammers offline.

Announcing her arrival at least meant that one of those monitors—barely larger than *Conviction* despite not needing to fit inside a nova bubble—was in position to greet her and Nightmare's fighters as the two women emerged.

"Nova fighters, this is Otovo monitor *Michael*," came over the radio. "You are expected; please verify your identification immediately."

"*Michael*, this is Commander Kira Demirci of Conviction Limited, operating under contract to the Redward Royal Fleet," she replied crisply. "Identification codes attached to this transmission."

A moment passed. Then at least ten seconds as Kira tried not to roll her eyes.

"Identity verified, Commander Demirci," the monitor's communications officer finally replied. It had apparently taken them fifteen seconds to validate the RRF identifiers she'd provided. It should have taken two.

"We are awaiting instructions from the Navy Department as to… what exactly to do with you, sir," the junior officer continued. "Your message only barely preceded your arrival."

"I understand, *Michael*," Kira replied. "If you can provide a parking orbit, my wing pilot and I will maintain position as ordered. I am operating on a time limit, as *Conviction* will be leaving the system in just over seventeen hours. I would prefer to carry out my business by virtual conference if possible."

All of that had been in the message they'd sent ahead. On the other hand, Kira had sent that message thirty-three minutes before she'd novaed, and they'd received it barely three minutes earlier.

"I will make sure that's passed on to the Minister, sir," *Michael*'s determinedly unnamed officer told her. "Orbital data is being transmitted now. Please maintain position on the course provided or we may be required to take drastic action."

The *words* were threatening…but the young officer's tone was so dryly ironic that Kira suspected he knew *exactly* how much of a threat the monitor posed to her fighters. Once the multiphasic jammers came up, everything was down to optics and computer image processing—and even *that* wasn't entirely reliable.

Kira was relatively sure the monitors wouldn't be able to find the Hoplites, let alone hit them, if she raised her jammers. On the other hand, small as the monitors might be for their type, they were still *monitors* and she hadn't brought torpedoes. The Hoplites' built-in guns would take forever to burn through their heavy armor.

Neither of them actually had a chance of hurting the other, which made it a good thing no one was planning on causing trouble today!

THE ORBITAL MONITORS might have taken longer to confirm Kira's identify than she would have expected, but it took the local government less time to get someone on a channel who could answer her questions than she'd feared.

Of course, Kira had half-expected that they wouldn't *manage* to get someone who could answer her questions in sixteen hours. Otovo might be a poor and lightly populated planet, but that still left its elected officials governing over four hundred million people.

"Commander Demirci," a cheerful older woman appeared on her coms without preamble after roughly three hours. "We apologize for the delay. Are you able to speak to the Minister now?"

"I am at the Minister's convenience for about the next thirteen hours," Kira replied. "I am able to speak to them now."

"Of course. Stand by for Minister Crystalline."

The older woman vanished, replaced by a rotating seal of a stylized caninoid of some kind. Kira didn't recognize it, which meant it had at least a thirty percent chance of being native to Otovo.

The rotating seal was replaced with a request for a virtual conference. Kira accepted and found herself inside an office on the corner of a glass-walled tower looming over a city.

From the look of things, either the tower was entirely illusory or it was almost alone in the city. She eyeballed it at about thirty stories, small by even Redward standards, but it was unmatched in the area she could see.

Clearly intentionally rustic wooden walls separated the corner office from the rest of the tower. The floor was plain white tile, and the only furniture being relayed into the virtual meeting was a table that she suspected was overlaid over someone's desk.

The posture of the man on the other side of the table certainly suggested he was sitting at a desk—though Kira's virtual avatar wasn't mirroring her actual body at all, so that could be deceptive.

"Commander Demirci," the man greeted her. He was a smaller bald man in a conservative black suit that offset skin the color of pale jade and eyes that glittered with unnatural color. "I am Minister Joseph Crystalline, the head of Otovo's Navy Department."

"I appreciate you making the time to speak with me, Minister,"

Kira said carefully. Politicians were *always* dangerous, even the ones you were reasonably sure were on your side.

"In all honesty, I've been waiting and hoping for someone to arrive from Redward for some time now," Crystalline said. "*Hope*'s silence has been even more terrifying for us than you, I fear."

"She was five days overdue at Redward when we left," Kira told him. "The RRF has a thousand demands on their time, so they sent us. I'm assuming she wasn't destroyed here, but it sounds like she didn't leave to continue her patrol."

"Captain Kopp and I spoke in some detail when she visited us," he said. "President Redding was involved in several of those conversations as we, frankly, begged for her help. I don't know how much of that detail you will need."

"All of the detail, none of the begging," Kira replied. "We need to know where *Hope* went and why. Our contract with the RRF is to locate *Hope* and retrieve her and her crew."

"That is what I presumed and hoped," Crystalline told her. "I will provide all the information I can. Are you recording to provide to Captain Estanza?"

"I am," she confirmed. "I am empowered to negotiate on his behalf as well, if that becomes relevant. With the lives of *Hope*'s crew potentially in the balance, we are worried about time."

"As we all are, Commander," the Minister agreed. He paused thoughtfully.

"Captain Kopp agreed to investigate a situation we are dealing with," he began. "The entirety of our nova-capable navy consists of three gunships purchased secondhand from Redward ten years ago. Obsolete by RRF standards, I know, but more effective vessels than we were capable of building.

"But when one of our mining outposts reported that they'd seen Costar Clan vessels in the system, we sent a gunship to investigate," Crystalline told her. "They didn't come back. We confirmed they arrived, but they were never seen after they left on a survey of the system."

"But you were still in communication with the outpost?" Kira asked. "What were you mining out-system?"

"Fissionables," the Minister explained. "For whatever reason, Otovo System doesn't have any easily accessible deposits of heavy metals. The DLI-O54 System is mostly asteroids, and some of those asteroids are readily minable for the same fissionables that we have difficulty extracting here.

"It was cheaper to set up mining outposts and a small fleet of ten-kilocubic freighters than it has been to operate deep-drilling operations on our own uninhabited worlds." He shrugged. "That may change over time, especially if the situation is as bad as I fear."

"Were you still in communication after you lost the gunship?" she prodded.

"We were, but we started to lose ships," he said grimly. "It started with every fifth or sixth, but by the time *Hope* arrived, we were losing a ship in three. We only had a hundred of the transports to begin with, Commander, and by that point, the government had already been forced to step in to keep them insured and operating."

"So, you asked *Hope* to investigate," she concluded.

"We did. Captain Kopp promised that she'd return within three days at most, with the intention of completing her overall patrol inside the allowed delays." Crystalline shook his head. "She never returned. There were fourteen transports in the system, Commander Demirci, and all of them should have come home by now.

"None of them have returned either."

An entire system gone silent. That sounded more ominous before taking into account that there were probably less than twenty thousand people in DLI-O54.

"So, you expected to hear from Captain Kopp fourteen days ago?" Kira asked.

"We did," Crystalline confirmed. "We dispatched a ship to Redward, but that was only five days ago. They will only be arriving now."

"I'm not sure the RRF has more resources to mobilize," she admitted grimly. "Our contract is clear: if *Hope* went to DLI, we're heading to DLI. Any information you can give us on the system is appreciated."

He tossed her a virtual file.

"That contains everything we have," he told her. "Ships, names, station positions, geography...everything." He chuckled bitterly. "If I was certain those people were alive, I just violated our privacy laws in eleven different ways."

"I won't tell anyone," Kira replied. "Is there anything else we should know, Minister?"

"My government would be willing to contract *Conviction* to investigate the Clan gunship sightings," Crystalline said quietly. "If you can secure our outposts and make certain our people are safe, we will happily pay. I am unsure what your rates are, but we do have a stockpile of both Redward kroner and Royal Crests."

Kira was torn. She knew she didn't make a very good mercenary, but that was both an offer she couldn't turn down—and an offer she couldn't help feel gross taking.

"We will have our people forward a contract," she said finally. "For one kroner in advance to make it official, plus a hundred-kroner bonus for each citizen rescued."

Two million kroner if they rescued all twenty thousand civilians wasn't...a lot. It would just about pay Kira's salary for a year, but she was offering the locals a deal. If they weren't already being paid by Redward—it cost the RRF a million kroner just to get *Conviction* to leave dock—she wouldn't have been so generous.

From Crystalline's expression, he understood both what she was offering and why.

"That sounds more than reasonable, Commander Demirci," he told her. "We will make certain all of the i's are dotted and t's are crossed before you leave."

9

"ONE KRONER, COMMANDER?" Estanza asked Kira as she entered his office. From his tone, he'd just barely stopped laughing. "You signed a contract for *one kroner*?"

"And bonuses," she countered. "Our expenses for going to DLI are already paid, aren't they?"

"They are," he conceded, still grinning. "And the bonuses aren't shabby. We might well find out that everyone is just panicking and sheltering in place, in which case we make a nice easy couple million.

"Of course, a couple million kroner is, what, three hundred thousand crests if we're counting real money?"

"I only keep up on the exchange rate as it relates to paying my people's salaries," Kira replied primly. "And buying their beer."

The Captain laughed again as the door opened behind Kira and Zoric joined them, shortly followed by McCaig.

The humor in the room faded as Estanza brought up the map of the DLI-O54 System above his desk. Like a lot of similar outpost systems, there were not only no habitable planets, there weren't actually very many *planets* at all.

DLI-O54 was a dim orange dwarf with a super-Jovian that was almost a binary partner. A single rocky world had survived, closer to the star than the gas giant, but the tidal forces had ripped everything else apart into an immense asteroid field that defied the term *belt*.

The Otovon outposts were barely a blip on the size of the asteroid field, a dozen stations assembled from prefabricated components. They were all close enough to the edge of the field to be easily accessed by the small nova freighters that delivered their supplies and carried away their production.

"None of those stations are particularly large or hard to sweep," McCaig said. "I know the type. They look messy, but all of the pieces are the same, so they're generally pretty easy to follow on the inside. Rescue ops should be straightforward if needed."

"Is it likely they'll be needed?" Zoric asked. "From the files we got and Kira's conversation with the Minister, it looks like we're dealing with pirates, not an invasion force."

"Raiding one of the processing stations is probably a better risk-reward ratio than anything else related to Otovo," Estanza pointed out. "More importantly, we know no one has sent any coms back and forth with Otovo since *Hope* would have arrived here. Otovo was holding the freighters until Kopp reported in, but there were fourteen ships in DLI that should have come home.

"Something happened to those ships and it might well have happened to the stations as well," he concluded grimly, "and that's ignoring that one of the most modern destroyers in the entire Cluster went into this system to check on these people and didn't come back."

The office fell silent around Kira now and she grimaced.

"We're bigger and my fighters are more dangerous than *Hope*," she noted. "We'll go in loaded for an alpha strike, torps on every bird. We'll stick to our official list strength for the first launch, but that's still two full squadrons.

"If someone thinks they can attack a civilian installation like this and walk away scot-free, I have another think coming for them—and it's bringing thermonuclear explosions with it."

Estanza snorted, but the humor was gone from the room.

"The fighting is always going to fall on the nova group," he warned. "We updated our surprise from the Kiln to be a permanent installation, but it's still a sucker punch not a sustained combat effort."

Heading into the Kiln, Labelle had assembled crude fittings along one side of the carrier to hold torpedoes. The one-shot weapons had saved the carrier from an unexpected attack by the Brisingr heavy fighters the Equilibrium Institute had given the Costar Clans, and they'd decided to repeat the trick.

The new installations were more permanent, but they were still relatively crude. Most importantly, reloading them required an EVA by the engineering crew to manually refill the box launchers with new torpedoes.

Conviction could now duplicate the onboard armament of a cruiser three-quarters of her size...once. After that, she was just as unarmed as she'd ever been.

"We'll have the Bravo Squadrons ready to go in case there's something seriously wrong out there," Kira promised. "I wish I had a chance to run my people through some scenarios, but we don't have enough time."

"What would you do this time, throw them at a SolFed carrier group?" Zoric asked. "That might be a bad precedent, given your apparent omniscience."

Kira managed a smile in response to that. In preparation for the operation at the Kiln, she'd thrown her fighter wing into an exercise against multiple Brisingr heavy destroyers and heavy fighter squadrons—mostly because she'd had simulation data files for those ships.

When they'd actually ended up fighting those ships, she'd acquired a reputation as a dangerous kind of prophet.

"I was thinking more along the lines of the same exercise I threw at them before the Kiln," she admitted. "It's a good disaster-proofing scenario, since we don't actually expect our fighter group to take on multiple modern destroyers."

"And that's being generous in calling Brisingr ships modern," Estanza pointed out. "But they're the most modern ships we have enough data to run simulations with."

He shook his head.

"I like exercises as much as the next commanding officer, but timing might make all of the difference. How long until we nova?"

"Three hours till the core has cooled enough," Zoric reported. "We've completed our tachyon-static discharge and refueled; just waiting on the exotic-matter elements to restabilize."

"If I have the time to take an hour to prep the fighters, I'll take it," Kira said grimly. "That doesn't leave us the time to run simulations. I'm better off making sure they've all showered and eaten."

"And the same for the rest of the crew," Zoric agreed. "Better fed and ready—I'm assuming we're going to battle stations prior to nova?"

"A good call," Estanza agreed. "We don't know what's waiting for us there—but *something* killed Redward's fanciest destroyer. Let's be ready to nova into hell, everyone."

Kira knew perfectly well that the ship was still two degrees above the normal temperature...and she still shivered against the chill—and she wasn't alone.

No one in this room had any illusions what "novaing into hell" could look like.

10

DESPITE THE FACT that every single person aboard *Conviction* and in her fighter crews had reasonably modern headware that could track time for them, there was a massive clock on the side of the flight deck counting down the time until the nova.

It currently sat at five minutes, and Kira's pilots and support crews were buzzing across the deck like angry ants. There was a pattern to the chaos, one she was intimately familiar with, and she wove her way through it with practiced ease.

"I can't help but notice that the plan calls for *your* fighters not to be carrying torpedoes," Joseph Hoffman told her as the gaunt pilot emerged from the crowd. "We both know a Hoplite flies like a garbage truck with a torpedo loaded."

"And against anything except other nova fighters, it won't matter," Kira countered. Her squadron commander fell in beside her as they dodged their way through the chaos. "The second strike group will have time to offload the torpedoes if we *are* looking at nova fighters or sub-fighters, but against the gunships and corvettes the Costar Clans field, we'll need those torpedoes."

"And the first strike group needs the extra maneuverability,"

Hoffman conceded. "I just don't like the stickiness of hauling it—and we *have* the PNCs."

"Each of whom is hauling *three* torpedoes for less of a maneuverability penalty, yes," she agreed. The PNC-115s could carry a single torpedo without problems, but the extra mass of three had a noticeable impact on what their Harringtons could achieve. The heavier fighter-bomber could still handle it better than the Hoplites, which were only intended to carry torpedoes in an emergency.

"If things go right, we won't even launch the second group," Kira told her subordinate. "But if things go wrong, I want to be ready for them going *very* wrong. If we're looking at a force that punched out a twenty-eight-kilocubic destroyer to see what they could lure out, well, we might need every torpedo we can field."

"If it's a trap, they have no idea what they've bitten off," he said brightly. "I don't like the torps, boss, but I know where to put them if we need them." He glanced up at the clock. "Minus one-eighty; I need to stop distracting you."

"Believe me, Longknife, you were nowhere near distracting me enough for me to miss the launch window," Kira said with a chuckle. "Lock and load, my friend. Fly straight."

"Break a leg, sir," he told her, snapping to Academy-precise attention and giving her a perfect salute. "We're right behind you, waiting for the call."

Kira returned his salute far more lazily as she reached her own nova fighter, a mental command folding out the entry ramp.

"See you on the other side," she said as the fighter closed up behind her, an automatic process that took her from standing on the ramp to seated in the cockpit. She could override it—the Hoplite didn't have *much* of a cabin outside the cockpit, but it did have one—but today, that was where she needed to be.

"*Conviction*-Nova-Actual," she said firmly into the tactical network. "Linked in, live. Sound off."

"Memorial-Alpha-Two, linked in, live," Cartman's voice told her. "Memorial-Alpha Squadron is clear and ready to engage."

"Darkwing-Alpha-Actual," Hersch added a moment later, sounding surprisingly calm. "Darkwing-Alpha Squadron is clear."

"Nova in sixty seconds," she reminded them. "We launch immediately upon clearance. Mission is search and defend. Priority is protection of local civilians and Redward military assets. Today isn't a day for kills."

At least half of the pilots in each squadron were already aces, anyway. Two of the ex-copilots Kira had co-opted for her own Memorials had flown for her before and made ace—three kills, all gunships that time around.

That left her five ex-copilots who had no kill markers on their fighters, and four ex-gunship pilots, one in each squadron, who had no kills earned in nova fighters.

Kira had no idea what was waiting in DLI-O54, but she was taking no chances. Twenty-four nova fighters was more than even existed in the Syntactic Cluster outside Redward. Green as her group was, she'd take them up against anything the Cluster had to offer.

"All hands, all hands, this is Commander Zoric. Nova in ten. Nine. Eight. Seven. Six. Five. Four. Three. Two. One.

"Nova."

WHILE NOVAING aboard a fighter was always an uncomfortable experience, bigger ships with their heavier hulls and class one nova drives didn't suffer from that particular side effect. Thankfully, that also went for pilots in nova fighters aboard said bigger ships.

"Ball is released," Angel Waldroup snapped on the tactical network. "Alpha squadrons, launch, launch, launch."

All Kira did this time was send a release command to the computers. They were launching twelve fighters in half as many seconds. Humans had written the program for the launch cycle, but no human could process fast enough to take on the task of actually carrying it out.

She barely had time to blink before she was in open space, her Harrington coils flaring to life as the reactionless engines gave her control of her fighter. The rest of her systems came online in seconds, her weapons warmly responding to her commands and her sensors seeking the enemy.

"Nova-Actual, this is *Conviction*, we are feeding you the download from our scanners," Zoric's voice said in her mental ear. "Geography is as expected, but…"

"But what, *Conviction*?" Kira demanded sharply. That didn't sound good.

"There's nothing here, Kira," the carrier XO told her, dropping radio security protocol. "No hostile warships, no jamming fields, no Costar gunships—but also no Otovon freighters and no Otovon mining stations."

Kira's stomach tried to drop through the bottom of her fighter. That was bad. That was *really* bad. A mining station wasn't a subtle presence, usually buzzing with the rockets and Harringtons of the small craft that did most of the grunt work, and radiating heat and energy from its own processing facilities.

If nothing else, most mining stations were firing off high-powered sensors on a regular interval to find their *next* high-value mining target.

"They were destroyed?" Kira asked grimly.

"We can't confirm from this far out," Zoric replied. "We have no sensor readings on any significant heat or energy signatures anywhere in the star system."

"The Otovons gave us *full* details on those platforms," Kira snapped. "Project their locations and send the coordinates to my people. We sweep by pairs, but we confirm what the *hell* happened here."

"I've got a team on it," the XO confirmed a moment later, long enough for her to have passed on the commands. "I need at least a minute, maybe two. You'll have those coordinates. What then?"

"*Search and defend* just became *search and rescue*, Kavitha," Kira said grimly. "We find out what happened and we save whoever's left. That's what Otovo is paying us for—and it's the best way for us to find out what happened to *Hope*, too."

It was possible, she supposed, that someone had committed a mid-scale atrocity in the system *after* the Redward destroyer had come through, but that seemed unlikely. All of this had to be linked.

Somehow.

"PASSING YOU COORDINATES for the six largest stations," Zoric finally confirmed. "There were two processing and residential facilities that counted for over eighty percent of the population of the system. The other stations were explicitly work camps."

She paused for several seconds.

"There were children on the residential stations," she said, her voice suddenly very tired. "Possibly as many as three or four hundred."

"Understood," Kira replied, assessing the data as it came through her headware. "And then twenty-three workstations, none of which should have had more than twenty people aboard?"

"Four thousand people total across them all, according to the files from Otovo, and twenty-two thousand on the bigger stations."

"Understood," Kira noted. "Gizmo, you get the data?"

"I have it all, Basketball," he confirmed. "I suggest you and I take our wings and check out the main stations, sending the rest of the squadrons to check out the others?"

"By pairs," she agreed. She considered the situation for several more seconds, then nodded to herself. "*Conviction* Deck," she said grimly as she opened a wider channel, including the second strike group. "Clear the torps from Memorial-Bravo. Darkwing-Bravo is to launch immediately, Memorial-Bravo will launch once the torps are out.

"All squadrons are to sweep facilities in pairs. Nova back to *Conviction* if there is any question of your safety. Even if it's just one gunship. There are thousands of people out here. A lot of them might already be gone—but we are the *only* hope for the ones left.

"We save everyone we can."

Even as she'd been speaking, she'd been mentally allocating the targets to her people. She and Nightmare took the largest, Gizmo and Lozenge got the second-biggest, and so on down the list.

"You have your targets," she said as she sent out the data. "First pass is quick, then report back to *Conviction* so we can collate data and make a plan."

"We'll have the boarding teams ready to go by the time you get back," Zoric promised.

"We'll be back soon enough," Kira replied. "Nightmare, on me.

"Maintain formation and *nova*."

11

THE STATION SHOULD HAVE BEEN easy to find. It should have been a blazing sun of energy and activity, clearly visible even from *Conviction*'s position seven light-minutes away. From Kira's new position, within a light-second of its projected position, she should have been able to pick it out with the naked eye.

"I have nothing," Nightmare reported grimly. "Wait...I had a debris field at sixty by one oh five."

"I see it," Kira confirmed, focusing her scanners. "Looks like..." She exhaled a long sigh.

"Looks like one of the Otovon freighters," she concluded. "I've got decaying exotic-matter signatures consistent with a standard one-thousand-cubic-class nova drive. Let's move closer," she ordered. "Most likely, the freighters would have been near the station."

"Wilco."

The two nova fighters dove through the dark. Kira didn't usually find space constricting or even particularly unusual. She'd spent most of her adult life behind the stick of a starfighter, after all. This was her life and her passion.

Today, though, the dark pressed in on her as she bounced around the outer edge of an asteroid belt. The radiation signatures in the belt weren't helping with her calm either. It would take some effort to hide in DLI-O54's asteroid field, but it would be possible. That wasn't true of most asteroid belts, let alone empty space.

"Wait," she whispered. "I've got…something. Nightmare, I'm sending you coordinates. Spread the view; let's collate the cameras and see what we can get."

The two fighters moved apart, synchronizing their sensors to create a facsimile of a single larger sensor.

"Heat signature," Kira finally concluded. "System is reading it at just over minus thirty Celsius."

Compared to the roughly three Kelvin or minus two hundred and seventy Celsius of the rest of the space around them, it was enough to be picked out. The asteroids were warmer than empty space, but they still wouldn't reach minus thirty.

A human-inhabited space station, which both created heat to keep the occupants warm enough and radiated that heat away to keep them cool enough, should be pinging at something closer to *positive* twenty or thirty Celsius.

"Form on my wing," Kira ordered. "Let's move in slow and careful. I'm picking up more debris field as well. There's at least three wrecked freighters here."

Depending on the ships, that could be anywhere from six to thirty dead. That number barely registered to Kira right now—because there were supposed to be twelve *thousand* people on the station she was investigating.

"I've got her!" Nightmare snapped. "Thermal signature verified by visual… What the fuck happened here?"

Kira's own computers were fractions of a second behind Cartman's, updating her with long-ranged optical views of the station.

Built from prefabricated components, a mining and processing station like this had to rely on artificial gravity. A cheap station built in the same system as its industrial base could be a ring, but rings didn't lend themselves to being moved in ten-thousand-cubic-meter chunks.

Instead, it was a collection of boxes, mostly twenty-meter cubes. Nothing bigger could be moved by the small but cheap ships used by Otovo. Kira could see where four of the cubes had been linked together in a row to create the primary ore-processing facility. At least a dozen of them formed a spiraling complex that had clearly been built to be as decorative as possible, given the components available.

The station should have been glittering with lights and activity, with an endless stream of transports and mining ships, massive solar panels and heat radiators extending off into the night, and at least one rotating sensor array to sweep the system for mining targets.

All of that was gone. Kira could see where the solar panels had been anchored, but plasma fire had shredded the external support structure. Any ships that had survived the attack had docked, but from the debris field surrounding the crippled space station, she wasn't sure any had.

"Power core is dead," Nightmare reported. "It's the only spot on the station itself that was shot, but someone took it out with what looks like a gunship's cannon."

"Sensor array and solar panels were obliterated too," Kira agreed. "Someone wanted to make damn sure they didn't see something. I'm not even sure killing everyone from exposure was part of the plan."

She shook her head angrily.

"It might just have been a happy side effect."

They couldn't even risk getting close. The debris field of wrecked small craft and peripherals was actively dangerous. Normally, Kira would set her ship's guns to defensive mode and sweep in, but she needed to be sure there was no one alive.

"Let's keep up the synchronized heat scan," she ordered. "With the fusion plant gone, they're not radiating a lot of heat, but we should be able to confirm if they're still generating power."

Normally, getting *rid* of heat was the biggest problem on a space station. But if the mining platform's power core and production systems were all offline, any survivors would be at risk of running out of heat. And air. And water. And...

The data from the detailed heat scans started to come back, and Kira gently bit her tongue to try to control her hope.

"I have multiple sections of increased heat," she said aloud, hoping Nightmare was following along. "It looks like they've concentrated whatever power and population is left into the bottom half of the spiral."

"The spiral has to be the residential section of the station," Cartman replied. "There's no way they put the effort into making something pretty into one of the industrial segments."

"So, they've got aux power running there to keep people warm and breathing," Kira agreed. She looked at the data again and shivered. "Or unfrozen and breathing. I'm not picking up any coms, though."

Even the *warm* sections of the station were hovering around zero. The structure was *designed* to shed excess heat. Without the fusion plant, that design would slowly but surely become a real hazard to the occupants.

Of course, they'd still probably run out of oxygen first.

"We need to nova back and bring *Conviction* in," Kira decided aloud. "Hopefully, the other residential is in a similar state. It's going to make our lives harder, but better to have two stations to save."

Because the alternative didn't bear worrying about.

MOST OF THE nova fighters were already back when Kira and Nightmare emerged from their nova. A three-hundred-cubic-meter nova fighter *shouldn't* have had anything that could count as body language, but somehow, they managed it.

Kira had a lot of experience at judging pilot moods by the way they flew, and she guessed the worst of the news before she even linked in with Zoric.

"*Conviction*, this is Nova-Actual. Brief me," she ordered.

"None of the smaller stations are left," Zoric said bluntly. "Each was hit by what appears to have been gunships and...obliterated. No survivors at any site we checked out."

"The primary station is badly damaged but structurally intact," Kira replied. "Solar panels, sensor arrays, and support craft have all been destroyed, but the residential sections appear intact and appear to have operating emergency power.

"There were no coms, but it appears that at least a portion of the station populace is alive and sheltering in place," she continued. "We need to move to provide relief immediately. Has Hersch reported back in yet?"

"Negative, we're still waiting on him."

"We need to assume that the secondary station is in a similar state to the primary," Kira told Zoric. "I'm not sure how much use nova fighters are going to be for this, *Conviction*. This is a ground and medical team problem now."

"Understood. Hold for *Conviction*-Actual."

Kira sent a wordless assent and paused, waiting for the Captain.

"How bad?" Estanza asked bluntly.

"Bad," she confirmed. "They don't have power, they don't have sensors, they don't have coms. They don't know anyone is here to save them. All they can do is hold out as long as they can and hope…and it's hard to say how much hope they have left."

"We don't have the ability to transport large numbers of civilians," the carrier CO said grimly. "There's a lot we can do, but most of it is just buying them time until Otovo can relieve them."

"I'm not sure Otovo has the ships left to relieve them," Zoric warned. "We can update them and see what help they can provide, though, can't we?"

"A nova fighter would have a twenty-six-hour delay after jumping back to Otovo, but we can make the jump," Kira reminded them. "We can send one of the PNCs back to update the Otovon government and request assistance while we move in to provide support.

"No one in this system has the sensors to know we deployed the full wing. We recall all fighters except for the CAP and send for help."

"Next closest system is Ypres," Zoric pointed out. "They'll have more ships and better gear than Otovo."

"And it would take a nova fighter almost four days to make a trip *Conviction* can make in sixty hours," Kira countered. "None of my Apollons can go to Ypres alone, either."

"We can't wait on Gizmo," Estanza decided. "Basketball, you and Nightmare head to the secondary station and check in on Gizmo. Once you find him, update him and nova back to *Conviction*. Do you have a crew you'd pick to send back to Otovo?"

Kira considered. Her first choice would be Lozenge, who had the distinction of being the oldest of her pilots. Lozenge didn't want a squadron command but he was still a mature and sensible individual who'd make a good courier.

Of course, Lozenge was Gizmo's wing pilot, so he was off investigating the secondary station with his boss.

"We'll send Purlwise," she decided. That was Alpha-Four, Akira Yamauchi, one of the original PNC pilots from before Kira's time.

"We'll collate the data into a package once we're in position to commence rescue ops," Estanza told her. "We'll confirm the other station's situation once Hersch arrives and you catch up with us. Priority has to be rescuing as many people as humanly possible, so we move as fast as we can."

Conviction was already moving, her Harrington coils accelerating the big ship at a rate rarely seen. They couldn't nova for hours yet, but they could cross seven light-minutes in less time than it would take the nova-drive core to cool down.

"We can send the nova shuttles on ahead," Kira suggested. "If we deliver portable power generators, that may buy us time."

"Agreed," Estanza said. "So long as no one is watching, we pull out all the stops."

"I'll confirm on the secondary station ASAP," Kira said. Her fighter had completed the far shorter cooldown on its nova drive. "Nightmare, form on me. Time to go check on the kids."

"Gizmo's fine," Nightmare told her. "He knows well enough to stay out of trouble."

"Then what's taking him so long?" Kira asked grimly. "Maintain formation and nova."

12

KIRA AND NIGHTMARE emerged from nova in time to watch one of the two fighters they were looking for disappear *into* nova. Kira managed to keep her expression of disgust out of the channel as she took in the situation in front of her.

It only took her a few seconds to find the secondary station, but that was because one of her fighter-bombers was sitting on the edge of the debris field, flashing an emergency code.

"Gizmo, this is Basketball," she hailed the fighter. "What is your status?"

"I guess we were late," Hersch replied dryly. "Good news is that I have coms with the people on board the station and have a status update for them—Lozenge is carrying it back to the carrier."

"And bad news, Commander?" she asked.

"They didn't know if anyone was listening and their signal was even weaker than they thought," he said grimly. "I had to get closer than was wise to establish communications, and I took several hits from pieces of debris. My Harringtons are offline. I *think* it's an alignment issue and I can fix it, but…"

"*Conviction* is on her way to the primary station," Kira told him.

"Scans suggested most of the populace was alive and concentrated around what power and air generators they still have."

"Casa Bravo is in much the same state, according to Administrator Bronx," Hersch told her. "Out of nine thousand five hundred people aboard, the Administrator says she's got about eight thousand settled down in an impromptu camp around what systems they have. She's in intermittent contact with several other groups that might make up most of her missing souls, but they didn't sound like they were in good shape.

"Help is needed sooner rather than later," her senior subordinate said grimly.

"We've already sent one of the PNCs back to Otovo to request assistance," Kira told him. "*Conviction* is en route to Casa Alpha to provide assistance there."

Now that Hersch had used the name for this platform, her head-ware happily confirmed the somewhat unimaginative names of the stations: Casa Alpha and Casa Bravo. They probably weren't even in the first ten thousand stations to use the names.

"We have no coms with Alpha yet, so establishing that link is the priority," she continued. "Depending on Bravo's situation, *Conviction* might be able to detach some support."

Kira was grimly aware that they could only split their resources so far. The best shot *she* saw was using the nova-drive-equipped shuttles to supply and assist at Bravo while the carrier and her regular sublight shuttles assisted at Alpha.

Depending on when Otovo's ships showed up, that could cause problems...but Kira wasn't going to prioritize keeping the extra class two nova drives secret over saving lives. If nothing else, her impression was that King Larry would be *furious* if they did.

"Can you act as a relay so I can talk to the administrator?" she asked. "The more I know, the better plans we can make."

"I'll ping her," Gizmo agreed. "My impression is that the core population will be fine for at least a little bit, but..."

Kira nodded silently.

"We'll see what we can do," she promised.

It only took a few seconds for her to feel an additional presence on the channel. From the feel of the link, it was audio-only, which made sense. There was no sense wasting energy to send video when the station was in this much trouble.

"This is Administrator Samantha Bronx," the woman said, her voice level. Her tone was flat with exhaustion. "Do you have an update, Gizmo?"

"Administrator Bronx, this is Gizmo's CNG, Commander Demirci," Kira told the woman. "Gizmo sent for assistance from our carrier, and we've already sent a courier back to Otovo to request additional ships.

"*Conviction* is heading to Casa Alpha as we speak, but they won't be there for several hours still," she continued. "We do not have communications with Alpha's crew, but it appears they were also successful in preserving most of the population of the station."

Bronx sighed in relief.

"Thank you," she said quietly. "My wife and daughters are on Alpha, Commander, visiting a family friend. I had no choice but to fear the worst."

"We still don't know who is wounded or dead, Administrator," Kira warned. "You have my word we are doing everything we can. We will have additional resources in play here at Bravo shortly, but most of our resources are nova fighters. Attack craft aren't very good rescue vehicles."

If she concentrated a squadron, she could probably cut the station off its asteroid anchor and pull the entire structure out of the debris field. The risks involved in that boggled her mind, though. They couldn't haul the asteroid itself, and cutting the station free was probably a bad idea.

"I understand," Bronx conceded. "We still have...probably sixty hours of air and power for the main shelter. But I have two groups in the processing center that I am extremely concerned over."

"We can likely move to rescue them first if necessary," Kira offered.

"It almost certainly is," the administrator admitted. "They... Commander, they should have run out of power sixteen hours ago. They're still going and they won't tell me how they're powering their heat and air. There are engineers in both groups, and I am almost certain they've rigged up decay generators."

It took Kira a mental moment to pull up the files on the type of device the administrator was talking about. Basically, a pile of radioactive materials allowed to decay to provide heat and electricity. A crude one could keep a small local life-support plant going, but...

"I'm guessing they'd have a harder time finding shielding than finding unstable heavy metals in a heavy metal processing plant," Kira said slowly.

"And they might not have bothered," Bronx warned. "If they've done what I think they've done, they'll have bought everyone in their pockets days of time...at the cost of giving everyone radiation poisoning.

"The engineers and workers themselves...they..." The administrator swallowed, unable to finish the sentence.

They're dead was what she couldn't say. The men and women were almost certainly still walking around and talking, but Otovon medicine wasn't up to repairing that kind of cellular damage.

Conviction's was, Kira was reasonably certain...but she was also certain they could handle at most five cases like that.

"I understand," she told Bronx. "Like I said, we'll do everything we can."

FLASHES of blue Cherenkov radiation marked the arrival of Kira's hoped-for help. The two nova shuttles emerged from nothingness, accompanied by Lozenge and two more of the PNC-115s.

Far smaller than any class one nova-drive ship, the shuttles still dwarfed the nova fighters three to one. Without torpedo mounts and carrying only the lightest of weapons, the shuttles had more than enough cargo space to *store* a nova fighter. It wouldn't be an efficient use of space, but it was theoretically possible.

Today, Kira hoped they were carrying a less-aggressive cargo.

"Shuttle one, shuttle two, this is Basketball," she greeted them. "Report status."

"Basketball, it's Milani," a familiarly languid voice replied. "I've got four medics and a dozen sets of hands, plus power generators, medical supplies, and O-two matrix. My understanding is the pilots are dumping us and going back for a second wave of supplies.

"Where do you want us?"

"How's that dragon-painted metal of yours at radiation?" Kira asked.

Milani joked that the only thing people needed to ever call them was "that scary fucker in the dragon armor." The mercenary wore black armor with a fiery red snarling dragon on the chestplate.

"Our armor is rated for twenty-four hours in deep space as a fully contained environment," they told her. "True rad suits are better, but we can take radiation better than just about anything else."

"We have two pockets of survivors that are operating unshielded radioactive decay plants to maintain air and heat," Kira told the mercenary. "We need to pull them out and I'm not sure where to put them just yet."

"We can handle the rads from an RTG," Milani confirmed instantly, "but regular civvies can't. We can move in, replace the decay plants with the ones we're carrying, and make sure there's no further damage until relief arrives." They paused grimly. "That might eat up most of our medics' time, sir. Do we triage?"

"If you have to," Kira ordered. She'd hate herself for that later, but so would a lot of other people. The engineers had almost certainly expected to die for their choice, but she knew that they *could* be saved. But if the same resources that could save one of the radiation-poisoned techs could save a dozen others…

"Understood." The nova shuttles dove toward the station. "Pilots are telling me that this is going to be a messy road. Can we get an assist?"

"Of course," Kira confirmed. "Nightmare, on my wing. We need to plow a road for the medics."

She didn't like vaporizing debris. Some of their answers might be in the mess they were blowing away—but between her answers and innocent lives, the lives came first.

Always.

13

PART OF KIRA had hoped that the Otovon ships would beat *Conviction* to Casa Alpha. It was certainly *possible*, since they could nova in closer than the carrier had. If someone turned out to be around to threaten the freighters, well, *Conviction*'s nova fighters were out in force.

The mercenaries had been in the system for eight hours when the first wave of transports arrived. *Conviction*'s ground troops, led by McCaig himself at Alpha, had made contact with the locals aboard Alpha.

They had similar isolated pockets as Bravo...and the engineers there had made much the same choice. By the time Kira returned to her carrier, part of the flight deck had been turned into an impromptu field hospital.

"The ball is *very* precise right now, Commander," Waldroup told her. "We can bring you in and out on computer control, but the effect field of the Harringtons is barely small enough to make this happen."

"Believe me, Deck Boss, I know when to take my hands off the controls," Kira agreed. "You have the ball, *Conviction*. Standing by for automatic landing."

The six ten-kilocubic freighters orbiting with *Conviction* were doing a good job of keeping clear of the carrier's launch and retrieval lines.

Even without being linked into the coms network, Kira could tell that everyone was deferring to *Conviction* as the central coordinating hub of the whole affair.

Casa Bravo was a bit more mixed, mostly because four light-minutes was a stretch to be giving orders at. Kira had left Milani in charge, the mercenary grimly determined to do their best.

An automated retrieval was normally faster than a manual one, but today, her fighter seemed to creep into *Conviction*'s deck, her Harring-tons running at minimum power as the fighter craft dodged around the shielded camp on the deck.

"Surely, we have other places we can put them?" Kira asked as her fighter settled into its cradle. "The shuttle bay is where they're coming in, isn't it?"

"And the shuttle bay is turning around a flight every seventeen minutes," Waldroup snapped. "We're rotating the nova fighters slowly enough that this *is* the best place for them. We're not set up to handle this many casualties."

"How bad?" she asked.

"Not my area," the deck boss replied. "I'm managing shuttle flights for us and our new friends. Available volume and life support says we can take a thousand at most, so I'm guessing less than that."

"Thanks, Angel," Kira told the other woman. "Let me know if you need support."

"I've got all of my hands on deck, and Zoric's people are backing us up," the deck boss told her. "CIC and flight control are swamped, but we've got a handle on it."

"Thank you."

"Thank me by coming up with a plan to save these people."

WALDROUP'S WORDS echoed in Kira's mind as she crossed the deck. She recognized cryo-hibernation gear when she saw it. Unless she missed her guess, every single set of cryo-gear on *Conviction* was currently on her flight deck.

It wouldn't save the critical cases, but it could buy them a few days.

Maybe a week. Even cryo-hibernation was just that: *hibernation*. The body still needed to live, and if the body was destroying itself or already critically damaged...

She spotted Ailin Devin passing between patients, but given that he was in the middle of having a nurse strip off one set of gloves with another nurse standing by with a fresh set, she wisely decided not to intervene.

"Zoric, what's our status?" she asked silently through her headware.

"Messy," the XO replied. "I've got most of this delegated to my people, but I'm keeping in the loop. We've got the administrators due aboard on the next round of flights, and the Captain's going to want you in that meeting.

"My advice? Go shower. You've got twenty minutes and then you're back in the mix."

Kira snorted.

"I'm a fighter pilot," she reminded the other woman. "I can do a lot more than just *shower* in twenty whole minutes!"

KIRA WAS SHOWERED, dressed and even somewhat caffeinated by the time she met Estanza in the shuttle bay. She was carrying a coffee bulb as she checked the status of the two approaching shuttles.

The older sublight ship was slightly smaller than the brand-new nova shuttle, but it was definitely in the lead. She wasn't sure if the pilots were jockeying to get in ahead of each other or if there was an agreed-upon plan.

If it was the former, she'd have to have words. While *Conviction*'s shuttles functionally reported to McCaig on a day-to-day basis, Kira was still responsible for their maintenance and the pilots. They mostly operated in their own little bubble, but they *did* answer to her.

Her planned remonstrances died unspoken in her headware, though, as she saw the party that offloaded from the first shuttle. Her guess was that the immense bald man with the same pale green skin as Minister Crystalline was the station administrator—but the redheaded woman and three young girls walking a step behind him, searching the shuttle bay for someone who wasn't there yet, could only be one group of people.

"They're Administrator Bronx's family," she told Estanza silently via her headware. "We still hadn't confirmed if they were alive or not, and she's assuming the worst."

"Ah," Estanza replied. "Administrator Jade didn't say he was bringing them. They might have only been found recently."

All that mattered to Kira was that her pilots had clearly known who was on each shuttle, and the pilot carrying Samantha Bronx had intentionally slowed down so the woman's family would be waiting for her.

Everyone in the shuttle bay looked up as the nova shuttle swept in and came to a calm halt, Harrington coils cooling down with an almost-inaudible hiss. The expression of hope and fear on the woman Kira guessed was Bronx's wife was heart-wrenching—right up to the moment where the ramp slid open to reveal a heavyset woman walking forward at an almost regimented pace.

Samantha Bronx looked like death. She looked like she'd *died* and her body was only managing to continue on because duty and compassion demanded it. If she wasn't broken, she was as close to it as Kira had ever seen someone—right up to the moment where a taller and svelter woman with long red hair leapt onto her and wrapped her in her arms.

The girls were only a few steps behind their mother, and Kira and Estanza pointedly turned their attention to Administrator Jade as every member of the family started crying.

"I hadn't had time to look for Amelia with everything going on," Jade said quietly. "I needed to make sure *everyone* was taken care of, not spend time checking in on friends and family. Once I knew Samantha was coming, I found a few people I trusted with spare time and sent them looking."

"It seems to have been worth it," Kira allowed.

"More than," the big administrator agreed. "This has been a damned nightmare, Captain Estanza, Commander Demirci. Your arrival here has saved thousands."

"But some may yet die," Estanza said grimly. "And I'm afraid I have questions for you and Administrator Bronx both. We were only partially here to check on you."

"No, I know why you're here," Jade told them. "I am grateful that you have acted to save my people, but you're here for the Redward ship."

"We also took a contract from Otovo to check in on the stations," Kira noted. "And no spacer would leave you in the state you were in. Common decency alone required our intervention."

The big man closed his eyes and bowed his head.

"I am not certain if the people who attacked were lacking that or relying on it," he said grimly. "Whatever you were promised for rescuing us, I will make certain my employers add to it. If they argue, I'll point out how expensive the processing units are. Money often talks where compassion is unheard."

"My experience is that even corporate executives are swayed by both," Estanza replied. "I appreciate the gesture, Administrator, but as unmercenary as it is of me to mention it, I am *quite* certain that the King of Redward will also reward us for our efforts here.

"It will make him look *very* good, after all."

"It will, and honestly, too," Jade agreed. He glanced past them. "It appears Samantha has some time to spare for us now. You have questions, Captain, and we have a desperate favor to beg. Shall we get to it?"

14

BRONX LOOKED SIGNIFICANTLY MORE ALIVE, having met with her wife, joining Jade on one side of the table with a sharply assessing gaze at the two mercenaries. Kira took advantage of the moment to pour herself more coffee from the side table—and poured coffees for the others.

They didn't know the administrators' coffee preferences, and this didn't feel like the kind of meeting where flashing *Conviction*'s small luxuries like coffee robots would help.

"You may as well get your questions asked, Captain," Bronx told them. "We owe you any help we can provide, but unless Jade has a different story than I do, I'm not certain we'll be much assistance."

"Whatever you can provide will be of value, I hope," Estanza said. "Otovo's government told us that this system was functionally under siege by the Costar Clans."

"The Clans have harassed us on and off for years," Bronx admitted. "Sometimes we buy them off, sometimes we ransom back ships and crews, sometimes the government sends gunships to protect ship-ments. It's rare for them to actually destroy anything, but they've been an iron weight around this operation's neck forever.

"Starting about eight weeks ago, it got worse. A *lot* worse.

Suddenly, ships weren't being offered the chance to buy their way out of being captured. No ransoms were being accepted. Ships that tried to run were destroyed outright.

"It was out of character for the Clans. They've always treated our operations as sheep they could fleece. Killing us and taking our ships might give them a short-term higher profit, but what they were continually stealing from us was worth far more in the long run."

"And, frankly, we were building that into our costing models at this point," Jade said. "Between insurance claims and the value of what we were extracting, we could lose ten percent of the final cargos and still come in cheaper than extracting in Otovo, so long as we could get the ships and crews back. But when they were taking a quarter? Wrecking ships?"

He shook his head.

"We asked for help, but we knew what the government's resources were. And then...your ship arrived."

"Our ship?" Kira asked.

"The Redward warship," Jade confirmed. "We didn't get a particularly good look at her, but they identified themselves as *Hope* before everything went to ever-loving shit."

"That's more than I got," Bronx said. "I barely saw their nova signature. We only picked out the beacon later."

"What happened?" Estanza asked.

"Those gunships that had been harassing our shipping? They'd also apparently been running detailed scans of the platforms," Jade told him. "I'd guess they were about as far away from Casa Alpha as Casa Bravo, since Samantha saw *Hope*'s nova signature.

"They'd just about finished telling me they were here to help deal with the pirate problem when the gunships novaed in on attack runs. They knew where everything they wanted to hit was. Our sensors were the first thing they took out, which left us blind to the rest of the attack until the damage reports started flowing in."

"It was the same at Bravo," Bronx said. "We spotted the destroyer's nova signature and then gunships burst out of nova, already shooting. The stations aren't armed, but we couldn't have stopped that even if we had been."

"*Hope* should have been able to deal with half a dozen gunships," Kira murmured. They'd have twice her cubage, but *Hope* was far more survivable and a significantly more advanced ship.

"I don't know what happened," Jade said. "Our sensors were gone. The freighters and other stations might have seen something, but…"

"Someone made very sure they weren't in a state to pass on any sensor data," Estanza agreed. "This doesn't make any sense. It's like the Costar Clans wrecked an entire star system to cover up the attack on *Hope*. But they had to know someone would come investigate."

"We can give you our sensor data, but we need something in exchange," Jade told them. "You might be able to extract something from our raw data that we can't."

"But you're not going to give it to me for free," the Captain noted. "Despite us saving your lives."

"Not everyone is saved yet," the administrator said flatly. "Between people too close to impact points, the engineers who set up those decay generators, and half a dozen other problems…there are over two hundred people you've pulled out of the stations that can't be saved by the medbays aboard our ships."

"Our doctors are doing everything they can," Estanza said. "But most are being put in hibernation until we can get them to a proper hospital."

"Otovo doesn't have the hospitals and gear to save many of them, do we?" Bronx asked quietly. "We're poor and we're lost, Captain. Can *you* save them?"

The room was silent for at least twenty seconds before Estanza sighed.

"Timing is the problem," he conceded. "From my understanding of the situation, we can treat approximately five of the worst cases every twelve hours. The hibernation process buys us four to six days, depending on the case. We can save at most…half of them."

"And so we come to my desperate plea," Jade said. "We need you to take the worst injured to Ypres. My corporation has offices in Ypres Sanctuary and Ypres Hearth. They should be able to arrange emergency treatment in hospitals there—Ypres *does* have the facilities to handle two hundred of this level of injury.

"No one else can get them there in time, Captain Estanza. Our transports don't even have the capability to keep them alive that long. I need...*we* need you to save them. Everyone else here you've already saved. The Otovon transports can get us all home now.

"I'll give you everything we saw of the gunships, of *Hope*...everything. But many of these people are the engineers whose actions saved the lives of hundreds of others. We need to do everything we can."

"I understand, Administrator," Estanza said calmly.

Kira looked sideways at her boss. *She* didn't want to go to Ypres—the divided system with its multiple factions was the home of the Brisingr embassy. Anyone trying to collect the death mark on her or her pilots had to bring the proof of that death to Ypres.

The *last* thing she wanted was to be in the same star system as the only Brisingr Kaiserreich consul in the Syntactic Cluster—but innocent lives were at stake.

Her Captain met her gaze and she bowed her head slightly in a silent nod.

"Our nova drive has finished cooldown," Estanza told the two administrators. "I'll touch base with my doctors and evacuation teams and make sure we have all of our people and all of the worst-injured aboard.

"Then I will do as you ask." He smiled thinly. "I was already considering it. These people willingly chose to give their lives so others could live. I see no reason to require them to fulfill that choice when I can save them as well."

15

THE DATA PROVIDED by the locals ran through Kira's office…again.

There was only about seven minutes of it, which meant that she'd gone over it at least thirty times since they'd left DLI-O54. The gunships slashed across the air in her office one more time and the data recordings ended.

Hope was still intact when everything froze. At the moment of Casa Alpha's sensor loss, she'd been less than five light-seconds away from the space station. Captain Kopp had probably seen the gunships emerge from nova by then, but her response hadn't reached the space station.

Seven point four seconds. If the gunship pilots had been Kira's, she'd have been impressed. They'd emerged from nova and destroyed the station's sensors *completely* in seven point four seconds.

There were damage-report codes for the time afterward. It had taken them another few minutes to destroy the power plant and the solar panels, but without sensors, the station had been blind.

Casa Bravo's data was less useful, Kira supposed, but that was a fine hair to split. They had an almost identical attack pattern but had been far enough away that they'd only seen *Hope* arrive.

Wait.

Kira blinked away fatigue—she hadn't slept in more than catnaps since finding the crippled stations. They were still forty-plus hours from Ypres. She'd sleep eventually, but she *needed* these answers.

She overlaid the attack run data from Alpha and Bravo and watched it run through. She dug into the parameters, cutting apart components of the recorded scanner information and moving, then rerunning them.

"They *are* identical," she said aloud. Not *almost*. Accounting for the different layout of the two stations, the attack patterns were identical.

That was a rehearsed, prepared, *trained* assault.

The Costar Clans were competent spaceship crews, determined to a fault and convinced that their thefts were the only thing keeping their homes alive. She'd fought them multiple times now and she was never going to begrudge their skill or their courage…but they didn't *train*.

Not as an attack formation.

She focused in on the gunships, bringing up every piece of data they had and comparing it to what they had on Costar gunships they'd fought before. The ten-thousand-cubic gunship was a near-ubiquitous spacecraft, outnumbered among starships only by the ten-thousand-cubic *freighter*.

There *were* differences between builders and tech levels. The low-end basic ships were closer to identical than more-advanced vessels, but…

Now that she knew what she was looking for, the answer was right there.

Her headware was linking her to Estanza before she finished the thought.

"Sir, I think I have something," she said urgently.

There was a long pause and she realized the Captain *had* been asleep. His response was verbal only.

"Define *something*, Commander," he said crisply.

"I've been going over the data from the attack on the Casas," she told him, more slowly now. "The gunships…they weren't from the Costar Clans. They were more advanced ships intentionally stepping down their power levels and adjusting their harmonics to *appear* to be Clan gunships.

"They didn't deploy like veteran pilots. They deployed like well-trained pilots following a plan. The attacks on Alpha and Bravo were practically *identical*."

"Damn." The single word hung on the channel for a few seconds. "I'm guessing there isn't enough to ID who they *were*."

"Not a chance," she said grimly. "I almost wish I'd sent one of the nova fighters to try and grab old light."

"All we'd have got is a bubble of multiphasic jamming," Estanza replied. "And the fighter would have been playing catch-up for days. We waited for Purlwise but that was as long as we could stay."

"I know," she conceded. "I don't know if knowing it wasn't the Clans is even *helpful*."

"Neither do I," Estanza said. "But it's valuable." He paused. "Kira, have you slept?"

She answered slowly enough that it clearly *was* an answer to the old man.

"Forward your data to Zoric and the analysis team and then tell your headware to knock you out for eight hours," her Captain ordered. "If the nightmares are bad enough, talk to Devin once we get everyone off-loaded. I won't have you hurt yourself in a manner we *both* know is a bad idea.

"Am I clear?"

Kira grimaced. She'd been a squadron commander for the Apollo System Defense Force before she'd joined him, and she'd led that squadron through a real war. She knew *exactly* what she was doing to herself and had talked a dozen younger pilots out of it in the past.

"Fair, sir," she admitted. "I just…I needed *something*."

"Well, you found something," he told her gently. "It's more than we had. It fits the puzzle. I don't like the shape, and I wish we could give Redward more than puzzle pieces, but…"

"I know, sir. I'll rest, I promise."

"I'll hold you to that," Estanza insisted. "But this is worth something. More, it feels, than our sweep of where *Hope* should have been."

Kira grimaced. She'd seen the data from that, too, but there'd been no point in reviewing it. The diffuse vapor cloud that *might* have been a warship wasn't going to give up answers to anything less than extensive spectrography.

There were more reasons than one she was having trouble sleeping.

16

"KAVITHA, have you spent time in Ypres before?" Kira asked the other woman. Zoric was currently in the captain's seat at the center of *Conviction*'s old-fashioned horseshoe-shaped bridge. The seat Kira was leaning on was intended for either the executive officer herself or an observer during combat.

Other stations were laid out in front of the captain's seat, wrapping around a holotank built against the far wall. As originally designed, the bridge had probably been spacious. That had been a century and a half and at least a dozen refits earlier. New stations and additional modules sprouted like mushrooms as ships were updated—and the fact that some of those stations and modules were built with cruder tech than the original ship didn't help.

There was enough space to reach each console and for someone to work at it. There wasn't much extra. The bridge avoided feeling claustrophobic mostly by keeping the majority of the consoles around a meter in height.

The main holotank was showing their current location, a trade-route stop four light-years from Ypres, with a slowly updating dashboard displaying the status of the nova drive. They were still over an hour from their final nova.

"A few times," the XO confirmed. "But you were here when we dropped off the prisoners from the Kiln—and didn't you fly through there on your way out to Redward?"

"*Fly through* is the most accurate description, yes," Kira agreed. "We stopped at one of the gas giants to refuel and discharge static, but the Captain of the freighter didn't have any deliveries in Ypres, so we moved on quickly. And when we dropped off the prisoners, everyone was being paranoid about the death mark, so I stayed aboard ship while we docked at the same gas giant."

A month of quiet on the bounty-hunter front meant she was a bit less concerned about people chasing the death mark now, though she was still going to be careful there in Ypres.

"Fair. They're a gateway system, which means a lot of people don't see much more than you did either time," Zoric told her. She conjured an image of the star system between her and Kira, a headware projection that only the two of them could see.

"We visited Ypres Flanders last time," the XO noted as she gestured to the innermost of the system's three gas giants. "That faction consists of the refueling installations and supporting colonies on the two gas giants: Zuidschote and Voormezele." Zoric waved a hand at the system's distant ninth planet. "Technically, they claim Zillebeke as well, but that's a forlorn ball of ice home to some scattered water-mining operations. Nobody cares."

"I remember that Ypres is divided, yeah," Kira agreed. "Redward is allied with Ypres Sanctuary? But I think that's also where the Brisingr Embassy is located?"

"Redward is mostly allied with Sanctuary, yes, but they try to remain on good terms with all five factions," Zoric agreed. She highlighted the third planet.

"Dikkebus is probably the most important planet, the one that often gets treated as *the* planet in Ypres. It's on the warm side of hospitable: no ice caps but habitable equators. Two mega-continents, whose official names are all but ignored on a day-to-day basis. The west continent is Sanctuary. The east continent is Hearth.

"Each of those continents supports an orbital asteroid fortress and a small fleet of both monitors and nova warships. They each represent as much wealth and industry as a good chunk of the star systems in the Cluster."

"And they share a planet?" Kira asked. "That must go...smoothly."

"The entire system has been at one level or another of cold war for about eighty years," Zoric said bluntly. "Hearth and Sanctuary used to use the outer worlds and the asteroid belts as patsies, but those unified against that about thirty years ago."

The innermost two worlds highlighted.

"At this point, everything outside of Dikkebus's orbit has basically flipped off Hearth and Sanctuary, so their main off-world industrial operations are at Dikkebus's Lagrange asteroids and on the two inner planets. Hearth and Sanctuary have been fighting a low-key war over those asteroids and planets for the last five years, but the fighting has been off Dikkebus so far."

Kira was studying the data codes for the three planets between Dikkebus and Voormezele.

"Wait, Ypres has *two* habitable planets?" she asked.

"Part of why they're as divided and as rich as they are," Zoric agreed. "What's colloquially known as Ypres Center is officially the Central Yprian Republic, the elected government of Elverdinge which is also in control of Hollebeke, the fifth world.

"Elverdinge is barely habitable and Hollebeke is a glorified mining outpost, which makes Center only a bit more powerful than Hearth or Sanctuary alone." Zoric shrugged. "They've tried to play peacemaker over the years, which has endeared them to many and...not to many others.

"The fifth faction is the Ypres Guilds, who are an alliance of asteroid miners and similar in the Vlamertinge asteroid belt. They have an official 'capital' on Sint-Jan, the sixth world, but it's mostly a formality and a meeting place.

"Unlike the rest of the Ypres factions, the Guilds have *no* nova ships at all. They do have a significant fleet of monitors and sub-fighters to protect their interests—and a *big* axe to grind against the two Dikkebus factions."

Zoric was looking at the model in between them with sad eyes as it glittered in five different colors.

"Unified with an integrated economy, Ypres could give Redward a run for its money on industry and finance," she noted. "Given twenty years as a unified power, they'd probably pass Redward—though the SCFTZ swings the balance to Redward now. Divided like this? None of them are actually important except for the system's geography. If Ypres wasn't the easiest stopping point for people entering the Cluster from coreward, they'd be forgotten."

"And I imagine that's in a lot of people's minds," Kira agreed. "Thanks for the briefing, Kavitha. Beyond the fact that there's a death mark for me based out of this system, what *else* should I be watching for?"

"We have nova fighters. Nobody in Ypres does, and they all want them," Zoric told her. "Even our birds are enough more advanced than the tech in the Cluster to give them a decent chance of knocking out an asteroid fortress."

Kira turned her gaze to the icons marking those formidable installations. Two above each of the habitable worlds and another one above each gas giant. Even assuming their tech was cruder than Redward's...

She shivered.

"I would *not* want to be the one coordinating and leading that strike," she admitted. "Even with the best-case tech advantage, I'm pretty sure we'd lose."

"They don't have nova fighters," Zoric repeated. "And most people who don't have them overestimate them. You command a powerful weapon, Kira."

"So, we buddy-system it and everyone who goes groundside goes with bodyguards," Kira concluded. "Because we can't risk kidnappings and ransoms."

"We do that everywhere in the Cluster but Redward, really," the XO said. "It's just more important here because these guys are *this close* to open war at the best of times."

Zoric held her fingers in the air a few millimeters apart.

"Given any chance to seize an advantage, even our theoretical allies here will take it," she concluded. "So, we need to be careful."

Kira tapped her finger in the air, on the illusory sphere of Dikkebus.

"And it doesn't help that somewhere on this planet is the embassy where someone can turn my people's heads in for hundreds of thousands a pop," she said grimly.

"It doesn't," Zoric agreed. "I'd prefer we not send any of your people off-ship here, to be honest, but I know the boss has work you'll need to do while we're here."

It took Kira a moment to remember what she meant, and then she shook her head with a sad smile.

"That's right. If there's anywhere in the Cluster I'm going to find nova-fighter pilots looking for a new start, it'll be here, won't it?"

"There's a Pilots' Guild that operates throughout the system," the XO told her. "They're officially headquartered on Sint-Jan and are part of the Guild Alliance, but their main operations are in Sanctuary. Problem is, they don't deal electronically. Leftover from cyberwarfare ops a few decades back, I think."

"Wonderful," Kira said drily. "Well, it's a good thing we have soldiers, isn't it?"

"Most of them will be moving the injured over to Yprian hospitals, but McCaig will make sure you have muscle," Zoric promised. "We'll probably stick around until we are certain the locals are taken care of. I know we've budgeted for couriers back to both Otovo and Redward to fill them in."

"I wish we knew more about what happened to *Hope*," Kira admitted.

"So do I." The XO shook her head. "The fact that the debris we found was so limited and so dispersed tells me one thing I really would rather not have known, though."

"What's that?" Kira asked.

"She didn't survive," Zoric said flatly. That hadn't been *officially* stated by anyone, though Kira had guessed. "We found enough bits and pieces across the area we were expecting to find her in to know she was obliterated. Not defeated. Not destroyed. *Vaporized.*

"That wasn't gunships, Kira. She ran into somebody's cruiser— quite possibly more than one—at extremely close range."

"A focused nova-bomber strike would have much the same effect," Kira pointed out. "But...cruisers are more likely, yes."

"I'm not sure why," the other mercenary officer said. "It makes no sense to me. But someone jumped *Hope* with overwhelming firepower and then stuck around to make sure there were no bits left.

"I don't know who they were and I'm not sure how we can find out...but I really, *really* want to know."

The best estimate that Kira had seen out of Zoric's analysts was that they'd saved twenty-three thousand people in DLI-O54...and that over ten thousand had died.

"So do I," Kira agreed quietly. "So do I."

17

"NOVA IN THIRTY SECONDS; all hands stand by."

Kira stood next to Angel Waldroup in flight control, going over the launch patterns for the CAP one last time. They'd launched and retrieved fighters around the impromptu hospital on the deck half a dozen times now, but she didn't want this to be the time they screwed it up.

"This is a pain in the ass," the burly deck boss grumbled. "Worth it, don't get me wrong," she continued, "but a pain in the ass."

"How many people on the deck, boss?" Kira asked, glancing at the camera feed.

"Three hundred and sixteen," Waldroup said instantly. "Another eighty in sickbay. It's worth it, like I said." She tapped a command, loading the launch profile into the four nova fighters waiting to deploy.

"Nova."

Zoric's calm voice rang through the ship, and reality *shifted*.

"CAP launch, CAP launch," Waldroup barked.

Kira's headware told her that the message had gone out through the flight deck. Moments later, four starfighters flashed out of the launch bay. She double-checked. The flight profile had been perfect.

"I don't think we even gave the tents a breeze," she told the deck boss. "Well done, Angel."

"Last time," the mercenary grumped. "We should be an hour from Dikkebus orbit, right? We'll have these guys on the ground before the birds come back in."

"Do the locals let us fly nova fighters into orbit?" Kira asked.

"They can't guarantee our security, so we do it," Waldroup said flatly. "Not when a war might break out in orbit."

"Commander, Boss, can you take a look at this?" one of the flight control techs asked. "I've got something odd-looking at the IFFs in Ypres orbit."

"Odd? What's odd about IFF beacons?" Kira asked, but she walked over to take a look. The identify-friend-or-foe beacons—more a general identifier beacon carried by every ship, though the military version had a few extra layers—would be visible more readily than the ships themselves right off the bat.

"There should be two main sets," the tech said slowly. "Sanctuary and Hearth...but I'm only reading one. Even the fortresses...they're transmitting the same code." The woman looked up at her bosses. "Sanctuary's code. I'm not reading any Hearth IFFs in Dikkebus orbit, sirs."

Kira had to pull the IFF baselines from her headware to confirm, but the tech was right.

"It looks like my political briefing on the system might already be obsolete," she said grimly. "That's not go—

She stared at *another* IFF code. One that had *no* business being in the Syntactic Cluster at all.

"I need that code validated *now*," she snapped, pointing at the flashing icon. "Triple-check it."

"It's not a familiar code; I was trying to—"

"I know that code," Kira told the tech. "Confirm that it's not an error."

"Yes, sir."

"Commander?" Waldroup said softly.

"That's a Kaiserreich warship code," Kira told her subordinate flatly. "And there's no way in *hell* one of those should be out here."

"Code is displaying correctly, sir," the tech replied. "Should we—"

"Zoric, I need full sensors focused on contact"—Kira checked the data—"twenty-one. I need you to tell me what the *fuck* I'm looking at."

Flight control and the bridge were silent for several seconds.

"I'm relaying you the data as we scan," Zoric said slowly, "but I think you might be the one to actually answer the question, Commander Demirci. I'm not familiar with the Brisingr Kaiserreich order of battle."

The data rippled in as *Conviction* moved closer to the planet and the orbiting warship. Energy readings first, heat and other radiation. Then, finally, the visuals.

"That is a K70-class heavy strike cruiser," Kira finally told them, the specifications falling out of her headware with the ease of years of practice. "Ninety-six thousand cubics. Twenty-four heavy turrets and a wing of twenty Weltraumpanzer-Fünf heavy nova fighters, assuming they haven't upgraded or swapped the starfighters."

The K70 was a quarter again the size of *Conviction* and probably counted as more modern at this point. Even if it wasn't more modern, the Brisingr warship was a direct-fire combatant. *Conviction*'s torpedo broadside could match roughly half the cruiser's firepower for one salvo...and the cruiser could keep up that bombardment for *hours*.

"So, she has us pretty badly outclassed," Zoric replied. "Any weaknesses?"

"She's between thirty-five and fifty years old; does that help?" Kira asked. "The K70s are first-rate warships, XO. They're about as old and small as you get around Apollo and still count as first-rate, but...she could take us apart without even launching fighters."

The K70's fighter wing was almost an afterthought, intended to chase down ships that managed to nova away from the cruiser while her drive was recharging.

"Zoric, Demirci," Estanza cut into the channel. "My office, five minutes. I'm going to prod some of my contacts here and see what I can learn, but the presence of a modern warship is concerning."

"It shouldn't affect our current mission, should it?" Zoric asked.

There was a long silent pause.

"No," Estanza finally allowed. "This is a humanitarian relief operation and we have neither the intention nor the need to be aggressive here. If you have any contacts I don't here, Zoric, now's the time to prod them.

"I want to know what I'm walking into!"

ESTANZA WAS STANDING FACING the wall of his office when Kira entered, his lips moving silently as he carried on a conversation with someone only he could see and hear. He was clearly aware of Kira, though, as he waved her to a seat.

Zoric joined them a few seconds later, waiting silently for the Captain to finish his conversation. Finally, Estanza nodded his head and made a cutting gesture. Blinking, he turned to face them and hooked his chair to him with one ankle.

"Well, I'm more informed if not necessarily more illuminated," he told them as he took a seat. "Kavitha, did you learn anything?"

"The ship is *K79-L*," the XO reported. Brisingr names were highly formalized and unimaginative by most people's standards. "She arrived twenty-five days ago, which means we missed the news reaching Redward of her arrival by about two days. She hasn't done much other than sit in orbit since, though I imagine her presence is *somehow* related to the 'peaceful' unity treaty Hearth signed ten days ago."

"I poked at her ident beacon in a bit more detail as well," Kira admitted. "She's flying a Brisingr code, but the modifiers are…interesting. Apparently, she's officially under private contract to an organization called Ghost Explorations out of the Syndulla System."

"I'm not familiar with Syndulla," Estanza admitted. "What do you make of it?"

"Syndulla is a second-rate power in the Apollo-Brisingr sector that stayed neutral during the war," she told them. "They certainly couldn't build a K70 and I doubt any private company there could afford to operate one."

"Could their government afford to run one?" Zoric asked.

"Probably, though not easily," Kira agreed.

"So, we're either looking at a cover for a Syndullan operation of some kind or a multi-layer cover for a Brisingr privateer," the XO concluded. "The latter seems most likely to me."

"And me," Kira admitted.

"Their activities here certainly suggest something of the sort," Estanza agreed. "They arrived and immediately their supposed civilian owners met with the Brisingr ambassador, and then with the leadership of Sanctuary.

"From what I'm being told, *K79-L* is being operated as a mercenary concern to cover the operating costs for her current lessors." The Captain shook his head. "Supposedly, she's a science and exploration vessel, but I don't think anyone is buying that for a second. Her owners and captain were heavily involved in the negotiations that brought about what is, bluntly, the unconditional surrender of Ypres Hearth.

"Given that my understanding is that she's powerful enough to knock out Hearth's orbital fortress...I imagine the fact that she was likely going to engage on Sanctuary's side tipped the scales."

"She couldn't take an asteroid fortress on her own," Kira said. "She's still an older ship for Brisingr. Combined with Sanctuary's fleet, though..." She pulled up Redward Intelligence's listing for the faction.

"She could have tipped the scales, as you said," she agreed. She shook her head. "I just don't see Brisingr releasing one of their first-rate ships for *anything*. When I left Apollo, the Kaiserreich had thirty first-rate warships. The K70s were the oldest, but they still had seven of them in active commission."

"I'm worried there's more at play here," Estanza admitted. "Bringing together the factions under one banner would create a counterweight to Redward and the SCFTZ—one that Equilibrium could quietly augment while no one was looking."

Zoric gestured and a set of ships appeared on the headware in the middle of the room.

"We know the Ypres factions are good at working up other people's tech, too," she pointed out. "There's twenty nova destroyers in this system, and despite belonging to four different factions, they're all basically identical."

"How does that work?" Kira asked.

"The Kingdom of Crest wanted to keep the gate into the Cluster open to keep their bank happy," Estanza told her. "They 'sold' Ypres Flanders two destroyers and a bunch of support systems twenty years ago. A year later, Flanders had built two more—and a year after that, every intelligence network in the system had stolen the designs."

"The locals are very good at both reverse-engineering and stealing each other's data," Zoric said. "The latter will be less necessary if Sanctuary succeeds in bringing the others in line."

"Center, Flanders and the Guilds are still a pretty tough nut to crack," the Captain said. "My contacts are telling me that Flanders has made several concessions the other two have been after for a while to bring them into a mutual-defense pact."

"So, two factions are now one and the other three are ready to fight to stay independent?" Kira asked. She shook her head. "Even with K79-L, that'll be a mess."

"Sanctuary and Hearth combined probably outweigh any two of the others," Estanza said grimly. "It won't take much to tip the scales, not when they can throw monitors at the asteroid forts."

The smallest monitors in the system were much the same size as *Conviction*. Some of the larger ones, orbiting high above Dikkebus, were at least two hundred kilocubics. Their lack of nova drives made them vulnerable to nova attack, but there was a reason capturing a planet was generally regarded as impossible.

"Let's not forget that while Ypres's defenses could stand off K79-L, there are a lot of systems in the Cluster who couldn't," Zoric said grimly. "Her presence is a seriously unbalancing strategic factor."

"If it's Equilibrium, though..." Kira trailed off. So far as she knew, Zoric was the only other person on the ship Estanza had told about his old conspiracy days. The fact that they'd transported a detachment of Equilibrium agents after the Kiln meant it wasn't as quiet as it had been, but only the three of them knew everything about the Institute.

"They've got to be far more in with Brisingr than I thought," she admitted.

"I always figured they were," Estanza admitted. "The Kaiserreich is far more the speed of their desired hegemons than Apollo's Council of Principals. By their standards, the Council combines the worst aspects of both democracies and dictatorships."

Apollo's government was a formalized oligarchy. It was far from perfect, even in Kira's opinion...but she couldn't help but feel it was better than the Kaiserreich's only lightly limited monarchy!

"Either way, she's not going to interfere with our mission," Zoric said. "If anything, the unification of Sanctuary and Hearth might help us. There'll be less arguing over who we need to talk to about hospitals if all of the Dikkebus hospitals are under one government."

"Agreed. I've already set the gears in motion on that," Estanza told them. "I'm waiting to hear back, but it doesn't look like we'll be limited to our own shuttles to transport our medevacs to the surface.

"We got them all here, people, and for all of the unexpected surprises, it looks like Ypres is going to take care of them for us. We might not have saved *Hope*, but we *have* saved four hundred lives no one else could have."

"And twenty thousand in DLI who might not have lasted much longer," Kira added. "I think we did okay. I don't know if Redward will agree once they have the news about *Hope*."

"We'll find out," Estanza said with a nod. "For now, we'll get these people into hospitals. And since we're here anyway..."

"I'll check in with the Pilots' Guild and the local recruiting boards," Kira promised. "They might drop some clues about *K79-L*, too. We'll see what we can learn."

"Be careful. I don't *think* the Kaiserreich Navy is going to try and collect that bounty, but these guys are operating behind enough screens and lies, I'd be surprised if there aren't Shadows aboard."

Kira nodded silently. The Brisingr Shadows had hunted her squadron across their own homeworld—and across multiple star systems as her old comrades had tried to flee. Those covert assassins were *why* she was in the Syntactic Cluster.

"You be careful too," she told him. "If there are active Equilibrium agents on *K79-L*, you've reminded them that you're their enemy of late. They might decide to get stabby about it."

"I will be," Estanza confirmed. "The biggest risk is that they'll point that heavy cruiser at *Conviction*—but that would start some fights I don't think they want to engage in yet. I think we're safe enough for now."

"So long as we keep our eyes open," Zoric murmured.

"Exactly."

18

THE FIRST WHITE-PAINTED medical shuttles met *Conviction* before she'd even fully decelerated into orbit. Kira stood at the side of her flight bay, watching as Dr. Devin's medical staff in their mismatched scrubs guided the neatly uniformed Sanctuary High Guard paramedics into the impromptu hospital.

The High Guard's medevac shuttles were designed to handle up to twenty patients apiece. They were capable midsized orbital craft—but the SHG only had six of them. Three of them were still on their way from the other side of the planet.

"Wonder how many of the shuttles belonged to Hearth a month ago," she muttered to Waldroup.

"Can't say I care right now," the deck boss replied. She gestured to the stretchers being set up to carry patients in hibernation. "With their help, we move a hundred people down on the first flight. A hundred and sixty on the second and a hundred forty on the last."

"And the locals have already flagged which hospital each shuttle flight is going to," Kira confirmed. She'd double-checked all of that in her headware a few minutes earlier. "I'm sure *someone* is going to be paying for their care in the long run, but it isn't going to be us and Sanctuary is prioritizing lives."

"Some of those folks are in the last few hours of lethal radiation poisoning, even with the cryo," Waldroup nearly whispered. "I've seen it before. Without us…"

"They'd have died. We did a damn good thing, Angel," Kira agreed. "It's always good to see an effort that *everyone* can get behind."

The deck boss shook her head grimly.

"Except whoever left those people to die," she said. "Someone has to pay for that."

"Someone will," Kira agreed. "Right now, though, we have more… immediate concerns."

"I'm guessing you mean something other than these guys." Waldroup gestured at the patients being moved off the flight deck.

"I do. Once the flight deck is cleared, I want Darkwing Group prepped for an emergency alpha launch," Kira ordered. "Full torpedo and fuel load, ready to go."

"What about the Hoplites?" the deck boss asked.

"We'll use the Apollo-built units for our CAP, but we'll stick to two at a time without PNCs," Kira said. "None of the new-build Hoplites fly in Ypres unless *Conviction* goes to battle stations."

There was a long pause.

"That Brisingr cruiser would be able to tell the new-builds from the standard, wouldn't they?" Waldroup concluded.

"They would, yes," Kira confirmed. "Just like how I can plug the specifications of that ship into our training sims, they've got full files on the Hoplite-IV. If we fly the ones we and Redward built anywhere that cruiser can see, Redward's secret is out."

If *K79-L* was under Equilibrium command, it wasn't that big a secret. *Conviction* had delivered the Equilibrium Institute engineer who'd given Redward the class two nova-drive fabricator to Ypres herself. But they'd promised to keep the secret, so they'd keep the secret.

"Are we actually expecting to fight the cruiser?" the deck boss asked slowly.

"*Fuck*, do I hope not," Kira said fervently. "But if we have to, a Sunday punch from the PNCs is our only chance of buying time to get

Conviction clear. We hit her hard, we hit her fast, and we hope we distract her enough to let us get clear."

She saw the engineer doing the math out of the corner of her eyes.

"You think she can take thirty-six torpedo hits?"

Kira grimaced.

"There are two K70s on my kill list, Angel," she told the other woman. "I flew Hoplites in both engagements. We were escorts for Peltast bombers, *real* bombers. The smaller force that bagged a K70 led with a full nova combat group, twenty-four bombers. A Peltast carries *eight* torpedoes. Sixteen survived to launch and we still only crippled her. It took a close-range gun pass by the Phalanxes once we'd cleared the fighter cover to finish her off."

Apollo's Phalanx-V heavy fighter, like the Weltraumpanzer-Fünf fighter that *K79-L* was probably carrying, fell somewhere between a Hoplite-IV and a PNC-115 in its design. It could carry two torpedoes, but like the lighter interceptors, it lost maneuverability if carrying a full weapons load. Instead, the Phalanx carried heavier plasma guns that gave it a limited ability to hurt capital ships if it could focus on them.

Kira personally felt that heavy fighters got the worst of both possible worlds, even more so than a fighter-bomber like the PNC-115, though she was quite sure no one could pay her enough to get behind the stick of a true bomber.

"An alpha strike by the fighter-bombers is meant to knock out some of her guns, maybe even cripple her flight deck, but all I'd really hope for out of our entire flight group would be to buy time for everyone to run," she admitted. "We are seriously outclassed by that ship, Angel."

"And she isn't going anywhere," Waldroup concluded. "So, what's your plan for dealing with her next time?

Next time.

That gave Kira shivers, but the deck boss had a point. If Sanctuary was going to attempt to unify Ypres and then try to exert dominance in the region—a likely scenario if Equilibrium was involved—*Conviction* was going to find herself pitched against the cruiser sooner or later.

"I think that actually answers the question of what we're doing with the twelve new class two nova drives we've been promised," she admitted. "Given all the data we have on the Hoplites and the PNCs, how comfortable would you be rigging together a design for a nova bomber?"

"Are you fucking kidding me?"

Kira waited for the larger woman to fully process.

"Maybe," Waldroup finally allowed. "I know Redward has a whole design bureau working on this shit. I can have a chat with them once we get back, see if we can pull together something. But I can't design a bomber from scratch, Commander. That's like…a three-person-century job."

"I know," Kira allowed. "But Redward's cruisers aren't going to be able to fight that thing. So, if they want to remove *K79-L* from the board, the only option *I* see is a coordinated mass nova-bomber strike."

"Which means Redward needs nova bombers."

The last of the current wave of paramedics left the flight bay, none of them having approached closely enough to have heard any of Kira's conversation with her deck boss.

"We're in orbit, sir," Waldroup told her. "Speaking of nova fighters…"

"Yeah. I need to go find us some pilots," Kira agreed. "Do we have a shuttle free for me to use?"

"Shuttle Eight," Waldroup told her. "You can fly it yourself; damn thing is smaller than a nova fighter. It and Nine are VIP transports, not much use for moving more than five or six people."

"Milani should be meeting me in the shuttle bay in five with an escort," Kira replied. "Hopefully, they knew they could only bring four guards!"

19

THERE WERE three mercenaries waiting for her in the shuttle bay, theoretically anonymous in fully encasing body armor.

Of course, Milani was obvious. The snarling fiery red dragon painted across their armor was distinctive at a significant distance. Kira's understanding was that the armor was coated in an intelligent nanopaint that could be programmed to look like just about anything. Usually, that was a stealth feature.

The other two mercenaries hadn't undermined their anonymity the same way as their boss, though the slight permanent twitch to the mercenary on the left revealed his identity. Kira had encountered Crush several times since joining the mercenary crew, and he'd been hopped up on combat drugs every time.

Somehow, he was still alive, but the twitching made him identifiable through the armor.

The junior two cleared their faceplates as she approached, revealing the third mercenary to be Jerzy Bertoli, another mercenary who'd served as her bodyguard before. He'd been shot on that duty in the past, but that didn't seem to dissuade him from grinning at her.

"Are you ready to go, boss?" Milani asked. They hadn't cleared their faceplate. Kira had, in fact, never seen the mercenary with a transparent faceplate, let alone out of their armor. That seemed to be how Milani was comfortable approaching the world, and so long as their headware confirmed their identity, that was fine by Kira.

"I am. Shuttle Eight," she told them. "I'll be flying us. Anything I need to be aware of, Milani?"

"Naw," the mercenary replied. "You armed?"

Kira opened her jacket sufficiently to show the blaster pistol on her hip. The hip-length leather jacket also concealed an energy-dispersing matrix that would stand up to a blaster shot. Maybe even two, if she was very lucky.

"Sanctuary gun laws are strict, but as registered mercenaries, we get some leeway," Milani told her. "No heavy guns, but personal blasters are fine and no one has *told* us we can't wear armor."

From Milani's tone of voice, they knew perfectly well that the armor wasn't going to be popular...but that it also wasn't illegal, so they were going to wear it anyway.

"Given that we're dropping into the same *city* as the Brisingr Embassy where someone has to report my death to get paid, that seems like a reasonable precaution," Kira agreed. "I think we should be safe enough here—the Embassy doesn't want trouble any more than we do—but keep that in mind."

"Will do, sir," Milani promised. "We're not here to cause trouble, just keep you safe."

"And you are permitted to cause every gram of trouble needed to do that," Kira assured them.

CLOTH HALL WAS a sprawling city that easily rivaled anything on Redward. There were fewer towers than in the cities of *Conviction*'s current retainer, but the fifty-story towers both Redward and Ypres seemed convinced were impressive just looked provincial to Kira.

A paltry forty or so towers wrapped around an immaculately landscaped kilometer-square park made for Cloth Hall's downtown and the apparent economic center of Sanctuary. A shuttle port occupied the north side of the park, allowing travelers from orbit ready access to the business and government offices around Menin Park.

It took Kira and her escort almost an hour to clear their way through security, which wasn't a surprise to her—or, so far as she could tell, any of her armored escort.

"All of your paperwork is in order," a senior bureaucrat in a dark green uniform finally conceded, the woman putting the electronic flimsy she was scanning down on the desk in front of her. "I do not approve, but I have no choice but to permit you your weapons and armor."

"As I told your subordinates, we are equipped solely for self-defense," Milani replied, their voice bored. "Commander Demirci is subject to an illegal bounty, and we are unprepared to let her travel anywhere without a proper escort."

"You will draw more attention in full body armor than you could possibly gain in protection," the immigration officer said sharply. "But your paperwork is correct and there is no restriction on weaponless armor. You may proceed.

"I must warn you, however, that these are sensitive times, as the rogues in the rest of the system are searching for opportunities to create trouble. The attention you will draw may well prove an opportunity for that scum…a detrimental one for you."

"That is my problem, not yours," Milani replied, their tone still bored. "Are we clear to proceed?"

"You are clear," the woman sighed, waving them forward. "Go on."

Kira gave the bureaucrat a mostly sympathetic nod—she'd left the entire discussion in Milani's more-than-capable hands, which allowed her to play "good cop" now that they'd won.

"May I get a download of the city map?" she asked. "I need to find the Pilots' Guild."

"Fine." The woman forced a strained smile, but the download appeared in Kira's headware.

"Thank you."

Kira allowed Milani to lead her out into the open promenade of the shuttle port as she studied the map.

"Oh, good," she murmured. "Thankfully, it looks like the people running a *ship pilots'* guild put their offices next to the shuttleport. Is our security up to walking about a hundred meters?"

Milani and the other two guards were scanning the entire shuttle-port around them as they dropped into a neat triangle around her without any verbal commands.

"It's exposed, but a taxi is even more vulnerable," Milani told her. "We'll keep our eyes open, sir."

"All right." Kira started toward the exit from the shuttle port, doing her best to ignore the way the crowd scattered away from her armored bodyguards.

"Let's get to work."

"YOU UNDERSTAND, Commander Demirci, that we can't just let anyone post to the guild job boards," the tall and painfully thin man across the desk told Kira. His head was shaved clean and there were indentations around his eyes, sign of a life using far cruder space equipment than even Ypres should be providing.

"I understand that you require an in-person meeting to set up an account, yes," Kira agreed. The office was on the corner of the thirtieth floor of one of Cloth Hall's squat towers, with glass windows over-looking the landscape of the park. The carpet underfoot was soft and the walls were painted a soothing pale blue. The desk matched the room and the carpet for sophistication, a smoothly carved wooden edifice with concealed computer systems and holoprojectors.

The *rest* of the decorations did not. A meter-and-a-half-long segment of hull, bearing most of the hull number of what Kira guessed to be a small mining ship, occupied an entire interior wall. The other interior wall was covered in small holograms and physical models of dozens of types of ships. The display was chaotic, with little or no pattern to it beyond "we added this ship where there was space."

"In-person initial meetings have long been a policy of my guild," the guild officer told her. "My name is Lucrèce Robin and I have the privilege of running this office of the Pilots' Guild. You got bumped to my desk as soon as my reception staff realized who you were, Commander."

"Beyond my name, who am I, then?" Kira asked, her shoulders tensing. They'd left Bertoli and Crush in the front reception area, which meant she only had Milani with her. She doubted the Ypres Guilds had enough of a need for money to jump her in their own offices, but you could never be sure.

"You are the Commander, Nova Group, aboard what is unquestionably the second-most-powerful warship in the Syntactic Cluster," Robin told her. "You are a veteran of the Apollo-Brisingr war, which means you are familiar with the latest stranger to show up in my star system.

"I must admit, Commander, that I'm curious what the Pilots' Guild can do for *Conviction*."

There was more to his tone and Kira mentally sighed. *Of course* the senior members of the Pilots' Guild on Dikkebus had enough connections back to the Ypres Guilds on Sint-Jan that he'd be interested in *Conviction* itself.

"We are looking to recruit nova-qualified small-craft pilots," Kira said. If Robin wanted to try and hire *Conviction,* he'd have to make his pitch more clearly that that. "If you have any former nova-fighter pilots among your candidates, we would be delighted to review their files and make an offer."

"We're not a recruiting agency to actively get involved in the contact, Commander," Robin told her. "We run a job posting board that is distributed across the star system. Given the current tensions, you may have difficulties making contact with pilots operating out of Ypres Center, Ypres Guilds or Ypres Flanders."

"We're a neutral party in this," Kira pointed out. "If I'm looking at sufficiently qualified candidates, I can visit any of the four remaining factions."

Robin exhaled a long sigh and nodded.

"You are a neutral party for now," he warned. "If Sanctuary continues their aggression, your connections with Redward may deny you that neutrality."

"Redward has been a long-standing friend of every Ypres faction, and their alliance with Sanctuary is purely defensive and economic," Kira said. Robin presumably regarded himself as a citizen of the Ypres Guilds, which gave him a very clear side in the conflict. "I can't see the Royal Fleet intervening in your war."

"I'd hope that we aren't going to have a war," Robin said sadly. "But that may be in vain. My own nation has signed an alliance with one of our oldest rivals and one of our oldest friends, in the hopes of somehow standing off this madness.

"Ypres has functioned well enough as five nations for a long time, Commander, but times are changing. I'm afraid I and my staff may soon be recalled to the asteroids."

"Is that going to interfere with my business here?" Kira asked.

He snorted.

"I doubt *Conviction* will be in system long enough," he admitted. "I expect the recall order sometime in the next week...and I don't think the war will start long after that. It's only really a question of what *K79-L*'s commanders and owners want from Sanctuary as a price."

"And the Guilds will fight?" she asked.

"We'll fight," Robin confirmed. "I'm certain my leadership is already making overtures to your Captain as quietly as possible, but consider this another quiet overture, Commander Demirci. The Ypres Guilds will pay to hire *Conviction* at the same rate Redward pays. Our alliance can handle even the combined Sanctuary-Hearth fleets, at least so long as we engage them in range of Elverdinge's orbital forts, but that Brisingr warship..."

"I am not authorized to negotiate on Captain Estanza's behalf," Kira told the Yprian man. "I'll pass on your message, but I'm here for quite specific business."

"So you are," Robin agreed with a nod, and conjured a virtual form in the air between them. "Let's go through what you'll want in the posting, and then we'll discuss appropriate pricing for what you need..."

20

THE LAST THING Kira was expecting on Ypres Sanctuary was to be recognized by *anyone*—which meant that someone calling her name immediately triggered a threat reaction.

And that was before she registered the distinctly Germanic Brisingr accent in the voice.

"Demirci? Kira Demirci?"

A wall of armored mercenaries almost magically materialized between Kira and the speaker before she'd even finished turning around. The speaker, a heavyset and well-muscled man with pale skin and short-cropped copper hair, raised his hands instantly.

"Apologies," he said instantly. "I may have made a mistake."

He looked familiar but Kira couldn't place him. Since he was clearly unarmed, she gestured for the mercenaries to stand down enough for her to approach the man.

"I am Kira Demirci, yes," she said. "Do I know you?"

The stranger chuckled.

"Yes, but I wouldn't expect you to remember as well as I do," he told her. "Konrad Bueller, Major Demirci. When we last met, um, I was your prisoner."

She blinked—but with the name and that bit of context, her

headware placed him. The last time a squadron under her command had gone up against a capital ship—not a K70 but one of the L150 battlecruisers, an even larger and more powerful warship —they'd crippled her and left her on a collision course for a gas giant.

The Apollo task force hadn't had the weapons or numbers left to press the fight against the crippled but still-deadly warship, so they'd watched it fall into the planet. That also meant they'd watched the ship shed escape pods like a weed seeding.

Kira and Moranis had argued long and hard for permission to retrieve the escape pods before they'd fallen into the gas giant...and won. They'd only saved a third of the battlecruiser's crew in the end, but that was still over six hundred officers and crew who'd lived and been repatriated.

And Oberleutnant Konrad Bueller had been the senior officer on the second escape pod Kira had retrieved herself.

"I remember now, Oberleutnant Bueller," she told him. "But it's Commander Demirci now. I am no longer an ASDF officer."

"Ah, I see, Commander," Bueller told her. He smiled. "I am a civilian engineer these days, working for Ghost Explorations. I did not expect to see you so far out into the middle of nowhere," he admitted. "It's oddly good to see a familiar face."

"Em Bueller, then," she allowed. She recognized the name of the company he worked for. Ghost Explorations was the company that supposedly was operating *K79-L*.

"Civilian engineer," my ass.

"We are a long way from home," she agreed. "But that only means, I suspect, that we are both very busy."

"That's true, that's true, and I hate to take more of your time," Bueller agreed. "But I find myself in possession of an opportunity that I suspect will never repeat itself and, well, I have to admit that being hauled out of an escape pod does make an impression.

"If you have the time to spare, Kira, may I buy you dinner before you return to space?"

For a moment, Kira was straight-up shocked. It was, as Bueller clearly recognized, an odd time and place for that request. On the other hand, if she'd made that kind of impression on him as his captor, he was right that he'd never have the opportunity again.

She, on the other hand, had almost no impression of the Brisingr engineer beyond that he had an attractive set of muscles and was smart enough to be a senior engineer on a Kaiserreich battlecruiser. That might have been enough if he *wasn't* a Brisingr, but…

Kira opened her mouth to gently turn him down and then remembered who he'd said he was working for: Ghost Explorations.

She was never going to be handed a more golden opportunity to find intelligence on their potential enemy.

"All right," she finally allowed. "My bodyguards will have to accompany us, but they're decent at allowing privacy."

She hoped, at least—though it wasn't like she wasn't planning on recording the entire meal!

BUELLER MIGHT NOT HAVE BEEN EXPECTING to run into Kira, but he was clearly more familiar with Cloth Hall than she was. That basically meant he'd spent any time at all there, and he was openly skimming through a headware window, looking at restaurant listings as they walked back toward the park.

"There's a steakhouse next to the starport that has rave reviews of their view of the park," he finally said. "They claim to do a Greek-Germanic fusion cuisine, which I will reserve judgment on, but their patrons seem impressed."

"I've seen what *Redward* calls 'Greek,'" Kira said drily. "I imagine the theoretically German food out here is about on par?"

"I haven't risked it yet," Bueller admitted with a charming grin. "I mean, it's only a couple hundred light-years farther from Germany than home, so theoretically, it's probably at *least* as accurate."

That took Kira a moment to process. It was easy to forget that the divisions of traditional cuisines were often based on Old Earth geography. She was conscious of the existence of a Greece on Earth—though Apollo's "Greek" colonists were originally from a Meridian world named Parthenon—but she didn't always draw the connection between the Deutschland of her military history studies and the German cuisine and Germanic language and culture.

"It seems worth checking out," she told him. "It seems unlikely they poison their guests, and what more can two strangers in a strange land hope for?"

Five strangers, really. She'd leave feeding the troops to Milani—assuming the mercenaries were willing to take their helmets off on the planet.

"All right. I've made a reservation," Bueller told her. "It's this way."

She fell in beside him and took a careful glance around, trying to spot the engineer's protectors.

"They let you wander around unescorted?" she asked. "If you're on that cruiser in orbit, you must be worried about hostages."

The engineer shrugged.

"I don't think anyone in Ypres thinks kidnapping people is going to make Captain Sitz play well with others," he said. "Plus, I have a tracker beacon and there are some *very* capable ground troops aboard *K79-L.*"

Bueller had avoided outright saying he was working aboard the cruiser, Kira noted, but he wasn't trying to conceal it, either.

"Thought you were a civilian these days?" she asked, making sure her tone was gently teasing.

He stiffened slightly for a moment anyway, then relaxed and shook his head.

"My situation is complicated," he admitted. "The Kaiserreich didn't do much force reduction after the war, but the Kaiser made sure there was an option for those of us who had been prisoners of war to muster out early.

"A civilian desk job proved more boring than I anticipated, so when recruiters came calling, looking for engineers with heavy starship experience, I listened." He shrugged. "I wasn't expecting to end up on an actual warship, I'll admit, but here we are."

Bueller paused for several seconds after that, as if distracted, before continuing.

"What brought you all the way out here?" he asked.

Kira considered softballing the Kaiserreich's post-war activities for the Brisingr man, but while she was hoping to pump him for information, she didn't have *that* much concern for his feelings.

"Your Kaiser sent assassins after all of Apollo's aces," she told him bluntly. "The entire Three-Oh-Three was marked for death—and your Shadows *got* most of us. Some of us made it out to the edge of nowhere with a handful of stolen nova fighters and found work."

That silenced the man for long enough to reach the restaurant.

"Reservation under Bueller. For two, with a second table of three as escort," he told the artificial stupid hologram acting as host. The artificially generated woman was wearing a little black dress that would *never* have stayed decent on a living person.

"Of course, Em Bueller." The hologram nodded cheerfully, then paused. "Please wait one moment; a host is coming to meet you."

That was different. Most restaurants that were set up enough to have an artificial stupid host at the front used holograms to direct people to tables. Either the restaurant was actively aiming for a human touch, or something about Bueller's reservation had garnered attention.

An older man with sun-darkened skin and pure white hair emerged from the doors a minute or so later. He wore a dark blue toga in a style that occasionally showed up on Apollo, usually to vanish under its own impracticality in a single season, and bowed slightly.

"Em Bueller and guests?" he greeted them.

"I am Konrad Bueller, yes," the burly engineer agreed.

"I'll admit, sir, that we're not used to the two-table escort arrangement," the host told them. "May I ask…"

Bueller pointed to Milani and the other two mercenaries.

"My companion has bodyguards to keep her safe," he explained calmly. "They will need to sit with us and will need non-alcoholic drinks." He looked back at the mercs. "Are you three able to eat? Put it on my bill if you can."

"In shifts," Milani allowed carefully, their faceless helmet staring at Bueller. "Your generosity is appreciated."

"Of course, of course," the host conceded. "That will work, of course. Follow me, please."

THE TABLE they were given was on the end of a balcony on the second floor, with an absolutely incredible view of the massive green space. The bodyguards were given the next table over, making sure that everyone approaching Kira had to go by them.

The steakhouse might not be used to the escort-table arrangement, but they'd worked it out quickly enough.

"Their idea of *Greek* appears to be *slathered in mint*," Kira said after skimming the menu. "Oh, no, wait. I missed the dolmades."

"The dolmades are an entire section of the menu," Bueller pointed out. "Do Apollons normally stuff tomatoes with ground beef?"

"Not...normally, no," she said. "More rice in vine leaves. Which, at least, they have."

"The German side is schnitzel," he said. "And I think the fusion is schnitzel in mint sauce, which...might actually work."

Kira made a face and Bueller laughed. He had a nice laugh, she realized. A deep warm rumbling, like the purr of a *big* cat.

"You can try the mint schnitzel," she told him. "I am having a steak. *Without* mint."

He chuckled again and grinned at her.

"I like to live dangerously," he said. "I'll take the mint schnitzel and see what happens!"

Their body language was clear enough that a togaed waiter materialized a moment later, passing the mercenary bodyguards with a sideways glance.

"Those men are also on my bill," Bueller told the waiter, gesturing at the soldiers. "I don't know how much they can eat before they're not being intimidating enough, but make sure they're served as well.

"Of course, sir," the waiter confirmed with a bow. "Are you ready to order?"

They gave their orders quickly and the waiter read them back in a crisp voice to make certain they'd been recorded correctly.

"And are you two celebrating anything?" the man asked.

It took Kira a moment to realize he was reading them as a couple—which amused *her* enough to leave the question for Bueller to answer.

"Only that we ran into each other at all," the Brisingr man said brightly. "We're both a long way from home."

"Of course, sir. Your food will be thirty minutes or so; I will be back with drinks in a few minutes."

The waiter stopped to check in softly with the mercenaries as Kira turned her attention back to her dinner companion.

"Careful with calling people in armor *men*," she warned. "Milani is *that terrifying fucker in the dragon armor* and accepts no other descriptor."

Bueller's gaze flickered over to the mercenaries, and he grinned sheepishly.

"Point taken, Commander," he conceded. "May I call you Kira? I suppose I should have asked that a *bit* sooner."

She laughed, surprised at how easily that came in the presence of her old enemy.

"Yes, Konrad, you can call me Kira," she allowed. "But I might exact some price in return!"

"Did you *look* at the prices on the menu?" Bueller countered. "But name it."

"Just what *is* Ghost Explorations doing with a Brisingr *heavy cruiser*?" she asked. "I know the K70s are old, but Ghost isn't even a Brisingr corp. It seems damn weird to me, I've got to admit."

"The K70s are being decommissioned," he told her slowly, carefully, as if considering every word. "The Kaiser isn't an unlimited dictator, after all, and he had to sell the Diet on a new round of battle-cruisers. In exchange, four of the K70s were stood down and sold to private interests."

The Diet was the Kaiserreich's mostly—but clearly not *entirely*—tame elected legislature.

"So, the whole threat level here is a bluff?" Kira asked. "K79-L is properly decommissioned?"

Conviction had been through that at one point in her career. She'd originally been built with a small but powerful array of plasma guns—and part of the reason she couldn't mount any *new* guns was that they'd hadn't been removed carefully.

"That would be saying," Bueller told her, holding a finger to his lips.

That could be jokingly attempting to cover one of two sins: either the Kaiserreich had sold fully functional warships to friendly powers, or *K79-L* was running a *massive* bluff here in Ypres.

"But you work for Ghost?" she asked.

"I do. I'm *Seventy-Niner's* chief engineer, actually," he told her. "Hence tracker beacons, hence my being on the surface organizing supplies." He shrugged. "Most of the crew are seconded from the Kaiserreich still, but the senior officers are mostly ex-Syndulla or ex-Kaiserreich military working for Ghost."

"I'd never even heard of Ghost Explorations," Kira admitted. "They're big enough to afford to rent a cruiser with crew?"

"We're not huge," Bueller said carefully, "but there are some investors with deep pockets and close ties to the Kaiser behind them. When you're making novas into the unknown, having the armor and firepower to deal with unexpected trouble doesn't go amiss."

He shrugged as the waiter arrived with their drinks.

"We're really here as backup," he said after taking his first sip of the almost-black beer he'd ordered. "There are half a dozen smaller survey ships pushing into the zones outward from the Cluster, areas that are only half-explored at best. They're mapping nova routes to unexplored systems, and once we've got enough of them on the docket, *Seventy-Niner* will move out to make the first novas into those systems."

That all made sense on the surface, but the amount of money and political influence necessary to create the operating environment Bueller was describing on *K79-L* seemed out of all proportion with the potential gains. Colonization rights for habitable worlds were valuable, but she wasn't sure they were *that* valuable.

"And in the meantime, your Captain plays politics in Ypres?" she asked.

That got an active grimace from Bueller.

"If we're sitting here, we may as well earn some money for Ghost," he said, but his tone was utterly flat. "We've done some poking around the area to validate local nova routes as well, but mostly...yeah. We've been here in Ypres, waiting for word from our scout ships while the Captain and the Director try to fix all of the system's problems."

Kira smiled. Bueller hadn't mentioned a "Director" before...but she also figured she'd pushed too much already. She could justify a lot of questions about what he was doing in Ypres, but she suspected he'd already let too much slip.

There weren't many candidates, after all, for "investors with deep pockets and close ties to the Kaiser." She didn't necessarily want to buy into Estanza's assumption that Equilibrium had been involved in the Apollo-Brisingr war, but it would make *K79-L*'s presence here make sense.

"It sounds like civilian life suits you, then," she suggested.

"The kind that puts me back on a starship suits me," Bueller agreed with a relieved-sounding laugh. "A desk? God, I was sick of spreadsheets and design software by the second week. All of that is fine, but I need to get my hands in hardware to feel right. I need to feel a starship under my feet and a nova around my head for the world to be right."

"You wouldn't say that if you'd ever novaed in a fighter," Kira said.

"I *have*, actually," he told her. "And you're right, that's an entirely different experience! I still wouldn't trade a nova ship for any other work environment in the galaxy. I get to do too many things, see...too many things."

Kira filed his mid-sentence hesitation away. There was something else going on, not just that the man she was talking to was either directly or indirectly an Equilibrium agent—and her guess was *directly*.

From what Bueller had said, she expected that every one of the "Ghost Exploration" civilian officers aboard *K79-L* directly worked for the Equilibrium Institute.

They had most definitely found their enemy.

"I GREW UP IN A SHEPHERDS' village on the hills above one of Apollo's big spaceports," Kira found herself telling Bueller as they finished their meals. "Dogs, drones, sheep. A *lot* of sheep."

She grinned.

"Spent my formative years watching people flee the bounds of gravity and go to space," she concluded. "I don't think my parents were even surprised when I signed up for the Defense Force."

"They weren't disappointed?" the Brisingr man asked.

"Nah, I had an older brother who loved dogs and sheep," Kira told him. "Still do, I guess. His wife hates me, so we haven't spoken since my dad's funeral."

She fell silent, wondering how she'd wandered into that particular minefield. Bueller was easy to talk to, with both of them sharing an interest in science and machinery. That might be more dangerous than she realized.

"I was *expected* to go to space," Bueller said after a moment of silence, sensing that family wasn't something to push on. "Are you familiar with Brisingr's old tech families?"

"Beyond knowing that Brisingr has a hidden aristocracy, not really," she admitted. That wasn't particularly uncommon. If anything, Apollo's open embrace of a minimum income level for the franchise was rarer.

On her homeworld, someone had a vote in planetary affairs if they paid taxes in the highest income tax bracket. Her understanding was that the balancing factor was the power of the local and regional governments—which followed a more traditional voting franchise and controlled the judiciary.

"We wouldn't *call* ourselves that," Bueller said in a false pained tone, "but it's true enough, I suppose. It was very clear that I would either join the Navy or be an engineer." He shrugged. "I chose both. The company I had a desk job at was owned by my cousin; it's that kind of network."

"I'm familiar with the idea," Kira conceded. "I saw it in action on Apollo, too. Nowhere's perfect."

"That's true enough," he agreed. "Our waiter is coming back. Dessert?"

"I really should be heading back to *Conviction*," Kira admitted, with a regret that was surprisingly unfeigned. "It's not fair to keep my bodyguards sitting in armor being bored, either."

"That's fair," he allowed. "This was my invitation, Kira, so you can get going if you need to. I'll handle the bill."

"Thank you," she said.

"I..." Bueller trailed off, then shrugged and continued. "I know neither of us has anywhere we're really guaranteed to be, but I think if we trade headware codes, we can check if you're here or I'm in Redward? I'd...like to do this again."

Kira arched an eyebrow at the man. She knew she was attractive enough, but it seemed both forward and optimistic to attempt to arrange a second meeting—she couldn't even call this a date—given their circumstances.

"There aren't many people out here I can talk to about home who aren't my coworkers," he admitted. "There's a lot of...*stuff* tied up in conversations on *Seventy-Niner* right now. It's refreshing to talk to someone who isn't mixed up in that—and I won't pretend that being pulled from an escape pod didn't make a lasting positive impression!"

She laughed and he joined sheepishly.

"All right," she told him, tossing him a digital file with her contact info. "I can't promise much of anything, Em Bueller. And even that..." She sighed and looked over at the shuttle port. "It depends on what your ship and crew get up to here in Ypres, doesn't it?"

Bueller's face fell, but he nodded his understanding as he passed a similar file back to her.

"I understand," he told her. "I don't call the shots on *Seventy-Niner*, Kira. I'm just one voice of a dozen—and, well, we're here."

"So you are," she murmured.

21

"WHAT'S UP, DEMIRCI?" Estanza asked as Kira stalked onto *Conviction*'s bridge. "You look like you're raising pet storm clouds."

"I need to borrow the tactical team for a minute," Kira replied. "To confirm a suspicion."

The trio of techs currently holding down a section designed for fifteen looked up with interest, the almost-synchronized movement making them resemble Apollo's imported gophers.

"They appear bored," the Captain noted. "You don't mind if I eavesdrop?"

"Not at all," she said as she crossed the bridge to stand behind the three mercenaries. "I presume we've been watching *K79-L*?"

"Yes, sir," the senior tech, a woman whose name tag read s connors confirmed. "She hasn't done much since we got here. Retrieve and launch fighters, that's all."

"Can you show me those fighters?" Kira asked.

The image appeared in Kira's headware a moment later, a trio of dark wedges flitting through space. At the same time, an icon on the main display flashed, highlighting the location of the craft she was looking at.

"Weltraumpanzer-Fünfs," a younger tech, a man with the elongated limbs and build of someone raised in low gravity and with the name tag WONG B told her. "We're pretty clear on what those look like at this point."

Kira studied the visual of the spacecraft for a moment before nodding in confirmation.

"The differences between the Vier and the Fünf are sometimes hard to spot," she noted, "but you're right. These are Fünfs. Thank you. Now, how closely have we been examining *K79-L*?"

"Closely?" Connors said. "We've been keeping at least one optical pickup on her the whole time and tracking her every movement."

"I don't want to know where she is; I want to know everything about her," Kira replied. "I want to read her Captain's *name tag*. Are we watching her that closely?"

"If we go active, she'll see that as a threat," Connors said.

"I don't think that's what Commander Demirci means," Estanza said. Kira glanced behind her to see that the Captain had moved up to join them. "Care to clarify, Demirci?"

"Passive scanners give us a lot of data," Kira told the techs. "Hell, we fight with optics and computer analysis, given how badly multiphasics hash everything else. I need heat signatures, detailed visuals, radiation profiles—hell, we should be able to do a spectrographic analysis of her hull."

"We probably have collected a lot of that data already," Connors admitted. "We passively scan for heat and radiation. Not sure about the spectrographics; that takes some careful watching on the light, and I'm not sure what we'd get out of it."

"It'll tell us whether the hull was all made at one point or certain sections were replaced," Kira replied. "That'll help us pick out potential weak spots where armor was repaired from prior damage, though that's not what I'm looking for."

"What are we looking for?" Connors asked, with a glance past Kira at Estanza.

"Officially, that ship was decommissioned from the Kaiserreich Navy and sold into civilian service," Kira told them. "I know Brisingr has a paramilitary wing that manages leasing arrangements and crew for recent surplus—but the ships are still supposed to be heavily demilitarized."

"In which case she would be missing most of her guns, wouldn't she?" the Captain murmured.

"Exactly. That they *have* Weltraumpanzer-Fünfs tells me they're not playing entirely by the rules, but if they were even partially disarmed, they're running one hell of a bluff here in Ypres," Kira told them. "Or 'Ghost Explorations' is most definitely *way* more than they're pretending to be."

Estanza was right next to her now, studying the scans as Connors started pulling them from the records and rapidly building a three-dimensional visual and energy-signature model of the Brisingr warship.

He almost certainly guessed what Kira was thinking. It was *his* paranoia she'd picked up, after all. It was *possible* that Bueller and his people were running a huge bluff—but it seemed far more likely to Kira that *K79-L* was still a fully functional warship.

And a fully functional Brisingr warship would never have been permitted to enter the type of service *K79-L* was engaged in.

"Her hull profile definitely suggests she's still fully armed," Connors said after a minute of analysis, highlighting the clear positions of the cruiser's turrets and fixed weapon mounts. "That could be faked—if I was running a bluff, *I'd* fake it—but the energy lines into the turrets and gun batteries can't be. There's too much power in play to do it safely. And *if* they're faked, that spectrographic analysis we're working will stick out like a sore thumb."

Energy and heat signatures were being overlaid on the model as the analysts worked. Kira waited silently and patiently. They knew the question now, which meant she was going to get her answers.

"Got the spectrography," Wong announced. "It's still preliminary, but I've got some initial comparisons."

"And?" Kira asked.

"I'd guess she's never even taken a hit," the tactical analyst told her. "Armor, hull, turrets, weapon mounts—everything is within a margin of error. I'd say it's all original material from one construction batch."

"And those weapons systems definitely have power," Connors

added. "They're not currently powered up—that would be a *lot* more obvious, but that style of plasma gun can't be held at full power for more than an hour without being discharged."

"So, she's fully armed," Kira concluded.

"Which is what we all figured," Connors pointed out. "We haven't really learned anything from this, though I think it's a useful exercise to carry out whenever we're this close to somebody else's warship."

"We haven't learned anything from this on its own, but I have some other information to run it against that *does* give me answers," Kira told the tech. She looked at Estanza. "I'm going to need half an hour of your time, sir."

"Zoric is due to relieve me shortly—or should she be in this chat too?" the Captain asked.

Zoric was the other person on the ship Kira knew was fully inside the secret of the Captain's past. Given everything she'd just learned...

"I think she should be in on this," Kira told him. "I've got a lot of new pieces to the puzzle, and the more of us who have them all, the better."

KIRA HAD RECORDED the entire conversation on her headware and sent the key fragments over to Zoric and Estanza as she picked up coffees from the station. All three of the drinks were black and hot and made with one of Redward's finer export blends.

Conviction's sojourn at Redward risked turning them all into coffee snobs at this rate, but Kira wasn't complaining about having good coffee as she ran through what Bueller had told her.

"'Investors with deep pockets and ties to the Kaiserreich,'" Estanza finally echoed. "That's a phrase that brings back memories. Not talking about Brisingr, but...*I* used almost that exact phrase a few times."

"When talking about the Institute?" Zoric asked.

"When I worked for them," the Captain agreed. "Every so often, we ended up working for someone who couldn't *possibly* have afforded to hire us, and that was the spiel. Our 'employer' had an interested party with deep pockets and local political ties backing them.

"Or some variant of that." He shook his head. "I figured this 'Ghost Explorations' for a front, but I was figuring I'd have to dig a few more layers to find Equilibrium."

"My guess is that Ghost is closer to Cobra Squadron than Cobra Squadron's employers," Kira said. "They're a direct Equilibrium front. I would guess that at *least* Captain Sitz and Bueller himself are Institute agents, and Bueller mentioned a 'Director' a few times who he didn't name."

"I have to wonder if those survey ships are even out there," Zoric said.

"Probably," Estanza replied. "I doubt they ever do any actual surveying, but survey ships can pass through almost anywhere without attention. I wonder..."

He trailed off, staring thoughtfully into his coffee cup before taking a large swallow.

"Captain?" Kira asked.

"I wonder if moving *K79-L* or another ship out here to push Yprian unification was always part of the Institute's plans," he said. "The timing is too tight for them to have put this all together in response to Deceiver's defeat at the Kiln. But if they were always planning on bringing a more-modern warship out here and putting it at the disposal of their chosen hegemon..."

"They could have accelerated that in the time frame we're looking at," Kira finished the thought. "Having the ship be available to Ypres to shut down Warlord Deceiver would have helped make sure the Clans didn't undermine their plan, either. Sooner or later, someone had to defeat them—and sending a K70 out would make sure that happened."

Kira and Estanza figured the Institute's plan had been for the ship-building complex they'd helped the Costar Clans build to fall into the hands of someone they could then encourage to establish their preferred military hegemony over the Cluster. It wouldn't have mattered to the Institute whether it was Ypres or Redward—they would figure they could convince anyone of the righteousness of their cause.

But Deceiver had guessed that plan and blown those shipyards to pieces, along with thousands of his own people, rather than allow Redward to capture them. In some ways, his nihilistic selfishness had been more of a wrench in Equilibrium's plans out there than all of Kira and Estanza's efforts.

"So, we now know what we'd guessed before," Zoric said. "We know *K79-L* is an Equilibrium asset pushing for the unification of Ypres to create a local hegemon for the Cluster. I wonder how in their pocket the Protector is."

The Protector was Sanctuary's ruler, elected for life to replace their predecessor as each died. If the Institute owned the Protector, uniting Ypres under Sanctuary gave them a perfect patsy for their mission.

"Deep," Estanza guessed. "For them to be moving this obviously in the region, they have to feel that he's either entirely theirs or entirely controllable."

"Makes sense." Zoric grimaced. "There's one thing in that conversation that worries me. Two things, really, I guess."

"What?" Kira asked.

"He said they'd been 'surveying local nova routes,'" the XO repeated. "And then later it sounded like he'd *recently* seen or done something he wasn't okay with."

Estanza's office was silent for a long time.

"The timing would be about right, wouldn't it?" Estanza murmured. "And there's no question: if *Hope* came up against *K79-L* with her nova drive in cooldown, she'd have been obliterated. I assumed we saw the debris cloud we did because her killers took care to make *sure* there was no identifiable wreckage…"

"But if you ran a small ninth-rate destroyer into an eighth-rate heavy cruiser, that's about what you'd end up with unless the cruiser was *trying* to leave debris," Kira said. "And…fuck me."

"Demirci?" Estanza prodded.

"Brisingr doctrine calls for 'testing engagements,'" she told them. "We ran into it a few times in the lead-up to and during the war: skirmishes or small battles where the Kaiserreich brought in overwhelming force so they could judge the quality of an unknown opponent.

"Intentionally trapping and overwhelming a representative of the class being touted as Redward's latest and most advanced would be entirely in line with their operational and strategic doctrine," she concluded. "*K79-L* might be an Equilibrium asset, but from what Bueller said, her crew is Kaiserreich Navy and her command staff is ex-Kaiserreich officers the Institute hired away from cushy desk jobs."

"Sorry, Kira, but it looks like your new boyfriend is in the middle of this mess," Zoric told her.

"I gave him my headware code; I think we're a ways away from *boyfriend*," Kira replied. "He seemed nice enough, but if he was in the middle of the mess at DLI, that might have been a cover."

"DLI was ugly," Estanza said. "I'd guess that was a mix of Brisingr doctrine and Equilibrium policy to create a worst possible situation. The Brisingr commander wanted to test his ship against a Redward warship, and the Equilibrium team lead, who I'm guessing is *not* the same person, wanted to make sure there were no witnesses."

"I don't like the answer, but it adds up," Kira agreed. It was a shame, really. Bueller hadn't seemed like the type, and she'd been considering the virtues of what would have effectively been a pen pal. "What a fucking mess."

"Still leaves one question," Zoric pointed out. "We know the gunships at DLI weren't Costar Clans. They weren't Yprian, either, I don't think. I'd have to poke a bit, but I think our sources would have mentioned if *half* of Sanctuary's gunships had vanished for a week during the negotiations around absorbing Hearth."

"That's another moving part, and it adds to the only conclusion I think I can take from this," Estanza said. "All of our medevacs are on the surface and in capable hands. We need to talk to Redward intelligence about all of this—even the parts that can't go on a courier."

"It's a shame to waste the money on the job posting, but we might be able to send one of your Commanders out here to follow up on it solo," he continued to Kira. "We need to get moving. Zoric—get everything in motion.

"If anyone is still off-ship, I want them back aboard ASAP. We nova by noon."

He shook his head.

"I want to be somewhere where I don't have to watch my back for surprise thermonuclear fire!"

22

"BOSS, YOU GOT A MINUTE?"

"For you, Mel? Always." Kira gestured for Cartman to come in and join her. She waved away the files she was working on—mercenary companies managed to have less paperwork than proper militaries, but not *no* paperwork—and focused on her old friend.

"What's up?"

Kira's office was still a plain space. She'd had decorations in her office when she'd served in the Apollo System Defense Force, but those had all been left behind when she fled her home. Now, the only "decoration" was her armored leather jacket hung on a hook by the door.

"You are," Cartman pointed out. "At oh-one-hundred hours ship time, when Hoffman has the formal group command and we're sharing a trade-route stop with an RRF gunship squadron. This is about as safe as *Conviction* is ever going to get, but you're awake. In your office, not even your quarters."

Kira grimaced.

"I lost track of time," she told her friend. "Not really paying attention."

"You have seventy-eight grams of high-density molecular circuitry in your skull, same as the rest of us," Cartman replied. "That's linked to your brain and doesn't really let you lose track of time unless you tell it to."

The CNG sighed.

"I'd blame paperwork, but that's a symptom, not a cause," she admitted.

"You feel like you've vanished on us, boss," the pilot told her. "A few months ago, we were throwing a wake together, but as the nova group expanded, you got more and more locked with Estanza and less and less with us."

"This ship has secrets, Mel," Kira said. "I don't even know if I should share them, let alone if I can. But some of those secrets seem to be impacting all of us more than I'd like, so Estanza and I keep working on it."

"You're still the CNG, Kira," Cartman replied. "But more than that, there's five of us on this ship who've been through hell and deep space with you. You haven't so much as shared a beer with us in a month. We're starting to worry."

"And the old hands elected you to come raise the topic with me?" Kira asked.

"I've known you longest and I fly on your wing," the pilot said with a smile. "I know when you're beating yourself up and I can tell when it's a man versus work—or grief."

"And which is it this time?"

"All of the above," her friend told her. "You're still hurting over Mbeki, even if you never did get a leg over there. And while you're not telling us those secrets, they're playing into everything you're dealing with.

"And Milani told me about your dinner on Dikkebus. Dining with the enemy, but he sounded nice enough, so I'm guessing you're feeling guilty over enjoying his company. Especially since you figure he's an Equilibrium agent."

Kira blinked, stared at her friend for several long seconds, then blinked again.

"I'm not sure how much of that you even *should* know, let alone put into words," she finally said.

"We had an Equilibrium Institute engineering team on the ship for over a week," Cartman reminded her. "After you rubbed their boss's face in who they actually worked for, they didn't really stick to their cover very well. Shitty field agents, in my opinion."

"They were techs, not field agents," Kira said. "I figured most people wrote all of that off as conspiracy theories and bullshit."

"I don't know exactly what the Equilibrium Institute is," Cartman admitted. "What I know is that they scare you and the Captain, that they provided a pirate warlord out here with a *lot* of tech, and that a shiny new warship just showed up in our area of operations.

"Somehow, I'm thinking these are connected. Am I wrong?"

"No," Kira acknowledged. She considered her old friend. "Let me call Hoffman in here," she finally said. "I'll keep some of Estanza's secrets, mind you, but I think the two of you are owed at least as much as I know outside of that.

"Assuming you believe a word out of my mouth, that is."

"THAT'S a hell of a pill to swallow," Joseph Hoffman said slowly after Kira finished laying out what she knew of the Equilibrium Institute and their operations in the Syntactic Cluster. "A conspiracy stretching all the way back to, what, the Heart? The Core?"

"Honestly, I think it's born out of the Meridian," Kira said. "They tend to bring tech from more advanced local systems rather than bring it out from the inner worlds. If they were based in the Core, even a single SolFed ship could turn the tide of most of their endeavors."

"That would be too obvious, though," Cartman replied. "The 'Ghost Explorations' front out here? I can just about see it being real. I mean, I'd expect the ship to be properly demilitarized, but I can see it. Warships get used for that.

"But if you even had a recent Fringe ship, you're talking something five hundred light-years from home with no real reason to be here." She shook her head. "They could move money from the Meridian to the Rim easily enough. Flow it through enough hands and enough systems, and no one is ever tracing the source. Hell, my understanding is we buried most of the money that founded the Memorials pretty cleanly, and we only went a hundred-odd light-years."

"Exactly," Kira agreed. "Some of that was using bearer credit chips; some of that was running it through chains of banks across multiple star systems. You can trace the money we started with back to Jay Moranis's personal fortune if you try hard enough, but it wouldn't be easy. Run it another hundred light-years and you're talking months to follow that line, if you could at all."

"I get...how, I guess," Hoffman agreed. "But why would someone sign on for something like that?"

"They've got a hell of a pitch, from what I saw when we had Burke aboard," Kira told them. Cameron Burke had been the Equilibrium engineer who'd coordinated supplying the Costar Clans. "Peace and stability for all mankind. You can get a lot of people in deep with that pitch, especially when you can run the Seldonian analyses to *show* what will happen if you don't act.

"I don't think they've really controlled everything and everyone forever and everywhere," she continued. "I'm guessing there's a wedge of the Rim and part of the Fringe where they've been influencing things for at least fifty or sixty years. Maybe longer...maybe even enough longer that we'd see their fingerprints in the Periphery, too, but I think we're looking at a wedge a few hundred light-years thick, not an entire layer of the sphere of human expansion."

"Bad enough, if it's true," Hoffman agreed. He sighed. "And I believe you, boss. I don't know what parts you're not telling us, though it sounds like the Captain had a damn close brush with them, but I believe you.

"It's just...a hell of a pill to swallow," he echoed.

"Believe me, I was shocked enough when Estanza briefed *me*," Kira said. "If I hadn't still been in shock and angry over Daniel's death, I'm not sure I'd have believed him until we had Burke aboard."

"So, what do we do now?" Cartman asked. "I'm guessing that the Captain isn't on great terms with the Institute?"

"No," Kira confirmed. "Worse, the Institute regards projects like the Syntactic Cluster Free Trade Zone as inherently unstable, inevitably doomed to fail in fire and death. I worry about what level of expediency they'll embrace to bring the Cluster into *their* form of stable government."

"Well, they seem well on their way to unifying Ypres by force," Cartman said grimly. "I'm guessing they follow that up with an injection of money and tech, probably at least including a class two nova-drive fabricator."

"And then the Cluster gets drawn into the same kind of bloody war that swallowed our home sector," Kira guessed. "And that's assuming that Equilibrium doesn't upgrade the unified Yprians fast enough to straight up overwhelm Redward and the SCFTZ fleets."

There was a long silence.

"We have to take out *K79-L*," Hoffman said flatly. "Preferably followed by having King Larry negotiate an actual peaceful solution to Ypres and bring them into the SCFTZ. If he gets Ypres in, in however many pieces, that tips the balance, right?"

"Right," Kira agreed. "If Ypres is unified—or at least, all of the remaining factions are in the Zone—there's no one left for the Institute to play games with. King Larry and his allies should be able to lead the Cluster into a fucking golden age.

"Assuming, of course, that we can take out a hundred-thousand-fucking-cubic heavy cruiser with two dozen nova fighters and no bombers—and *then* negotiate a peaceful solution to a set of two-century-old divisions. Easy."

"If it was easy, someone would have already done it," Cartman said with a chuckle. "And they wouldn't have needed *Conviction* and Memorial Squadron, would they?"

23

THE TRIP back to Redward passed with a surprising lack of trouble. With everything they knew to be going on, Kira half-expected every nova to be followed by a full scramble order—and she kept her people ready for exactly that.

"We're about to nova *into Redward*," someone finally complained as she issued the orders to prepare again. Jowita "Lancer" Janda was Memorial-Alpha-Six, the only ex-RRF gunship pilot in Kira's own squadron. "You seriously want us prepped for a scramble in safe territory?"

Kira stood just inside the door of the flight officers' lounge. Less than a bar and more than a mess, the lounge acted as the beating heart of flight country. Currently, it held about a third of her pilots and copilots, the only ones to get the order verbally instead of by headware.

All four of the ex-Redward Royal Fleet pilots were in the room, though they were at least not clustered together. That had been one of her fears—and was why the four had been split across three of her squadrons.

"We last received updates on Redward news eighteen hours and a nova ago," Kira reminded them all. "The ship giving us that news was twenty hours out of Redward themselves. It will be another seven hours before we nova into Redward, since I'm giving you all enough warning to grab a decent chunk of sleep in advance.

"That means, for those of you who are math-challenged, that when we arrive in Redward, our news will be forty-five hours out of date," she concluded. "Two days, basically. A lot can happen in two days."

"Against a defended star system?" Janda asked drily. "Seems unlikely."

"It is," Kira agreed. "But I'd rather put us all through a bit of minor inconvenience that makes for good training by being paranoid than take that risk. We're making a four-point-seven-light-year nova, people. We can't make that long of a jump straight into orbit, which means we're outside the range of the asteroid fortresses' guns. I have seen systems lose control of their space outside of the range of their fortresses.

"I don't expect it here, but it was Brisingr cruiser groups that pulled that off," she told them. "And while I will freely admit I'm on edge from my old enemies showing up, well, I have the privilege of being in command of you lot.

"So, unless you want to *quit* and give up your claim on bonuses for this little trip, you follow my orders. What do you say, Lancer?"

Janda threw up her hands in defeat.

"You're the boss, boss," she said. "Just seems like a lot of effort for nothing."

"It almost certainly is, Lancer," Kira replied. "And if that K70 hadn't shown up, I wouldn't be doing it. But that ship isn't supposed to be here, so we're going to be a bit more paranoid for a while. Hopefully, it's a waste of effort."

The room was silent as everyone considered what it would look like if it *wasn't* a waste of effort. *K79-L* and her fighters couldn't challenge the monitors and fortresses above Redward itself or around the fueling stations at the gas giant Lastward. They could, as Kira was grimly aware, probably take on the entire RRF.

Redward only had three cruisers and those were sixty-thousand-cubic ships, smaller than *Conviction*. *K79-L* had enough of a technological edge to make up for being outnumbered three to one.

With the RRF's long list of commitments right now, Kira would be surprised if there were more than a cruiser and maybe three destroyers in the system. *K79-L* would have a harder time fighting the RRF's non-nova-capable monitors, but the nova warship could easily avoid engagement with warships limited by the speed of light.

One heavy cruiser couldn't blockade the entire system, but they could cause a lot of trouble without ever fully cutting Redward off. It didn't seem likely to Kira, but it was a situation she had to plan for—though, if nothing else, they'd left *K79-L* behind in Ypres and it would have been extremely difficult for the cruiser to beat them here!

LIKE EVERY PILOT under her command, Kira spent the nova in her nova fighter. The Hoplite-IV was a comfortable cocoon, a familiar reminder of times past. To her surprise, though, she didn't necessarily qualify those times as *better*. Just more familiar.

Conviction and its more-casual atmosphere were growing on her. She'd lost a lot of friends getting there, but it was more comfortable out there than she'd expected…especially since she still had friends willing to yank her up short when she got too tied up in her own head.

"Nova in ten seconds," Zoric's voice said in her head. "All hands stand by. Nova in five. Four. Three. Two. One. Nova."

There was no clear sign when the world changed. It took about half a second for the sensors to catch up to the fact that *Conviction* was now here instead of there, a blink of discontinuity that showed even computers missed the change.

Then Kira's sensors updated, new data flickering in as she examined their position. *Conviction* had novaed in just over ten million kilometers from Redward itself, and everything looked…normal. She even recognized the cruiser in high orbit above the planet: *Last Denial* had been part of the fleet they'd gone to the Kiln with.

"All scans show clear," Zoric told her. "Everything looks calm and orderly."

"Thank you, Commander," Kira replied. She switched to the nova group channel. "Nova Group, you may stand down. Nightmare, Indigo, Purlwise. You're CAP on me. Launch on the ball."

The ball dropped into her mental sphere as she spoke, and she triggered the initiation command without hesitation. A few seconds later, her fighter flashed into space. Three more followed her in perfect sequence, the designated Carrier Air Patrol falling into formation on *Conviction*.

This was probably even less required than having the nova group ready for a full scramble launch. Despite that, it was a more regular part of their operations. Everywhere *Conviction* went, at least two and usually four fighters flew escort.

"We are cleared for our usual dock at Blueward Station, Basketball," Zoric told her. "You'll cover us in then report aboard?"

"We'll RTB once we're inside the coverage of the fortresses," Kira confirmed. There were points, after all, where it became even *more* redundant to have the fighters out than usual.

Black Ward, White Ward, Green Ward and First Ward were the four asteroid fortresses orbiting Redward. Each had been carved into and out of a nickel-iron asteroid ten kilometers in diameter. They weren't invulnerable, but they were the next best thing available to the Syntactic Cluster. The weapons and other systems in Redward's defenses were advanced enough that Kira wouldn't have wanted to take Apollo or Brisingr nova ships against them, either.

Sub-fighters, the non-nova-capable siblings of her nova fighters, carried out more distant patrols around the planet. Eventually, they'd be replaced with true nova fighters to cover up the one weakness of the monitors and fortresses they supported.

Right now, though, every nova fighter Redward was building was going to their carriers. Those ships, crude freighter conversions, *sucked* in Kira's opinion...but they were carriers and could deliver thirty fighters to anywhere in the Cluster in a week.

Once their sub-fighters were replaced, they'd make for a core striking force no one in the Cluster could match...or could *have* matched, before *K79-L* had arrived.

The presence of the new fighters meant that Redward could at least regard *K79-L* as "merely" a threat to the structures and alliances they'd been building for two generations, instead of an existential threat to their own freedom and safety.

Either way, Kira was grimly certain that the local military wasn't going to handle suddenly being completely outclassed very well.

As they approached, her sensors continued to update, and she felt a spike of not-quite-grief as she spotted *Sensibility* herself detaching from Green Ward. Pound for pound, the destroyer and her remaining sister were the most advanced and powerful warships the Cluster had ever built, intended to act as the heralds of a new age of peace.

Against *K79-L*, they were toys.

That said, the shipyards that had built those destroyers were busy. There had been three construction slips concealed under Green Ward's rocky bulk when *Conviction* had left. Those were swarming with robots and small craft as the keels of new warships were taking shape—and other, similar swarms were crawling through empty space as they began the process of assembling at least two more construction slips.

The cruiser yard under First Ward was alive with activity as well, for the first time since Kira had entered Redward. Her files said it had been two years since the RRF had commissioned their last cruiser, and the king had been struggling to find the money to build more.

That struggle, it seemed, was over. Kira had to wonder if that was in answer to the vastly expanded responsibilities inherent in the finally solidifying Free Trade Zone...or a direct response to the sudden arrival of a probably hostile warship that could match the entire Redward Royal Fleet.

24

KIRA DISMOUNTED her fighter to find John Estanza waiting for her. *Conviction*'s Captain, the primary shareholder and sole director of the mercenary company that owned the warship, had changed from his usual insignia-less shipsuit into a dramatic dark teal uniform she'd never seen before.

The cut of a space-force shipsuit was relatively standardized across the galaxy, but dress uniforms were *far* more varied. Estanza's uniform was the most basic, though, a long-jacketed suit over a white turtle-neck. Like most space-force dress uniforms, it could cover the shipsuit that acted as an emergency safety system in space.

And unlike his usual unmarked outfit, Estanza's dress uniform incorporated a stylized golden rocket worn over the left breast. The location varied, but the golden rocket was a reasonably standardized starship-captain insignia.

"Did I miss a memo?" Kira asked, eyeing her fully dressed-up boss.

"Several," he said crisply. "My attendance has been requested as *Conviction*'s representative at a briefing the RRF command wants to hold in roughly two hours."

"That's a good sign, right?" she said. "That they're treating you like a senior officer?"

"Oh, it is, but you need to check *your* messages," Estanza told her. "Because they tried to hire *you* as the main speaker at the briefing through me."

Kira blinked.

"Okay, I can do that..." she said.

"That's outside your contract with me," he pointed out. "For that kind of engagement, they have to talk to *you*." He grinned. "I did give them a suggested number to offer, though."

Kira pulled the message into her headware. She nodded and grimaced as she processed the text.

She'd *met* Admiral Vilma Remington, the senior officer of the Redward Royal Fleet, but she still hadn't been expecting a direct message from the woman. The precisely blunt language of the note suggested that Remington had written it herself rather than having her office send it, too.

"They want me to give them a full briefing on the K70 heavy cruiser and the likely fighter wing," she said aloud, grimacing. "That makes sense, though I'd have liked a little more time to prep."

She reached the number and swallowed. Remington was offering as much money for one two-hour briefing as they'd pay to deploy *Conviction* for those two hours. It wasn't exactly "retire on this paycheck" money, but it was still more than her time was worth.

"If you don't want to give the briefing, you can probably just sell them your simulator files on the K70," Estanza noted. "I doubt we'll get more than a half a million for them, but they'll take them."

"I can give the briefing," Kira admitted in a somewhat-choked tone. "I basically gave you and Zoric the short form at one point."

And she'd been refreshing herself on everything she had on the K70 for a bit now—and she hadn't ended up a nova-group commander by lacking in self-confidence. She nodded firmly.

"I can definitely give them what they need, though I'm not sure it's what they want," she said calmly. "I shouldn't need more than a few minutes to pull files together for it."

"Good," Estanza told her. "Because Hoffman tells me you didn't set a dress uniform for the Memorials, and no one appears to have brought a pattern for an Apollo System Defense Force dress uniform, either.

"That means we're putting you in *Conviction*'s uniform, and even *our* fabricators need some time to make that happen!"

KIRA'S ASSUMPTION had been that, as a mercenary, she'd wear civilian formal wear to any event that would have required a dress uniform from an officer. The concept of attending military briefings with most of the senior officers of a planet's military hadn't occurred to her.

Certainly, *giving* that kind of briefing hadn't. If she'd considered it, she might have had something made up for her people—and it *wouldn't* have been Apollo's dress uniform.

There had once been a distinct combat value to a stylized linothorax cuirass. That had been in an era where untrained Greek citizens had marched out into the field and stabbed each other with spears. For the modern Apollo military, it was an uncomfortable affectation.

The dress uniform *Conviction*'s fabricators had run up for her—in well under an hour, giving them plenty of time—was far more comfortable, even worn over a shipsuit.

Where Estanza wore a golden rocket, Kira had the ancient insignia of pilots' wings over a single five-millimeter thick gold bar. The insignia was that of an ASDF Colonel, the commander of a full Nova Combat Group...her current role, if not the rank she'd retired from the ASDF at.

The insignia cost her some of the overall comfort of the uniform, but she couldn't argue with it. She was the senior nova fighter pilot in this star system. Even the RRF's handful of nova-fighter pilots had willingly conceded command to her at the Kiln, recognizing that she knew *far* more about the tactics required than they did.

It still took her every scrap of the self-confidence, even arrogance, of an experienced fighter pilot for her to walk down the steps of the amphitheater-style briefing room. This was not the small space set aside for the senior officers of *Conviction* or even a flight-country-style ready room for the two combat groups aboard an Apollo fleet carrier.

The space was sized for at least two hundred people. It held maybe half of that, but Kira had enough experience with reading Redward insignia by now to realize that the room was full of Captains and Admirals.

For there to even *be* that many senior officers, she had to have basically every senior officer from the monitors and asteroid fortresses in the room, plus the commanders of every nova ship currently in-system. Redward was taking *K79-L*'s presence deathly seriously.

Admiral Vilma Remington was alone on the stage at the center of the room when Kira reached it. The tall and gracefully aging woman looked perfectly at home controlling a room of a hundred senior officers, but this was her home environment.

Kira was actually surprised by how much actual nervousness she had as she stepped up and shared a nod with the Admiral.

"Officers of the Redward Royal Fleet and allies," Remington said loudly. "By now, you are all aware of the change in the situation in the Ypres System. Ypres Hearth, a longtime trading partner of ours if not exactly our friend, has ceased to exist. They have been absorbed by the Protectorate of Sanctuary and have joined forces with their neighbor and age-old enemy.

"This was enabled by the presence of a new factor: a warship from the Apollo-Brisingr Cluster whose crew appears to be acting as both mercenaries and political opportunists," the Admiral continued. "While the Brisingr ship *K79-L* has official reasons for being in Ypres that don't involve unifying the system, her commander appears more than willing to involve the ship and her nova fighters in that long-standing conflict."

Remington leveled flinty gray eyes on her audience.

"While Redward has not yet chosen a position on this and Sanctuary is our traditional ally in the Ypres System, the situation has grown far more complicated, and understanding the level of threat represented by *K79-L* has become utterly critical to all of our strategic and operational planning.

"Fortunately for us all, we currently have a retainer agreement with the Memorial Squadron mercenary company. The core members of that force are refugees from Apollo, enemies of Brisingr who have fought this type of vessel before. Their senior officer and shareholder, Commander Kira Demirci, has agreed to brief us all on the capabilities of the K70 class heavy cruiser and her fighter wing."

Those gray eyes flickered away from the audience to meet Kira's gaze, warming as they did.

"You've got this," her voice said in Kira's headware, the Admiral apparently reading her like a book despite Kira's years of practice at self-control. "Remember that not all of this audience is cleared for Project Sinister. They *are* cleared about Lancer Squadron and the Battle of the Kiln."

There was a pause as Kira mentally affirmed her understanding. Project Sinister was Redward's top secret development program for the new nova fighters. Kira wasn't even fully informed on it, but she knew it existed. From Remington's instructions, most of her audience didn't even know that much.

"You have control of the projection system," the Admiral concluded. "Good luck."

AS THE ADMIRAL stepped off the stage, Kira turned to face the audience and made a small gesture. A hologram of the K70-class heavy cruiser appeared above her head, filling most of the space with the blocky and utilitarian lines of the Brisingr warship.

"Officers, this is your subject," she told them. "A Brisingr Kaiserreich Navy K70-class heavy cruiser. I'm not certain of the age of this particular unit, but her number suggests a later-series construction, making her between thirty-five and forty years old.

"By BKN standards, she is near-obsolete but remains a front-line first-rate combatant. She is two hundred and forty-three meters long and totals ninety-six thousand cubic meters. That makes her the largest single vessel in the Syntactic Cluster by over fifteen thousand cubic meters."

She gestured at the image and the ship broke apart into a rough schematic.

"I don't have full specifications on the K70 class," she noted. "Some of the information I do have may well be out of date, depending on the updates *K79-L* received. She would have been originally built with a point-six-rated dispersion network under her armor but was almost certainly updated to point six five during her career.

"It is certainly *possible* that she was updated to point seven, but Brisingr has primarily reserved networks of that rating for brand-new construction."

Kira tried to ignore the consternation in her audience. The rating of an energy dispersion network was a rough approximation of how much of the energy of a plasma bolt it would dissipate harmlessly. The *effective* rating went down with each hit, but *K79-L* would disperse sixty-five percent of the thermal energy of the first hit on her hull.

She didn't know the rating of Redward's dispersion networks, beyond knowing that the most advanced ones had been installed in the *Sensibility* class. Given that many of the Cluster powers didn't include the networks at all, she guessed it was around point two to point three. At best.

"Her Harringtons would have been harder to update, leaving her relatively clumsy by the standards of her newer cousins," Kira told her audience. Numbers flashed across the screen, and she carefully didn't let her concern show.

"Relatively clumsy" in this case meant that the cruiser could outmaneuver *Conviction* and anything in Redward's order of battle. Her audience was following the numbers, and the verbal consternation was fading into grim silence now.

"As you can see from her profile, she mounts twenty-four dual heavy plasma-cannon turrets in four six-turret broadsides," Kira continued. "At any given angle, usually twelve turrets can bear on a target. She *also* mounts six spinal dual-emitter heavy cannon capable of firing forward or backward. The most dangerous place to be is in front of her, where she can bring those spinal guns and twelve of her turrets to bear. The spinal guns are also used to cover her rearward arc, where only eight of her dual turrets can be brought to bear."

Firing arcs were drawn in red cones on the hologram above Kira, and her audience was completely silent now.

"In addition to her own weaponry, approximately ten percent of *K79-L*'s volume is dedicated to the deployment and support of two ten-ship squadrons of nova fighters. BKN doctrine calls for any nova group of this size to be made of multipurpose craft, usually heavy fighters."

The line between *heavy fighter* and *fighter-bomber* was fuzzy at best, even to Kira.

"In BKN service, a K70 would carry twenty Weltraumpanzer-Fünfs," she concluded. "The Fünf is an extremely capable fighter, with some of the heaviest plasma guns I've ever seen on a nova fighter. Those are both its biggest strength and its biggest weakness: it empties its gun capacitors and needs to recharge significantly more often than ships with lighter weaponry."

A holographic breakdown of the Weltraumpanzer-Fünf joined the K70 above Kira's head.

"Nonetheless, the Weltraumpanzer-Fünf represents a nova fighter capable of engaging both other nova fighters and nova starships with a high success and survival rate against both opponents," she concluded. "A number of these fighters were in Warlord Deceiver's hands, but we were spared the worst of their capabilities because his pilots were recently transferred gunship crews."

She studied her silent audience.

"I have a question, Commander Demirci," Vice Admiral Ylva Kim said, the tall blonde woman rising to her feet in the second row.

"I hope to have an answer, Admiral," Kira allowed. Kim had commanded the fleet at the Kiln, and while she was a bit of a pain, she had also led that fleet to victory.

"Do you have any idea what would cause the Kaiserreich to send a first-rate capital ship, even an old one, this far out? We are well outside their sphere of influence or all but the most extended trade routes."

"Thanks to our time in Ypres, I actually have some idea what brought them out here," Kira admitted. She wasn't going to admit to things like the Equilibrium Institute, but she could tell them what was *officially* going on.

"*K79-L* has been decommissioned from the Brisingr Kaiserreich Navy. Instead of being scrapped, since she's still a quite capable unit, she's entered what they call the Secondary Service Reserve. These are former Navy ships that are at least partially in civilian hands but mostly used as political-influence tokens by the Kaiser.

"SSR ships come in two varieties: ships that have not received their latest upgrades but retain all of their warfighting gear, and ships that have been at least partially demilitarized."

"And *K79-L*?" Kim asked.

"That's where things are complicated," Kira admitted. "Our current understanding is that *K79-L* is officially leased to a company named Ghost Explorations, out of the Syndulla System. No non-demilitarized SSR unit would be leased to a civilian company."

She held a hand to forestall comment and waved away the generic hologram, replacing it with the scans of *K79-L* itself in Ypres orbit. Her audience was more than familiar enough to tell the difference, and there was a new tone as every officer in the room leaned forward.

"We confirmed the presence of Weltraumpanzer-Fünf nova fighters flying air patrol around Dikkebus in the Ypres System," Kira said quietly. "We also did detailed passive scans of *K79-L* herself. Barring an *immense* investment in a deception that would be just as complicated as reinstalling the cruiser's guns, *K79-L* is fully operational. She has not been demilitarized at all.

"That tells us that her official role is bullshit," she concluded. "Either she is still in Brisingr service, or she has been leased to the Syndulla system government, not a civilian corporation. Not unless that corporation has access and influence at levels of the Kaiserreich that I have never seen."

She couldn't explain to this audience that that last was almost exactly what she figured had happened. That started to get into conspiracy theories she didn't want to be the one selling the RRF on.

"Why she is here is irrelevant, in the end," Remington said, rejoining Kira on the stage. "What matters is the threat she poses. In your opinion, Commander Demirci, can the RRF defeat *K79-L*?"

Kira swallowed. She'd half-expected the question, half-hoped it wouldn't be asked.

"No," she said calmly. "Not in open battle in open space. *K79-L* is a nova warship, with all the limitations that entails. While she is more advanced than your monitors and fortresses, she is simply too small to practically engage either.

"She is, however, large enough and powerful enough to take on your entire nova fleet in a single engagement. If she entered that engagement with only her own nova fighters for support, she would be badly damaged in that fight but she would win."

"Could *Conviction* engage her? Or, I suppose, *Conviction*'s fighter group?" Remington asked.

Kira glanced out at Estanza in the audience and shrugged.

"If the entirety of *Conviction*'s nova group arrived at the perfect time while *K79-L* had no nova fighters deployed and no other allies or escorts in play, it is possible we could launch a fatal torpedo strike on her," she told them. "At no point in our time in the Ypres System was *K79-L* that defenseless. For twenty-four nova fighters to destroy a heavy cruiser of *K79-L*'s scale and capability would require complete incompetence on the part of our enemies."

The only scenario where *Kira* could see *K79-L* being defeated was a combination of both the entire RRF *and Conviction*'s nova group *and* significant numbers of Redward's own new-build nova fighters *and* a strike group of nova bombers no one in the Cluster even had a design for.

"Before we open this to general questions, Commander, I have one last important one," Remington told her.

"I am at your disposal, Admiral Remington," Kira said.

"Have *you* seen one of these ships destroyed?"

"I have participated in the bombing runs that destroyed two K70-class heavy cruisers during Apollo's war with Brisingr," Kira told them. "In only one of them did I launch a torpedo to be given partial kill credit, but I have seen two K70s taken down. I was also present for the destruction of a hundred-and-twenty-thousand-cubic Brisingr battlecruiser, though *that* ship was defeated by two Apollo warships of equivalent scale.

"This ship is not invulnerable. She does, however, badly outclass your current fleet."

"I appreciate your honesty, Commander Demirci," Remington told her. "And while you have made the limits of your knowledge of this particular ship clear, you still know more about *K79-L* than anyone else in this star system. I suspect we have a great many questions."

"I will answer as best as I can," Kira replied. She grinned. "It's not like Apollo is going to mind me telling everything we knew about our enemy to someone else on the wrong side of the Kaiserreich!"

25

BY THE TIME the briefing was over, Kira was completely wrung out. The RRF, for all that it was the tiny navy of a ninth-tier power, was still a professional and well-trained force. They had a solid idea of what they needed to know about a potential enemy warship, and their officers had sucked her brain dry.

"I'm not sure that was worth the money," she admitted to Estanza as she collapsed into a seat on the shuttle. "Damn. I keep half-writing off the RRF because their ships are crap."

"And most officers from even Fringe space forces would do the same to the ASDF," he reminded her. "Technological advancement does not inherently lead to a more professional or capable military—or vice versa, really.

"Remember that a single SolFed destroyer would be an even greater unbalancing force than *K79-L*." He grimaced. "Hell, a single modern *Griffon* destroyer would be about as bad, and half our nova fighters are old Griffon birds."

"It's easy to think of the most advanced folks in your neighborhood as the top dogs," Kira conceded. "Especially when you *are* the most advanced folks in your neighborhood."

"Something both Ypres and Redward struggle with, I suspect,"

Estanza said. "You did a good job of helping them realize how much trouble they're in. Though I think the odds are not quite as bad as you painted."

"Remington asked me not to talk about Project Sinister," Kira told him. "Since that's the big odds-evener in play, well."

"How many of their new fighters would it take to really even the odds?" he asked.

"If they packed all three carriers with Hoplite and One-Fifteen equivalents…" She shook her head. "Maybe. If we filled *Conviction* all of the way and they did the same, we could hit *K79-L* with a hundred and fifty nova fighters of comparable vintage, plus the rest of the RRF…then they start to look like they're in trouble."

"They've given us half of their class two drive production so far," Estanza told her, his tone weary. "I'm not supposed to know that, but I keep my ears to the ground. We got twelve drives and are due another twelve shortly. They've kept twenty-four and they only have one of the two designs complete."

"Fuck." Kira had assumed they'd been getting a quarter of the production at best. But…a class two nova-drive fabricator produced one drive unit a day. Forty-eight units in two months made sense, given setup times and learning curves.

"How many actual fighters?"

"Twenty Sinister-Alphas," he said quietly. "Based on the One-Fifteen, and what I've seen says they're actually a decent fighter-bomber. But that's it. They decommissioned the Lancers to crew them, which was a good call even if it kept their total numbers down."

The Cavalier-II nova interceptors flown by Redward's one nova squadron had been problematic hangar queens that their home system had happily sold to the RRF—and a lot of other people—without bothering to downgrade. The Cavalier-*III* was a solid fighter that could go toe-to-toe with Kira's Hoplites.

The II was not. Standing them down to have experienced pilots for the new fighters made perfect sense to Kira.

"Three months to fill their carriers," she calculated in her head. "By then, whatever's going to happen in Ypres is going to have happened."

"Give Redward five years, and even Crest or Brisingr is going to hesitate to clash with them," Estanza told her. "Some of that is what we've sold them. Some of that, they've stolen or bought elsewhere. Some of that is going through the wreckage in the Kiln."

He snorted.

"And some of that, I suspect, is that my 'allies' have spent more time in my nova drive than I'd really like, but I'm not going to point it out," he concluded.

"Sir?" she asked.

"The Syntactic Cluster, including Redward, is still building Ten-X nova drives," he told her. She nodded her understanding—10X was the base standard, a nova drive that would take ten times its own volume through the nova. That was the design that every colony had had in their data banks when they were founded.

It was hard to build a bigger nova drive after about two thousand cubic meters. It was even harder to raise the multiplier. That was what limited most systems to ships in the ten-to-twenty-kilocubic range.

Of course, her home system was building ten-thousand-cubic 12X drives to support hundred-and-twenty-kilocubic battlecruisers and carriers.

"*Conviction* runs a Twelve-X drive—and the *Sensibilities* run an Eleven-X drive," Estanza told her. "I wonder how much they learned watching us jump around." He shrugged. "Of course, the class two drive plant we stole for them is a Brisingr design, so those are Twelve-X systems."

"So, their new ships might be bigger than anyone expects?" Kira asked.

"They're burning the candle at both ends to get a second cruiser slip online at First Ward," he said. "And if I'm reading everything right, they've upped their drive size as well. Their current cruisers are sixty thousand cubics. The next generation is slated for *seventy-five*. Almost as big as *Conviction*."

"That'll help," Kira conceded. "In two years."

"Exactly." He shook his head as the shuttle dipped back toward *Conviction*. "And I suppose it's certainly an option for Redward to fall back behind their fortresses and wait for those ships to finish before engaging the Yprians and *K79-L*, but..."

"Who pays for the cruisers, then?" she asked. "Why am I figuring it's not coincidence that it's only as the Free Trade Zone really starts to get implemented that Redward can afford these ships?"

"They're showing a bump in trade already, from what I'm told," he agreed. "I don't know the numbers, but I'd bet it's helping pay for the new fleet. If Ypres is suddenly in a position to blockade Redward, all of that goes away."

"And the Institute has their military hegemon…one way or another," Kira said grimly. "Because I can't imagine that Redward will stay quite as optimistic and friendly if they're besieged for several years."

The shuttle was silent.

"No," Estanza conceded. "So, I'm going to go look for an answer in a collection of military history books." He chuckled. "I don't expect to *find* one, but I'm going to look. I suggest you get some rest as well. That briefing did not look easy."

"It wasn't," she agreed. A ping in her headware interrupted her before she agreed to rest. A message from Simoneit?

"I think I need to watch this," she told Estanza. "Give me a moment?"

"Of course."

She activated the message and the image of her lawyer appeared in front of her. Simoneit was grinning like the proverbial cat-eating canary.

"Commander Demirci, I'm not sure what your evening plans are, but I've been asked to pass on an invitation. Please get back to me ASAP so I can make arrangements if you are available.

"Her Majesty, Queen Sonia, has requested the pleasure of your company for dinner at the Solitary Lodge in six hours from the time-stamp of this message. As I mentioned when we last spoke, she uses these dinners to help build support networks for people she likes—and people she thinks will benefit Redward.

"If you can at all make it happen, I beg you to," he concluded. "Her Majesty is a powerful ally, and while she's unlikely to take offense at a refusal or a request for a later date, one does not generally turn down offers from royalty."

The message ended and Kira closed her eyes, doing mental math. If "dinner" was in six hours, the Solitary Lodge definitely wasn't in Red Mountain, the capital city. The fleet ran on Interstellar Meridian Time, which was currently *mostly* aligned with Red Mountain time in Redward's twenty-four-and-a-half-hour day, and it was late afternoon on the station.

"I might need to get this uniform washed while I take a quick nap," she finally told Estanza. "It appears I have a dinner invitation for later this evening."

"This evening, Kira? You look pretty wiped... Whose invitation is *that* urgent?"

"The Queen of Redward's."

26

THE SOLITARY LODGE was aptly named. It was three entire time zones west of Red Mountain, hidden on the side of a lake in the middle of a planetary park three hundred kilometers wide. From the name, it was almost certainly intended as a private and secure retreat for the royal family.

And the threat indicators on Kira's shuttle's displays told her it was *very* secure.

"Shuttle *Conviction*-Four, do not deviate from your assigned course," a cheerful young voice said in her ear. "You are cleared to landing site two. Follow the given course, please."

Kira wasn't sure how many shuttles would have had the sensors to recognize they'd been locked in by surface-to-air missiles. The thick forests that swept down to the lakeshore concealed at least three defensive batteries—and the hills rising a dozen kilometers away concealed another three.

The batteries had probably been brought into the park by antigrav and installed as single-piece installations, minimizing the environmental impact while making sure they were easily concealed.

Conviction-Four was a combat shuttle with more advanced technology than was available to Redward's defenders. Kira could see the threats and she was reasonably confident that she could evade or confuse the local missiles...but not several dozen of them.

Even if she'd been inclined to cause trouble, she'd have meekly brought the shuttle in on the assigned course. The final approach was across the lake surface, suspended half a dozen meters above the water by her antigrav coils as she drifted slowly toward the docks.

As she approached, a computer handshake requested control of the shuttle. Kira checked the appropriate security protocols were in place and surrendered the landing to the local computer. A concrete pad slowly rose out of the water next to the long wooden dock, water cascading off the surface in a short-lived waterfall.

Looking past the docks, Kira was surprised to see that the Lodge itself was surprisingly small. Despite the defenses and security, there were only three buildings on the side of the lake. One was clearly a boathouse, presumably holding a mix of pleasure craft for the royals and security craft for their bodyguards. Another was likely a hangar for whatever aircraft had brought Queen Sonia and her other guests there.

The last was clearly the main house, larger than the hangar or the boathouse but still a modest two-story structure built of stone and local wood. Massive windows looked out over the lake, though Kira's practiced gaze picked out the telltale shimmer of defensive screens in front of them.

It was intentionally rustic, blending into its forested surroundings with an ease and grace that suggested true talent on the part of its architects. A brook wrapped around the house and burbled down to enter the lake next to the dock.

The whole place had been intentionally designed to feel as isolated and secure as it was. It was a haven, and Kira felt herself relax as the shuttle touched down.

The architects had probably been extraordinarily expensive, but in Kira's opinion, they'd clearly been worth every penny.

EVEN THOUGH THE invite had been from the Queen herself, Kira was surprised to exit the shuttle to find the tall and delicately built monarch waiting for her on the dock. There were two conservatively suited young men standing behind her, their gazes surveying the calm lake water around them.

"Commander Demirci, welcome," Sonia greeted her warmly. "I understand that you had a busy day, and I appreciate you making the time for this."

"I may not be your subject, Your Majesty, but when royalty calls, few dally," Kira replied, smiling to take some of the bite from her words.

"I appreciate it regardless," the Queen told her. "And please, call me Sonia. The Lodge is a place for quiet reflection with no ceremony or formalities."

"And politics one does not want seen or overheard, I presume," Kira said. "If you insist, you should call me Kira."

"Of course, Kira," the taller woman agreed, then grinned. "On both your points, I'm afraid. Much is done in secret—or at least quiet—at the Family's assorted retreats. It's not like Larry has the stomach or time for hunting."

Kira fell in beside the Queen, letting the guards drop back behind them. She'd flown the shuttle herself and come alone. That had been the request, and this *was* Sonia's planet.

"I suspect anyone who assumes your husband lacks *stomach* is going to come to some rude surprises," Kira noted.

"And you would be correct," Sonia agreed. "But that is when duty drives him. To inflict unnecessary fear and pain for entertainment? Let us not pretend the King must hunt for his dinner, after all. My husband does not have that in him."

"And you, Sonia?" Kira said.

The Queen smiled.

"There is a reason, Kira, that *I* run the Kingdom's intelligence services," she said calmly. "But that is not why I brought you here. I have ulterior motives, I won't deny them, but I also found you refreshing when we met before, and I wanted a chance for us to get to know each other better."

They were walking beside the brook now. There was no way, in Kira's opinion, that water could burble that consistently cheerfully without intentional design.

"I am not one of your subjects," Kira pointed out. "But I'm also no noble. Not even an elector, as my people calculate such things."

"And I am supposed to care?" Sonia asked with a chuckle. "I have many...*networks*, Kira. Few friends. It is difficult to be true friends with subordinates and subjects. Not impossible, but difficult. You command. Have you found it any different?"

"Most of my friends are my subordinates," Kira said. "But it has its problems, yes." She was a little taken aback by Sonia's forthrightness. She wasn't quite sure how to respond to the Queen of a world saying she wanted to be friends.

"I'll admit, I'm hoping to find your perspective valuable," the Queen told her. "Nothing a Queen does is without secondary motives. Or tertiary, or..." She sighed. "I'm also our chief of intelligence. Very little I do is without layers and levels, though inviting you to my dinners was *supposed* to be simple enough."

"And then *K79-L* happened, at a guess?" Kira asked.

"Exactly," Sonia confirmed. "Come on. There is food waiting and it's good. The Lodge chef signed on to feed royalty and only gets to do so once or twice a month; she will be *irritated* if we let her food get cold!"

THE DINING ROOM was attached to the tall windows Kira had noticed. While the windows didn't reach the entire height of the building, they were more than enough to give the dining space a floor-to-ceiling view of the lake to go with the smoothly finished natural wood floors and walls.

The center of the room was home to an immense and amazing table. At some point, a giant of the forest had been felled and its heart milled into a single slab fifteen feet long and six wide, ending at the living edges all around.

There were two more women already at the table, neither of whom

Kira recognized. One looked like an engineer stuffed into a dress, pale green eyes staring wistfully at Kira's dress uniform as she wrapped an auburn curl nervously around a finger, undoing another measurable fraction of her hairdo.

Someone had put a great deal of effort and product into the arrangement but the woman's nervous tic had left it lopsided and with stray hairs everywhere. Kira wasn't even interested in women, and she wanted to smooth the other woman's hair and tell her everything was going to be all right.

The other woman looked like someone had liquefied a cobra and poured it into a woman-shaped mold. She had dark skin and hair, combined with a whip-thin build and unusual golden eyes. Most of all, though, she moved with a twitchy lethality Kira could identify after spending months with *Conviction*'s mercenaries.

She might be wearing a dark golden sheath dress that matched her eyes, but the woman was soldier-boosted to the nines. Even assuming she didn't have implanted weapons, she could probably take both of the suited guards now flanking the door behind Kira and Sonia. Assuming, of course, that the guards didn't have concealed tricks of their own.

"Kira Demirci, meet Dr. Alexandra Talos, one of our top design engineers, and Colonel Hope Temitope," Sonia introduced the two women, indicating the auburn-haired engineer and the Black soldier in turn.

"A pleasure," Kira said, nodding to the two women as she took her own seat. "I don't believe I'm familiar with either of your work; I apologize."

"You shouldn't," Temitope said, her words swift and precise. "If you had heard of me, Em Demirci, I would be bad at my job."

"Dr. Talos works on a side effort of Project Sinister," Sonia told Kira. "Even in such classified endeavors as that, some things are more secret than others."

"I take it I'm learning some of those more-secret items?" Kira asked.

"After supper," the Queen insisted. "That goes for all three of you," she said with a warning finger and a warm smile. "The Lodge's staff is cleared at the highest levels, but dinner is a time for personal conversation, not work."

Sonia had almost certainly sent a headware message, as a set of doors Kira had missed in the back of the room swung open to admit a pair of waiters balancing trays.

THEY MOSTLY FOLLOWED the Queen's instructions through dinner, helped by the fact that the food was incredible. The one thing that was missing, and it wasn't really a surprise to Kira, was alcohol. A new drink came out with each of the four courses, but all of the drinks were either fruit juice mixes or delicately flavored iced teas.

As the last plates were cleared, the waiters delivered coffees. Leaving a carafe by each of the guests' left hands, they then withdrew as silently as they'd worked all along.

"My compliments to your chef and your staff," Kira said before taking a sip of the coffee. She looked down at the cup after tasting the drink and blinked. She'd thought the Astonishing Orange coffee she'd made sure was stocked on *Conviction* was good.

Sonia's grin suggested she'd been expecting the reaction.

"The coffee is the Redward Royal Reserve," she told them. "Grown on South Tangerine on *very* carefully positioned farms for the exclusive use of the royal family. It's..." The Queen chuckled. "The Redward Royal Family actually has very few privileges that wealth alone couldn't purchase. Military-grade security...and our own coffee varietal."

Kira wasn't entirely clear on where the Redward Royal Family's money came from, but her impression was that even their security was only partly funded by tax kroners. There'd probably been government influence used to build Solitary Lodge in the middle of a park, but it would have been paid for from the Stewarts' private money.

"I will pass your compliments on to the Lodge's staff, Kira," Sonia assured her. "This room is now locked down; even the staff won't be entering for the next bit. Your headware couldn't reach the main network from here anyway, but a Faraday field is being activated."

Kira felt the field wrap around them. As Sonia had said, they'd lost a lot of the usual back-and-forth with the main planetary network just from how far out the Lodge was, but Kira had been relaying anything she needed up to *Conviction* via the shuttle. Now she was truly cut off.

Which was normal for high-security meetings, she supposed.

"You are all here because I value your diverse points of view. Dr. Talos and Colonel Temitope have been subjected to my soirees before and are very much part of the network of competent women I have stretched across the surface of this planet.

"The rest of our conversation tonight, however, will be classified Top Secret Scarlet Topaz," the Queen told them, her voice suddenly noticeably more formal. "You are all aware of the criteria in your contracts and commissions around the violation of top-secret classifications, so I won't belabor them."

Kira leaned back in her chair with her coffee and studied the room.

"A nova ship engineer, a special forces commander, and a nova pilot," she observed. "You're planning something clever, Your Majesty, and you're planning on using us all to pull it off."

"Not bad, Kira," Sonia told her. "You're fundamentally correct. As I'm sure you made clear to our military when you briefed them earlier today, there is no way our conventional forces can engage *K79-L* in open battle. She represents a destabilizing piece on the board, one we have no way to control or mitigate, and appears to be in the control of our longer-term enemies.

"If those enemies succeed in their plan, Ypres will take over as the leading force of the Cluster and the SCFTZ will be ended even as it takes shape," the Queen stated calmly. "Therefore, I see no option but to remove *K79-L* from the board."

The other three women in the room were silent, waiting for the Queen to explain. Instead, she smiled thinly and gestured to Kira.

"First, however, I think we all need to be aware of just who our enemy actually is. Kira, could you please brief Hope and Alexandra on the Equilibrium Institute?"

KIRA PAUSED for long enough for the other two women to look at her questioningly, then she grimaced and nodded.

"I've been operating under the assumption that Redward wasn't going to buy in to Captain Estanza's conspiracy theory," she admitted. "We certainly haven't tried to conceal anything, but it all does sound rather paranoid."

"You're not paranoid when people are actually out to get you," Sonia said. "The mess of gear that Warlord Deceiver was in possession of was the final piece I needed to be certain we were looking at an outside force interfering in the Cluster.

"When the Equilibrium Institute came up in the files we extracted from the nova drive fabricator Em Burke traded us for his freedom, it fit far too well with what I was already looking for." She smirked. "I don't think Burke expected us to be able to decrypt those particular files, or he'd have done a better job of deleting them.

"That Burke wanted to be transported by *Conviction* and the fact that Captain Estanza didn't appear surprised by this told me that *he* knew something—and you were very clearly in his full confidence."

"You were testing me," Kira realized aloud as Sonia laid out her thinking.

"A little," Sonia conceded. "Mostly, I suspect you have a better understanding of our enemy than I do, and we need Hope and Alexandra to know what we're getting into."

Kira nodded and considered her words carefully.

"I won't go into how Captain Estanza and I know about the Equilibrium Institute," she told them. "That's not my story to tell. But, as Sonia has asked, I can tell you what they are.

"The Institute is a cell-based organization with access to massive, if not infinite, resources," she noted. "We believe they're based out of our side of the Meridian and have been influencing regions through a large arc of the Fringe and Rim to shape them toward their ideal.

"Their goal is to create a stable peace for humanity via the implementation of Seldonian analyses and behind-the-scenes influence. They have calculated that the safest structure for humanity is a series of regional hegemons capable of preventing war and piracy in their own territory but incapable of projecting power against the next hegemon over.

"In my home territory, I now believe they funneled money and intelligence to the Brisingr Kaiserreich to allow them to overcome Apollo and our allies," she said grimly. "*K79-L*'s presence in the Cluster is at least partial repayment for that help."

"But...wouldn't they be backing *us* here, then?" Talos asked. "The SCFTZ sounds like exactly the kind of thing they'd want."

"I would agree," Kira said. "I'm not certain of the basis—I've been told there's incorrect assumptions baked into their Seldonian models, but I haven't seen those models. And it's not like I can follow psychohistorical math in the first place!"

She shook her head.

"But what matters is that they've decided that anything less than a stable militaristic state with a force-based hegemony over their region is inherently unstable. They'd give the SCFTZ a decade or two at most before it collapsed into anarchy again."

"And they're going to poke at us and make that happen, creating a self-fulfilling prediction," Temitope said grimly. "That's...a hell of a conspiracy theory. A hell of a threat, if it's true."

"It's true," Sonia said flatly. "Kira has given me a bit more context for the logic of their operations, but the shape of the threat had been taking form in the Office of Integration's analyses for at least a decade.

"We're not blind to what happens outside the Syntactic Cluster, and the pattern of manipulation is subtle but ever-present. The trick is seeing past the first-tier deception to the real source. Take *K79-L*, for example. It's clear that Ghost Explorations is a front to get the cruiser out here, so we assume it's a Syndullan or Brisingr covert operation. We then look for motivation and build a model around that logic.

"But if Ghost Explorations truly *are* the people leasing *K79-L*, because they have money and influence they wouldn't normally have, then we can draw a model that includes a dangerous interstellar third party. One of my analysts starting using that as a secondary model about ten years ago—more as a joke and a methodology test than anything else."

"And out of a joke fell a monster," Kira murmured.

"Exactly." Sonia looked at the three women grimly. "I will not permit a bunch of armchair psychohistorians from over a *thousand light-years away* to dictate the fate of the Syntactic Cluster. They hoped to put the shipyards they gave Deceiver in our hands, hoping to tempt Redward into becoming the kind of conquerors they want.

"Deceiver screwed them there. Now they attempt to enable the Protector of Sanctuary to conquer his system and move on to the rest of the Cluster. *K79-L* is unlikely to be the only string to their bow, but it's the strongest one. We need to remove it."

"You said that before," Kira pointed out. "But we can't fight her. My assessment is that given six months of production of the new nova fighters, the RRF and *Conviction* should be able to put a force into play that can challenge on an equal footing, but..."

"In six months, they'll have conquered Ypres and begun challenging us for domination of the trade routes," Sonia agreed. "The likelihood that the Institute won't have provided Ypres a class two drive fabricator by then is low as well.

"My Office's calculations are that we need to neutralize *K79-L* in the next twenty-one days to prevent Sanctuary from conquering Ypres." The Queen sighed. "We've spent thirty years working to try and achieve Yprian unification, and now I'm actively planning to stop it."

"To neutralize her in the next twenty-one days, the forces involved would need to leave in the next five," Temitope pointed out. "And Kira just said that we don't have the forces."

"We don't have the forces for an open battle," Sonia agreed. "Which means our options become deception and a knife in the back. Dr. Talos, can you brief Kira and Hope on *Forager*?"

Now the engineer had everyone's attention, and she smiled. The shy nervousness faded almost instantly as everyone looked at her and she activated a concealed holoprojector.

"When the decision was made to decommission the Lancers in favor of the new Sinister fighter-bombers, officially the Cavalier-IIs and their drives were judged unusable," Talos told them. "This was a deception. While the Cavaliers weren't worth preserving, they still contained Eleven-X class two nova drives. Inferior to the ones our new fabricator produces, but still class two nova drives.

"Those six nova drives were detoured into a project code-named Nightfall. We borrowed data and files from Sinister and modified an existing special-purpose vessel, named *Forager*."

The hologram showed the ship. It didn't look particularly unusual to Kira. At thirty thousand cubics, the freighter was midsized by Redward standards and largish by the standards of the overall Cluster. It would have been small in Apollo, but it still would never have drawn a second glance.

"*Forager* is carefully designed and modified to conceal every unusual aspect of her structure and purpose from external scanners," Talos told them. "A key component of that is a set of sensor baffles manufactured in a Periphery state I can't name that were purchased on the black market. My understanding is that the reason they made it out this far without being sold was that they were classified enough that covert agents of that state were actively pursuing them."

The engineer coughed.

"We arranged affairs so that it appeared the sellers had left Ypres without managing to sell the baffles. We later learned their ship was destroyed at a trade route stop near Crest. So far as we know, the manufacturer believes this particular set of baffles was destroyed.

"Certainly, they are far beyond our ability to duplicate, but they do provide us with exactly the kind of concealment necessary to build a vessel like *Forager*."

Talos gestured and the freighter hologram expanded into an exploded-view schematic.

"*Forager* possesses a single spinal heavy plasma cannon equivalent to those mounted on our cruisers," she continued. "The original plan called for concealed turrets but was heavily revised after the Battle of the Kiln for multiple purposes."

"That's a miniature fighter hangar," Kira said quietly, pointing at the back of the ship.

"Yes," Talos confirmed. "Retrieval and rearming of the fighters would be complicated, sufficiently so that I would recommend against doing so in anything resembling hostile space, but we have constructed a hangar capable of holding four Sinister-Alpha fighter-bombers modified to read as Cavaliers and two nova-drive-equipped assault shuttles.

"We also borrowed Captain Estanza's trick and *Forager* mounts a total of ten torpedo launchers. The load time on them is not what we would like, but she can duplicate one of our cruisers' broadsides and *repeat* that action every few minutes."

"That's better than we managed on *Conviction*," Kira admitted. "Ours are box launchers that need to be externally reloaded."

"*Forager*'s launchers contain four torpedoes before requiring an equivalent reload," Talos told her. "The nova shuttles are modified versions of our Peregrine-IXs, Colonel," she told Temitope. "Other than the addition of a class two nova drive, they are in fact identical."

"That's thirty combatants a shuttle, then," the special forces commander said slowly. "With the nova, we can get a lot closer than they expect...but you're still talking sixty people against the entire crew of a heavy cruiser."

"Commander, how many soldiers would a K70 carry?" Sonia asked.

"In BKN service, two hundred weltraumsoldats," Kira replied. "I'd presume less in SSR service, but we don't know what the Institute might have put aboard themselves."

She studied the ship. "Even from complete surprise, there's no way that this ship could disable *K79-L*," she told them. "Even with four nova fighters."

"No, the plan would be to deploy Colonel Temitope's commandos via the nova shuttles with antimatter demolition charges," Sonia said flatly. "Would I be correct in that it is dangerous but possible to nova from inside the ship?"

Kira exhaled sharply as she considered the hologram.

"None of your people could do it," she said slowly. "Maybe...three of my people could."

It went without saying that *she* was one of those pilots.

"That's what I expected, Kira," Sonia said quietly. "I want to contract with the Memorials, Kira. I want *your* best pilots in those Sinisters—and I want *you* to command the mission."

"Me? I'm not a starship captain."

"No, but you know combat novas better than anyone else in the Cluster," the Queen told her. "My understanding is that you made connections in Ypres that might be useful as well."

Kira considered Konrad Bueller and sighed as she nodded. It felt a bit abusive to use the man as a link back to his ship, but if he was the chief engineer…that opened up possibilities too.

"I'll want to bring some of *Conviction*'s ground troops as well," she said. "Apologies, Temitope, but I want some people I know at my back."

"Conveniently, I'm currently short ten troopers," the woman admitted. "A training accident. They'll *be* fine, but I only have five squads to deploy instead of six."

That a *Colonel* commanded a force that apparently regularly only had sixty people was interesting to Kira. Just who *were* Temitope's people?

"I hope I can count on all three of you to put this together," Sonia told them. "Kira, the Office of Integration will be in contact with your people around the contract and the money. But—"

"It's not about money, Your Majesty," Kira said quietly and formally. "I trust you to be generous, but it's not about money. I'm in."

She shook her head as she considered the warship that represented both her old and new enemies alike.

"I'm in," she repeated.

27

LOGISTICS AND DETAILS consumed another two hours before Kira even returned to her shuttle, which meant it was beyond late according to *Conviction*'s clock by the time she returned to the carrier. Those same logistics and details, however, meant she had a lot of work to do.

She set a meeting with her Apollo veterans for ship's morning—barely five hours away, she realized with a groan—and then pinged Estanza as she reached her quarters.

The note was simple enough:

We need to meet ASAP. Let me know when you're awake.

She wasn't expecting a response until later and was stripping off her dress uniform to fall asleep in her shipsuit when her headware chimed.

"I'm awake," Estanza's voice said calmly in her head. "Is this an in-person problem or a call problem?"

"It's not a problem, I don't think," she told him. "I need to shower first at the minimum, but it's urgent."

"I'll meet you in your office in fifteen, then?" her Captain suggested.

Kira could probably shower and be in *his* office in fifteen minutes, but her office was closer to her quarters.

"That'll do, sir," she agreed.

KIRA MADE it to her office with five minutes to spare, but wasn't really surprised to find Estanza sitting in the chair she kept for guests. He had the vaguely unfocused look of someone looking at headware files on a virtual screen in front of them.

As she came in, he blinked whatever he was looking at away and smiled at her.

"As you get older, you'll find you need less sleep," he told her. "You'll also find that, sooner or later, *everything* hurts."

"So I'm told," she admitted. "I've got enough of the aches and pains to wonder when the needing less sleep starts."

"Cybernetics can help with that," he admitted. "I had it turned off, but I have a system to help purge fatigue toxins and organize memories. I only need three or four hours of sleep with it."

"I should look into that," she said. "Though some days, I feel like I already have enough metal in me!"

Meeting Temitope, who was significantly more heavily augmented than most people, had brought her own list of implants more to mind than usual. In addition to her headware, she had the standard nanotech medical suite, a uterine controller, an emergency oxygen reserve in her lungs, and a spleen augment to handle a blood disorder.

Without thinking of her implant, Kira tended to forget that she even *had* Evans Syndrome. It had been identified when she was three, and even the clinic in her village had been able to provide the genetic and nanotech supplements to handle the immediate problem. They'd sent her to the nearby city to get the implant designed and installed, but she'd been five the last time she'd even had a procedure related to it.

The uterine controller gave her a similar forgetful attitude to the concepts of things like periods and fertility. So long as that device was functioning, she had complete conscious control of her fertility cycles and the attendant functions.

"We have a few mercenaries that are more metal than flesh by body mass," Estanza pointed out, clearly thinking of similar soldiers to Temitope. "It's not the *preferred* form of soldier boost, in my experience, but it can work."

Soldier boost was a generic term for any suite of augmentations that made someone a better fighter. They could range from genetic modifications to artificial organs to cybernetic implants. Many would include the ability to administer combat drugs on command...but all of them were generally regarded as pointless to obsolete.

Even the armor worn by the mercenaries aboard *Conviction* could withstand several blaster shots. No augment had yet been designed that could permit human flesh to do the same, rendering the armor an absolute necessity—and everything that could be built into a soldier could be built into armor.

With the advantage that the armor didn't need to retire back to a civilian population later.

Soldier boosts were the territory of very specialized forces, usually elite units made of veterans who'd already proven themselves in armor before being boosted, intended to do jobs where the priority was stealth and discretion.

"The locals seem to prefer slightly more discreet boosting," Kira told her boss.

"Huh," he said, then arched an eyebrow at her. "If you *met* Redward's boosted troops at dinner, something very interesting is going on. What has Her Majesty recruited you for?"

Kira couldn't help but laugh. From an almost completely unrelated comment, her boss had put together what was going on.

"Why does anyone bother having secrets around you?" she asked.

"I am old, Kira," he told her. "I have seen a lot of things and *done* a lot of things. Sonia had multiple reasons to want to talk to you, but the timeline suggested she wanted to recruit you for something specific."

"Yeah," Kira confirmed. "She's hiring me and the Memorials to spearhead a covert operation. I'm authorized to talk to *you* about it, but nobody else on *Conviction* is supposed to be briefed yet."

"If it's your contract, not mine, I'll respect that," Estanza said promptly. "Am I getting you back afterward?"

"I'm leaving my nova fighters with you, so I'm *damn* well coming back," Kira told him. "I'm taking five other pilots with me, probably the Apollo vets. We're moving aboard a Redward covert-operations ship I won't be naming.

"It's equipped with nova shuttles and nova fighters, as well as a surprisingly deadly onboard arsenal. Most importantly, it can fake being a civilian transport at quite short range."

Estanza nodded slowly.

"So, you're going to try to sneak up to *K79-L*," he concluded. "Risky business. Nova fighters as cover for a boarding action, use the transport's guns to cover the final retreat?"

"Basically. Details are still being worked out, but I have most of two platoons of boosted commandos that we're trying to insert, along with some demolitions that should gut the cruiser if we can get them onboard."

She shook her head.

"I want to borrow Milani and their squad," she continued. "We can fit ten extra gun hands on the shuttles, and I want backup for my people. We're using Redward's crews and fighters, and I don't want to be alone on a strange ship with just the six of us."

"Done," Estanza agreed instantly. "Am I billing you or Redward for them?"

"Ah, mercenaries." She grinned. "Me, I think. Avoids a layer of complication—and I expect Sonia to be generous enough. She is hiring me to *command* this operation as well as fly one of her nova shuttles."

"Elite nova fighter pilots at the helm of shuttles," the older man said. "I don't want to know what you're planning on doing with those shuttles, do I?"

"What we have to," she told him, humor fleeing as she considered the task ahead of her. "That ship...we can't just let her run rampant over the Cluster."

"Agreed. I hope the plan works," he agreed. "I have one request, a modification to your plan if you'll accept it."

"Which is?"

"Leave Hoffman if you can," Estanza asked. "We're already going to be short an entire squadron of nova fighters while you're gone. If you take the entire command structure of the Memorials with you, our interceptors are going to be badly handicapped.

"Where if you leave Memorial-Bravo's commander, I trust Hoffman to keep the other five or six in order on his own if he has to."

"I still need six pilots on my side," Kira warned.

"Take Maina," the Captain told her. "With Mbeki gone, the only two pilots on this ship *I'd* trust to make a suicide jump in a nova shuttle are Lozenge and myself."

He smiled gently.

"I trust your judgment of your Apollo vets as to which ones can make that jump, but I know Maina can make it."

Kira nodded slowly and thoughtfully. Joseph Hoffman had been the person she'd been planning on putting in the other nova shuttle—and Estanza clearly understood the plan they were aiming for. A jump from inside another ship was dangerous and complicated and wasn't something that could really be practiced.

Boyd Maina was the oldest pilot on the carrier other than Estanza himself, and the man had every scrap of the skill expected from thirty years behind the controls of a nova fighter.

"I'll talk to him once I've talked to my people," Kira promised.

"That makes sense, but timing is everything. I need to report aboard the covert ops ship with my pilots and troopers by twenty hundred hours IMT tomorrow."

She checked the time and grimaced.

"Make that today."

28

"WELL, boss, this is the meeting you decided to call sometime after midnight," Cartman pointed out drily as she slid a large mug of coffee across the table to Kira. "I don't know how much sleep you *actually* got, but you thought this was important."

They'd avoided the main pilot briefing room for a smaller conference room that was more easily secured, another sign to Kira's people that something unusual was going on.

"So, spill."

Kira took a long gulp of the coffee and nodded to her friend as she looked around the table. The Apollo System Defense Force's Three Hundred and Third Nova Combat Group had been an elite force, present at half a dozen key battles of the war. They'd lost friends and colleagues along the way, but the twenty-four pilots still standing at the end had been deadly competent aces to a one.

Seventeen of those pilots had died at the hands of the Brisingr Shadows. Some of those were still officially listed as natural causes or accidents, but Kira was perfectly willing to blame the assassins for all of them. One had chosen to retire, taking the money Jay Moranis had set aside for him and buying a freighter.

That left these six, Kira and her comrades in arms. Her *friends*.

The six deadliest nova fighter pilots she knew.

"The Memorials have a new contract," she told them. "One that's going to take six nova-qualified pilots and ten soldiers away from *Conviction* for an unknown but probably short period of time. I've already arranged the troops," she noted with a wave of her hand, "but the pilots are on us."

She met Hoffman's gaze.

"Unfortunately, Longknife, Estanza has asked that you stay behind to keep our collection of new recruits in order," she told him. "You get to stay in the briefing so you know what the rest of us are up to, but I need you to mind the deck while we're gone."

"I get it," he said with a long exhale. "But I'm guessing I'm going to be worried sick the whole time, aren't I?"

"We'll be fine, Dad," Patel told his wingman, commanding officer and boyfriend with a massive grin.

"We hope so, anyway," Kira agreed. "But let's not pretend this is going to be easy or straightforward. We're being hired to provide the nova pilots for a covert-operation ship that is tasked with eliminating K79-L."

The briefing room was silent.

"Okay, Longknife, you can worry," Cartman told the squadron commander. "Damn, Basketball. We have a plan?"

"We do, but it's not a pretty one. We have two nova-equipped assault shuttles and four nova fighter-bombers that have their lines and emissions fucked with so no one is ever going to identify them as anything in specific."

She'd looked at the data for the fighters on the flight back to *Conviction*. They were supposed to look like Cavaliers, but Cavaliers were medium fighters and the Sinisters were PNC-derived fighter-bombers.

They weren't going to flag as Sinisters, even once those fighters were acknowledged to exist, but they definitely weren't going to flag as Cavaliers. They were Uglies, unidentifiable mixes—which was perfect for this task.

"I am in overall command of the operation and will also be flying one of the nova shuttles," Kira told them all. "I'm also going to bring Lozenge along with us, and he'll be flying the other shuttle.

"We're going to assess the situation once we arrive in Ypres and see if we can come up with a *better* plan, but our Plan B is to launch the nova shuttles from *inside* our covert-ops ships, jumping to within boarding range of *K79-L*."

"That's insane," Cartman said bluntly. "Who in all..." She glanced around the room thoughtfully. "Okay, so you could, maybe. Hoffman could, maybe. I guess Lozenge has been around and seen it all, so maybe. But..."

"You were the next on my list to try it," Kira told her friend. "It's not safe or sane, hence hoping to find another option. But if push comes to shove, we use a suicide jump to insert Redward commandos with antimatter bombs onto the cruiser.

"Then we try to get the commandos *out,* using the nova fighters and the covert ops ship herself as a distraction. A few half-kilogram antimatter charges won't leave much behind of the cruiser."

The briefing room was silent as a tomb as her people considered her words.

"This is a dangerous op and I won't order you to take it on," Kira admitted.

"Well, we're in," Evgenia "Socrates" Michel said brightly. "We're not letting you make that jump without us at your back. We're in this together, aren't we?"

"Agreed," Abdullah "Scimitar" Colombera agreed. He and Michel were the Memorials' jokers, the youngest of the original Apollo veterans. "If anyone can take down a Brisingr heavy cruiser with hope, gall and surprise, it's us."

"I'm in," Cartman confirmed.

"Sorry, Joseph, I'm afraid you'll have to worry," Patel concluded. "I'm in too. Don't like leaving you behind, but..."

"It's part of the job I took when Kira made me Squadron Commander," Hoffman conceded. "Just promise you're coming back."

The question might have appeared addressed to the whole room, but Kira knew better. It was addressed entirely to Patel, and she concealed a smile as the two men ignored everyone else for a few seconds.

"Of course," Patel promised. "Always."

"We're all coming back," Kira told Hoffman. "This is where I'm leaving my stuff—and my *fighter*!"

29

"CAN we all at least *pretend* we're real soldiers for ten bloody minutes?" Milani barked through the mostly organized cluster of intentionally non-uniformed mercenaries gathered outside *Conviction*'s loading tubes.

The mercenary carrier had been docking at Blueward Station for long enough that the cargo and personnel loading bay had been reconfigured to handle her needs as best as it could, but the truth remained that it had been designed to handle six gunships, not a single capital ship.

Kira shook her head as she dodged around a stack of coffee containers and grinned up at the armored mercenary.

"Half of them are nova pilots, Milani," she pointed out. "We definitely *aren't* real soldiers, but there are tricks."

She cupped her hands around her mouth.

"Hey, *idiots*," she barked. "We're moving out as a group and sticking together as we make our way to the military docks and our ride. Play nice with the people in augmented battle armor, please. We're on a schedule."

Between her and Milani, the mercenaries and pilots fell into a chaotic-seeming cluster that was at least moving in one direction as a group.

The mercenary squad leader shook their armored head.

"I can already tell how much fun this whole side trip is going to be," they noted. "Have I said yet how glad I am you picked my squad?"

"You're the only squad leader on *Conviction* I actually know," Kira admitted. "And I like your style. It'll work."

"Of course it will work," Milani agreed, falling in beside her as they set off through the station. "You know me because I'm the *best*. And you're putting us next to what the locals call the best, which means my grunts are going to do their damnedest."

"Competition is the sincerest form of flattery?" she asked.

"Exactly," the squad leader confirmed. "Put up against real commandos, my people will want to show they're just as good or even better. Mission brief is a fucking nightmare but still looks better than the alternative."

The alternative was an open battle between the heavy cruiser on one side and the massed fleets of the SCFTZ on the other. Even assuming that King Larry could get his allies, who'd signed on for a *trade* deal, to muster their fleets for that fight, it wasn't a battle they were likely to win.

Plus, everything looked like Ypres Sanctuary would throw their ships in on *K79-L*'s side, and while they might only have destroyers, they were modern destroyers by Syntactic Cluster standards.

"Plus, this way you actually get to do something," Kira told Milani. "As opposed to waiting aboard ship feeling bored."

"Believe me, Commander Demirci, I have *never* felt *bored* during a space battle," the merc said drily. "I don't lead a squad of heavily armored mercenaries because I like my life being in other people's hands."

"Then this mission should be right up your alley," she said. "Fate of our mission in your hands. Fate of worlds in your hands."

"Fuck that, fuck you, fuck me," Milani said calmly. "Let's not remind my collection of misfit killing machines of the pressure if we can avoid it, yes?"

THE SHUTTLE they rode out from Blueward Station was aggressively nondescript. It was neither new nor old, neither large nor small, neither in disrepair nor gleamingly clean. If Kira had been asked to pick it out of a lineup of other spacecraft, she'd have failed—and she was *good* at recognizing spacecraft.

The interior was much the same as the exterior, except that they were riding out with a squad of Redward commandos. The ten soldiers introduced themselves politely, took their seats at the front of the shuttle…and then ignored the mercenaries for the rest of the trip.

That was fine by Kira. She was curious as to what *Forager* looked like from the outside and had the codes to access the shuttle's sensors.

With the information and holograms from the prior night, she was able to pick out the covert-ops ship as they approached it but, like the shuttle, it was nondescript. There was nothing in the hundred-meter-long cylinder to suggest that it was remotely unusual.

"Dock contact in two minutes," the pilot announced. "Stand by for boarding."

The shuttle's sensors weren't amazing, but Kira would still have expected to pick out *something* unusual as they came closer to *Forager*. To her surprise, there was nothing. Not even the slightest hint that the innocent-looking freighter they were docking with concealed guns, torpedoes and fighters.

She felt the moment they made contact, the shuttle vibrating gently as the vehicles connected.

The commandos were on their feet instantly, the mercenary troopers following suit as rapidly as they could. Kira could already see the competition Milani was planning on using for motivation taking shape.

Conviction's soldiers were good, but the commandos were supposed to be the best of an entire planet of two billion people. They should, in theory, be better—but Milani's squad wasn't going to accept that.

Kira waited while the armored soldiers of both groups got themselves sorted and in motion before rising from her own seat and following them out. With the soldiers in front of her, she wasn't worried about running into unexpected threats.

Her pilots fell in behind her like lost sheep as she left the shuttle, each of them accompanied by a small robotic case trundling along behind them. They exited the shuttle into a loading bay that continued the nondescript theme of the ship.

So far, *Forager* looked like a regular freighter, and if it hadn't been for the commandos, Kira might have wondered if she was on the wrong ship.

A group of three crew was waiting for them in unmarked shipsuits. Two directed the commandos while the third, a heavyset woman with broad features, stood back and surveyed everything.

Spotting Kira, that woman stepped forward and offered her hand.

"Commander Demirci?" she asked. "I'm Šiwa Como. I was *Forager*'s Captain, which I guess makes me your second?"

Kira held up a hand.

"I think we need to clear up a misunderstanding immediately," she told Como. "I am the *mission* commander, not *Forager*'s commander. If you're *Forager*'s Captain, you're *Forager*'s Captain."

She shook her head.

"Everything I've seen of our ops plan says I'm abandoning *Forager* right before she goes into battle," she continued. "I am not taking command of your ship away from you, Captain Como."

There was a moment of silence, and then she watched as concealed tension slowly drained from Šiwa Como's face and shoulders.

"I appreciate that clarification, Commander," Como told her. "Would you like the tour of the ship I had planned regardless?"

"I would," Kira said with a smile. "Everything I've seen says she's an incredible piece of work—not least because I haven't seen *anything* of her that looks unusual in person so far. If one of your people can show my pilots and troops to their quarters?"

"Landry!" Como barked. One of the other crew members stepped forward. "Get the pilots settled. Commander Demirci and I are taking a walkabout. Let me know if there's any problems ASAP."

"We want to be moving sooner rather than later," Kira said quietly. "Any delays expected?"

"Last of the commandos are due aboard at exactly twenty hundred hours," Como told her. "And then we're on our way whenever you give the order."

"We get clear of Redward as soon as everyone's aboard and nova as soon as we can without drawing attention," Kira ordered. "This show needs to be on the road yesterday."

"Can do, Commander. We'll make it happen."

30

THE TOUR ENDED in the only place that made sense: *Forager*'s under-sized launch bays. The space around the fighters and shuttles was barely larger than the spacecraft themselves. Each of the six nova ships was in a bay of its own, pressed against the outer hull.

"Concealed hatches?" Kira guessed, stepping up next to one of the fighter-bombers and studying the end of the bay.

"Underneath false hull plating, yes," Como confirmed. "We have a small stock of replacements, but if we need to deploy more than a couple of times, we'd need to fabricate more."

She chuckled.

"We need to have the bays open to reload torpedoes, anyway," the covert ops ship captain admitted. "We didn't have the volume to spare for a proper loading setup. We can refuel them, which handles the guns, but torpedoes are EVA work."

"So, they're already loaded?" Kira asked. "Not the safest, but I see the logic."

It could be worse, she supposed. Her torpedoes were one-shot plasma cannons. Fusion explosions were hard to trigger by accident. Rumor said that some of the powers closer to the Core—*much* closer, potentially SolFed itself—were using *antimatter* weapons as their fighter munitions.

Kira had no idea how that would work unless SolFed had solved the problem of getting enough computer power and optics into an expendable missile to allow an actual tracking munition to be used inside a multiphasic jamming field. Then she supposed they could load a missile with an antimatter warhead—if they wanted to risk carrying antimatter around with them.

"We have our limitations," Como admitted. "We still need to have enough of the original freighter left to be able to take inspectors through. Add in the gun, the torpedo launchers, the commando barracks...*Forager* doesn't have a lot of excess space to spare."

"I saw that," Kira conceded. They'd walked a good chunk of the ship's cramped spaces on her tour. The commandos were stacked ten to a room. Even the ship's officers were sharing rooms. A ship of *Forager*'s size would normally have a crew of twelve, though a freighter would have been at least three-quarters empty space waiting for cargo.

"She is what she is," Como said. "We've got a lot of surprises, but squeezing them in was a pain. I'll admit, Commander, I'm not necessarily expecting this to go well for us."

Kira glanced around the shuttle bay as she rested her hand on the nova shuttle she was going to be flying.

"We currently have a Plan B," Kira told her. "That's the one where we nova from inside *Forager*'s hull to deliver commandos carrying antimatter bombs to *K79-L*."

She shook her head.

"I don't know what Redward's soldiers call them, but the ASDF ground troops called antimatter bombs *suicide charges*," she admitted. "I give Plan B about a fifty-fifty chance of actually taking the cruiser out—with about ten percent of *any* of us getting out alive."

"And less for the commandos," Como said.

"Basically zero for the commandos," Kira agreed. "Not much better for the nova shuttles. I don't *like* dying, Captain Como, so I'm really hoping to put together a Plan A. That requires more data."

"So, Ypres."

"Ypres," Kira agreed. "And then I call a gentleman who gave me his phone number who happens to work on *K79-L*."

She grinned.

"I do have a plan, Captain Como," she said. "I just don't know where it goes *after* we kidnap their chief engineer!"

FORTUNATELY, one of the spaces that had been kept to show inspectors was the freighter's mess, which gave them a place where Kira and Como could pull a dozen people together for a meeting after they'd novaed out of Redward.

"We are five novas and just over four days from arriving in Ypres," Como told them all. "We'll try and keep up on news from ships heading the other way, but right now, our news is five days out of date.

"According to that news, the Ypres Alliance has served Sanctuary with an ultimatum," the captain continued. "As of five days ago, they had forty-eight hours to withdraw their troops from Dikkebus's eastern hemisphere and return control of all Hearth territories, facilities and ships to the duly elected government of the Democratic Principality of Hearth."

"So, we can assume that as of three days ago, Ypres was at war," Kira concluded. "I did not get the impression while we were there that anyone on the Sanctuary side was planning on giving up."

"They've wanted to rule the entire system since the colony first landed two centuries ago," Temitope said grimly. The commando officer looked at the others. "As Demirci said, it's war. The only question is whether the shooting starts before we arrive."

"Our worst-case scenario," Kira told them all, "is that the fighting is underway when we arrive. In some ways, our mission might be easier if the fighting is over."

Milani was the only person in the room wearing armor and a mask, but their wince was still clear to Kira.

"Surely, Sanctuary can't overrun half a star system in six days," they asked.

"It seems unlikely that all of the fighting will be over," Kira agreed.

"But it is entirely possible that *K79-L* will have forced an open engagement with the Ypres Alliance fleet and destroyed their mobile forces.

"Central and Flanders have fortresses, but the Guilds are dependent on their monitors. They might have thought that they had enough of an edge in mobile units, if not nova-capable ones, to accept an open space battle."

"And if the Alliance's mobile forces are destroyed, the war is over unless the SCFTZ and the rest of the Cluster intervenes," Como told them. "Our best case is that the fighting hasn't started yet, I assume?"

"Yes," Kira confirmed. "Six days isn't much time, all things considered. *K79-L* is ready for the fight, but Sanctuary still needs to make sure they have reliable control over the ex-Hearth ships. *K79-L*'s biggest vulnerability would be the ex-Hearth monitors turning on her during the battle.

"I expect that there will have been opening skirmishes," she told them. "Most likely, both sides are down a couple of monitors, maybe a nova destroyer. Sanctuary will be mustering their forces and *K79-L* will be at a lower state of readiness."

"How likely is it that she's a low-enough state of readiness that we can get aboard her?" Temitope asked.

"If we play it hard and fast, we have a decent chance," Kira said. "Without knowing what kind of defenses they've set up around her, I can't be certain what it looks like. I know what *I'd* have in place, though.

"At least three nova fighters flying carrier patrol. Similar number of local monitors cycling alerts. With the tools at our disposal, we might be able to get in…but we won't get out."

"My commandos understand the odds," Temitope replied, but her voice was bleak.

"So do I," Kira agreed. "So does everyone on this mission, Colonel. If we take everything we've got and take the risks we're all prepared to take, we can destroy that ship. What's eighty lives against the stability of the entire Cluster?"

The room was silent.

"The logic adds up, doesn't it?" she asked. "Except that these days, I'm a mercenary, not a patriot. And there's no point in getting *paid* if I die along the way. We are going to take that ship out of the equation, people. One way or another.

"But if I can find a way that doesn't involve us all dying, I'm going to take it. We have options. We have a ship that can fly right into Dikkebus orbit as a civilian and go unnoticed while we scope out the area and make a plan with all of the damn information.

"I have contact information for *K79-L*'s chief engineer, an ex-Brisingr officer I once rescued from a wrecked ship. We agreed to meet up for dinner again if we were ever in the same star system.

"People: in five days, I'm going to be in the same star system as him. I'm going to feel guilty as hell using his request for a date to kidnap him, but I don't think that's an option I can afford to leave unused.

"So, that's where we start," she told them. "We go to Ypres. We look all normal and innocent while we drop into orbit. We use local Redward Intelligence assets to fake making a delivery so no one questions us.

"We find out *everything* we can—from our sensors, from Konrad Bueller, whatever comes to hand—and we assemble a plan. One with all of the information. One that lets us take down that ship and live."

"I do have one question, though," Milani said into the silence as Kira finished.

"Which is, Milani?" she asked.

"Are we aiming high enough?" the mercenary asked. "We're talking about dropping sixty of the best troops in the Cluster on that ship. Why don't we try to capture her?"

Kira stared at the mercenary in surprise for several long seconds, then laughed.

"I wish," she told them. "It's theoretically possible, yes, except that the ship will be surrounded by half of Sanctuary's fleet. There is no way we can break through her security systems enough to even nova out before a counter-boarding force gets aboard.

"Much as I'm sure handing Redward a heavy cruiser would earn us all some nice paychecks and medals, I think the best we can hope for is to take her out," Kira concluded.

31

"MAY I INTERRUPT, COMMANDER?"

Kira looked up at the door of the shuttle and saw Temitope standing just inside. The interior of the shuttle was probably one of the larger open spaces on *Forager*—and it was definitely one of the least occupied ones. By the end of the third day of the flight, Kira had retreated to the nova craft to familiarize herself with it.

And if that kept her out of rooms that were crowded even for extroverts, so much the better.

"Sure," she told the Colonel. "I'm just making sure this girl and I know each other as well as we can."

Temitope swung a small bag in one hand as she stepped into the spacecraft and walked up to the cockpit. A bottle emerged onto the shuttle console, followed by two glasses.

"I'm not used to the new-shuttle smell," she admitted, sniffing the air. "Redward spends most of the military's money on having shiny nova ships. I agree with the logic, but it means the army gets about one new assault shuttle a year. I have literally flown boarding operations on the same shuttle my mom was maintenance chief on fifty years ago."

"Even with the resources of an entire star system, some choices have to be made," Kira conceded. "Even in Apollo, I knew freighter captains whose ship had been originally purchased by their grandparents. There's probably choices like that even in SolFed."

Temitope chuckled.

"What, we don't think everyone in SolFed is choosing whether to use the gold toilet or the platinum one?" she asked drily. "Some of the rumors we hear from the Core…"

"They're still human and their butler-robots still put their pants on them one leg at a time, just like us," Kira said with a chuckle of her own. "What's the bottle?"

"Tradition," Temitope told her. "My family runs an orchard and meadery on Redward. Back when she was a maintenance chief, Mom always split a bottle of apple mead with the pilot before they went into action.

"I've kept it up, started by splitting with my fire team leader. Then, my CO as I got mustanged and kept going. Today, you're the CO."

Temitope poured generous helpings of the golden liquid into the glasses, a rich smell of apples and honey filling the cockpit as she offered the glass to Kira.

"Thanks." Kira took the glass. "Did you know what you were getting into when you accepted the Queen's invite to dinner?"

The commando laughed.

"I think everybody had already volunteered by the time you showed up," she admitted. "I didn't know quite *how* deep the Queen was dragging us, I'll admit. The Equilibrium Institute…that's a new wrinkle on me."

"When Estanza told me about it, we'd just finished the wake for *Conviction*'s last CNG. Estanza's protégé—and a man I was busy falling head over heels for," Kira replied. "I wasn't sure I believed him either.

"I still have my days, and I've *met* Equilibrium agents now."

"Like this engineer?" Temitope asked. "I'm surprised you're cold-blooded enough to use a date as an opportunity to kidnap him. *I* would, but I'm special ops."

"He seems nice enough, but if I'm reading this correctly, he's Equilibrium," Kira said bluntly. "That means he's bought into a line of thinking and an ideology that says the whole galaxy has to work the way *they* say it must. Regardless of what the rest of us think."

She shook her head.

"Also, I'm about seventy percent sure *K79-L* ambushed and destroyed *Hope*," she pointed out. "Which came along with the deaths of about fourteen thousand innocents to keep us from being able to confirm that. So, if he signed off on that, I have *no* issue using his interest in me as a trap."

Temitope took a gulp of her mead and nodded.

"That's a whole different mess of blood and murder," she agreed softly. "Word is that you guys took the rescue contract for a single kroner, too."

"Don't go thinking we were being charitable," Kira replied uncomfortably. "We took the rescue contract on a price-per basis with a nominal upfront cost. Otovo owes us quite a chunk of money for the rescue op; they just didn't have to pay in advance."

"That was being uncharitable and selfish, of course," Temitope said, with irony thick enough to cut with a knife. "You really think the Brisingrs were behind that?"

"Ambushing *Hope* would be Brisingr doctrine," Kira told the other woman. "Wiping out the witnesses, though? I suspect that was *Equilibrium* doctrine."

She shook her head.

"And it looks like they got Ypres to play along with that, too," she continued. "They had gunships from somewhere, anyway."

"Sanctuary's going to have a lot to answer for when this is over," Temitope said grimly. "I hope I'm here to see it."

Kira sighed, grabbing the bottle and emptying it to refill their glasses—it was a surprisingly small bottle.

"If it comes down to it, we will do the suicide option," she conceded. "But if we can come up with *anything* else, we're going to do that. I wasn't a fan of *do and die* even before I was a mercenary!"

As Temitope took another sip of her mead and both women were studying the empty bottle, a chime sounded behind them as the shuttle door slid open.

"Thought I'd find you here," Cartman said, her voice pitched to carry through the tiny spacecraft. "Ah, Colonel Temitope. I wasn't expecting to find you, but you're welcome to join us."

"Join you where, Em Cartman?" Temitope asked carefully.

"Apparently, Lozenge snuck a case of beer aboard in his luggage," Cartman said cheerfully. "Well…more than one, I think. One went to the mess, but there's a pilots' and officers' party in the other shuttle, if you'd care to join us."

Kira downed the rest of her mead and met Temitope's gaze.

"Well, we're out of mead here," she told the Commando. "And I suspect too many of us are going to find corners to mope in on the last night if we don't make an effort to keep ourselves distracted!

"Come on, Colonel. Let's go make sure the party reaches the appropriate level of rowdy!"

32

THE NEWS UPDATES they'd received as *Forager* had followed the trade route between Redward and Ypres left Kira with more than a few misgivings. Things had progressed much as everyone had expected: Sanctuary had rejected the Alliance's ultimatum and begun a pressure campaign against their enemies.

She could see the pattern of Sanctuary's strategy in the attacks, and it suggested they had the time to carry out their plans. Sanctuary was hitting vulnerable points belonging to the Guilds, seizing or destroying military and civilian infrastructure throughout the star system.

Most of the heavy lifting was being done by Sanctuary's nova destroyer squadron, though Kira was reasonably sure she saw the signs of nova fighter strikes in some of the reports.

The point of the attacks was to convince the Guilds, the member of the Ypres Alliance physically between the other two, that Flanders and Center were unable to protect them. She wasn't sure it was going to work, but even if it failed, it could force the Guilds to disperse their sublight monitors.

So far as Kira could see, the key to everything was probably Elverdinge. The Guilds and Flanders had moved most of their monitors to the system's second habitable planet—and Sanctuary had pulled its old and "new" monitors together on Dikkebus as the two planets' orbits drew them closer together.

Neither force could move on the other without being intercepted. Neither force could leave without leaving a critical position uncovered —nova warships would hesitate to challenge orbital forts, but both sides had enough sublight monitors to make taking the forts possible.

Sanctuary was using their nova warships to unbalance their enemy, to force the Ypres Guilds to pull monitors back to defend their own territory. The math of an in-system war was personally unfamiliar to Kira, but she'd studied it.

The joker in the deck was *K79-L* and her fighters, a force capable of ambushing and obliterating any of the larger but cruder and slower monitors in the star system. Ignoring the cruiser, the two forces in the system were roughly matched in both sublight and nova-capable warships.

So far, however, *K79-L* remained in Dikkebus orbit while Sanctuary's destroyers harassed the Alliance. As *Forager* entered the system, the cruiser was exactly where they expected: orbiting slightly above one of Dikkebus's orbital forts, well inside the arc of the massive asteroid's guns.

"Well, there's our target, everyone," Como announced as the freighter accelerated toward Dikkebus. "Time to orbit is estimated at just over two hours, so let's all get a good look at the problem."

"Most dangerous warship in the system, well inside the defenses of the most powerful fortress in the system," Temitope noted. "Not sure I'd trust Sanctuary that far."

"Equilibrium seems to think they've got Sanctuary well under their thumb," Kira agreed, studying the position of the heavy cruiser. "Though…can we tell if her nova drive is charged from here?"

"No," Como admitted. "From the files you gave us, I'm not sure anyone in the Cluster would be able to tell if her drives were charged from anything but point-blank range."

"Really?" Kira asked, surprised. It wasn't always easy to detect the charge level of a nova drive, but the binary answer of "charged or not" should be straightforward.

"The thermal shielding around her drive cores is too dense," the covert ops ship captain replied. "It helps control the static buildup and it also keeps us from scanning her drives."

"But you only need thermals for charge-level analysis," Kira replied. "If the drive is online, she's leaking Jianhong radiation."

The bridge was silent for a moment until Como coughed delicately.

"The smallest Jianhong radiation detector Redward can build would occupy a third of this ship's volume, Commander," she pointed out. Jianhong radiation, named for the original inventor of the nova drive, was an inevitable side-product of running power through the exotic matter arrays at the heart of a nova drive.

"I take it Apollo's is smaller?"

Kira nodded apologetically.

"Large enough that we don't mount it on fighters, but yes," she admitted. "Sorry, I don't always remember that."

She turned her gaze back to the sensors.

"Would the fortress have one?" she asked. "At a hundred thousand kilometers, the drive would be detectable if they do."

"Quite possibly not," Como admitted. "Which would make it possible for *K79-L* to have her drive online and ready to go."

"I'd like to know if she did," Kira replied. "It would tell us a lot about the relationship between Sanctuary and Equilibrium."

But they worked with what they had, not what they wanted to have.

"We'll get our orbital slot shortly, which will give us a better idea of our options and barriers," Como said. "It looks like most of the civilian shipping is being kept well away from the fortresses and the monitor fleet. Getting close will draw attention."

"That's why we brought nova shuttles," Kira said, with a confidence she wasn't sure she felt. "No approach. We jump straight from *Forager*'s launch bays to the shadow of *K79-L*. It should work."

"I'd love at least two backup plans," Temitope admitted.

"I'm still treating making the nova jump as a backup plan," Kira replied. "Which means I need to start pulling on some levers."

She looked at Dikkebus itself.

"Anyone have a suggestion for a restaurant in Cloth Hall that will make kidnapping my date easier?"

KIRA PROBABLY SPENT LONGER agonizing over the message to Konrad Bueller than she would have if she was *actually* trying to ask him on a date. No one aboard *Forager* really knew Cloth Hall's food scene well enough to make a useful suggestion of a restaurant, and she also needed to come up with a reason for her even *being* in Ypres without *Conviction*.

"Hi, Konrad, this is Kira," she finally began the message. She was running a virtual background to conceal the fact that she'd retreated to the shuttle for privacy again. "You suggested that I reach out if I was ever in-system again, and I'm here to try to follow up on my job posting I made last time.

"I'll be on the planet in a couple of hours, but I'm not sure how long I'll be able to stay. If you want to meet up for dinner again, let me know as fast as you can."

She paused, considering how to close it. Most of the things that came to mind just felt too false for the situation.

"We'll see what we can make happen," she concluded, then ended the recording and sent it.

There was only so much stressing she could do. If Bueller walked into her trap and was cooperative, they might manage to expand their options for neutralizing the cruiser. If he smelled a rat, though, it might not even change the difficulty of the task before them.

Their backup plan was sufficiently suicidal that Kira didn't think K79-L was likely to prepare for it, even if they thought someone was trying to kidnap the chief engineer.

To her surprise, she hadn't even left the shuttle before she got a ping. It was a request for a live call, with her headware advising her of a half-second transmission delay.

Exactly the right amount of delay for Bueller to be aboard the Equilibrium cruiser.

Reactivating her virtual background—an obviously false scene of a mountain chalet—Kira accepted the call.

"Konrad, I didn't expect to hear back from you that quickly," she told the engineer as his image materialized in front of her. He was also running a virtual background, she noted. His was a calm beach looking out on Brisingr's dark green oceans.

"You're a soldier, Kira; you're familiar with *hurry up and wait*," he replied with a smile. "The Director has inserted us into the local politics, but we're not acting yet. I've done my part in making sure *Seventy-Niner* is ready, and now I just check occasional reports."

He was almost certainly down-selling what he was doing, of course. Kira would be doing the same in his place.

"If you're aboard ship, I guess dinner isn't an option?" she asked. That could be a problem...

"I'm actually expecting to make a trip to Cloth Hall this evening, local time," he told her. "It's a work affair, but I'll be free afterward for several hours. I might need to make some arrangements, but I'm reasonably sure I can manage to do dinner. Did you have a plan in mind?"

"I don't know Cloth Hall at all," Kira admitted. That sounded like there'd be more Equilibrium operatives on the planet than they'd like, plus those arrangements might include bodyguards. But...they could work with that.

She had sixty elite commandos, after all.

"We could do the same restaurant as last time?" she suggested.

"Their idea of fusion still makes my teeth hurt," Bueller said with a chuckle. "Do you have transport on the surface? I will be out near the main spaceport, and there's an excellent pasta restaurant on the outskirts of Cloth Hall, roughly halfway between the two ports."

"I can rent a taxi once I'm done at the Pilots' Guild," Kira agreed. Something in the outskirts sounded far more workable for a quiet kidnapping than a restaurant in the main downtown. "I can make that work."

"Awesome!" He grinned at her with enough enthusiasm that she couldn't help but return it. "Shall we say twenty hundred hours local time? I'll make a reservation."

She chuckled.

"All right, I'll make sure it works," she told him. "Send me the address?"

It pinged in her headware even as she was asking.

"Good luck with your job-posting review, Kira," Bueller told her. "I hope you find the pilots you need."

"I don't have much hope," Kira admitted with an honest grin. She'd *never* actually expected to find a dozen ex-nova fighter pilots in Ypres.

There was, she realized, only one place she could find the pilots she needed: on board *K79-L.* Which wasn't happening, for obvious reasons!

"I'll speak to you tonight," she told him. "I need to go check my shuttle flight and make sure everything is in order."

And make sure the restaurant had appropriate surroundings to infiltrate commandos. Bueller was charming enough, but she couldn't forget why she was meeting with him.

Even if she liked his laugh.

33

"WE'VE RENTED four local aircars from four different rental organizations," Temitope told Kira as they slid down the road toward the restaurant in a rented groundcar. "Plus the groundcar, plus two airtrucks."

Antigravity coils were in the core database that every colony world started with. They couldn't get a vehicle to orbit on their own, but they certainly made the process easier. They were also useful for creating cheap low-flying vehicles.

"Does that get us everyone on site?" Kira asked. She checked the temperature as she adjusted the knee-length skirt of the light blue summer dress she was wearing. The garment went well with her leather jacket, but the weather didn't justify the jacket. That left her with only the stunner the dress concealed at the small of her back.

"No. I've got my first three squads and Milani's people," the Colonel said grimly. "Forty troopers; three in each car and fourteen in each truck."

"I hope we've passed out stunners," Kira said.

"This isn't my first kidnapping, Commander," Temitope pointed out. "Or Milani's, I suspect, from their part in the planning. Everyone is carrying stunners and hand blasters. There are heavy weapons in the trucks, but the aircar fire teams don't even have blaster rifles. If this goes sideways, we could end up badly outgunned."

"I know," Kira conceded. The car's autopilot warned them they were almost there. "The main plan is still subtlety."

"Agreed. Let's go over it one last time," Temitope said.

"I bring him out after dinner and have him walk me to the car," Kira recited. "You'll still be in the back seat. We stun him and dump him in the back and head back to the shuttleport like nothing ever happened. We move him into a case along the way so we can move onto the shuttle without drawing attention."

"Aircar teams will deal with any bodyguards he brings with him," the commando told her. "Nonlethally. We'll follow up stunners with sedatives to buy us a few hours, enough time to get into space."

"If we go according to plan, there will be nothing to draw attention to us once we leave Dikkebus," Kira agreed. "That will give us time to work with."

"If we have to shoot our way out, primary objective is to break contact and get you and Bueller removed from any tracking," Temitope told her. "We want to get everyone back aboard *Forager* without pursuit, but if necessary, some or all of the commandos can go to ground on Dikkebus for a few days or weeks.

"Resources are in place to protect us. You just won't have us for the strike on *K79-L*, so the engineer better make up the difference."

Kira nodded and exhaled as the groundcar rolled to a halt at the far end of the parking lot. The restaurant was of a suburban style that hadn't really changed in hundreds of years. Flat parking lot, square structure standing alone.

The style had grown rarer over time, but it was still common enough to be recognizable.

"All right," she said. "Now I just need to get through an entire dinner with a surprisingly nice man who I'm planning to kidnap."

"Good luck," Temitope said drily. "You might need it. Air teams are sweeping the area; scans suggest there is at least one bodyguard team trailing him. Give us a cue for when to move on them."

Kira tapped her temple, roughly where the radio transmitter for her headware was concealed.

"Will do."

AN AIRCAR DROPPED out of the sky abruptly as Kira approached the entrance to the restaurant. While the vehicle wasn't marked any differently from the others traveling the computer-controlled lanes above Cloth Hall, something about the way it maneuvered made her want to find cover and a heavy blaster.

Unfortunately, even her usual hand blaster was illegal on Ypres and she wasn't officially pushing the mercenary license this time. Temitope and Milani's people had smuggled the non-stunner weapons out of the shuttleport and she hadn't asked how.

Her stunner wasn't going to do much against an aggressively piloted aircar. Whoever was flying the car had learned in military VIP protection courses. She recognized the style and they probably weren't threatening her.

The door to the aircar opened just as she paused at the restaurant door, and Konrad Bueller emerged. Unlike the first time they'd met, he was in a Kaiserreich Navy uniform. A *dress* uniform, even, though he'd removed the heavy jacket with its gold embroidery to leave him in only slacks and a black turtleneck.

"I'll call you when I need you, Brian," he told the driver of the aircar. "Go check in with the Director; he might need a driver more than I do."

Kira didn't hear the response but the aircar lifted off on silent anti-gravity coils before whipping away. Bueller looked after it for a moment, shaking his head before turning to Kira with that damnable grin.

"We asked an ex-weltraumsoldat pilot to fly an aircar," he said drily. "We should know better, I suppose. According to Brian, everything is a threat."

"I know the type," Kira agreed, opening the door for Bueller as the engineer reached her. "I've probably *been* the type. I recognize VIP-protection driving when I see it."

The engineer chuckled and opened the inner door for her.

"You would, wouldn't you?" he asked. Stepping inside the restaurant he nodded to the artificial stupid hologram running the seating. "No bodyguards today?"

"Distant coverage," Kira allowed. "They're keeping an eye on things. I imagine you know that drill."

She wasn't going to *tell* him she knew he had his own distant bodyguard team.

"I'm familiar with it," he agreed as a hologram led them to the table. Kira had spotted a human in the back keeping an eye on things, but it looked like the restaurant was almost entirely robot-manned.

"Sometimes, it's less…friendly than others," he continued, closing his eyes. "Security and protection are always an interesting game, aren't they?"

"They can be," she murmured. He was doing something in his headware, and Kira didn't know what. That wasn't a good sign, with everything going on.

"Ah, I was right," he murmured. "How curious are you, sir?"

"Konrad?" Kira asked, a chill running down her spine and her fingers twitching toward the stunner.

He opened his eyes and grinned.

"Just taking some security precautions," he told her. "The security on this restaurant is good, but it's not good enough. I own their computers now. There are two humans on staff: the one you can see keeping watch on the tables and serving robots, and a chef in the kitchen doing final assembly and review on the food.

"Enough of a human touch to keep people coming back," he concluded. "Neither is expecting us to do more than talk to the holograms, so they haven't noticed my taking control and futzing with the security feed. No one outside this restaurant is seeing a live feed anymore. That leaves us some much-needed privacy."

Kira glanced around the restaurant at the almost two dozen other patrons.

"Privacy from whom?" she asked carefully while nonverbally letting Temitope know about the change in environment. "We are hardly alone."

"Yes, but the other patrons are here for a meal and don't care about us," Bueller told her. "Where my employers are now watching a sophisticated artificial construction of the two of us having a regular ordinary meal."

"And what *else* would we be doing?" Kira asked slowly. This was not going the way she had expected.

"Please, Kira, I am not stupid," he said. "There are a very limited number of reasons why you'd be in Ypres without your carrier—and right now, I find it extremely odd you'd be here trying to recruit fighter pilots as a war is going on.

"So, you're here for other reasons, and the fact that you reached out to me gives me some very interesting clues as to what those reasons are."

A chime told them that an artificial stupid was about to arrive, interrupting their conversation and leaving Kira confused and silent as she ordered spaghetti without even looking at the menu. The hologram vanished a few seconds later, and Bueller grinned at her.

Despite herself, she couldn't help returning it.

"Unless I've badly missed my guess, Kira, you're planning on kidnapping me," he told her brightly. "Which is *damn* convenient from my perspective, because I would very much like to defect."

34

FOR AT LEAST TEN SECONDS, Kira just stared at Konrad Bueller in silence, then she started laughing.

"I'm going to guess that Ghost Explorations isn't quite this paranoid about people going missing," she told him. "So…who exactly do you work for?"

"You know who I work for," he said. "You worked it out the last time we met, though I didn't realize it until I researched what you'd been up to out here. I was recruited by Ghost Explorations, yes, but was rapidly brought into the inner circle of Ghost employees who work for the Equilibrium Institute.

"And let's not play the game of you not knowing who they are," he continued. "If we want this to look convincing while still avoiding my supposed friends, we have only so much time."

"Okay, so let's say I know what the Equilibrium Institute is and what's going on here; why would you want to defect?" Kira asked. "And to who, for that matter?"

"You were looking for the Redward ship *Hope*," Bueller told her, his voice suddenly distant and sad. "I was already…" He sighed. "Look, the Institute's pitch is hope and peace for all humanity. They have a dream, they have a plan, they have resources. It's seductive as hell, especially if you're the kind of person who wants to leave the universe a better place than it was when you arrived.

"The degree of secrecy around *Seventy-Niner*'s mission and deployment was already bothering me. Maybe half the officers know our real masters, and the rest think our whole involvement in Ypres is opportunistic. The crew are Kaiserreich Navy, not even seconded. Active-duty, under direct orders to follow the Director and the Captain."

Bueller shook his head.

"I understand the concept of a testing engagement," he admitted, "but the Director insisted on absolute secrecy. I could have lived with myself for ambushing and destroying *Hope*.

"Destroying every station that saw what happened? Damaging the main stations so they couldn't see and so they were at risk? We and our allies killed ten thousand people to keep our allegiance and actions secret."

"Twelve thousand, five hundred and ninety-three," Kira said flatly. "I was there, Konrad. I saw the aftermath."

"I know," he said softly. "I don't *think* Captain Sitz realized how badly that pissed me off. I couldn't stop it, but I can't bring myself to believe that our cause is worth that kind of ruthless unnecessary massacre."

"Some will always believe their cause is worth any price," she told him.

"I'm not one of them," he countered. "There are lines that should not be crossed. Actions that should not be taken. Crimes that cannot be forgiven. The blood of those innocents is on my hands, for all that I did not command it or carry out the attacks."

"*K79-L* wasn't even involved in the attacks on the civilians," Kira noted. She wasn't trying to absolve him. More...testing him. The answers so far were about as good as he could give, even if he *had* been part of one of the worst atrocities she'd seen.

"That does not forgive my part nor exclude any of us from our guilt," Bueller said flatly. "I owe a debt that cannot be repaid to the dead. I cannot repay that debt on my own." He grimaced. "Even as chief engineer, there are safeguards to keep me from destroying the entire ship...and it turns out I am unwilling to embrace suicide."

"And what do you think you *are* willing to do?" she asked.

"I'm willing to help *you* deal with her," he told her. "I'm guessing you have a plan. I have access and knowledge of that ship that no one else does. Get me out, Kira Demirci, and I will hand you that cruiser on a platter."

"What happens after that?" Kira said. "You just admitted to being a war criminal, after all."

He was silent as their food arrived, staring down at his pasta in silence.

"If Redward wants me to face a court for my involvement in that crime, I will," he finally said. "I'd rather join *Conviction* or the RRF and try to undo some of what I've helped be done, but I will face the consequences of my actions, Kira. I will not run."

"All right," she concluded, considering the situation. "This is not what we were planning for, but I think we can make it work. Eat your lasagna," she ordered. "I need to talk to my team."

"HE WANTS *WHAT?*"

Temitope's voice sounded loud and clear to Kira, though she knew no one else around her could hear it, and the sheer incredulousness came through perfectly.

"To defect," Kira repeated. Her own words were just as silent. Headware communication could be intercepted or hacked, but it was at least unlikely to be overheard. "*K79-L* was apparently behind *Hope's* destruction, and their 'cleanup' after that was too much for him. He wants out."

"We can certainly oblige him, I suppose," the Redward woman said with a chuckle. "We think we've IDed his escorts. I'm guessing he has no way of making them go away?"

"Probably not, though we might be able to buy ourselves some time," Kira realized with a chuckle of her own. "If his people think we're on a date, after all..."

"You can take him to a hotel, his people can settle down for a long watch, and we can sneak you out without even engaging them." Temitope immediately filled in the details for her. "I'm guessing they're not overhearing you in the restaurant?"

"Apparently, Bueller has control of the restaurant's computer systems," Kira replied. "He seems a useful gentleman. If he *wasn't* both Brisingr and Equilibrium, I might have been considering a one-night stand by now."

"Hold that thought, Commander," the commando suggested. "Pulling him into a situation where his bodyguard doesn't expect to see him for at least a few hours gives us a window of opportunity. The moment they realize he's gone missing, *kidnapped* or *defected* doesn't matter; a whole bunch of his codes will get locked out.

"The longer those codes are active, the better."

"I think he'll be willing to work with us," Kira told Temitope. "Get me a hotel address while I talk to him."

She blinked away the communication and took another bite of her spaghetti. The pasta was surprisingly good, which would help explain her and Bueller's silence to the rest of the restaurant.

"I'm guessing you have no actual authority over your guards," she said softly.

"Not really," he admitted. "They're an Institute security policy in more ways than one. They're not from Brisingr. Operatives from somewhere with covert boosts installed in the Fringe, I believe. I can only speak to their cybernetics, I'm no doctor, but the implants I've managed to scan were higher-quality than anything I'd seen back home."

Kira nodded slowly.

"Will they buy it if we go to a hotel from here?" she asked. "If they're expecting us to have sex and spend the night, that clears us some time to work with."

The engineer actually *blushed* at that suggestion, but he maintained his composure enough to nod.

"The Director is playing a dangerous game, but it's one that calls for *Seventy-Niner* to remain out of the fight for now," he admitted. "Captain Sitz has strict orders. That's the only reason she hasn't already tested the theory that our nova fighters could cripple the Alliance's fortresses."

"The Director needs Sanctuary to *lose* at least one battle, enough to justify bringing in the rest of the battle group as 'mercenaries.'"

"*Battle group?*" Kira echoed, then shook her head as she got an address from Temitope. "We have to talk about that later, Em Bueller," she warned. "Right now, you and I need to wander out of here looking like our date went extremely well. My team has a hotel picked out."

"I'll tell you everything you want to know," he promised. "I've paid our bill. Shall we, Em Demirci?"

He rose from his chair and offered Kira his arm. Grinning at him, she took it. To anyone who didn't know the context, it hopefully looked flirtatious.

The way Kira intentionally molded herself against Bueller's side *definitely* looked flirtatious. She'd talked enough attractive men back to her hotel room in the past to know how to make it look good.

From Bueller's strained cough, that was a bit more than he'd expected, but he went along with it. The engineer led the way out of the restaurant, carefully opening the doors for Kira to let her sidle through.

"I've called us an autotaxi," he told her. "You have the address?"

"Yep," she said with a wink. The taxi should be fast enough, but she slid up to him anyway. "Warned your escort off?" she whispered.

"They know the 'plan,' yes," he confirmed, then chuckled with a smile. "Of course, they know who you are, so I got told to check for knives and blasters."

"You were never senior enough in the Kaiserreich to get *that* much attention from me," she told him with a purr.

The autotaxi arrived before Bueller could parse that, and he stepped over to open another door for her.

"I look forward to seeing this hotel of yours," he told her in mock seriousness. "I presume it has many amenities?"

"Oh, it has *all* the amenities we need," she replied with equal seriousness.

In another circumstance, she'd have been referring to the bed. In *this* case, she was referring to lightly monitored service accesses.

35

KIRA AND BUELLER weren't even the first people into the hotel room. Milani was sitting on the bed, their dragon drawn in line art on their armor's automatically changing camouflage pattern.

"Hotel security is ours," they announced. "Looks like Em Bueller's friends are trying, but we're feeding them the same false line as everyone else."

"May I check?" Bueller asked. "I know their tools."

"My cyber is watching, but go ahead," Milani told him. "Your security has split into two teams of three. They've pulled the plans for the hotel and are positioning to watch all the accesses."

"I expect competence from them," the engineer said, his voice distracted. "Your cyber is good," he continued. "Even knowing what they're doing, I can barely tell. I'm as certain as I can be that the team is fooled."

"Good," Kira said, letting the flirtatious act drop and eyeing Milani. She suspected the mercenary had been in the room as a precaution, just in case Bueller had been playing some kind of multilevel game.

She didn't necessarily *need* that level of protection, but she appreciated it regardless.

"What's the plan from here?" she asked them.

"There are nine accesses to this hotel," Milani replied. "Bueller's escort is good. They have eight directly covered and there is no way to exit the ninth without crossing their field of view.

"Unfortunately for them, *we* got to the plans before they did and made a selective edit."

"A tenth access?" Bueller asked.

"An underground service tunnel," Milani said. "The plans currently on both the hotel's and the city's servers show it connecting to a nearby reservoir and terminating. There is an exit there via the service access for the reservoir, and your team has it covered.

"*However*, there is another tunnel connecting to that reservoir from a water treatment facility down the road. It's a maintenance system for checking the water supply for the district, and it isn't a short tunnel— but it's three kilometers long with an exit every kilometer before reaching the treatment facility.

"We'll exit through the facility to avoid attention. There's an aircar waiting for us that will take us directly to the shuttle port."

"They'll track all of that eventually," Bueller warned. "Did you have a plan for my tracker?"

Milani produced a handheld scanner.

"I need to locate and remove it," they admitted. "We were planning on you being stunned for this part."

The engineer nodded grimly and pointed to his left shoulder.

"I *know* there's one there, but checking for one they didn't tell me about makes sense," he told them. "I have a device I can use to set up a decoy for my headware, but they'll be validating it against the tracker. Supposed to be for my safety, but…"

"Also to make sure you don't disappear," Kira confirmed. "Milani, find it, cut it out. How tight is the timeline?"

"Depends on what you want to do afterward," the mercenary told her as they ran the scanner over Bueller. It chirped as expected over the engineer's left shoulder. Milani pulled up Bueller's shirt and marked the spot with a black marker before continuing the sweep. "Exfil is going to take a while. We have a plan to cut the trail, but getting us back to the ship may take as much as three hours."

"We're hoping to get into position with Bueller's codes intact," Kira said. "Three hours…"

"Three hours to make sure we're not traced down in three *minutes* the moment they realize there's a problem," Milani replied, the scanner chirping again above Bueller's right thigh. The engineer sighed and shucked his pants, allowing the mercenary to mark the spot.

"Probably worth it," Kira conceded. "I have more use for your knowledge of the ship than your codes, I have to admit."

"I also have back doors coded into *Seventy-Niner*, Kira," Bueller told her as a *third* tracker beacon chimed in his lower back. "Chief engineer's codes open a lot of doors, and I have access to a few I shouldn't.

"I know you're planning on destroying her, but I do have an alternative that doesn't require my shipmates to die."

Milani took advantage of the engineer's moment of pleading to extract an ugly-looking oversized needle. They paused, judging Bueller's distraction, and then stabbed the device into the first black mark.

"*Fuck.*"

"One down," the mercenary said cheerfully, ejecting a bloody hunk of flesh and silicon into a tray. They sprayed the wound with plasti-skin before it bled too much, and moved down to the mid-back tracker.

"I'm open to alternatives, Konrad, but *K79-L*—*Seventy-Niner*, whatever you want to call her—has to cease being a threat," she told him.

"More than you know," he agreed, then hissed in pain without cursing this time as Milani jabbed the extractor into him again. "Captain Sitz could have ended this war already. The Director wants it to get ugly, to force the Protector into a position where they can *support* him more."

"And it being an ugly war helps make the society left over more aggressive and militaristic, doesn't it?" she asked.

"That's my understanding of the Seldonia—*fuck*."

Milani had taken him by surprise with the last extraction.

"You're done," they told him. "Set up your decoy. The plasti-skin should keep you together for the walk."

"I'll be fine," Bueller said grimly. "I ran three hundred meters with a ten-centimeter chunk of shrapnel in my leg once. I can make a few kilometers with some tiny holes."

He shook his head and focused back on Kira.

"If you just destroy *K79-L*, the Director still has a fucking fleet to finish the job with," he told her flatly. "You need to turn her against Equilibrium, Kira, and bring in Redward as well. You have to capture my ship."

Kira stared at him in disbelief, then met Milani's gaze.

The mercenary shrugged, the line art dragon showing her a wide toothy grin.

"We were going to get paid well for taking her out," they pointed out. "Just think of the paycheck you'd get for *selling* Redward that ship!"

36

BUELLER MANAGED to live up to his determined statements. He didn't make a single complaint as they made their way along the underground maintenance tunnel, even though Kira could tell that the extraction wounds in his thigh and lower back were hurting him.

Her own complaint that the tunnel was *far* too cold for a knee-length summer dress was sufficiently minor in comparison that she kept her mouth shut as she brought up the rear, her stunner finally drawn.

"Here," Milani told them. "Proper stairs at this exit, even!"

Except for the exit at the reservoir, each of the promised "one every kilometer" exits had been a ladder with a manhole cover. Kira was perfectly willing to take one of those, but she suspected that would be too much for their defector with the extraction wounds.

The tracker beacons had been placed with malice, she suspected. It couldn't be coincidence that removing them was slowing Bueller down as they tried to escape, even if the man was stubborn enough to push through.

But the door Milani had found opened into a neat set of steps ascending to the surface. The mercenary paused, then nodded.

"Surface team is in position; facility is clear," they reported. "There are some civilians on site, but we have eyes on and I will be able to maneuver us around them."

"Where's Temitope now?" Kira asked. The commando had been staying in her rental car, currently abandoned at the restaurant parking lot to allow Bueller to call her a taxi.

"She slipped out of the car after the escort moved on," Milani replied. "She's with the surveillance teams watching the escorts at the hotel. They'll exfil on their own later."

"Let's get to the aircar," Kira said with a nod. "Thanks for the update."

She stayed at the back as the other two headed out. Milani stopped them at several seemingly random intervals, presumably keeping them out of sight of the night shift workers.

It took them five minutes to make it through the relatively small facility, finally emerging back into night air to find the liveried rental aircar waiting for them.

"Subtle," Bueller said drily. "You know those are all tracked, yes?"

"Counting on it," Milani replied brightly. "We've got a few where we're spoofing the tracker, but this one is active. Draws less attention right now and gives them a trail we *want* them to follow for later."

"I'm starting to think I should have asked for more details on this plan," Kira muttered.

"No time," the merc said. "Get in the 'car."

Kira obeyed, ushering Bueller in at a vague gunpoint in case someone was watching. Milani got in the front compartment, taking manual control of the vehicle and sending them whipping away across the cityscape.

"I'm starting to worry about what I agreed to," Bueller told her. "Kira..."

"I don't like killing people I don't have to," she said. "If we can capture *K79-L*, I'm down. But she's a capital ship. One in the hands of a bunch of conspirators whose job requires professional paranoia."

"The destruction of *K79-L* will only work to the Director's advantage," he countered. "It's proof of the threat of the region, proof that Protector Daniels needs Equilibrium's help. Sitz has been trying to talk him into launching an offensive for a week, but he's been pushing for a guarantee that we'll deploy alongside his ships.

"If *K79-L* is gone, he has to either move against the Alliance or find a basis they'll accept peace on," Bueller said. "If he *loses* that fight, then he has no choice but to accept whatever terms Equilibrium imposes."

"And what kind of terms are those?" Kira asked. She hadn't missed that the engineer had started using the same name for his ship that Kira did.

"I don't know," he admitted. "Hell, Kira, I don't even know the Director's *name*. All I know is that he's in charge of everything Equilibrium in the Cluster. I've seen the rest of the battle group; I can give you numbers and weight of metal. It's more than enough to turn the tide of this little war, and they'll give the Protector a 'mercenary' counterweight to *Conviction* and the other mercenaries Redward uses."

"So, even if we take out your ship, we lose?" she said grimly.

"The odds get a bit more even, but the Director has options," Bueller told her. "I'm not sure what his plan is, but I know that he wants a real battle here. Sitz had three different plans that would have ended this war with a surgical strike using *K79-L* and Sanctuary's nova destroyers. The Director vetoed them all."

That suggested that Equilibrium wanted to make sure they had far tighter control over Sanctuary than they'd had over their pet Costar Clan warlord. If the Protector had to beg for help and was clearly going to lose without it, the balance of power between Ypres and their off-world sponsors was made *very* clear.

"The games are fun and all, but we're at the shuttleport," Milani said in their headware. "It's time to move."

THE AIRCAR TOOK off automatically behind them, linking into the city's computer navigation systems to return to the rental agency. A second mercenary had joined them now, the aircar's original driver turning out to be Jerzy Bertoli.

"Come on, let's move," Milani instructed. "For the next few

minutes, we're on a very tight timetable and I need you to trust me completely."

"All right," Kira allowed.

"Bueller, my merc here is going to have you subtly at gunpoint the whole way," Milani continued, gesturing to Bertoli. The big mercenary stepped over to loom over Bueller—and to conceal the hand blaster he was holding. "Right now, we are on the shuttleport's cameras but we're running a masking program."

"And when they unpeel that?" the engineer asked.

"Then they see you being marched at gunpoint to your fate," Milani said with a chuckle. "Now march!"

The four of them moved into the shuttleport at a decent clip. Their shuttle—not one of the nova boarding shuttles; it was *Forager's* only conventional shuttle—was parked in a commercial section that had less active security than other parts of the port.

As they walked up to the shuttle, a port officer stuck her head out of a nearby door.

"Hey, that bird isn't cleared for launch for at least a few hours," she told them.

"We know," Milani replied. "Just need to grab some things."

The woman regarded them suspiciously but let them go.

"Stay slow," Milani whispered to the rest as they came onto the pad. "Follow me. Do *not* hesitate."

They led the group across the pad and onto the ramp of *Forager's* shuttle...and then, without slowing down, jumped off the top of the ramp and ducked underneath the shuttle.

Bueller and Bertoli followed. Concealing a moment of concern, so did Kira.

From under the shuttle, Milani was moving toward the arrivals gate for the commercial landing at a brisk pace. Kira had to accelerate to catch up, her concern growing as they left the shuttle behind them—and then solidifying as the ramp on the spacecraft closed behind them.

"What are you *doing*?" she demanded via Milani's headware.

"Providing a thread for them to follow—and then cutting it off," the mercenary told her. "We now don't exist in their computers; everything after we left the ramp is being excised from the files as cleanly as possible."

Dodging through a closed gateway into the arrivals section, Milani swiftly delivered them to an unliveried air truck.

"Come on, get in," they ordered.

"We're not getting a shuttle?" Bueller asked slowly.

"Not yet, not here," Milani replied. Behind them Kira heard shouting and realized what her team had set up.

"Get in the truck, Konrad," she ordered. "I'm guessing this one has a spoofed transponder?"

"Cash purchase on the black market," Milani said. "No transponder, no trace. Let's *move*."

Kira made sure the two men got on board before she followed suit, looking back to see *Forager*'s shuttle rising out of the shuttleport on its antigravity coils.

"We weren't cleared for launch?" she asked Milani as the door closed behind her.

"Nope. And the autopilot isn't going to reply to hails as she runs for the hills," the mercenary replied. "Registry and port records now list her as coming from a completely different ship—which is, of course, a false front...for another ship. We've got the records completely mixed up at this point, so they'll never be able to say where she came from."

"And when they shoot her down, they'll know where she went," Bueller finished. "I take back my doubts, Em. But...where do we go from here?"

"Main spaceport, where we have tickets waiting for us on commercial transport to the cargo transfer station our ship is docked at," Milani replied. "It's slow and we'll need to ditch the guns, but we'll make it back safely without drawing attention to ourselves."

Kira eyed the two armored mercenaries. *Drawing attention* was probably going to happen...but there were ways to do that that didn't usefully stick in people's memories.

Somehow, she was certain Milani was a master of them.

37

CARTMAN WAS WAITING for them when they stepped off the commercial shuttle, Kira's second-in-command having traded in her uniform for an ankle-length form-fitting dark blue dress. She was accompanied by one of the Redward commandos, trying to appear inconspicuous but only managing to radiate *bodyguard*.

"Ah, Kira, good to see you," Cartman greeted her cheerfully. "Come on, come on, we don't want to keep everyone waiting!"

Kira let Cartman's "mom friend" aura sweep over her own little group of four as the other pilot urged them along and out of the main crush of the space station access.

"This is him?" Cartman finally asked once they were clear of everything, indicating Bueller. "I guess he's big enough to suggest some uses for him."

The engineer just gazed impassively back at her, and she giggled.

"Come on; *Forager* is docked at the civilian loading bays," Cartman told them. "We're moving containers off and on."

"What about the rest of the surface team?" Kira murmured.

"That's what the containers coming *on* are," her subordinate replied. "Some came up by cargo, some by mass transit. We've got about half back and we figure we'll have everyone in about two hours."

Cartman pointed a finger at Bueller again.

"Which means this one has two hours to make himself worthwhile, because we're running short on time."

"The good news is that my former compatriots will almost certainly believe me dead when they realize I'm missing," the engineer murmured. Even on the glorified surface-to-orbit bus they'd ridden to the station, the news had been playing and everyone had been able to watch the scene as an "accidentally launched shuttle" was "destroyed by Sanctuary High Guard to protect the citizens of the Protectorate."

Milani had left a convincing trail to suggest they'd been moderately competent but had blown their launch plans. Then, having attracted unwarranted attention, they'd fled in a panic until the locals had vaporized them.

If everything had worked right, Equilibrium would think Konrad Bueller had died in a botched kidnapping.

If was a big word in Kira's mind, though.

"We have maybe a couple of hours until they realize he's missing," Kira replied. "When we were actually kidnapping him, we were hoping to move by now."

She glanced around as she realized what she'd said, making sure they were alone. Thankfully, they were, but Cartman still wagged an admonishing finger at her.

"Be more careful, boss," Cartman warned. "Maybe all of this should wait until we're back aboard?"

"Probably," Bueller said levelly. "If it helps, I *do* have a plan of my own. We'll see what we can integrate of your resources and mine, but if you have half of what I think you do, we can make this happen."

"But as Mel said, we should talk about this on the ship," Kira replied. "Right now, we're two groups of friends meeting on the space station and heading back to our ship for a party. Better not to fragment that illusion just yet."

"We have cyber overwatch," the Redward commando pointed out. "The more smoothly we move, the less work they have to do to make us disappear."

"Slow teaches smooth, smooth teaches fast," Kira replied. "Let's move, people. *Smoothly*."

———

THEY MADE it back to *Forager* without interruption, joining Captain Como and Colonel Temitope in the mess hall they'd turned into their main briefing room.

"Em Bueller," Temitope greeted the engineer as she offered a handshake. "I'll admit, this wasn't how I expected to meet you."

He shook her hand briskly.

"I imagine there was supposed to be a stunner involved," he said. "Hopefully, my involvement in my sudden change in status will be as large a surprise to the Institute."

The commando shook her head.

"You know, I still didn't quite believe in a galaxy-spanning conspiracy to shape human society," she admitted. "To hear someone admit to working for them is weird."

"I can't say anything about *galaxy-spanning*," Bueller said. "I was recruited by one cell, worked mostly with a second, and interacted with the remnants of a third whose operation you people *shredded*.

"Outside those three cells, I have no information on the larger Equilibrium Institute," he admitted. "Hell, I suppose it's theoretically possible that Ghost Exploration *isn't* even a front and uses the deception of the Institute as cover for their social engineering projects. The government of Syndulla could be behind all of this."

"But you were recruited for the Institute?" Como asked. "Is that correct?"

"I was recruited for Ghost Explorations and then I was introduced to the concepts and ideology of the Equilibrium Institute as we prepared the survey work that *K79-L* theoretically supports," Bueller agreed. "By the time *Seventy-Niner* was actually involved, I'd been brought into the Equilibrium cell that runs Ghost.

"*Seventy-Niner*'s senior officers constitute the second cell I was working with," he continued. "Of the three hundred and seventeen people aboard *K79-L*, fourteen are Equilibrium Institute operatives.

The remaining twenty officers are ex-Kaiserreich Navy or ex-Syndulla Security Force. The noncoms and crew are active-duty Brisingr Kaiserreich Navy operating through a covert ops branch."

"How many of those people are weltraumsoldats?" Temitope asked. "A K70 has, what, two hundred in active service?"

"Two standard companies, yes," Bueller confirmed. He wobbled slightly. "Can I sit down?" he asked. "Grab a coffee, maybe? I napped on the shuttle, but it's been a long night."

"This is a mess hall," Kira pointed out. "Someone grab him a coffee. Get me one, too—and then you can all sit down so we don't burn calories we might need later."

Temitope seemed to consider objecting but realized this wasn't an interrogation and nodded.

Coffees materialized for everyone and Bueller took a grateful sip. He then paused, blinked, and took a more considering sip.

"This is *good*."

"Astonishing Orange," Kira told him. "It comes from Redward's South Tangerine continent; I make sure every ship I fly on has it these days."

"I begin to see unexpected perks of defecting," the engineer said with a chuckle. "In answer to the terrifying woman's question, there are no weltraumsoldats aboard *K79-L*. She is carrying two hundred and forty BKN NCOs and crew, thirty-three officers from Ghost Explorations, thirteen of them Equilibrium operatives, and forty-four security personnel from a separate Institute front."

"You can call her Colonel," Kira said calmly. "And this is the Captain." She gestured at Como. "You'll forgive me if I don't give you their names just yet."

"I can work with that," Bueller agreed, glancing around and studying the room. "This appears to be a standard freighter," he admitted. "I know you have at least some troops around, which should give us enough."

"We have more than that," Temitope said grimly. "If there are only forty-four security agents, we will have a numerical edge if we can get everyone aboard."

"Many of the BKN personnel are trained in firearms and will

attempt to repel boarders if given the chance," the engineer warned. "I have some answers for that, but perhaps we should discuss just what kind of plan we are operating with."

"You came to us at this point," Kira told him. "How about you lay out *your* plan and then we'll tell you what resources we have?"

Bueller nodded with a long exhalation.

"Trust has to be earned," he admitted. "I get that. All right. You know that I was *K79-L*'s chief engineer. Most of the NCOs in Engineering are people I trust. BKN special ops are carefully selected, but that doesn't mean they're down with the kind of witness elimination carried out in DLI.

"I won't lie: a lot of people on *K79-L* would have been okay with it if it was in defense or support of *Brisingr's* objectives," he admitted. "But even the people who aren't aware of the real chain of command know we're not out here to directly support the Kaiser. Patriotism is only a shield against crimes you can justify as helping your country."

"Your point, Em Bueller?"

"If I can get into the ship's internal coms, I can get most of the engineers to stand down," he told them. "With my chief engineer's codes, I can shut down most of the ship—even lock people out of the armories from anywhere I can link to the network. I have coded back doors throughout *K79-L*'s systems, and I can take full control of her if you can get me to her bridge."

"That's a hell of a promise," Como said. "Chief engineer or not, I'm not sure I believe that."

"Given the choice between enabling you to kill all of the people I've been working with for the last year and helping you *capture* them, I'm going to take *capture*," Bueller said. "I don't like what Equilibrium has had my ship do. A lot of people on that ship went along out of fear, habit or discipline. Only afterward did we really think about what we'd seen.

"Worst-case scenario, I am one hundred percent certain I can get you on board *K79-L*," Bueller concluded. "You can bring whatever bombs you have with you, and if my plan fails, you can blow her up from there.

"But as I warned Kira, destroying *K79-L* won't be the end of this."

"You promised us details on that, too," Kira pointed out.

"Captain Sitz answers to an individual who is occasionally aboard *K79-L* who is only known to us as 'the Director,'" Bueller told them. "He's *not* Cameron Burke, if that idea has occurred to you. I met Burke after you pulled him out of the mess he created."

Kira grinned and nodded. She had been wondering that, since Burke had been in charge of the previous Equilibrium cell they'd encountered.

"As we have grown closer to the date of intended action here in Ypres, the Director has been spending less time on *K79-L*," the engineer said. "Most of his time has been spent on Dikkebus dealing with the Protector directly, but my understanding is that he has access to at least one courier ship and has been out with the battle group since."

"The battle group being the ships that took out the stations at DLI," Kira said.

"Exactly. I suspect that the Director has kept anyone aboard *K79-L* from being fully aware of the battle group's strength, but the intention was to allow Sanctuary to lose the first real battle against the Alliance and have *K79-L* save the day.

"At that point, the Protector would be forced to 'hire' the battle group to carry the war. Combined with *K79-L*, they were expected to be more than enough to take down the monitors and fortresses of the Ypres Alliance."

"And they're nova ships, by necessity," Como said softly. "How many ships are we talking about?"

"I saw three Crest-built assault destroyers and twenty gunships of various Inner and mid Rim provenances," Bueller told them. "I would be very surprised if there isn't at least a light carrier in the mix, though I doubt there's anything bigger than thirty-kilocubic destroyers for main-line combatants."

That was a force that could tangle with any of Redward's carrier battle groups. *Conviction* could tip that balance easily enough—if Kira and her other five veterans were aboard. Short six of her most experienced pilots, *Conviction* was badly weakened at the moment.

"We can be reasonably certain that the Director has assembled a larger force than you were allowed to see, yes," Kira agreed. "If they're planning on stacking them up against asteroid fortresses—even ninth-rate asteroid fortresses—three destroyers and twenty gunships isn't going to cut it."

"Triple that and layer in a pocket carrier with half a dozen bombers and proper escort, though…" Cartman suggested softly.

"Then Ypres is in real trouble," Kira agreed. "We just added a critical component to the mission, I think."

"Which is?" Como asked.

"If Bueller can get us aboard *K79-L*, we move forward on his plan," she told them. "But *before* we do that, we need to find the fastest courier we trust in the Ypres System and send them home. If the Institute has a proper destroyer flotilla ready to move in to 'stabilize the situation,' we need backup.

"A lot of backup."

38

"OUR NEW ASSET has disclosed that there are additional forces in position near Ypres to reinforce Sanctuary," Kira said into the recorder. "These forces appear to be mid and Inner Rim mercenary units, currently in the employ of a third party retaining them to back up *K79-L*.

"We have reason to believe that the seizure or destruction of *K79-L* will result in the deployment of these forces to either support Sanctuary or, in a worst-case scenario, engage in an overall hostile takeover of the Ypres System."

She studied the data packet she was sending along with the transmission for a long moment. There were limits to how much she could put into a general message to the RRF. Queen Sonia accepted the existence of the Institute, but it would still sound like a conspiracy theory to most of the admirals.

"We are certain of a minimum strength of three destroyers and twenty gunships," she told them. "Given that the force is expected to be able to engage and neutralize the Ypres System planetary forts, I would estimate that we are looking at at least triple that strength, likely with at least one carrier carrying bombers.

"While I believe we have a high likelihood of neutralizing our primary target, the intervention by this hostile force will represent a similar imbalance in the Ypres System. However, unlike *K79-L*, the individual units of this force are only moderately superior to the RRF on a ship-to-ship basis.

"It is not my place to recommend a course of action to His Majesty's commanders," she said drily, "but I feel I would be remiss in *not* suggesting that the nova combatants of the RRF and your Free Trade Zone allies may suffice to neutralize this enemy while being seen as the defenders of the Cluster against an outside invader.

"I have attached all solid information we have. Regardless of the success of the next stage of my mission, we will be falling back to the previously agreed rendezvous point for this information. We will await updated orders there."

She closed the message, stared at the holographic models of Crest-built Sabertooth assault destroyers floating in the air in front of her. They were newer than should have been in the hands of mercenaries, but *K79-L* could have taken all three ships without blinking.

With a sigh, she activated a set of encryption protocols that *should* frustrate even the Redward Royal Fleet's analysts. Facing the recorder again, she didn't force the same professional expression she had for the RRF.

"John, you've been copied on my message to the RRF," she told Estanza. "I'm sure you've already realized that the fleet in question is Equilibrium-controlled. They might well *be* Inner Rim mercenaries—the security troopers on *K79-L* are apparently employees of an Equilibrium front company that handles their ground troop needs—but they operate on the Institute's orders.

"I can't give you much more information on the asset than I gave RRF, but realize that I have an Equilibrium defector aboard," she continued. "Most of *K79-L*'s senior officers are Equilibrium. We might even be able to take some more of them alive."

She shook her head.

"You're going to need to talk to him when this is done," she admitted. "He wasn't inside for as long as you were, but he was there for the massacre at DLI. You're probably the only person who can help him work through the trash that's left him with.

"If everything goes according to plan, we'll hit the rendezvous with a heavy cruiser under our control. That'll help turn the battle that's coming. I don't know how deep the Protector is with Equilibrium, but my impression is that they don't quite own him yet. If they did, this would already be over."

The fact that the Institute wanted Sanctuary to end up with a serious loss before they even let *K79-L* turn the tide was a warning sign all on its own.

"My biggest fear at this point is that the RRF won't get here in time," she admitted. "It's five days for this message to reach Redward and five days for reinforcements to get back. I need you to make sure they don't waste time.

"If they're coming at all, John, I need them to be here in ten days. Even that might not be soon enough."

KIRA ENTERED *Forager*'s bridge to find Konrad Bueller sitting at one of the consoles under Temitope's careful gaze.

"It's done," he announced, looking up to see Kira. "Good timing, Commander. We are now officially booked for a delivery of parts to *K79-L*."

"That was easy," she said. "How does that work?"

"I'd set up a bunch of purchase orders and shipping orders in advance that I was working through to get everything fully stocked," Bueller said. "While I wasn't *planning* on using them for this, it was easy enough to break into the supplier's system and mark the order as fulfilled. Once that was done, I assigned the shipping order to *Forager*."

He shrugged.

"The manifest and order come with the clearance to dock with *K79-L*. There's a secondary clearance structure, but it's supposed to be run before the shipping order is assigned. *K79-L*'s system is supposed to stop the shipping order being assigned without that clearance, but I sent a bit of code along with the order to override that."

"But if they look, we're not cleared?" Como asked. "That seems risky."

"It's possible," he admitted. "I don't think I've seen that triple check performed since we made it to Ypres, but it is possible. That's part of why I'm glad to be doing it in the middle of the ship's night—they'll be on hour five of a dead dog shift when we arrive. They'll do their jobs, but an extra security check beyond what's in the process book?"

"Risky assumption," Kira agreed. "But we don't have much choice. What's our timeline?"

"Our delivery slot is in sixty minutes, so we'll want to get moving quickly," Bueller told them. "The Colonel's people will need to be ready. If this works, we'll be boarding through *Forager*'s cargo bay instead of whatever shuttles you have."

"And these security troops, they're competent?" Temitope asked.

"They aren't weltraumsoldats, but I never noticed the lack," the engineer admitted. "I'd assume they're professional, at least as good as Brisingr troopers. Their gear is good."

"We can work with that," the Colonel agreed. "The maps are accurate?"

"As of twenty-four hours ago," Bueller confirmed. "I'm coming with you, Colonel, so it's in my interest to have this go smoothly."

"I'm not sure I like that part of this plan," Como grumbled. "We're putting a lot of trust in someone who defected today."

"The Colonel's people bring the bombs," Kira said. "I'll fly the secondary strike team over to the cruiser's shuttle bay while the first wave goes aboard. That will give us a nova escape route if things go sideways."

She was far happier novaing out of the bay of a ship she *didn't* care about, after all.

"I suggest that Bueller goes with the shuttle," Temitope replied. "It will delay our main operation by a minute or two, but I'd rather not have the person who we need alive in the middle of the main crush."

Kira checked the orientation of the cruiser and the distance from *Forager*'s shuttle bay to *K79-L*'s once they'd docked. "Not even a minute, I don't think," she said. "But I will draw attention, no matter how careful I am."

"Once the shooting starts, attention is unavoidable," Temitope said.

"I can shut down a lot of internal systems, but not until I'm physically aboard," Bueller told them. "That's a security protocol even I couldn't work around."

"Then I'll fly quickly," Kira said with a confident grin. "Everyone else stands by in their own nova craft as well. If I give the order, Como, you nova the fuck out of here."

"What happens if they pop multiphasics?" the freighter's commander asked.

"You nova the fuck out of here," Kira repeated. "At that point, we'll cram everyone onto the nova shuttle and run if we need to."

"All right."

The room was quiet. The unspoken assumption of Kira's plan was that if they *needed* to run, she probably didn't need to worry about carrying all sixty of the people they were boarding with.

39

"CLEAR A PATH!"

Milani's bellow was probably unnecessary as the mercenaries and commandos that filled the passenger compartment of Kira's shuttle were already moving aside to let her and Bueller through.

The Brisingr engineer was awkwardly clad in a hastily resized set of Redward commando armor. Like most armor, it had a long list of features and capabilities...most of which Temitope had promptly turned off to avoid information overload.

It would allow him to keep up and let him take a blaster bolt if needed. More than that would be more harmful than helpful.

Kira gave Bueller a nod as Milani peeled him off to a seat at the front of the compartment—on the right side of thirty armored killers—and stepped into the cockpit. Her headware interfaced with the shuttle's systems, guiding her instinctually to her seat as the chairs and displays were replaced with a representation of the space around *Forager*.

She blinked back a step, to an augmented reality display instead of a virtual reality display, and looked up to make sure she *had* a copilot for this. The seat was currently empty and she checked the network.

Milani was apparently copiloting for her themselves. That would work. They were probably more familiar with assault shuttles than Kira was, though she had no concerns about her ability to move the agile and deadly spacecraft the hundred meters she needed to.

"We are on approach to *K79-L*," Como's voice said in her virtual ear. "My god, that's a big rock."

Kira focused on the world around them. *K79-L* was still barely a dot in the distance, though her headware told her where the cruiser was. The Sanctuary nova destroyer keeping her company wasn't even a dot, just an icon marking its location.

Similar icons marked another destroyer and a dozen gunships within a hundred thousand kilometers of their position. They were already well into the lions' den—but the *alpha* lion was the source of Como's comment.

Rising Glory was the asteroid fortress positioned in a geostationary orbit above the equator near Cloth Hall, linked to the surface by a forty-thousand-kilometer-long cable it acted as a counterweight for.

Of the two fortresses that orbited Dikkebus, it was the one that had belonged to the Protectorate of Sanctuary all along. Like most asteroid fortresses, it was the linchpin of its owners' defenses and had been lavished with care and wealth.

Even *Forager*'s sensors were enough for Kira to tell that *Rising Glory* was visibly less sophisticated than even its Redward equivalents, with lighter guns and less capable sensors, but she made up for at least part of that by being built in an asteroid fifteen kilometers in diameter.

Glory was, as Como said, a big rock. One festooned with guns and sensors that made up in numbers what they lacked in sophistication. In a region of space where sixty kilocubics was a big starship, Sanctuary had probably built something close to a full cubic *kilometer* of battle station into the surface of the asteroid—approximately a *billion* cubic meters.

K79-L was no match for the fortress, even if it was a far more flexible vessel in a thousand ways. But...*Rising Glory* was the most powerful fortress in the system, and Kira could see ways to use a heavy cruiser and its twenty nova fighters to challenge the weaker stations.

It would be more easily done with multiple nova ships and made *vastly* easier with real bombers—but it could be done. Kira wasn't used to thinking of the defensive stations above planets as attackable. The entire war between Apollo and Brisingr had been predicated around securing the trade route stops and blockading a handful of systems.

The fortresses and monitors had made the planets invulnerable. But when the modern warships from her home sector were brought there, to a region with notably cruder technology, that paradigm shifted.

"We've transmitted our codes to *Rising Glory* Control," Como reported. "We are on final approach to *K79-L* and, I'll note, currently in range of three monitors, two destroyers, twenty-two gunships, the heavy cruiser we're targeting *and* the biggest asteroid fortress I've ever seen."

"And if any of them shoot at us, we've done this very wrong," Kira replied. "Time?"

"Just over three minutes to contact...codes have been accepted," the Captain told her. "We're cleared all the way in, people. Places, everyone. The dance starts shortly."

A countdown clock appeared in Kira's vision as Milani stepped into the cockpit and took their seat.

"Ready?" they asked.

"Born ready. You?"

"I'm the terrifying fucker in the dragon armor," Milani replied. "Everyone *else* needs to be ready for *me!*"

40

THE SHUTTLE'S systems were linked into *Forager's*, allowing Kira to watch Como's entire approach to *K79-L*. The freighter was large enough that she figured someone *had* to be getting suspicious as they pulled up alongside. The size gave them options they hadn't considered, though, and Kira smiled coldly as the ship rotated.

They were adjusting into a position that would line up the freighter's cargo bay with the cruiser's loading bay. That would allow for the easiest transfer of the containers of supplies *Forager* was supposedly carrying.

But the slight adjustment that Como had added meant that for a few precious seconds as they approached, the freighter's shuttle bay would be lined up with *K79-L's* at a distance of about two hundred meters.

Como highlighted the moment for Kira silently, the hatch over Shuttle One's exit sliding open.

K79-L, thankfully, went for gravitic containment on her shuttle bay while she was resupplying. The entrance was open, a ten-meter-by-five-meter weakness in the cruiser's armor. Kira had been expecting to have to cut through the armored hatch protecting the bay, so that took a minute off her expected assault time.

"Go," she whispered, making sure Como could hear her, and triggered the shuttle's Harringtons.

They were clear of *Forager*'s bay in under a second and inside *K79-L*'s five seconds later. Kira held her breath as she slammed the spacecraft into a hover inside the enemy ship, waiting for alarms, weapons fire...any response at all.

"Unidentified shuttle, what the *fuck are you doing*?" a voice, presumably the bay controller, exclaimed in her headset. "This isn't a cargo shuttle deliv—"

Kira guessed that the controller had just looked at her displays and realized just *what* was hovering in her bays. She'd spent those critical seconds locating the bay's defense weapons and targeting the shuttle's smart munitions.

A hatch popped open on the bottom of the shuttle and six missiles flashed out. Kira slammed the assault shuttle into the ground a moment later as the weapons hammered into the defensive turrets around the bay.

Alarms were already starting and Kira grinned as she checked her displays.

"*Forager* has made contact and Temitope is moving," she told her passengers. "Our turn. *Go*."

Milani was already out of their seat and swinging into the passenger compartment. Ramps and side doors slammed open, and blind-fired blasters swept the space around the shuttle as the commandos and mercenaries swarmed out.

There was no one *in* the shuttle bay, but the thought was still there. As her ground troops spread out around the shuttle, Kira picked up her own blaster rifle and put her own helmet on.

Her armor was less capable than the suits issued to the mercenaries, but it could take blaster bolts almost as well and she knew the functions it did have perfectly.

"You're up, Bueller," she told the engineer, not quite pointing the blaster at him. "The three kilos of antimatter the commandos just disembarked with says we've achieved the minimum objective, but *someone* sold me on a better plan."

"Working on it," he said in a distracted tone. "I'm into the network and telling the people I trust to stay in their quarters. Wait...what the—"

"Konrad?" Kira asked, now concerned.

"That paranoid fucking *goddamn witch*," Bueller snapped. "Sitz locked out my codes. They must have realized I was missing and she immediately cut off my access, regardless of whether they thought I was dead or not."

"Then fuck this, we abort," Kira replied.

"No, no, I'm not out of tricks yet," the engineer told her. "I can't take control of the ship, but..."

There was always a degree of background noise to a starship. A whirr of life support. A buzz of lights. A faint hum of displays. None of it was really consciously noticed after more than an hour on a ship... until most of it stopped.

"Emergency shutdown," Bueller said flatly. "I told you I had back doors, Kira. I can't do as much with them from here as I could if I had actual authority codes, but I've put the ship into shutdown. I also activated security lockdowns. They can't get into the armories and the ship is cut into pieces."

"I'm hearing a *but* coming," she said.

"Yeah. So long as I'm actively in the system, Sitz can't undo any of that—but so long as *she's* actively in the system, I can't do more. I need to be physically in the bridge to override her, and even then, I need *hardware* access to take control at all."

"Well, then, Em Bueller," Kira told him. "You always said we needed to get you to the bridge; it just sounds like that got more urgent. Let's move."

He stayed frozen for a moment, then nodded. His shakiness was visible even through the armor suit, but he took her arm as she levered him to his feet.

"I said I'd deliver you this ship," he finally said, his voice shaky but determined as he selected a spare blaster from the mostly stripped weapon rack. "So, I'll deliver you this ship. No matter what it takes."

"SWORD, HAMMER, THIS IS WINGS," Kira said over the radio. At this point, very little could be considered secure—and their plan had been to hijack the ship's internal communications if multiphasic jammers came up. Code names were essential.

Sword was Temitope and the assault force headed toward Engineering and Life Support from the loading bays. *Hammer* was Milani and the assault force headed for the bridge.

"Pliers had their access burned out," she told them. "They shut down the ship, but we need bridge access to complete the job. Hammer, we're with you."

"Understood," Milani replied. "Minimal resistance so far. Sticking to stunners."

"Harder resistance this way," Temitope said. "Mostly crew without serious gear. Stunners are carrying us forward, no casualties." She paused. "Do we adjust?"

"No," Kira replied aloud. "Maintain objectives. Pliers and Wings will rendezvous with Hammer and continue on plan. Secure your targets and stand by."

"Understood."

If nothing else, Temitope had another set of one-kilogram antimatter charges. There were enough of the bombs on the ship to blow her to very small pieces, even though the *fifty*-kilo containment devices were a pain to haul.

Even one in Engineering would leave *K79-L* crippled, even if she somehow survived.

"Dropping you waypoints for rendezvous," Milani told her. "There's still a team with the shuttle. Leave *some* of them, please."

"Wilco."

Kira stepped out of the shuttle, glancing around to locate that team. It took her a few seconds, since the commandos were in full camouflage mode and had taken up defensive positions. The armored figure that appeared from under one of the Brisingr shuttles nearly gave her a heart attack.

"We got the update," the woman said briskly. "Four of us will accompany you to catch up with Milani. Everyone else stays here to make sure we still have a ride."

"Sounds good," Kira said. "Let's move."

BY THE TIME they caught up to Milani, resistance had definitely intensified. The distinctive *crack* of blaster fire echoed down the dimly lit corridors, a harsh contrast to the scattered stunned-and-restrained remainders of previous encounters Kira and her companions passed.

"Hold back four meters," Milani's voice said in her headware. "I think we found the security goons."

"How bad?" Kira asked.

"There are as many of them as there are of us and they have better gear," the mercenary admitted. "Our people and the commandos are better and they've lost more than we have, but they've got the only path I can see to the bridge locked down.

"We can push through, but it isn't going to be fast. Five, ten minutes at least."

Kira didn't even need to ask Como if taking ten minutes to press through the bridge was possible. Every one of those ships they'd flagged within a hundred thousand kilometers was already on their way—most, including the fortress, would have already launched at least one shuttle of boarders.

They had maybe *five* minutes to take the bridge, bring *K79-L*'s nova drive back online, and get the hell out of the system.

"Konrad?" she asked the engineer. "You got something? *Anything*? The security troops have the bridge locked down, and we don't have the time to push through them."

If they'd had more people, a frontal assault might have traded lives for time, but they didn't have the numbers. Milani would have suggested it if it was an option—they knew the time constraint as well as Kira did.

"Not enough space for an assault team, but there *are* maintenance accesses," the engineer said after a second. "Enough for...us six?" he gestured around at Kira and their escorts. "They're locked down," he admitted. "I'll need physical access to open the hatches.

"Do it," Kira ordered.

"This way." Bueller said, taking off back the way they'd arrived at a steady clip.

"We have a plan, Hammer," she told Milani. "Keep them pinned."

"That's easy enough," the mercenary replied. "Dare I ask *what* plan?"

"Nope." Kira turned a corner to discover that Bueller was apparently part of the large minority of humans with an external physical dataport. He'd lifted his helmet and pulled back the hair behind his ear to expose a small circle of metal. He'd then connected a cable from that circle to a panel in the wall.

Moments after she reached him, he disconnected the cable and a section of wall slid open.

"It's cramped," he warned them. "But—"

"We go first," the commando leader said flatly. "Neither of you is expendable *and* we're more dangerous."

Kira couldn't argue either point, so she gestured the armored soldiers forward. The accessway was big enough for just one of them to fit in at a time, but the commandos seemed to have themselves oriented and were moving before Bueller could give them instructions.

She glanced at the engineer as the fourth commando climbed through the hatch, and shrugged.

"Ladies first," she told him, and clambered into the tunnel herself, blaster rifle in hand.

THEY DIDN'T HAVE FAR to go. Ten meters took them past where they estimated the defenders were positioned. Five more would have taken Kira and her companions to the bridge—except that there was a bulkhead in the way to stop them doing just that.

The ship's designers hadn't been stupid, after all.

"Link the cable into the panel," Bueller instructed as he passed the wire from his port to the commandos. "There are two ports; you want the blue one."

"Got it," the lead commando replied. Kira just barely made out the sound of the wire connecting. "Give us a count?"

"Five count," Bueller agreed. "Ready?"

"Grenades," the commando ordered her companions. Each of them produced a small silver orb the size of a child's fist. "Now we're ready."

"Okay. Five. Four. Three. Two. One. *Opening.*"

"*Throw!*"

The hatch had only completed a third of its meter-long route by the time the order was given. The four silver orbs flashed through the hatch.

Kira heard one shocked curse, perfectly clearly, before the high-powered multi-pulse grenades activated. Even through the bulkhead, she felt the EMP effect on her headware. It passed, thankfully, but the defenders didn't have the benefit of the hardened bulkhead.

"Move!" the commando leader barked. "Clear the hall!"

The four commandos spilled out of the hatch in a single wave of angry soldiers, blaster rifles sweeping the hall. The distinct harsh buzz of an under-barrel stunner sounded twice, followed by the *crack* of a blaster firing.

"Clear!" the commandos reported.

Kira was out the hatch before they'd finished speaking, Bueller only two steps behind. A quick glance down the hall toward Milani showed that the commandos had been feeling merciful: the grenades' actual *detonation* had been disabled.

The EMP had fried the defenders' armor and headware, leaving them vulnerable to the stun wave that had followed. The third stage would have turned the casing into high-speed plasma, flash-cooking even armored humans.

Instead, Kira's helmet happily informed her that most of the defenders were alive. Unconscious and in need of implant resets, but alive.

"Milani, leave a team to secure the prisoners and fall in on me," Kira snapped. "Bueller, the bridge."

"This way," he told her. "No grenades now, please. One EMP in the wrong place and everything to get us this far has been for nothing!"

The four commandos were already formed up around them again as Milani's team began to pick their way past the defenders. Kira checked the time and realized they couldn't wait. Even *seconds* were going to matter now.

"Move," she snapped. "Move *now*."

The commandos didn't argue. They were at the heavy blast door sealing the bridge a moment later, covering Bueller as he physically linked in.

"What now?" Kira asked.

"Ready?" the engineer asked.

"Yes," she said flatly.

"This."

The blast doors slid smoothly open, their power sources coming to life at the engineer's command. The commandos opened fire in the same moment, stun pulses flashing into the room on the other side.

Blaster fire responded and one of the commandos went down. Kira stepped into the fallen Redward soldier's place—and she hadn't mounted the under-barrel stun gun on her blaster rifle.

Her fire joined the commandos' and an armored guard went down as three bolts hammered into their chest. Counter-fire slashed into the wall and then someone started shouting.

"Stop! Stop shooting or I'll blow us all to hell!"

41

THE SHOOTING STOPPED and Kira slowly stepped into the bridge, her blaster trained on the remaining armored guard. There were only half a dozen people in the space, scattered around a circular room designed to hold twenty.

Two of those people were dead, armored soldiers who'd drawn the commandos' fire. A third guard was holding a blaster rifle as Kira's people focused their weapons on them. Two more people were clearly mid-ranking NCOs, the people who'd hold down a quiet night watch under the supervision of the officer of the watch.

The woman in the middle of the room was definitely not mid-ranking. She'd traded in the uniform of the Brisingr Kaiserreich Navy for a plain black civilian shipsuit, but she still wore the gold eagle of her old rank on her collar and the stylized golden rocket of a starship captain on her left breast.

"Captain Sitz, I presume," Kira greeted her. "Well, you've managed to stop the shooting for a few seconds, but I do believe we're all on fascinating timelines right now."

"I don't know or care who you are," Sitz replied. "I'm guessing you've co-opted my chief engineer, which is a problem *I* at least saw coming. Bueller never had the stomach for what needed to be done."

"Most people blink at mass murder to keep stupid secrets," Kira agreed. "But right now, I have physical control of your ship, and possession is rather more than nine-tenths of the law out here."

"You have nothing. The ship's self-destruct is armed and linked to my vital signs," the Captain told her. "Shoot me or refuse to surrender and I blow us all to hell."

"I have no inclination to surrender, so I suggest you try another pitch," Kira said. "I should note that Burke already made the 'join us and rule the galaxy' one, so I advise you find a new one."

She stepped forward, clearing a space for Bueller to enter the bridge, while moving the focus of her blaster to Sitz.

"Burke," Sitz cursed. "That makes you one of Estanza's lackeys, doesn't it? Like Bueller, you lack the stomach to finish what you start. Lay down your arms, *mercenary*, and I will spare your pitiful lives."

"Assumptions, assumptions," Kira taunted. She *hoped* Bueller had a plan. "You see, the problem is that my mission is to neutralize *K79-L* by any means necessary. I brought bombs with me to make sure you didn't survive this."

Even as she spoke, she was watching the screens behind the Captain. The bridge had its own power source, it seemed. However it worked, they clearly had some scanners up—and they showed at least a dozen shuttles were heading their way, the closest only a few minutes out from *K79-L* and *Forager*. They were running out of options, and she sent a headware message to Como.

"Get out. Either we take her or we blow her. We'll meet you at the rendezvous point or we'll see you in hell, but there's nothing you can do now."

"You don't have the stomach to die for your beliefs," Sitz reiterated. "One word, one *thought*, from me and we all die. A galaxy worth living in is worth the sacrifice."

"Captain, look!"

One of the NCOs had noticed *Forager* departing. The freighter swung away from the cruiser, keeping the bigger warship between her and *Rising Glory*, and then vanished in a blue flash of Cherenkov and Jianhong radiation.

"I have the stomach to commit to this," Kira said softly. "I left my home because of people like you. Fled to the edge of civilization and took a job fighting people like you. Now five dozen systems claw their way toward the light and you would drag them down because you don't like their story.

"I won't let you do that, Captain Sitz," she told the other woman. "So, you have two choices: surrender *K79-L* to me, or blow us all to hell."

For a moment, Kira thought she saw *K79-L*'s Captain's resolve waver—and then the harsh *crack* of a blaster rifle echoed in the space as Sitz's head blew apart in a bolt of bright plasma.

"Drop them, drop them!" Milani barked, the mercenary having apparently followed Bueller in. "What the *hell*, Bueller?"

"I told you I could do more from the bridge," the engineer said calmly. "I could stop her self-destruct, but the moment I locked it out, she'd know...and there's a physical trigger in the Captain's seat's controls which you will *not* go near, Em Callahan."

Bueller's blaster rifle, the weapon that had just blown Sitz's head off, was now trained on one of the noncoms.

"What do we do now?" Milani asked quietly.

"You keep these idiots away from the Captain's seat while I jack in," Bueller told them all, crossing the bridge to where Sitz's body was slumped on the ground. He gently stepped over the dead woman and sank into her seat, his access cable already linked to his dataport as he flipped open the arm of the chair.

"You have maybe two minutes," Kira pointed out. "No pressure."

"It takes more than that to cold-boot a nova drive, doesn't it?" Milani asked, their voice fatalistically curious.

"But it takes more than five for a nova drive to cool down, so we should be basically live," Bueller replied as new icons came alive on the screen. "With Sitz out, I have basic control. Not much, but navigation is live and the nova core is coming back online."

He pointed to a console. "Kira, can you jump a nova ship?"

"In my goddamn sleep," she told him, crossing to the console and taking a seat as it came alive. The operating system wasn't quite what she was familiar with, but she'd trained on Brisingr gear at one point.

"Thirty-five seconds to docking," one of the NCOs—not the one

Bueller had called Callahan—told them. He sounded more curious than anything else. "Several of the shuttles might have detected that you've powered us back up; they are boosting their Harringtons to close faster."

Kira checked the console in front of her and smiled. The core wasn't fully warmed back up after losing all power for five minutes, but it wasn't like she could make a full jump from this close to a planet, anyway.

"Doesn't matter," she said aloud. "Novaing *now.*"

Reality shifted and the ship rippled around her as she punched it across a light-month in a fraction of a second. The bridge was silent.

"We'll need to recharge for a bit before we can move on to the rendezvous point," Kira told the others after a few seconds. "But we are no longer in Dikkebus orbit."

She leaned back and looked around the bridge, her confident grin returning as she looked at Bueller and Milani.

"Folks, it appears we just stole a cruiser." She indicated the three remaining Brisingr crew. "Restrain those people, please. Milani, link in with Temitope. We need to sweep the ship and make sure everyone is contained."

The NCO who'd given the sensor report calmly rose from his chair and proffered his hands.

"That's Bueller in the Captain's seat, isn't it?" he asked.

Bueller reached up and removed his helmet.

"Yes," he confirmed. "Commander Demirci is in charge; I'm just a useful asset."

"You trust her?" the man asked Bueller.

"She saved my life once, and her people have been *trying* to use stunners as they stormed the ship," Bueller replied. "I trust her more than I trusted Sitz or the rest of the folks in Ghost and their puppeteers."

"Good enough." The noncom didn't even blink as one of the commandos put restraints around his wrists. "I'm Chief Iyov Waxweiler, tactical. Technically still active-duty in the Brisingr Kaiser-reich Navy, but I didn't sign on for blowing up civilian stations and knifing ninth-rate powers in the back."

"So?" Kira asked bluntly.

"If Konrad Bueller is with you, I'm with him," Waxweiler told her. "Not going to argue with cuffs until you can check everything out, but I doubt I'm the only one, either. I fought for the Kaiser, but even for him…this would be beyond the line.

"I don't know what you're planning on doing with *Seventy-Niner*, but I doubt you've got a crew in your back pocket. If you've got something to say…I'm willing to hear the pitch."

42

WAXWEILER'S WORDS hung in the back of Kira's mind as the commandos escorted the Brisingr crew from the ship's bridge. She had commandos aboard the captured cruiser, but the only people qualified to *operate* the ship were her and Bueller.

"We're going to have a problem," Bueller said grimly from his seat in the center of the empty space.

"I can think of a few, not least of them that battle group you've told me about," she replied. "Which one are you thinking of?"

"Sitz wasn't nearly as confident about you surrendering as she was pretending," the engineer told her. "She activated an anti-mutiny protocol I was only partially able to counteract."

Kira grimaced, checking the console she was working at.

"I appear to have a nova drive," she noted. "What did we lose?"

"Everything else," Bueller said flatly. "It looks like she overloaded key fuses and capacitors throughout the ship. I had protocols in place to prevent something like that in Engineering, so we have power and we have the nova drive and life support, but…"

"No plasma guns, no sublight engines, no nova fighters?" Kira guessed.

"Only basic sensors, minimal internal control, no internal defenses," he reeled off, and sighed. "We have the nova drive and that's about it. If I had a list of what she'd done, my team and I could probably undo it in a day or so.

"Without that team or that list? We're looking at weeks, Kira."

"Then it will take weeks," she said. The cruiser was out of the fight. That was the main victory they needed right now. "Do we have internal coms?"

"We do; I'm linking the commandos in," he confirmed. "What I don't have is internal sensors to guide them to any holdouts."

"I caught the last of that," Temitope's voice said in Kira's headware. "How screwed are we?"

"We can nova and we won't run out of air, so we're fine," Kira told the Redward Colonel. "We just don't have much else."

"I like your definition of *fine*," Temitope replied drily. "I'll coordinate with my team leads and we'll set up a sweep to make sure the ship is clear. What the hell do we do with these people? *K79-L* only has prison space for fifteen at most."

"For now, stun and restrain," Kira ordered. "Lock anyone who voluntarily surrenders in their quarters. Even if we don't have internal control, we should be able to seal them in pretty effectively."

"I have ways," the Colonel agreed. "That only buys us time, Commander."

"We'll rendezvous with *Forager* in a couple of hours at most," Kira said. "We'll try and triage the prisoners as quickly as we can. Actual threats move to Captain Como's ship."

"She doesn't have that much space either."

"Maybe not designed for this," Kira agreed. "But we left *K79-L*'s carrier air patrol behind in Ypres, so we can fit those four Sinisters on the deck here. If we move the nova fighters over, that opens up some nice empty spaces she can secure and set cots up in. It won't be comfortable, but it'll meet conventions."

"Any chance we can use this ship against Bueller's 'battle group'?" Temitope asked.

"Fighters will be individually locked down, and it sounds like our guns might be physically disabled," Kira admitted. "We can get through all of that, but it will take time. Anyone want to take the bet that Equilibrium is going to give us a few weeks to nova her back to Redward and repair her?"

Neither Temitope nor Bueller were apparently feeling lucky today.

"I CAN'T BELIEVE you did it," Como told them.

With *K79-L* unable to move sublight under her own power, *Forager* was left to close the distance herself. The rendezvous two light-years from Ypres wasn't a neatly mapped trade-route stop, which meant they'd arrived almost thirty light-seconds apart.

"We did something," Kira agreed. "Thirty-plus dead still leaves us with almost three hundred prisoners being managed by fifty commandos and mercenaries. On a crippled ship with no weapons, jammers or fighters."

"Mission accomplished, I guess," the Captain said. "What's next?"

"First steps, Nightmare and the others fly their fighters over here," Kira ordered. "You set up a POW camp in your fighter bays and we offload as many of these prisoners as we can. Lozenge and the second nova shuttle will stay with you.

"Then we see if we can get any of *K79-L*'s systems back online while we wait for a courier from Redward," she continued. "We're nine days from an update, but I'm hoping that there's enough confusion in Ypres and the battle group to buy us that much time."

No one would be dispatched to the rendezvous point until they received her messages. If she was lucky, there'd been a fleet ready to go when the courier arrived—except that Redward was unlikely to have more than a single carrier group ready to deploy. A junk carrier with forty sub-fighters and a single sixty-kilocubic light cruiser weren't going to counterbalance the Equilibrium battle group.

"I'll pass the instructions on to Nightmare," Como promised. "I'll need some of those commandos back if you're sending me prisoners, though. *Forager* only has a crew of twenty-six."

"I know," Kira conceded. "See what space you can clear up and let me know how many prisoners you think you can handle. You get a commando per five you're handling, which should be enough."

"*Should* is always a dangerous word," Como said. "We'll rig things up once the fighters are on their way." She shook her head. "Interesting set of problems to have, I suppose."

"Could be a lot worse," Kira agreed. "I don't know what I'm going to do with her, but apparently I have a cruiser now."

Como laughed and signed off, leaving Kira sitting in the navigation console on *K79-L*'s bridge, running through the limited information she had.

"We need hands, Kira," Bueller told her, disconnecting himself from the captain's seat and rising. "And you should be in the captain's seat, I think."

"Does it even matter?" she asked. "You have control of this ship as much as anyone right now. I really do hope you're on our side."

He chuckled.

"*Your* side," he said with careful stress. "I'm not planning on going with the ship if you sell her to Redward, to be clear. I hope *Conviction* has a space for an engineer."

"You'll have to talk to Commander Labelle about that," Kira told him. "They run our engineering space." She shook her head. "Got any ideas on finding those hands?"

"Yeah, but it depends on how trusting you're feeling right now," he admitted. "We've got three hundred-ish prisoners. I can directly vouch for about forty of them, almost entirely Engineering techs —*exactly* the people we need if we want this ship to play a part in Ypres."

Kira turned her chair and studied the Brisingr man. Bueller had earned her trust—or, at the very least, created a situation where she *had* to trust him. But to loose forty Brisingr engineers on an ex-Equilibrium starship seemed *damned* stupid.

"I don't know if we can go that far yet, Konrad," she admitted. "Talk to them and we'll keep them aboard ship. If they seem amenable, we'll even keep them in quarters arrest rather than in the brig, but... right now, *K79-L* can do all I actually need her to do."

It would be a few hours before the cruiser's drive had recharged enough to nova, and she wasn't planning on leaving until the courier arrived. She could get to Redward before the courier could reach her...

but if they *did* end up being needed in Ypres, better one nova from Ypres than six.

"There's very little I can do on my own," Bueller told her. "But I understand. I'll talk to my people, see what they say. I think they'll get it too."

He paused.

"What *would* it take for you to trust them?" he asked.

"Trust? Time," she said. "To *use* them? Necessity. I need eyeballs in Ypres."

"Everything we're seeing is two years old," the engineer said.

"Konrad...we're about to have four nova fighters on hand," Kira pointed out gently. "They might not recharge from a two-light-year jump as quickly as a proper ship with a class one drive would, but they can still give me eyes in Ypres that no one is going to bother."

STEPPING into *K79-L*'s fighter bay gave Kira a moment of nostalgia. It wasn't an exact match for Apollo-style flight decks, but it was closer than *Conviction*. The old carrier had automation and tools that no one in Kira's home sector could match still.

The bay was small compared to an actual carrier of any variety. Even Redward's sub-fighter carriers had larger flight decks, but then, *K79-L* only carried twenty nova fighters. Four had been left behind in Ypres, leaving their cubicles neatly empty.

Now Kira watched as Nightmare carefully manually slotted her fighter into one of those cubicles. Scimitar was already aboard, with Dawnlord and Socrates hovering outside the bay doors, waiting their turn.

"Glad for the manual landing drills now?" Kira asked the youngest pilot as Colombera stepped up to her and saluted.

"Even you never made us manually dock the fighters to this extent," he admitted. "I'll be happy never to do it again."

Cartman's fighter settled into place and her systems audibly cooled down, tiny noises descending into silence.

"Dawnlord, you're up," Kira ordered. "Nightmare, come join me."

Cartman was out of her fighter thirty seconds later, watching as Patel brought his fighter in and landed. Once the Sinister was on the ground, Kira's wing pilot crossed the deck to her.

"That was fun. Please tell me I don't have to do it again," she said, unconsciously echoing Colombera's words.

"You're going to have to do it again," Kira replied brightly. "Once all four of you are aboard and you've had a chance to poke at the systems here, I need you to set up a schedule. At least one fighter needs to swing through Ypres every twelve hours."

Cartman grimaced.

"Which means manual launch and landing," she noted. "To be fair, it's not like *Forager's* systems are any better. She wasn't originally designed for fighters."

"We're going to need to figure out refueling without a deck crew," Kira told them as Socrates's fighter made her final approach. "We didn't burn much fuel getting over from *Forager*, but novaing to Ypres and back will burn through fuel fast."

The amount of fuel burned by the nova drive wasn't entirely proportional to distance, thankfully. A combat nova of a light-minute or two would use up about five percent of a fighter's fuel supply, where a two-light-year nova would only use about fifteen percent.

"We can manage deck-crewing for ourselves, I hope," Cartman said. "Scoot 'n snoop?"

"Exactly," Kira replied. "We need to know what's going in Ypres. Hopefully, there'll be Redward reinforcements heading our way, probably with *Conviction* in the mix, but we're sitting in what's supposed to be the most powerful warship in the Cluster."

"And how much of her works?" Michel asked, the youngest of Memorial's squadron's veteran women wringing sweat out of her ponytail as she joined them. "We've got four fighter-bombers we trust. What about that lot?"

She gestured at the neat ranks of Weltraumpanzer-Fünf heavy fighters lining the rest of the deck. Kira now had sixteen of the beasts. They weren't her preference for nova fighter, but they would certainly pull their weight.

If she had pilots. If she could even turn them on.

"Physical lockdowns initiated by the Captain and not a pilot we can trust," Kira said. "And, sadly, not a priority for the *one* engineer I've got."

"I wonder if he still thinks the date was worth it," Michel said with a wry grin. "You are working the poor man's butt off."

"Given that I was planning on kidnapping him and he was planning on defecting, I'm not sure that dinner counts as a date," Kira pointed out. She returned the wry grin, though, when she realized that *she* wasn't necessarily counting it out as one.

And wasn't that interesting? Bueller was certainly proving more intriguing than she'd expected.

"I'll take the first scoot once I've got coffee," Cartman replied. "We stirred up a hell of a hornet's nest; I'm guessing you want data ASAP?"

"Six-hour turnaround, so yeah," Kira agreed. "I doubt this ship's coffee is—"

She stopped as Cartman produced a familiar bag from behind her back.

"Astonishing Orange?" Cartman asked with a grin. "I brought some. You're not the only addict in Memorial Squadron, boss!"

43

BUELLER LOOKED exhausted when Kira finally tracked him down in Engineering several hours later.

"Have you *slept*, Konrad?" she asked.

He blinked up at her.

"Not since…napping on the shuttle to *Forager*," he admitted. "Thirty-six hours? Maybe forty. I've lost track."

"Right." She sat down next to him and looked at the power coupling he was prodding. "I know enough to know that this is a power feed to a primary Harrington coil," she told him. "What am I looking at?"

Bueller snorted and tapped a small panel he'd opened in the side of the coupling.

"Fuse box, basically," he told her. "Rated for one point two one gigawatts. Three fuse boxes per coupling, two couplings per primary coil. Ten primary coils needed for a ship this size, *Seventy-Niner* has twelve."

"And?" Kira asked.

"Every one of those fuse boxes appears to have been overloaded," Bueller said. "The droid controller is in even worse shape—unfortunately, it appears to have been shot when our people stormed Engineering."

"So, manual replacement by hand?" she said.

"Bingo. Sitz might only have fried half at random, but it doesn't matter. Without a list of which ones she overloaded, I need to at least check every single one of them. Sixty fuse boxes. Without the droids, it's a couple of minutes to get into each coupling.

"Then, once the system is online, I need to find the physical anti-mutineer lock that Sitz *also* appears to have activated and remove it," he continued. "That'll take testing and luck." He shook his head. "We're looking at three days to have sublight engines if I'm doing this alone."

"How long to fix the droid controller and have them do it?" Kira asked.

"About half a day just to get a fabricator online, another day or two to fabricate parts. Then I have to basically rebuild the controller and resequence it, plus making sure Sitz didn't activate any surprises in the robots themselves..."

"So, focusing on the drives and manually fixing them, right," Kira said with a smile. "You talked to your people?"

"Yeah. Some were disappointing, if at least honest. I gave Temitope the list. We've got about thirty-five willing to defect—but, to be clear, that's defecting to you and me, not Redward."

"I don't know if *Conviction* needs thirty-plus extra engineers," Kira admitted. "Settling you all on Redward with Royal help might be the best I can offer."

"That's fair and we'll cross that bridge when we come to it," Bueller said. "What happens to the ones who don't sign on?"

"Arguably, we've committed an act of war against Ypres Sanctuary, and we've *definitely* committed an act of piracy," she told him. "They'll be treated as POWs and likely released with a transport back to Brisingr in a couple of months at most.

"We don't have a fight with your home system, after all. Sanctuary has chosen to be aggressive in a way Redward can't support, and I was hired to help stop that. Equilibrium was definitely on the radar of my hiring as well, but..."

Kira shrugged.

"I'm being paid to neutralize *K79-L*," she concluded. "Mission accomplished. Regardless, *you* aren't doing me or this ship any good falling asleep on your feet. Go sleep, Konrad. Right now, nothing is urgent. We can nova back to Redward once the situation is under control."

"You say that," he said quietly, "but we're going to be here, one jump from Ypres, when everything goes to hell. Aren't we?"

"Probably," Kira said. "But that's a problem for then. Right now, if you *don't* go sleep on your own, I might have to stun you and drag you to your quarters."

"All right, Kira, all right," Bueller chuckled. "I'll rest. I'll check in once I'm awake. *You* should probably rest too."

"Maybe," she agreed. "But *I'm* in charge, so I have different rules. No one can threaten to drag *me* to their quarters."

She was tired enough that she didn't realize she'd misspoken until Bueller started laughing, a deep rumbling that made her smile almost instinctively.

"You know what I mean," she told him.

"I do," he agreed. "And it sounds like you should *definitely* rest."

KIRA HAD TAKEN over the Captain's office next to the bridge, with its emergency cot, and set an alarm to wake her when *Nightmare* returned from Ypres. Years of practice meant she was awake instantly and the proximity of the cot had her on the bridge by the time her subordinate was sending the data download.

There wasn't anyone *else* to receive it, after all. Milani was holding down the fort on the bridge, but they weren't really qualified to run the tactical systems of a warship.

"How messy, Mel?" she asked.

"Messy," Cartman said. "We stirred up a hornet's nest and the Alliance poked it. If my math adds up, they lost half their nova destroyers and most of their gunships doing it...but they destroyed or disabled *every* nova-capable combatant Sanctuary had."

Kira whistled silently as she threw the data onto the bridge's many screens. There was no one else using any of them, so she filled the space with the data she wanted.

"That's a hell of a kick in the teeth for Sanctuary," she said aloud. "Combined with us stealing *K79-L*, they're in a much worse spot than they were two days ago. What about the nova fighters we left behind?"

"I didn't see them at all, so either the Alliance got them or they're laying low until they get orders from the Director," Cartman replied.

"Or they jumped out to the battle group," Kira guessed. "Assuming they were briefed on that."

They might have been. Now they had a solid idea of who their prisoners were, she knew that *K79-L*'s Commander, Nova Group, had been on the CAP when they'd stolen the ship. The man was definitely Equilibrium, so he might have had enough information to fall back on the Director's second-string force.

"So, the nova side of the fight is over until Equilibrium gets involved," she said aloud.

"Looks like. The Alliance needed that win, from what I was seeing, too," her friend said. "They have the most scattered small assets, but now the only people with a force capable of attacking far-flung assets is them. Helps keep the Guilds in."

"And if I'm reading this data right, it means the Guilds are moving more of their monitors to Elverdinge," Kira noted. There had been a dozen of the sublight ships scattered through the asteroid belt, attempting to protect those far-flung stations and mining asteroids.

Now ten of those ships were heading to join the fifty monitors already orbiting Elverdinge. Another half dozen were moving inward from the gas giants, presumably on similar logic. Sixteen of the sublight ships would tip the balance of numbers and firepower distinctly in the Alliance's favor.

Not enough for them to want to tangle with Sanctuary's fortresses, but enough that they would feel confident challenging the Protector in open space. If Equilibrium intervened, that could go poorly enough for them as it was.

"I make it two days for the Guilds' ships to reach the fleet. Three for the new ships from Flanders," Cartman told her, clearly following

Kira's thoughts. "There's no way for Sanctuary's fleet to reach Elverdinge before the Guilds' force, even if they were ready to move immediately."

"And there's no sign of that in the scan data," Kira noted. "Their losses are probably making Sanctuary hesitant."

There was a long pause.

"Is Equilibrium going to *let* them be hesitant?" her old friend asked.

"I have no idea," Kira admitted. "And that's the problem, I think. In the Protector's place, now is a time to negotiate—lean on that alliance with Redward to get a neutral arbiter in and maybe give up some concessions to keep the annexation of Hearth."

But Equilibrium needed a counterbalance to Redward, either a rival to be overcome and force Redward to become more militarized, or a military power to overcome Redward. Sanctuary leaning on Redward to negotiate peace wasn't in their plans.

"The Director apparently wanted a defeat," Kira reminded Cartman. "It looks like he got it. Now…now we see what his next step was."

"Swordheart novas out in six hours," her wing pilot said after a long, grim pause. "Twelve hours till the next update. What do we do?"

"We wait, we make sure the fighters we have are solid, and Bueller sees if he can get us sublight engines," Kira replied. "I doubt that Equilibrium had their little fleet ready to jump straight in—or that they don't have a plan for this."

She counted taking *K79-L* as a major victory, but the cruiser had been an obvious target. There was no way the Director hadn't planned for her being lost one way or another.

44

IT WAS CARTMAN, two days later, who brought back the news they'd all been waiting for. *Something* had to break, as the two sides in Ypres circled each other and prepared for a battle that Sanctuary was going to lose.

"I've got a bunch of scans of what's going down," she told Kira as her fighter decelerated toward the cruiser, "but I think you can get the gist of it from the news reports. Forwarding them to you now."

Kira had been waiting for the nova fighter's return and had established a virtual conference of her senior officers slash command council: Temitope, Milani, Como and Bueller.

Temitope was coordinating the security for the prisoners still on K79-L—roughly half of them—while Milani guarded the bridge to keep an eye on Kira. Como was on her own ship, and Bueller was only leaving Engineering when Kira made him.

He was determined to get the cruiser to as useful a state as possible with his own two hands, despite Kira repeatedly telling him they didn't *need* more than the nova drive.

"I've got her upload," Kira told the others. "Let's take a look, shall we?"

The role of news anchor hadn't changed in centuries. News could shift fast enough sometimes that most agencies kept a human in the camera rather than a computer-generated avatar. The image was three-dimensional and the anchor had access to media tools that would have made her distant ancestors green with envy, but the basic structure was identical.

"Reports of blaster fire near the Protector's Palace have been confirmed by multiple sources," the dark-skinned woman in the broadcast announced. "Despite the reasonable concerns of people near to the Palace, and the concerns of all right-minded citizens of Sanctuary, we have made contact with Palace officials.

"We have spoken with Major Jeremiah Lyons of the Platinum Guard, and he has confirmed that local citizens may have heard what appeared to be blaster fire over the last twelve hours." There was something in the woman's body language, Kira realized. The anchor was wearing a mask of utter professionalism, but she still couldn't quite conceal her skepticism of what she was reporting.

"Major Lyons informs us that the Platinum Guard, the army unit tasked with the security of the Palace and the personal protection of Protector Daniels, was carrying out unscheduled live field exercises. While citizens may have seen Platinum Guard soldiers in the streets and even seen and heard what appeared to be blaster fire, he asks us to assure all citizens of the Protectorate that only training weapons were in use."

A map of the region of Cloth Hall around the Protector's Palace hovered next to the anchor now, visible from any angle a viewer might choose. Bright white icons marked something.

"As you can see on the map, these were widespread exercises," the anchor said drily. "Each of the white icons marks a report of blaster fire or soldiers over the last twelve hours."

The icons made a near-complete circle around the Palace in multiple layers. It certainly could have been a large-scale exercise—but there was a *reason* that militaries usually didn't carry out large-scale exercises with fake blasters in metropolitan areas, let alone metropolitan areas around executive residences.

"Major Lyons notes that the exercises appear to have identified multiple weaknesses in the Palace's defenses against an unexpected ground attack," the anchor said. "To secure the Protector's safety and to allow for upgrades, he has asked us to inform our citizens that a temporary lockdown is being imposed on the region within two kilometers of the Palace itself."

An orange circle around the Palace replaced the icons of the "exercise."

"Citizens inside the lockdown zone are asked to shelter in place or evacuate until the Guard has completed their work," she continued. "Further information is attached to the broadcast if you live in the lockdown area, and the Guard has set up a help line for you to get assistance in hotel costs."

Kira cut off the transmission and looked grimly at the virtual representations of her officers.

"Well?" she asked.

"Coup," Milani said instantly.

"Coup," Temitope agreed.

"Pretty sure it's a coup," Como said.

"I *know* the Director had assets in the Palace, though I wouldn't have thought enough to co-opt the entire Platinum Guard," Bueller told them. "But if they'd *failed*, the Palace would be touting their victory. So..."

He nodded grimly.

"Coup."

Kira started pulling the rest of Cartman's data into a display she was sharing with the rest of the team.

"Unfortunately, Nightmare arrived in system after most of this had played out," she told them. "I doubt it was intentionally timed to line up with us not having a fighter in Ypres, mostly because that lines up with oh-dark-fuck-it in Cloth Hall.

"Their timing does mean that we don't have active scan data for while it was going down. Not that the Sinisters have the kind of scanners we'd need for useful data." Kira considered the situation, then sighed.

"I'm going to owe my team so many drinks after this, but we need to start cycling every six hours," she decided. "We need continuous data now. More than anything, though, I need to know when that damn battle group arrives."

With Sanctuary's nova-capable fleet out of commission, the only numbers that really mattered were the monitors. Between the old Sanctuary fleet and the ex-Hearth units they'd co-opted, they had sixty of the ships, averaging two hundred kilocubics apiece.

The Alliance's ships were smaller, around a hundred and fifty kilocubics on average, but the combined fleet they'd mustered was now over eighty of the ships, with the extra ships inbound from Ypres Flanders bringing it up to ninety.

Both sides had very similar tech, from what Kira could see. Their nova destroyers had all been functionally identical, and monitors were generally assembled from multiple modules that could have been nova-capable ships if the drives were installed.

Dikkebus had two asteroid fortresses to Elverdinge's one, which made an open attack on either world a losing proposition. The worlds were nearing their closest approach, so the Alliance could intercept any attempt by Sanctuary to take their sublight fleet at any other target.

"If they're smart, they'll hold it out-system until the Alliance moves," she guessed. "Even with the Equilibrium ships, they can't take on the monitor fleet *and* the asteroid forts."

"Could the Equilibrium fleet take down, say, the fort at Voormezele?" Bueller asked.

"Maybe," Kira said. "But that would only extend this mess. Invading planets is a fool's game; the only reason we're even looking at a monitor-on-monitor fight is because Ypres had two habitable planets.

"If they want to unify Ypres, they need to wipe out the Alliance's monitors," she told the rest. "They need to convince the Alliance to come out from Elverdinge to where the fortress can't reach, and jump them with the nova ships."

"Okay. So, what do *we* do?" Como asked. "We're still at least six days from even hearing from Redward, let alone having reinforcements."

Kira looked at the display of the Ypres System and swallowed a curse. If *K79-L* was functional, she and her fighters could easily dance around four or five times her cubage in monitors and rip them to shreds. She probably wasn't a single-handed match for the entire Equilibrium battle group, but the cruiser would make everyone hesitate.

"Two things," she finally said. "Firstly, Konrad, would Sitz have known about the coup plan?"

"Probably," the engineer agreed slowly. "I didn't, but Sitz was far more inside the Director's plans than I was."

"And the Director himself was aboard this ship," Kira said. "They had to have had files, people. We need to break open this ship's archives and logs."

"My cyber team is working on it," Temitope said. "We've been focusing on undoing software locks on the systems, though. Archives and logs might be doable, but then we're not working on getting the ship ready." She paused. "And it would help a lot if we had Bueller."

"I can only do one thing at a time," the engineer admitted.

"And that brings me to the second thing we need to do," Kira told them. "We're releasing the engineering crew and the rest of the Brisingr hands who wanted to volunteer. We *watch them*, carefully, but we need them.

"I don't know if we can get this ship combat-ready before everything goes to pieces again, but the closer we are, the better off everyone is going to be. Forty-some extra hands will go a long way to getting the drives, droids and guns online."

"Sir, bluntly…we have almost nothing to go on on these people," Temitope told her. "We know nothing about them, and a few days ago they worked for Equilibrium. Bueller has proven himself, but the rest…"

"We're trusting Bueller, not them," Kira snapped. "And we don't have a choice, Colonel. Six days for Redward reinforcements. Once things start moving, it will be *maybe* thirty-six hours before the real fight starts in Ypres.

"I need to know everything that Equilibrium was planning and did in Ypres so I can use that as psychological warfare—and I need a ship that can fly and fire its guns! The only way I'm getting any of that is if we give these people enough rope to help us out."

"Or hang us," Temitope said.

"Making sure they don't is your job," Kira countered. "If we don't have internal surveillance back online, set some up. Make it work, Colonel.

"Because we are out of options and starting to run out of *time*."

"BEEN WAITING FOR THAT," Patel said calmly as Kira finished the update to her pilots. "Well, not the coup," he continued after a moment's thought. "The six-hour cycle. Should we be bringing Lozenge in?"

"The shuttle has a class two drive," Cartman said. "And from my last chat with him, he'd jump at the chance to do something. Anything."

Kira felt a moment of guilt at that. She'd left the one Darkwing pilot she'd borrowed on *Forager* and then left the man almost entirely to Como. She had touched base with him once, but it sounded like she should have been doing so more.

Somehow. Amidst trying to put an entire ship back together, watching a star system come apart, and coordinating three hundred prisoners.

"The good news is that you're going to have deck crew shortly," Kira told them. "Three of them have volunteered to get back to work. They'll have one of Temitope's commandos watching them at all times, but they should be able to fuel your fighters."

"Guess we don't need to worry about rearming unless we actually fire the torpedoes, do we?" Michel asked.

"Not really," Kira agreed. "And if you are firing those things on your scouting missions, we're in real trouble."

"We're cycling locations, but we are vulnerable," Cartman warned. "Sanctuary might be short nova craft right now, but we know Equilibrium's got a few and the Alliance might try and send a destroyer or gunship to check us out."

"I know," Kira admitted. "If Ypres Alliance tries to poke us, you flash RRF codes and run for the hills. If the Equilibrium ships come after you, you do what you have to—up to and including firing all three of your Sinister's torpedoes.

"I need you, your fighter and your data more than anything else," she told them. "In a perfect world, we'd have everything functional on this ship, plus crew, plus fighter pilots for the Weltraumpanzers.

"Instead, right now, I don't even know if I'm going to have sublight engines when things hit the fan. I need as close to live data from Ypres as I can get, and that means I need you guys to get it for me."

"We know the drill, boss," Colombera told her. "We're snooping, not fighting."

But the problem with sending a nova fighter on a long-range jump was that the class two drive took *longer* to cool down after long jumps than a class one. Its advantage in cycle was entirely for in-system jumps.

She was going to worry for every single damned second she had people in Ypres.

45

"KIRA, can I borrow you for a moment?" Bueller asked.

Kira blinked away the simulation she was running—an analysis of just how heavy the Equilibrium nova force would need to be to turn the tide in favor of Ypres Sanctuary—and looked up from the captain's seat.

"Sure, Konrad, what's up?" she said.

She hadn't been alone on the bridge even before the Brisingr man had arrived. Bertoli, the most familiar of Milani's mercenaries, was standing guard inside the entrance.

That the mercenary hadn't warned her when Bueller entered the room said a lot. There was no way Bertoli would have let anyone he regarded as a potential threat get that close to Kira without a warning.

Bueller seemed to have earned the trust of Kira's people. The *rest* of the ex-Brisingr volunteers were operating under tighter supervision, but they hadn't almost single-handedly delivered the cruiser.

"It turns out I'm even more of a bloody idiot than I thought, and I need to confess that to somebody," he said dryly as he dropped into a seat near hers. "I'm also stuck wondering how long I could have stayed inside Equilibrium before this kind of shit seemed normal to me."

Kira studied the engineer. He looked exhausted, but that wasn't new. There was something more to it today.

"You cracked Sitz's files?" she asked.

"We did," Bueller confirmed. "Her commentary on *me* is…fascinating." He looked ready to vomit. "But worse is that she was the Director's coordinator for ops in Ypres when the Director wasn't around."

"So, she was in on the coup plan," Kira concluded.

"Among other things," he said. "Did anyone tell you that the President of Hearth was a war hawk? He was elected on a promise of forcing Sanctuary to fall back to the borders agreed thirty years ago on the inner worlds—borders Sanctuary has been ignoring for at least a decade."

"Doesn't sound like a man who'd surrender because you had one more cruiser," Kira said slowly, a grim certainty settling into her heart.

"No. He had a stroke and died two days after Captain Sitz and Ambassador Andreas started *facilitating solutions* between Sanctuary and Hearth," Bueller told her. "Full autopsies and medical workups; everything said it was perfectly natural."

Kira froze.

"What kind of stroke?" she asked softly.

"There was a blood clot, I think?" the engineer said. "Brain hemorrhage, basically."

That was *exactly* how her old CO, Jay Moranis, had died. He'd been old and in treatment for cancer, so everyone had taken it as an unfortunate side effect of the cancer—especially when the medical workups came back clean.

"And?" she prodded.

"Sitz's files say we did it," Bueller told her. "Apparently, it's a weapon the Institute made available, a self-destructing nanite matrix that is indistinguishable from hemoglobin once it does its work. The matrix goes to a targeted location and triggers a clot."

"Fuck," Kira snarled.

"Kira?" Bueller looked shocked.

"That's how my old CO died," she told him. "It was supposedly natural, but when so many others were turning up dead from the group—and Moranis was ex-Equilibrium."

Bueller looked even sicker.

"Something to look forward to," he half-whispered. "Didn't know that."

"Right," Kira sighed and studied him. "All of Cobra Squadron was. You know them, right?"

"Seriously?" Bueller coughed and shook his head. "What a fucking galaxy. I *think* the President's assassination is the kind of thing you were after, though, right?"

"It was," she agreed. "Any proof of their coup plans?"

"Enough bits to know that Sitz would have calmly detailed it if it had taken place while she was in charge," the engineer told her. "We're still hitting blocks on the Director's files."

"Did Sitz know his name?"

"If she did, it's not in her files," Bueller admitted. "But…there's also proof in there around *Hope* and DLI, though I think we assumed we'd get that."

"Well, that turns our seizure of *K79-L* into an appropriate response instead of an act of piracy," Kira said. "Proof of that is always handy. Saves me from needing an eye patch and a jolly roger."

Bueller nodded, swallowing his apparent queasiness.

"You knew an ex-Equilibrium officer before?" he finally asked. "How did…how did they live with it? Even what I knew was happening was bad enough, and now I'm learning about all of things I didn't know."

"I didn't know Moranis was ex-Equilibrium when I worked with him," Kira admitted. "But John Estanza was also Cobra. My *boss* is ex-Equilibrium, Konrad. He spent the last few decades running from them, but they keep expanding and poking at stars as they go.

"Estanza's done running, Konrad. Redward knows who their enemy is now, it seems, but even if they didn't, *Conviction* does. We'll fight them," she promised him. "They won't win here."

He nodded slowly.

"I don't know what else to do," he admitted. "I'm with you if you'll have me. We'll throw this cruiser in their fucking teeth, Kira."

She grinned, sharing his moment of determination.

"Can we yet?" she asked.

"We figure we'll have Harringtons back in a couple of hours," he told her. "Fabricators twelve or so after that. We'll be able to maneuver and make new parts, but you won't have guns or fighters for a while yet.

"It's going to take about eighteen person-hours per fighter to get them clear for operations," he noted. "I can get one or two back online easily enough, but that won't make much difference."

"No, I need *K79-L*'s guns if we're going to do anything in Ypres."

She exhaled and leaned back in the chair.

"Anything in the files on the battle group's strength?" she asked.

"I don't think even Sitz knew," Bueller told her. "The Director, whoever he is, appears to have held a lot of things close to his chest."

"If we're very, very lucky, we'll get to vaporize the son of a bitch," Kira said. "I'm looking forward to it."

Before Bueller could reply, an alert flashed to life on her console, and Kira was on her feet.

"That's not right," she snapped. "Dawnlord isn't due back for two more hours."

"Kira?"

"Nova contact," she told him. "Unidentified vessel at two light-minutes!"

46

"LAUNCH, LAUNCH, LAUNCH."

It was strange as all hell for Kira to be listening to someone *else* give the cadenced bark of an emergency scramble. There was no fighter for her on *K79-L*'s flight deck, though. There were only the three Sinister fighter-bombers not currently surveilling Ypres.

Nightmare gave the call and her fighter screamed out into space first. Scimitar and Socrates were only seconds behind her, a risky operation with the minimal flight control they could offer right now.

"I'm moving *Forager* between you and the unknown," Como told Kira. "If they're at our rendezvous, either they're friendly or we're fucked anyway, but I'm clearing the hatches and charging the main gun."

"This is Nightmare; we have the target," Cartman's voice echoed on the general channel. "Your orders? Do we deploy?"

The three nova fighters could close two light-minutes in an eyeblink, their multiphasic jammers evening the odds against just about anything in space. They couldn't take down a capital ship, but even most of the Cluster's true nova warships would have a bad day running into Kira's veterans.

Kira was scrambling with the systems. A warship's systems were different enough from a nova fighter's to give her pause on their own —and Brisingr systems were different enough from Apollo systems or even *Conviction*'s systems to give her another headache.

She was reasonably sure she'd know if the stranger was hailing her, but if *K79-L* could identify the ship, she didn't know how to.

"Sir!" Bertoli snapped behind her. "One of the volunteers is here; he's offering to help."

Kira looked up to see that Chief Waxweiler, the man who'd been on the bridge when she took control of the ship, was standing at the door to the bridge. A commando was trailing behind him, and he was calmly staring down the barrel of Bertoli's blaster pistol.

"Send him in," she ordered.

The Brisingr NCO crossed the bridge with confident steps, dropping into the tactical console with the ease of long practice and adjusting the entire bridge screen with a few deft motions.

"Target is at thirty-five point four million kilometers," he reported. "Jianhong radiation signatures suggests she is in cooldown and unable to nova. Resolving heat and energy signatures to establish size."

"And?" Kira asked.

"Estimate ten kilocubics, energy levels too low for a warship," Waxweiler reported. "I am not detecting any identification beacons, but I'm guessing they're not at a random empty bit of space by accident."

The NCO looked up at her.

"She's a courier, Commander," he concluded. "But since we scrambled fighters and started securing the volunteers, I'm going to guess you didn't expect her."

"We sent a message to Redward, but that should only have arrived in the last day," Kira said. "Nightmare, this is *K79-L*-Actual," she said, bringing up the general channel. "Stranger appears friendly, high likelihood of a courier. Take your wing out and say hello."

If Waxweiler was right, they'd know more in an hour or so once the courier could close the distance. And if the NCO was wrong, well, there were very few ten-thousand-cubic-meter ships in the galaxy Kira wouldn't back three of *her* pilots against.

TWO MINUTES LATER, the lightspeed signature of Kira's fighters appeared next to the stranger. The unknown ship had remained almost perfectly still since arriving—like prey in the eyes of a predator.

Or, well, an unarmed ship that had shown up to a rendezvous to find a massive warship.

Presumably, Cartman managed to allay the stranger's concerns. The ship's identification beacon turned on shortly after the fighter wing arrived at her location, identifying the ship as the RRF fast packet courier *Kenobi*.

When *Kenobi* brought her engines online, Kira had to concede that *fast*, at least, was an accurate descriptor. While it wouldn't make much of a difference in long-distance travel, *Kenobi* had similar straight-line acceleration to the nova fighters escorting her.

Long experience told Kira that the nova fighters would still be more maneuverable—and that achieving that kind of thrust on a larger hull meant major compromises had been made elsewhere. *Kenobi* would have no weapons and limited cargo space—but her cargos would get to their destinations slightly faster than most other ships and she was better able to avoid trouble as well.

K79-L chirped a notice at her, the cruiser informing her of an incoming transmission.

It took Kira a few seconds to work out how to *play* that transmission, but since *Kenobi* was two light-minutes away, there was no rush.

A young-looking man in an RRF uniform with Lieutenant Commander's tabs appeared in front of her.

"Commander Demirci, Captain Como," he greeted them. "I am Lieutenant Commander Ovidio Baldi of the RRF courier *Kenobi*. We were detached from First Fleet after Admiral Remington reviewed your message.

"I apologize for the radio silence; we were expecting to rendezvous with *Forager* alone and weren't quite certain how to take the cruiser's presence." Baldi paused, considering the situation and how to proceed.

"I unfortunately require multiple validation keys from both Captain Como and Commander Demirci before I can release my dispatches," he admitted. "The presence of *K79-L* raises questions as to whether or not you are uncoerced, and I have to be certain.

"I am attaching the validation requests to this message. The sooner I have the response keys from you both, the sooner we can continue this conversation. I make my ETA to close rendezvous one hour and twenty-two minutes."

The message ended and Kira checked for the attachment. This kind of validation was a series of encrypted ask-and-response electronic keys. Even if someone had managed to acquire Kira's encryption keys, they wouldn't necessarily know which response went with which code.

That allowed for options like responses that meant *I am being coerced* without a captor being able to know what she was doing. She had a number of them for working with the RRF—and more for *Conviction*.

The validation requests were mostly RRF, but there were also several messages that appeared to be from Estanza.

Either way, she triggered all of the responses and sent them back. A quick check confirmed that Como had done the same, which meant now they needed to wait.

Just over five minutes later, a new message arrived from *Kenobi*. Baldi looked a bit more sure of himself now, and he grinned at his recipients.

"From what Admiral Remington told me, you weren't expecting backup for a while yet," he told them. "Details are attached in the encrypted files I'm forwarding you, but First Fleet should only be two days behind me.

"Admiral Remington is in command of a combined allied fleet heading to Ypres to try and resolve the situation," Baldi continued. "They were still waiting on final detachments when I was sent forward, but they'd deployed to the trade routes already.

"When I left, First Fleet was three carriers, including *Conviction*, two cruisers, and twenty destroyers," the young officer told them. "There are forces present or promised from every SCFTZ system. The Syntactic Cluster stands as one."

Kira exhaled in surprise. Two days instead of four was a huge difference. She was pretty sure she saw both Estanza's and Sonia's hands in this. The envoys to gather this fleet had to have already been in place when Kira had left for Ypres.

K79-L would have been enough to break that fleet, but Kira had neutralized her. The Equilibrium battle group might still be able to *match* it, but just the presence of a combined fleet from half a dozen star systems would send a message that the Institute *might* listen to.

Might.

"I look forward to speaking with you both in real time," Baldi concluded. "I have spare torpedoes and parts for *Forager* and your fighters, but I don't have anything for *K79*."

That made sense. No one had expected Kira to capture the Brisingr warship.

"How many different derivations of the name does this ship have?" Milani asked from behind her as she was considering the situation. "Because I think the courier might have used a new one."

"We'll rename her sooner or later," Kira promised. Bad luck or not, everyone *except* the BKN preferred to have actual names for their ships. "Once all of this is done and we have a clue what the hell happens next."

"Well, it sounds like we sit this one out now, right?" the mercenary said. "That's a real fleet, Commander. Though...how many nova fighters do those carriers have?"

"Not enough," she told Milani quietly. "*Conviction* has three properly manned squadrons, and the RRF...might have about that between their two carriers. Thirty-six nova fighters."

"But Equilibrium probably doesn't have cruisers?" the squad leader asked.

"Last time, they had D9Cs from Brisingr," Kira pointed out. "Those might be destroyers, but they can go toe-to-toe with Redward's cruisers."

"Right." The mercenary was silent. "My job's to keep you safe, boss, not get in the way of the mission."

"Still working out what the mission is, Milani," Kira said. "I need to go over these messages. Chief Waxweiler?"

She turned to the ex-Brisingr NCO, who'd been silent during her conversation with Milani.

"I'm going to be locked in virtual for a bit," she told him. "Ping me if anything odd comes up."

"Will do." He paused, then sighed. "I didn't see any D9Cs, though the Sabertooth assault destroyers are nasty pieces of work for their size. If they've only got the three of those we saw, then that 'First Fleet' has them outnumbered and outgunned."

"But if they've got twenty destroyers of their own, they're going to have the locals badly outgunned," Kira agreed. "I know, Chief. I guess the answer is Yprian monitors—if we can pull it off."

He didn't answer that. There really wasn't an answer.

47

THERE WERE a number of messages in the queue. Kira quickly reviewed the headers and established that most were text and data, probably information on the position and capacities of the fleet. There were two video messages included, one from Admiral Remington to her and Como, and one from Estanza directly to her.

She started with the one from Remington.

"Commander Demirci, Captain Como, Colonel Temitope," the rigid-spined old admiral greeted them. "I have now been briefed on your mission by my intelligence officer, a woman I did not know reported to my Queen as well as me."

There was a clear expression of discontent with that on Remington's face, but it passed quickly enough. The uniformed commander of Redward's military knew the realities of her job well enough.

"While I'm not certain I approve of your mission, if you're receiving this message, you hopefully succeeded," she continued. "Given the news around this additional potential hostile force, the presence of *K79* would be an obstacle we cannot afford."

Kira was definitely going to need to rename the ship. She'd have to think about that.

"The situation has changed dramatically since you left," she continued. "The decision by Ypres Sanctuary to refuse the ultimatum and accept war with the rest of the system has escalated the Yprian situation from unfortunate to untenable.

"His Majesty has activated mutual-support agreements with the Syntactic Cluster Free Trade Zone systems. We are not expecting major support from many of those systems, but at least token contributions have been promised."

She snorted.

"I'm not going to pretend that one gunship from Otovo is going to make or break what's coming, but the effort is appreciated nonetheless," she said. "We have received your updated intelligence and have factored it into our plans.

"If you have further updates, please send them back to us with *Kenobi* as soon as possible. I trust your sensors and judgment better than, say, the news media out of Ypres."

There was a moment of silence as Remington looked at the camera.

"I wish we knew more about this backup group," she admitted. "I assume by now we know more about the trustworthiness of the source, at least. Any updates you send will hopefully reach us before we arrive in Ypres.

"I still hope to prevent a war, people, not fight one. But regardless of what I want, I must be prepared."

Kira nodded to herself as the message froze. The next fighter was due back from Ypres before *Kenobi*'s drive could recharge. That would give Remington intelligence that was only a day out of date when they had to make their final nova into Ypres.

That was the best Kira could do—and was probably better intelligence than most fleet commanders were used to.

She blinked away Remington's message and loaded Estanza's. Her ex-Equilibrium Captain was recognizably in his office, most of the room coming through with the message if she let it.

"You do have a way with trouble, don't you, Kira?" he asked brightly. "You managed to get an Equilibrium agent to defect? I'm impressed...and you're right, I probably will need to talk to them. The Institute got us to do a lot of things that seemed acceptable at the time but are worse in hindsight.

"Everything started moving damn fast once the news of the ultimatum and Sanctuary's refusal arrived," he told her. "Reading between the lines, Larry had been pushing for an intervention already. Faced with a hostile out-Cluster warship and an active conflict, everyone signed on.

"If I have a fear, it's that a third of this fleet are mercenaries," he admitted. "I trust Shang, but he's one commodore of three. I don't know the others well."

Commodore Shang Tzu had gone into the Kiln with the Redward fleet and fought the Costar Clans' new warlord there alongside *Conviction*'s crew. Redward had repaired and upgraded his fleet as part of his payment for that, but if his three destroyers were part of the fleet...

That was a lot of mercenaries. Kira knew the Cluster—hell, a lot of the Outer Rim in general—had more mercenaries than she was used to, but it was still an odd thought. It was cheaper for a system like Otovo to occasionally hire someone else's destroyers than to keep their own, but that always struck her as a terrible idea.

"We're waiting on the last detachment. Bengalissimo at least has a real fleet, so that detachment is going to be a proper cruiser group with at least five escorts, but I'm not sure of their timeline. We should only be a day or two behind the courier carrying this message."

Estanza paused and sighed.

"If you're on *Forager*, I'd ask that you follow *Kenobi* and rendezvous with us if you possibly can," he admitted. "Your detachment is six of my best pilots; I *need* you. I'm assuming you've got fighters over there, but I need you on my decks, flying *your* fighters.

"Not on some godawful retrofitted freighter flying Redward's birds. If I'm going to war, Kira, I need my CNG and I need my veterans. Come home."

The message ended and Kira stared into space as she downloaded the information from Remington.

Between Baldi's estimate of the strength and Estanza's read on Bengalissimo, she now knew roughly what the Cluster was bringing to the party. Three carriers, three cruisers, probably twenty-three to twenty-four destroyers, and forty-plus gunships.

It should be enough. The Equilibrium force was only expecting to tip the balance between two relatively evenly matched forces of monitors, after all. They weren't going to be coming in expecting to do that *and* face a nova fleet with a decent fighter group.

"Chief," she said to Waxweiler, letting the virtual office she was using fall away as she turned her attention to him. "Honest question. How large a force do you really think the Institute put together to try and take Ypres?"

The ex-Brisingr NCO looked up from his console and met her gaze.

"I don't know," he admitted. "But...everything I've known them to do was with utter overkill. We went after *Hope* with *Seventy-Niner* and twenty gunships. Some of that was apparently so we could make sure there were no witnesses, but...it was overkill."

Kira nodded grimly. Three assault destroyers and twenty gunships might tip the balance between the two sides in the Yprian war, but the Institute wasn't going to rely on *might*.

"That's what I was thinking, too," she admitted. "If you were putting together something like that, with an infinite budget and the kind of influence they seem to wield...what would you show up with?"

Waxweiler snorted.

"You're basically talking a planetary assault," he pointed out. "I wouldn't do it. Even with *Seventy-Niner*, we were never actually a threat to any of the asteroid fortresses without a *lot* of luck. There were ways we could hurt them, but people treat planets as untouchable for a reason, Commander."

"But assuming you have Sanctuary's monitors and armies for the actual assault," Kira prodded.

"I'm not sure what I'd even regard as enough," Waxweiler admitted. "But I'd be bringing everything I could. If I couldn't get proper carrier groups, I'd be scraping every mercenary destroyer I could covertly hire within a hundred light-years."

"Twenty destroyers, thirty, forty?" Kira suggested.

"As many as I could find, depending on my cover story," he said. "We were out here as a survey ship. Most of us had figured out that was bullshit, but I was on the bridge and didn't really know what Sitz was doing until Bueller told me."

"Mercenaries might be more willing to do what they're paid for without asking questions than you were," Kira countered, considering the numbers.

How many mercenary destroyers could there be within a few weeks' travel of the Cluster? The Cluster itself, from what she understood, had ten. So, if someone tried to hire every destroyer within fifty light-years of Ypres except the Cluster's ships…

Thirty to forty, she figured. Enough that if the Institute attached some more modern ships under front companies, even First Fleet could be facing a real battle.

"Dawnlord is due back shortly after we make rendezvous with *Kenobi*," Kira said quietly. "Then we'll know everything we're going to know."

She shook her head.

"There'll be a briefing, a senior officers' meeting," she told Waxweiler. "I'll want you there. For the moment, Chief, it looks like you're *K79-L*'s new tactical officer."

KIRA WAITED on the bridge until Dawnlord's fighter exploded back into reality. Socrates was ready to go to replace him—and then they all saw the code Patel's fighter was broadcasting.

Hold position, situation update incoming.

"Hold your nova, Socrates," Kira ordered. Michel was smart enough that the order was probably unnecessary, but double-checking was wise.

"Dawnlord, what is your status?" she continued on the general channel.

"Uploading scan update," Patel told her. "Sanctuary's fleet just sortied. Their course suggests they're trying to bypass Elverdinge and reach Voormezele or Vlamertinge. Both are on much the same line right now."

Kira grimaced. Vlamertinge was one of the largest asteroids in the Ypres main belt, which made it one of the primary population centers for the Ypres Guilds. Voormezele was the center of Ypres Flanders, with most of the refueling stations and refineries that underpinned Flanders' wealth and power.

"They're trying to get the Alliance to sortie to meet them," she guessed.

"They succeeded," Patel confirmed as the data began to load into the virtual displays on *K79-L*'s bridge. "The Alliance picked their time well, too. There's no way the Sanctuary fleet can evade them, even if they turned around the minute I novaed out.

"Vectors are in the upload, but I estimate they'll pop long-range mode multiphasic jammers in twenty-five hours and enter combat range in thirty."

"Understood," Kira said grimly. "There's a SCFTZ fleet under Redward command heading to Ypres right now. We'll relay that information ASAP.

"Socrates, wait until you have the full download, then nova out," she continued. "Be careful. At this point, it's just a question of when the Equilibrium fleet shows up. Don't get caught by their nova fighters."

"Not planning on it, boss," Michel told her. "See you in six."

The Sinister vanished in a flash of light and Kira studied the data continuing to flow in.

"Como, it's Kira." She opened a private channel to *Forager*. "You have the estimate of First Fleet's location?"

"I do," Como confirmed. "What are you thinking?"

"The rocket just went up and the battle is on. Remington needs to know—and the four hours *Kenobi*'s drive still needs might make all the difference. More of a difference than having you hanging out here will, anyway."

The covert ops officer sighed and nodded.

"I'll send over the rest of the commandos on Lozenge's shuttle," she told Kira. "We've got our prisoners pretty locked down and I'll be able to offload them when we catch up to the fleet. Once they're clear, I'll nova out."

She paused.

"What are you going to do?" she asked. "I may as well tell Remington and Estanza, right?"

"I don't know," Kira admitted. "But I don't think I'm just going to sit out here and *float*. Even if all I'm doing is delivering four more Sinisters to the fight, that's something."

"All right." Como paused. "I guess I'll see you in Ypres, Commander."

"Godspeed, Captain Como."

48

"I COULD USE GOOD NEWS, PEOPLE," Kira told her "officers" drily.

Neither Waxweiler nor Milani were officers, no matter how she stretched the term. Bueller could be argued but, like Waxweiler, was also technically a prisoner of war. Hope Temitope and Mel Cartman were the only other actual officers in the office attached to *K79-L*'s bridge.

"I think I can provide that, actually," Bueller reported. Now that he had support in his monumental task, he was looking much more confident and much less exhausted. "I can, in fact, declare that we are approximately thirty percent of an actual warship again."

"How are we calculating that?" Temitope asked. "I'm pretty sure we don't have guns, after all."

"The primary Harringtons are back online," the engineer replied. "We haven't done any maneuver tests yet, but all of the power conduits and couplings check out. Secondaries will take a bit longer, but we can now maneuver at about eighty percent of standard."

"That helps," Kira allowed. That *was* good news. "Not sure that brings us to any ratio I can count of *warship*, though."

"I wouldn't count engines alone as enough, but our three brave flight-deck techs, combined with your pilots, have the deck running,"

Bueller said. "We only have four operational *fighters*, but we are fully capable of guiding automated launches and landings as well as refueling and rearming any fighters we do bring in.

"They're working to clear some operating space and we'll still be shorthanded, but it looks like we'll be able to turn around a six-ship short squadron in roughly five minutes."

Six nova fighters *were* a squadron by Apollon or *Conviction* standards, but Kira knew Brisingr used the ten-ship standard. Five minutes was on the long side for a combat turnaround, but for three techs relying on droids and automated equipment, that was fantastic.

"Okay, that is useful," she conceded. "If we had multiphasic jammers, I might even buy that thirty percent number."

"Sitz never touched the jammers," Bueller countered. "We've *always* had our full jammer suite."

"All right. We have thirty percent of a warship," Kira said with a chuckle as she looked at the rest of them. "We need to stay the hell away from anything that's actually a functioning warship, given that our *only* weapons are on those four fighters."

"I can't see us doing anything else," Temitope said slowly. "If repaired, *K79* becomes the most powerful warship in the Cluster, but right now she's a cripple. I can't in good conscience recommend that we do anything but run back to Redward.

"Our presence here supporting the fighters as scouts has been valuable to date, but with First Fleet almost in play themselves, our role here is done."

"Speaking of which." Kira gestured at Cartman. "We now have two nova shuttles. Once Socrates is back, we stop sending the fighters out. We cycle the pilots through the two nova shuttles, but we keep all four fighters on the deck."

She turned her attention to Bueller.

"Konrad, do you think your team can get two of the Weltraumpanzers online?" she asked.

"If I leave the flight deck on it, they can probably manage it if we give them a couple of days," he confirmed. "Two?"

"One for Lozenge and one for me," Kira replied. "I'm not a starship captain. My place is in a cockpit, not a bridge."

"Right now, you're the closest thing we've got," Temitope said. "You can't seriously be planning on taking six nova fighters into the heart of the battle that's about to happen.

"I'm not seeing a lot of other options," Kira said quietly. "This ship isn't battle-ready, but her presence will add to First Fleet's intimidation value. The intelligence we've acquired will have a hell of a lot more weight being sent out by *K79-L* than by First Fleet.

"And I don't have it in me to quietly slink away and let other people do my fighting," she admitted. "Even if we keep *K79-L* standing back and use her solely as a nova fighter platform, no one is going to try and screw with her, because they have no idea how functional or not she is.

"We are maybe twenty-six hours from the largest battle the Syntactic Cluster has ever seen," Kira reminded her officers. "Which means, sorry, Konrad, your team has *twenty-four* hours to get those two Panzers online. And the rest of your team has those same twenty-four hours to turn on whatever the hell you can."

Bueller sighed but nodded.

"I don't think we can give you guns, Commander," he warned. "*Maybe* one. Maybe. There are triple-layered anti-mutiny measures in those guns, and we won't even know where to look for the lockouts until we've got power running to them.

"We can handle acting as a fighter support base, but that's it. We'll keep working for as long as you can give us, but…"

"This is the job, people," Kira reminded them all. "I don't know what Equilibrium's plans for Sanctuary and Ypres and the Cluster are, not really. But nothing I've seen so far suggests that anyone here comes out ahead except *maybe* Sanctuary.

"So, we fight. With whatever happens to be to hand—and today, people, we have this cruiser to hand."

49

THE LAST TEN minutes were the hardest.

That wasn't news to Kira. She'd done it before, locked in the cockpit of a starfighter aboard a carrier, waiting for a nova drive to tick into cooldown or a scout ship to return. The tension. The waiting. The almost exact time that things would explode.

Today, it was the wait for Lozenge and the nova shuttle. At some point in the next eighty minutes, the two Yprian forces would clash. They'd already begun flickering the inviolable cloaks of their multi-phasic jamming on and off to frustrate long-range targeting when Scimitar had jumped back six hours earlier.

Somewhere in there, two separate nova forces would arrive. If one of them arrived and the other *didn't*, this whole mess was going to end very quickly. First Fleet aligned with the Ypres Alliance would have Sanctuary badly outmatched.

Kira didn't think it was going to be that straightforward.

"Nova flare," Waxweiler said softly. "It's our shuttle…Commander, someone shot at her."

Kira was seeing the signs as well. The shuttle's Harringtons were off-balance and she was leaking atmosphere badly.

"Lozenge, report, do you require assistance?" she barked over the radio.

"I am mostly in control," the pilot replied in a flat voice. "I would... suggest clearing the shuttle bay, though; I don't think this is going to be my best landing ever."

"Waxweiler?" Kira snapped.

"On it."

"Got jumped by a pair of nova fighters before I saw the arrival of the fleet," Lozenge continued in that flat tone. "Uploading the data now, but the keystone is a problem. They've got a Crest *Liberty*-class strike carrier with what looks like a full deck and a swarm of destroyers."

"Commander?" Waxweiler said quietly. "He doesn't have it. The Harrington balance is completely out of whack."

The upload chimed as complete.

"Adjust our course to match his; we'll do a scoop," Kira ordered. "Lozenge, your coils are frying all over the place. We're going to swing and try and scoop you up. I need you to kill your Harringtons."

There was a long silence.

"I can't, Commander," he reported, his voice even flatter now. There was no emotion in his words, just the clipped tones of a professional. "Power couplings appear to have melted into each other.

"Harrington shutdown has failed."

"Kill your fusion plant, Lozenge," Kira snapped. "Your coils can't run without power, and we can pick you up before you're in trouble with life support, even with the leak."

"Understood," he confirmed. "Trying to lock in a vector. Initiating emergency shutdo—no! No! N—"

The shuttle detonated and a spike of anger rammed into Kira's heart. She could recognize containment failure without even needing to check the scans. Something had been cracked or damaged in a way that didn't show so long as the magnetic bottle was operating without change.

As soon as the system started to adjust for the shutdown, the mag bottle had failed. A contained fusion reaction became uncontained.

"Containment failure," Waxweiler said, the words a cold echo of her thoughts. "I'm...I'm not picking up any significant debris, sir."

"I wouldn't expect you to," Kira replied, recognizing the clipped tone of her own voice. "Do we have the stats on a *Liberty*-class in the system, Chief?"

"We should," he confirmed.

"Pull them for me," she ordered. "And get everyone ready to nova."

IT WAS STILL, technically, just one battle group, Kira reflected.

The strike carrier—sixty kilocubics, standard load forty nova fighters—was the centerpiece. She was supported by a pair of fifty-five-kilocubic light cruisers. Neither Kira's files nor *K79-L*'s had a source for those capital ships.

Eighteen destroyers and eighty-four gunships filled out the rest of the Equilibrium battle group. It was a powerful carrier group—devastatingly so by the standards of the Syntactic Cluster—but it would have only been weighed as a medium battle group in the war Kira had fought.

They'd clearly been getting data from someone in the system, because they'd known exactly when to send their fighters after they'd emerged from nova. Lozenge hadn't been able to confirm if the new fleet was talking to Sanctuary's fleet before their fighters had jumped him.

"Boss, Bueller's here," Milani told her from the door.

Kira waved for the engineer to come in. He obeyed, dropping into the executive officer's seat as always and leveling a steady gaze on her.

"We're novaing in less than a minute," she told him. "What's so important it got you to the bridge?"

"Two things," he said calmly. "Firstly, nobody else on this ship seems to have the stomach to tell you your place isn't a cockpit today."

"We might have only got one Weltraumpanzer online, but Lozenge is dead," Kira ground out. "Someone has to fly it."

"One nova fighter is not going to turn the tide of this battle, Kira,"

Bueller told her. "*Seventy-Niner* might, if we use her right. My people will listen to me, but they won't listen to Temitope or the commandos.

"The commandos are technical enough to be bloody handy, and we'll need them if we try and do anything with this ship, but they won't listen to me or my people. Temitope and I can work together and try and make it work, but neither of us would accept the other actually being in overall command," he admitted. "I know this ship better than her, but she won't trust a stranger. Neither of us is really wrong; neither of us is right.

"The answer is what it has been all along: you. You are in command of this mission and in command of this ship, and you can't do that job from the cockpit of a nova fighter somewhere else in the battlespace, tied up in multiphasic jamming."

"One nova fighter is going to make more difference than a crippled cruiser we can only use as a support platform," Kira snapped.

"If all we're using *Seventy-Niner* as is a fighter platform, I can't help but feel we're missing our greatest advantages," he told her. "Remember that nobody else knows she's crippled."

She glared at him.

"Maybe," she allowed. She didn't *want* to be on the bridge of a starship. She could fly *K79-L*, but she wasn't comfortable *commanding* her.

"Which brings me to the second reason I'm here," he said. "We cracked the Director's files."

"The timing could have been better," Kira admitted. A clock to her designated nova time was running down in her headware.

"I have the full data on his Operation Condor Flag," Bueller told her. "Everything from the plan to detain the Protector and force him to issue the orders they wanted, to their plan to use these mercenaries to raid shipping to force an increased militarization of the newly unified Ypres.

"It's everything, Kira, down to the fact that he had *minimum acceptable casualties* from the battle we're about to fight," he snarled, his calm façade breaking. "The bastard will have told these mercenaries that *at least half a million people have to die* today. No matter what, no matter how overwhelming the force, they won't let the battle end until at least a hundred of those monitors are wrecks filled with the dead."

"My god," she whispered. "We already had proof of the assassination of the Hearth President. But...are you serious?"

"Deathly," he told her. "That file might be as deadly a weapon as any plasma cannon I can give you, Kira. I don't even know the Director's fucking *name*, but I know what orders he was planning on giving those mercenaries—and I don't think the Yprians are going to like them."

Kira exhaled a long sigh and nodded.

"I'll stay on the bridge," she promised softly, reaching out to touch his shoulder across a space that wasn't *quite* large enough to prevent it. "Get me those files in a format I can send to every receiver in the system.

"And then I need you to get me at least one gun, Konrad," she said. "I don't care if we're faking it with a torpedo strapped to the turret, but I need at least one bloody gun."

"Are we going to have time for the torpedo option?" he asked, covering her hand with his own.

"No. We're novaing *now*. Go," she told him, not pulling her hand away until he rose. "This war does not happen today, Konrad. The Institute does not win today.

"We stop them. You get me?"

"I do."

50

K79-L ERUPTED into the Ypres system in a blaze of radiation. Unlike *Lozenge's* nova shuttle, she wasn't multiple light-minutes from the action. The heavy cruiser was barely twenty light-seconds from where Kira estimated the Sanctuary fleet was going to be.

She'd been slightly wrong, but the difference was less than half a million kilometers, and the time delay bought her and Waxweiler time to go through their scan data.

"All the players are here, sir," the ex-Brisingr Chief told her. "Flagging Sanctuary Force, Alliance Force, Equilibrium Force and First Fleet."

First Fleet's arrival had been just as cautious as Kira's, but they'd been aiming to reinforce Alliance Force. From the dispersing radiation, Admiral Remington had beaten Kira to the system by less than ten minutes.

First Fleet had brought every single ship they'd promised. *Forager's* familiar identity code was lost in the list of ships running into Kira's headware. Three carriers, three cruisers, twenty-four destroyers and forty-eight gunships.

It *should* have been more than a match for Equilibrium Force, but Kira was all too aware of the balance of technology. There were thirty-six nova fighters on First Fleet's carriers, supported by another seventy-odd sub-fighters.

There were forty nova fighters on the strike carrier—and the strike carrier was more heavily armored and armed than *Conviction*, let alone the converted freighters that hauled Redward's fighters.

Kira's four starfighters evened the nova fighter numbers, but the destroyers and gunships in Equilibrium Force were mostly mid Rim designs. They were probably at least twenty percent more powerful than the average Cluster warship facing them—and the cruisers were the same breeds.

First Fleet had more proper warships, but that swarm of gunships was going to be a problem.

The edge probably went to Equilibrium…which meant the edge for the entire battle went to Sanctuary and Equilibrium combined.

"All right," Kira said aloud, letting the numbers process through her brain. "Time to battlespace, Chief Waxweiler?"

"Everyone is still in pulse mode on their jammers, so we have clear visibility. Looks like…forty minutes, sir, until everyone is in the last couple of light-seconds."

Most ships didn't even carry weapons that were usable beyond a light-second. On the other hand, any warship's fabricators were perfectly capable of assembling smart missiles or lasers. So, the entire approach to final engagement was filled with random maneuvers and pulses of the multiphasic jamming, to make sure any toys like that didn't connect.

Once they were into the last few light-seconds, the multiphasic jamming would go online and *stay* online, rendering everything except direct visual analysis useless—and even that was distorted enough that human intuition was required to be certain of targets.

Most importantly right now, though, was that multiphasic jamming shredded *communications* as well. Once the jammers were online, Kira couldn't talk to anyone.

"Do we have Bueller's Operation Condor Flag data in a transmittable format?" she asked.

"We do, sir," Waxweiler confirmed.

"Send it to *everyone*," Kira ordered. "Then give me a directional transmission point at Sanctuary Force."

"Sanctuary, sir?" the Chief asked.

"Everyone else in the field, Chief, *knows* Equilibrium Force is their enemy," she pointed out. "But Sanctuary Force...they probably think their cavalry just arrived."

"Transmitter ready whenever you are," he said after a moment.

Kira took one last look at the battlespace, the four forces rushing toward each other. First Fleet and Equilibrium Force wouldn't be able to nova the capital ships for an extended period, but the nova fighters were already in space from both fleets.

Those fighters would open the battle soon enough. She needed to get her message out before they did.

Swallowing, she faced the recorder.

"Sanctuary forces, this is Commander Kira Demirci aboard the cruiser *K79-L*," she introduced herself. "This ship was seized under the authority of the Kingdom of Redward, as we believed it was responsible for the destruction of their destroyer *Hope*.

"We have now confirmed that. If that was the only thing I'd confirmed, I'd be moving into formation with the Free Trade Zone moving to reinforce the Ypres Alliance." She smiled thinly.

"With access to *K79-L*'s files, however, we have learned of a hostile operation being carried out against *all* of the Ypres System. The details of the plan have been transmitted in this system, but I am communicating directly with *you*.

"It is your leaders who have been assassinated and detained," she told them. "It is your government that has been quietly overthrown to force this conflict. And it is your presumed allies who are entering this battle with a minimum requirement for casualties. They'll drag this fight out until enough of you are dead.

"The Syntactic Cluster has sent their ships to stop this war. The fleet they've gathered doesn't want to *fight* you, but they will. We are not here because we want to pick a victor in Ypres's age-old war.

"We are here because an outside power has brought you here, to this point, where a million citizens of this star system are riding warships against each other. Do I understand everything about this enemy and this conspiracy? No. If you look at the files we transmitted, you'll know almost as much as I do about what was intended for Ypres.

"I beg you to look. To understand."

An alert flared across her screen as her transmission suddenly ended, cut off in the chaotic disaster of multiphasic jamming.

Instinct yanked Kira into the cruiser's control systems, and she flipped *K79-L* through a tight circle that sent plasma bolts scattering past her.

"Chief?" she barked.

"Incoming nova fighters," he said drily. "Someone *really* wants to shut us up!"

KIRA'S VIEW of the wider solar system was gone now, and even aboard *K79-L*'s bridge, the entire struggle condensed down to a bubble about six hundred thousand kilometers across. Inside that bubble, computers struggled to run visual analysis to identify the spacecraft swarming around the heavy cruiser.

At least the computers aboard a cruiser *could* do most of that work themselves. The computers that could fit in a nova fighter mostly flagged possibles that a human had to review. They did so in an intuitive fashion, zooming in on them as the pilot looked around the cockpit, but they still needed the human to confirm the identifications.

Chief Waxweiler could do the chunk of that that was still needed, which allowed *K79-L*'s screens to show a *mostly* accurate representation of the dogfight swirling around Kira's ship as she dodged the heavy cruiser through the chaos.

Four Sinisters piloted by her oldest and dearest friends were chasing three times their number in what the system told her were Crest-built Hussar heavy fighters. Kira's reflexes had allowed them to evade the Hussars' first wave of torpedoes, but they had at least one more salvo in them.

Kira's Memorials were doing everything in their power to make sure the mercenary fighters didn't line up for long enough to get that shot. As she watched, two of the heavy fighters vanished, torn apart by the streams of plasma fire from her guardian angels.

Then the rest vanished, flashing away in tactical novas to allow them to set up a second strike.

"They know we have no guns now," Waxweiler said grimly. "We're screwed, sir."

"They already guessed," Kira told him. "Twelve heavy fighters against a K70 cruiser? That wasn't a real strike—that was a goddamn test. And you're right." She glared at the screen. "We failed."

She couldn't let her four fighters go into the main battle *and* she couldn't lower her own multiphasic jamming. Not until she knew the strike on *K79-L* was over.

"What do we do, sir?" the Chief asked. "I'm not overly in favor of *lie down and die*, but the next time they come back, they'll only be evading the fighters. Not us. They *know* our guns are dead."

Something shivered in the software that was feeding the computer in Kira's head. Not an alert...this wasn't something that *required* an alert; it was supposed to be entirely normal.

"Then they might just be wrong," Kira told Waxweiler. "Bueller?"

"You have Turret Three, Commander," the engineer replied in the network. "We got lucky on finding the lockouts, and they're gone. We haven't run power-up tests, but there *shouldn't* be a problem. You have two guns. I don't know if you're going to get more today."

"You heard that, Chief?" Kira demanded.

"I heard."

"Then kill me those fighters—and Konrad?"

"Yes, Kira?"

Using first names was entirely inappropriate, but he'd just saved everyone's bacon—and she needed him to do one more thing.

"The moment we fire turret three, I need a full power-up test on every gun," she told him.

"That will hit the lockouts; we'll risk losing the couplings," he warned her.

"We can lose the couplings. We can't lose this battle—and you were right. If we use *K79* as a fighter platform, we're using her wrong.

"She's the biggest, baddest nova warship in the star system—and we need our enemies to remember that!"

THE FIGHTER WING was back almost exactly on schedule. A nova fighter cycled their drive in sixty seconds, and the attackers returned sixty-five seconds after they'd fled.

They emerged into *K79-L*'s multiphasic jamming field in ten matching bursts of light, maintaining a steady line for the critical seconds necessary to fire their torpedoes in a deadly swarm. They were varying their position and velocity but were on a direct line for *K79-L*.

As Waxweiler had predicted, they were evading the fighters and treating the cruiser as a non-threat—and the lead fighters never got a chance to realize their mistake.

The heavy dual plasma-cannon turrets weren't the best weapons on the cruiser for engaging fighters, but they could do the job. Turret Three was in position almost instantly and fired before the fighters did.

The dual guns couldn't target independently. They didn't need to. Waxweiler walked his fire across the incoming formation, plasma bursts easily a tenth of the size of the starfighters hammering into the attacking spacecraft.

Nova fighters couldn't survive hits from a heavy cruiser's turreted main guns. Ten fighters became six in the blink of an eye, and the same hail of fire obliterated most of the torpedoes before they could detonate.

Six fighters became four, and Kira made certain the surviving fighters got a good view of the energy signatures as power surged to the *rest* of *K79-L*'s guns. That power wasn't going to do anything, not with the hidden lockouts still in place...but the fighters had no reason to believe that now.

The Memorials dove onto the scattering Hussars. The cruiser's sole functioning turret kept up enough fire to add to the confusion until the sole survivor of the strike vanished into nova.

"We took a hit from one of the torpedoes," Waxweiler reported. "Armor held, no serious damage. They might be back with more," he warned.

"They don't have enough 'more' to send," Kira told him. "I know what it takes to bring down a K70, Chief. I've done it. That pissant little carrier? Her entire fighter wing couldn't take down this ship if it was fully operational—and now they think it is."

She smiled coldly.

"Start pulsing the multiphasics, Chief," she ordered. "We're clear for now. I need to see what's going on everywhere else."

There was a blink of calm in the chaos surrounding *K79-L*, and the cruiser's sensors greedily sucked up data. The situation had changed in the five minutes they'd been out of communication, and it had changed for the better.

"How are you reading this, Chief?" she asked.

"First Fleet and Alliance Force are maneuvering to converge about a million kilometers from Equilibrium Force," Waxweiler told her. "Sanctuary Force..." He grinned. "Sanctuary Force is in full reverse; course suggests an emergency return to base.

"Alliance Force is choosing to let them go to enable the intercept of Equilibrium Force."

"That's my read as well," Kira said in satisfaction. It wasn't necessarily a victory—in the Sanctuary commander's place, she'd have just classified everyone as potential hostiles and decided to get the hell out of Dodge.

She ran through the maneuvering system, bringing *K79-L*'s systems up to their current full power and heading toward First Fleet.

"It looks like we can join First Fleet and the Alliance at the rendezvous to me," she noted. "Take us down to standard approach pulse for the multiphasics, but watch for a renewed fighter strike."

Kira smiled and looked over to meet Chief Waxweiler's gaze.

"Well done, by the way," she told him. "You got those jammers up faster than those fighters expected; you might just have saved everyone."

"Part of the service, skipper," the Brisingr NCO told her.

Skipper. That sent a shiver down her spine. Like Bueller had kept gently pointing out to her, their defectors regarded *her* as the team they'd defected to.

That was going to be...complicated.

51

WITH THE MULTIPHASIC jamming down to intermittent pulses, Kira kept up evasive maneuvers as she flew the heavy cruiser toward the rendezvous with the SCFTZ fleet.

It really was a Free Trade Zone fleet, not a Redward one, too. That was going to have long-term consequences for the region, ones that Kira figured were going to be overall positives. In the face of a potential outside threat, Redward's allies had come out in force to stand together.

The responses certainly seemed to have left the collection of mercenaries Equilibrium had gathered without a clear response. They'd thrown fighters at *K79-L*, but that hadn't worked out for them. *Conviction*'s fighters were the only *visible* nova fighters in First Fleet's formation, but they were supported by dozens of sub-fighters.

And since Redward had stolen their class two drive fabricators *from* Equilibrium, the Institute's strike force had to know the Kingdom had nova fighters now. For that matter, Kira suspected there were other nova fighters out there.

Bengalissimo, for example, was supposed to have four to six of them in service. If *she'd* been sending out a cruiser group under these circumstances, she'd have sent out the cruiser with the nova fighters on board.

No one had *admitted* to that, though, which left Kira's known number of nova fighters at thirty-six—which was still at least six more than the *Liberty*-class strike carrier had left.

The distance was down to five light-seconds when Remington finally directly hailed them. The silver-haired Admiral was smiling as she appeared on Kira's projectors.

"Commander Demirci, that's a rather larger ship than I was expecting to see you in," she said. "*Forager* updated us, but I'll admit I wasn't counting on you getting her online and into Ypres for this fight."

"We're here," Kira agreed. Remington would hopefully get the hint that *K79-L* wasn't necessarily fully online. There was a limit to what she was prepared to put into an interceptable radio conversation.

Seconds ticked by as the messages flew back and forth, and then Remington nodded what Kira *thought* was understanding.

"Once you've rendezvoused with us, we'll need your nova fighters to slot into *Conviction*'s wing. Will that be a problem?"

"No, sir," Kira replied. "They know where they fit."

"Admiral!" a disembodied voice shouted on the other end of the call. "Bandit One is changing profile."

Kira checked her own displays. "Bandit One" was apparently her "Equilibrium Force," a logical difference, given that the RRF wasn't officially fighting Equilibrium just yet.

"They've flipped their vector and are opening the range," Waxweiler told her. "Enough of their ships have better acceleration than the Cluster units that…yeah. Only a portion of the local fleet can catch up."

"What about us?" Kira asked.

"Barely right now," he admitted. "Normally, we'd be faster than those cruisers, but we still don't have our secondary Harringtons."

"Understood."

She turned her attention back to Remington.

"We can theoretically catch them, Admiral, but we'd be pushing the current state of our engines," she told the Redward officer.

Seconds ticked by and Remington grimaced.

"The sub- and nova fighters could catch them," she admitted. "Plus some of the destroyers and *Civet*, the Bengalissimo cruiser. Even with K79-L for support, that's not a force that can win. They're refusing to communicate and I *really* want to kick their asses, but…"

She sighed and nodded slowly.

"We have no choice but to let them go," she decided. "Demirci, bring your ship to the rendezvous and stand by for further orders. I'm going to talk to the Yprians and see just what the hell the next step is going to look like."

The channel cut off and Kira exhaled as she studied the system map. If Equilibrium was running, the worst was over. The Yprian war might not be over, but *her* role was definitely done.

She hoped, at least.

"NICE TOY, KIRA," Estanza's image told her as the heavy cruiser slid toward *Conviction*. "Got a plan for her yet?"

"A plan?" Kira laughed. "I've been bouncing from confusion to disaster to miracle to disaster for a week, boss. I don't have any plans yet."

"Just a ninety-six-kilocubic heavy cruiser," he said. "I don't know what Queen Sonia's expectations *were*, but I'm guessing you exceeded them."

"Yeah…let's just say I need to find a home for a few kilograms' worth of antimatter," she told him. "Somewhere *not* on the ship I'm currently on board."

"I know *that* one, too," he said with a chuckle. "How's your ex-Equilibrium 'asset'?"

"Burying himself in turning the ship back on, along with about forty people who were working for the Equilibrium's front with different levels of awareness. They're all volunteers—defectors, I guess." She shook her head, glancing at Waxweiler, who couldn't hear the virtual headware conversation.

"They're good people, but they did some awful shit for the Institute," she told him. "Not sure how to deal with or cover for that, especially when Redward comes looking for *Hope's* killers."

"I did some awful shit for the Institute," Estanza reminded her. "They fought for you; you feel responsible for them?"

"Yeah," Kira admitted. "Think *Conviction* could use an extra forty crew?"

"Maybe, but that might not be the best use for them," he said. "And I'm back to the plan, Kira. If you don't have one, one is going to get made without consulting you. I can guarantee you that Remington regards that ship as Redward's, and all *she's* thinking is a nice bonus on your contract."

Kira straightened her spine as irritation spiked in her mind.

"This ship might have been captured on a mission for Redward, but Redward didn't turn her back on or bring her into action," she said coldly. "They better be planning more than that."

"And that is why I say *you* need a plan," he told her. "Remington will defer to Sonia and Larry—and I suspect Her Majesty, at least, will have your back."

Estanza grinned.

"So will I, but that goes without saying. Right now, Remington is busy making sure everyone doesn't shoot at each other for the next ten days."

"Ten days, sir?" Kira asked. Then she picked up what he'd said. "Wait, the King and Queen are coming *here*?"

"A lot of people are coming here," Estanza said. "Pretty much every major power in the SCFTZ is sending an ambassador if nothing else, but I'd be shocked if King Larry is the only head of state who shows up.

"Ypres has been the Cluster's problem child for a long time, Kira. Larry wants that problem to *end*, and he's going to use that as a lever for the FTZ. If he can get enough people in one place at one time to arbitrate and impose an answer on Ypres, he's got enough people to get the Cluster truly on board for the Free Trade Zone."

"That's a hell of a step," she conceded.

"It's a hell of a conference they're putting together," he agreed. "All of it was dependent on this battle either going in our favor or not happening. So, what happens next, Kira? It's because of you. That won't be on everyone's mind, but I'm pretty sure that Larry and Sonia will remember it."

"So, I need a plan, huh?"

"Ten days," Estanza told her. "Make your choices, Kira. I'll back you. Hundred and ten percent."

"Thanks, boss. It's good to know that," she admitted.

52

"DEMIRCI?"

Kira looked up from what had been Captain Sitz's desk to find Colonel Temitope standing just inside the door.

"The door's unlocked for a reason, Colonel," she told the Redward commando. "What's up?"

"We're being transferred out," Temitope told her, tentatively taking a seat in the chair facing Kira. The furniture hummed, adjusting itself to the correct ergonomic pose for the Colonel's build.

"The fuck?" the commando snapped.

"Sitz liked her comforts," Kira replied, gesturing around the room. "All of the chairs self-adjust. The tapestries came from Brisingr."

Every wall was covered in those. Where Kira might have put trophies or ship models or bookshelves, Sitz had eight-foot-high cloth hangings. Kira wasn't sure if they were hand-woven or machine-made, but the brilliantly multicolored forests and animals were certainly attractive enough.

The cot Kira had stuffed in a back corner stood out more than anything else did.

"That would take some getting used to, but I guess it's comfy," Temitope admitted. "But yeah. My commandos and I are transferring over to *Odysseus*. I wanted to make sure you were comfortable with just your mercs to watch over the volunteers."

"Can I send the prisoners who didn't volunteer with you?" Kira asked. "I'm keeping the volunteers for now."

"That's part of what I wanted to talk to you about," Temitope said. "My orders are to bring all the prisoners. That seemed, ah, *presumptive* to me."

Kira grimaced.

"Sounds like your boss doesn't think this is my ship," she said quietly.

"You commanded her in action, Demirci," the Colonel replied. "So far as I'm concerned, you're the CO. Which means you need to sign off on the prisoner transfer, regardless of what orders I'm getting."

"I appreciate that, Colonel," Kira said. "I like your people, but if they want this ship, they're paying me list price at least."

Temitope chuckled.

"Does Brisingr have a catalog of those?" she asked.

"Not that I know of," Kira admitted. "I'll sign off on the non-volunteers, Colonel. But the crew who fixed her and crewed her in battle for me? They're *mine* now, and they're staying with me. If I leave, they go to *Conviction* with me."

When had *when I leave* become *if I leave*?

Temitope's nod of understanding made it clear she'd picked up that distinction as well.

"I'll make sure my superiors understand," she told Kira. "If nothing else, you've got my word no one in Redward is going to be trying to arrest those volunteers without some *long* conversations."

"That helps…Hope," Kira told the other woman, rising to offer her hand. "It's been a hell of a journey to get here, but you and your people made it possible."

Temitope took her hand and shook firmly.

"No less than you and Milani and Bueller did," she agreed. "We did good, Kira. We did good."

"I know. It's what happens now that's in question."

"No, it isn't," Temitope told her. "The Sanctuary Army will storm the Protector's Palace sometime in the next twenty-four hours. King

Larry will get the factions to sit down and agree to a confederation of some kind. Having all of the leaders in one place will turn the Free Trade Zone into something real. Everybody wins."

"Do they?" Kira murmured. "You're an optimist for a commando."

"All commandos are optimists, Kira. We wouldn't sign up for this if we weren't!"

"All mercenaries are pessimists," Kira countered. "It's how we stay alive!"

Temitope chuckled and saluted.

"I'll get the prisoners off your ship, *Captain* Demirci," she promised. "Everything after that, well, you'll get it sorted.

"After all, I was planning to die blowing this ship up. Everything after that was thanks to you!"

KIRA WAS STUDYING one of the tapestries, the only one with sheep on it, when she felt as much as heard Konrad Bueller walk into the office.

"Am I interrupting?" he asked.

"No, I'm just wondering if Brisingr brought different breeds of sheep than Apollo did or if the artist took some liberties," she replied. "The heads and wool aren't quite right."

"Probably a mix of both," he told her, coming up behind her. "I wouldn't know myself, though. I think I might have seen some sheep on a field trip once? Maybe?"

Kira laughed.

"I grew up with them," she reminded him. "There's something left there, some memory of the shepherd's responsibility to the flock. It's how I ran my squadron and then *Conviction*'s nova group."

"You're sounding introspective," Bueller said. "What's going on, Kira?"

"A lot of things," she said. "You sound like you've got a specific question, though."

"Flight of shuttles just left," he noted. "Temitope and her people, plus all of the prisoners who didn't volunteer to sign on with you. So…

here we are. Forty-two ex-Ghost employees, ten mercenaries under Milani, and you.

"One working turret, one working nova fighter—and the biggest, baddest warship in the Cluster," he said, intentionally echoing her words during the fight. "We'll have more of both soon enough, but I've been hesitant to have my team do *too* much without knowing what happens next."

"And what do you think should happen next?" she asked.

"We committed crimes against Redward," he reminded her. "Not sure of exactly what bucket we'd dump them in, but we did."

"Did you?" she said. "Even Chief Waxweiler wasn't on the bridge when that went down. Even *you* weren't involved in the decisions. None of you were senior. None of our volunteers were even really in a position to refuse orders in a meaningful manner.

"The crew will be repatriated unless they ask to stay," she continued with a shrug. "No one has said it yet, but it's not in Redward's interests to piss off Brisingr. Brisingr has focuses back home, but they could still cause real trouble out here if they wanted to.

"Larry doesn't want that, so he's going to play nice. You and all of the volunteers can probably get a ticket home."

There was a long silence.

"Some of the crew might take that, depending on what the other offer was," Bueller rumbled. He was still several feet behind her, she noted absently, respecting her personal space when they were alone.

She turned to look at him, studying his face and considering him. They'd faked a date—hell, they'd faked going back to a hotel together —to set up the kidnapping-turned-defection. She hadn't been interested in him then, though everything they'd been through since had definitely helped his case.

"What kind of other offer were you thinking?" she asked with an arched eyebrow. He had the good grace to blush and step back a pace before realizing she was teasing him.

His chuckle was still pleasant. She wasn't sure she'd ever get tired of it, which was a *bit* concerning.

"If Redward were to put *Seventy-Niner* into commission, they'd need a training cadre even if they wouldn't trust us for crew," he told her. "A chunk of us would be willing to do that. I know I'm pretty unimpressed with the Kaiser right now. A new home with...new friends might be worth checking out."

"Friends with someone from Brisingr?" she teased. "That's asking a lot."

"Maybe," he conceded, "but a man can hope, can't he?"

Kira smiled at him, then turned to check the tapestries again. Everyone was dancing around the point, no one *quite* willing to say what clearly everyone thought she should do.

"I'm really not qualified to be a starship captain, you know," she finally said, answering the suggestion he *didn't* make. "I'm a nova fighter pilot and I belong in a nova fighter."

"So, find a captain," Bueller suggested. "Hire someone you trust. You can run the mercenary company but lead the nova group as your main role. Wasn't your company separate from *Conviction*'s in the first place?"

"It is, though I wouldn't want to separate that just yet," Kira murmured. "Estanza is too damned useful for advice and backup. The RRF will be *pissed*."

"I know this ship inside and out," the engineer told her. "Fabrication patterns, everything. I can't necessarily tell them how everything in her is built, but I'm pretty damn sure I can walk their yard techs through building a ten-thousand-cubic Twelve-X nova drive."

He grinned.

"*K79-L* wasn't the ship I ran the drive gang on, after all."

"Seriously?" she asked. "You can do that?"

"Pretty sure. Think that might be enough to tip them over into letting you keep the cruiser?"

She shook her head at him.

"Maybe," she agreed. "They gave me a stack of class two nova drives for the design files of the interceptors I brought out here."

She touched the tapestry with the flock of sheep and their blue-cloaked shepherd. There were a couple of dogs in the scene but none of the drones and similar modern gear a shepherd would be using, even on Brisingr.

"We'll have to find a crew," she told him. "We can borrow some from *Conviction,* and I'm sure the RRF will help us at least a little bit, but we'll want to make sure everyone is reliable and clean. The last thing we need is Equilibrium infiltrators."

"Agreed," he said. "We'll keep an eye on my volunteers, even. I trust them, but…"

"Yeah." She nodded. "Two requirements from me, then, Konrad Bueller."

"Beyond my agreeing to commit high treason to help buy Redward's support?" he said with a smile.

"Beyond that, yes," Kira told him. "Firstly, we're changing the goddamn name. No ship I own and fly aboard is going to have a fucking *serial number.*"

"If you insist," he conceded. He didn't look *happy* about it, but that was reasonable. No one liked changing ship names. Superstitious, but still a real factor.

Kira was more bothered by the serial number than by changing the name.

"You have an idea?" he asked.

"We name her for how we got her and how we stopped a war, my friend," she said. "We call her *Deception.*"

He looked thoughtful, then nodded.

"Makes sense to me," he agreed. "And your second requirement, my Captain-to-be?"

"When we get this ship back to Redward, you and I are going on an actual damned date that *isn't* planned to be a kidnapping!"

JOIN THE MAILING LIST

Love Glynn Stewart's books? To know as soon as new books are released, special announcements, and a chance to win free paperbacks, join the mailing list at:

glynnstewart.com/mailing-list/

ABOUT THE AUTHOR

Glynn Stewart is the author of *Starship's Mage*, a bestselling science fiction and fantasy series where faster-than-light travel is possible–but only because of magic. His other works include science fiction series *Duchy of Terra*, *Castle Federation* and *Vigilante*, as well as the urban fantasy series *ONSET* and *Changeling Blood*.

Writing managed to liberate Glynn from a bleak future as an accountant. With his personality and hope for a high-tech future intact, he lives in Kitchener, Ontario with his wife, their cats, and an unstoppable writing habit.

VISIT GLYNNSTEWART.COM FOR NEW RELEASE UPDATES

f facebook.com/glynnstewartauthor

OTHER BOOKS
BY GLYNN STEWART

For release announcements join the
mailing list or visit **GlynnStewart.com**

STARSHIP'S MAGE
Starship's Mage
Hand of Mars
Voice of Mars
Alien Arcana
Judgment of Mars
UnArcana Stars
Sword of Mars
Mountain of Mars
The Service of Mars
A Darker Magic (upcoming)

Starship's Mage: Red Falcon
Interstellar Mage
Mage-Provocateur
Agents of Mars

Pulsar Race: A Starship's Mage Universe Novella

DUCHY OF TERRA
The Terran Privateer
Duchess of Terra
Terra and Imperium
Darkness Beyond
Shield of Terra
Imperium Defiant
Relics of Eternity
Shadows of the Fall
Eyes of Tomorrow (upcoming)

SCATTERED STARS
Scattered Stars: Conviction
Conviction
Deception
Equilibrium (upcoming)

PEACEKEEPERS OF SOL
Raven's Peace
The Peacekeeper Initiative
Raven's Course (upcoming)

EXILE
Exile
Refuge
Crusade
Ashen Stars: An Exile Novella

CASTLE FEDERATION
Space Carrier Avalon
Stellar Fox
Battle Group Avalon
Q-Ship Chameleon
Rimward Stars
Operation Medusa
A Question of Faith: A Castle Federation Novella

VIGILANTE
(WITH TERRY MIXON)
Heart of Vengeance
Oath of Vengeance

**Bound By Stars: A Vigilante Series
(With Terry Mixon)**
Bound By Law
Bound by Honor
Bound by Blood

TEER AND KARD
Wardtown
Blood Ward (upcoming)

CHANGELING BLOOD
Changeling's Fealty
Hunter's Oath
Noble's Honor
Fae, Flames & Fedoras: A Changeling Blood Novella

ONSET
ONSET: To Serve and Protect
ONSET: My Enemy's Enemy
ONSET: Blood of the Innocent
ONSET: Stay of Execution
Murder by Magic: An ONSET Novella

FANTASY STAND ALONE NOVELS
Children of Prophecy
City in the Sky